THE PAINTER AND HIS POET

PRINCETOWN HEIRS
BOOK 3

BEA PAIGE

THE PAINTER AND HIS POET

The Painter And His Poet

Bea Paige

Copyright © Dec 2024 Kelly stock writing as Bea Paige

www.beapaige.co.uk

Cover Design: Everly Yours Cover Design

Cover Photography: Michelle Lancaster

Cover Model: Andy Murray

NOTE TO READERS

This book is a work of fiction, but with everything that I write, I do delve into difficult topics.

This book contains abusive, overbearing and narcissistic parents. Talk of past childhood abuse. Dub con. Vi*lence against the female lead (not from the love interest). Threat of r*pe (not by the love interest). Threatening and s*xually explicit messages, and some scenes of vi*lence (not between the love interests). Mention of a past eating disorder.

It also has a neurodivergent male lead, and whilst being neurodivergent is not a trigger, how he is affected by his specific condition of synesthesia may be triggering.

Please be mindful when reading.

BOOK PLAYLIST

As you all know I love a book playlist! I write to music always, and scenes are often inspired by the songs I choose. All of the songs that inspire this story can be found on my Spotify playlist - **The Painter And His Poet**

Princetown Heirs is a series of interconnected standalone romance books that can be read in any order, but to get the best out of your reading experience Bea suggests reading in this order:

- #1 The Thug and His Doll, a single mom / cinnamon roll, protector hero with all the spice.
- #2 The Rogue and His Flower, a brother's best friend / arranged marriage / enemies to lovers, spicy romance with all the heat and tension.
- #3 The Painter and His Poet, a stepbrother / off limits / neurodivergent male lead, angsty romance with all the smut.
- #4 The Thief and His Jewel, a second chance, indecent proposal, forced-proximity romance with all the delicious angst, tension and spice

Harlow and Sterling

"I see your true colours shining through, I see your true colours
and that's why I love you..."
True Colours - Cyndi Lauper.

PROLOGUE

Closing my eyes and pressing my fingertips to the bridge of my nose, I try in vain to stop the kaleidoscope of colours from forming in my mind. There are shades of cobalt blue, radiant sunlight yellow, soft hazy pink, spring meadow green, and deep blood red blending together to create a masterpiece that I have yet to bring to life with my paintbrush. Each hue shimmers and shifts behind my closed eyelids, tempting me to run from this goddamn hotel and back to my studio so that I can capture the image on canvas and relieve myself of the fucking turmoil.

And it's all because of her, Harlow Richards. A woman whose voice is as enchanting as an angel's and as seductive as the Devil's.

Despite drinking five shots of whisky, I still can't shake the insatiable desire to create art that was inspired by Harlow's performance at my father's wedding.

Fuck.

She's the woman I had a one night stand with several months ago. The woman who gave me a false name after I heard her sing at a dive bar in New York, who spent hours tangled up in my arms as we talked and fucked. The woman who I've been trying to find ever since.

The shock of seeing her again hit me like a ton of bricks as she walked down the aisle, and if that wasn't enough, she was also singing. Her voice, so fucking alluring, had triggered my synesthesia and caused a riot of colourful emotions to explode within me.

Emotions I've been battling ever since.

As I sit here with my three friends, Benedict, Drix and Dalton, in the bar of the five-star hotel my father was married in last night, I can't help but wonder what I did in a former life to deserve the pain of this one. Then again, I'm not the only one in turmoil. The bottle of whisky we've consumed between us only seems to deepen the shadows of our thoughts, making it even more difficult to come to terms with the fucked-up reality we've found ourselves in.

"What a fucking night," I mutter, swiping my hand through my hair as I catch Dalton's own weary gaze.

Drix shifts in his seat beside him, turning his attention to Ben who's lost to his own thoughts. "I'm assuming you've had just as little sleep as the rest of us," he says pointedly.

Ben glances up at him, his lack of words, and harrowed gaze, conveying a multitude of emotions we can all relate to.

"Yeah, that would be none then," I say, blowing out a sharp exhale of breath.

We're four heirs to our family's riches. Four men who've been rocked to the core by the women who have entered our lives and felled us just like the giant oaks surrounding my father's estate.

There's Benedict Pike, my best friend, whose brilliant mind is consumed by a forbidden love for a married woman who once shattered his own heart into a million jagged pieces. A woman whose bastard husband is willing to accept two million pounds in an indecent proposal so that Ben can spend a month alone with her.

Opposite him sits Drix, adopted son to the late Hubert Hammer, who was forced into the role of enforcer for our families in order to pay off a debt and putting his new relationship, to a single mum fleeing domestic abuse, in jeopardy.

Sitting beside him is Dalton, womaniser and self-confessed playboy, who has been manipulated into an arranged marriage with the one woman off-limits to him—Drix's younger sister—all in order to fulfil his duties as son and heir to the Gunn's immense wealth.

And then there's me, Sterling Blade, a secluded artist, and a perpetual source of disappointment to my overbearing father who wants nothing more than for me to take over his businesses and turn my back on the only thing that has ever made me happy.

This morning I had every intention of leaving town and never looking back. My relationship with my father has always been strained, but how can I leave now knowing that the woman I've been searching for will be moving into our estate?

A woman I want but can't have.

I should leave. I should put the past behind me and never look back.

And yet I won't.

Because everyone knows that an artist needs a muse, and ever since that fateful night, that person for me is Harlow Richards.

My goddamn *stepsister*.

ONE

Four months ago

Adjusting my noise cancelling headphones over my ears, I keep my attention focused on the pavement beneath my feet then turn left onto 52 Street, which leads back towards my apartment in the heart of Brooklyn. The open plan loft has bare brick walls, a raised area where my bed is situated, kitchen, bathroom and, more importantly, there's another room on the top floor of the building with floor to ceiling windows that bring in lots of light, making it perfect to rent out as a studio to create my art.

Since leaving the picturesque English town of Princetown a month ago, I'm finally beginning to feel as though I've found a place I fit, but perhaps not in the way you might think. In Brooklyn, everyone is too busy with their own lives to be interested in what the heir to a billion pound fortune is up to. I can disappear here. No one gives a shit about my family name, my father's money, or the fact that I have synesthesia, which is both a blessing and a curse.

A blessing because it enables me to express myself through art, a curse because every time I hear music, or more specifically, someone singing, I have this desperate need to paint and can't stop until the piece is done. Ten hours, twenty-four hours, days even, it doesn't matter. I'll barely give myself a moment to take a piss, and throw back some water, let alone eat. I'm in this indescribable place where nothing but putting colour to canvas is important. I'm just a vessel for the art to flow through, like the music notes that tantalise my ears and fuck with my senses, which is why I have to wear noise cancelling headphones and listen to white noise on a loop when I'm not holed up in my loft in blissful, soundproofed silence.

Sound is as vibrant as Brooklyn itself, and I learnt very quickly upon arrival that if I were to survive here I'd have to protect myself from the incredible array of music pouring out of every bar, night club, shop, and street corner where buskers perform daily. Occasionally, however, I spot someone singing and I remove my headphones, close my eyes and just *listen.*

And fuck me, the sensation is always immediate and overpowering.

With my eyes shut, and my fingers twitching, desperate to grab hold of my paintbrush, I become someone else entirely. No longer me, I become *more.* I become a vessel through which magic flows, a body filled with colour, with sound, with light and dark, with pain and elation, with suffering and freedom.

I get a physical reaction as much as a mental and emotional one. I *feel* the notes seeping into my skin, flooding my veins, travelling through my bloodstream with every frantic, overstimulated heartbeat. Musical notes reform into startling swathes of colour, the singer's voice exploding into violent paint strokes behind my eyes. Then a kind of magic descends, and I can see the artwork begin to form with every rapid fluttering, frantic, throbbing of my pulse. Each note is a metaphorical dip of my paintbrush into colour, reshaping, twirling, swirling into glorious, painful, all-consuming, delirious art.

In those moments, as I allow myself to listen, I become obsessed. I fall deeply in love with the sound, the voice, but mostly, the mesmerising, mind-altering *colour*. I'm both trapped and wholly, and completely free. My body trembles, my jaw grits, my bones rattle, my cells spark and alight.

Then, as the last notes linger in the air, other sounds filter in, adding more stimulation to an already overstimulated brain. It's in that moment, as the music is replaced with everyday sounds, that an unknown force drives me back to my loft to paint. Overcome with the need to purge myself of the colour swarming in my head and onto the canvas, immortalising it forever.

Nothing else matters.

Not the grumble of my belly needing sustenance. Not the lonely ache in my chest for companionship, understanding, acceptance, and certainly not the buzz of my phone in my back pocket telling me my father has called me for the fiftieth time that week. No doubt in an attempt to guilt-trip me, or bully me into returning home. All that matters is my need to paint.

It's all that has ever mattered.

Art is freedom, expression, hope. My neurodiversity, a colour-splattered palace I never want to escape from.

For years my father tried to cure me of my 'sickness', his words not mine. He spent thousands of pounds on private healthcare, on endless hours of therapy, and when that didn't work he'd try to use cruel words to drive the so-called sickness out of me.

I'm everything he hates.

I'm different.

Unable to shape me into the perfect son, my father made my life a misery. Divorcing my mother a year ago was his final attempt at breaking me. He knows that she's the only person who truly understands the real me. Her love has always been a grounding force that has kept me from falling headfirst into depression. To her my uniqueness is a gift, something that should be nurtured, encouraged, *welcomed.*

She was the one who gave me my first set of paintbrushes and paint. She was the one who stood me in front of a blank canvas as a young boy and pressed her lips against my ear whispering to me those sweet words I've never forgotten.

"You're father is wrong. You have a gift. So when it all becomes too overwhelming, paint, my darling. Paint what you hear, what you feel. Embrace who you are. Embrace the music and the colour it fills your existence with. You are loved. I love you. Trust in that. Always."

But for my father, my existence is nothing but a curse. My paintbrush, the blade he never wanted his son to yield. I'm a disappointment, an embarrassment.

Well, fuck him.

Fuck that man and everything he stands for.

Fuck that person he wants to mould me into.

Fuck that life.

So here I am, focussing on the ground beneath my feet, thousands of miles away from home as I traverse through a crowd of people, most of them heading out for a night dancing at the clubs, or drinking at one of the bars that line the streets. Unlike them, I walk against the tide, heading back to my loft for a night of solace, needing those moments of silence to regroup, to recentre myself until I'm ready to remove my headphones once again and fall into a world where only colour exists, and my soul is free to express myself with art.

"Look where you're going, asshole!" a burly fucker shouts as he shoulders into me, knocking my headphones off as he passes by.

"Fuck," I grunt, shoved sideways as a sudden flood of sound bombards my ears as the prick strides off, giving me the middle finger as a parting shot.

I open my mouth to curse his retreating back, but the words don't come. Instead, my spine snaps straight and a cascade of goosebumps covers my flesh as a haunting voice rises above the tide of Brooklyn's orchestra and floods my senses, swamping my vision with a dazzling array of colour. Bright red pulses at the corners of my vision, blurring into burnt orange and sun yellow, narrowing into a pin-prick of virgin white, teased and tormented by swirls of cerulean blue, and damask pink that bubbles outwards, consuming a velvety purple. Ripples of colour form and reshape, constantly moving, ever shifting and changing form.

"Christ!" I exclaim.

Unable to move, my discarded headphones forgotten, I find myself stuck in a vortex of stimulation that batters every part of my mind, body and soul. I'm vaguely aware of thunder rumbling overhead, the humidity caused by a long week of scorching late August sunshine finally making way for a cooler few days. Rain begins to fall, and the squeals of laughter and shouts of surprise barely register as people rush past me for shelter from the sudden deluge.

I'm drenched in seconds, my headphones shunted across the pavement by another passerby as my mouth parts on a guttural moan.

Who the fuck is that?

A woman, definitely.

I've heard, and dissected enough voices that I'm pretty certain I'm correct. The pitch and intonation is uniquely feminine, it's bone-achingly chilling. Fuck, her voice is both light and angelic, yet rich and smooth, darkly devilish. It's a catastrophe of possession, a cacophony of emotion, a symphony of sound that engulfs every single part of me.

My reaction is bone-deep, and I feel my body vibrate with the uniqueness of her voice. It's a voice that's so pure, so filthily perfect that the delicate notes, the soft, sultry cadence is like a beacon of light drawing my attention like a comet ripping through the pitch black of night.

I don't hear the words, yet I *feel* them, I *see* them, translated into a language only I can comprehend. Perfect notes of colour trip through my nervous system, making my skin itch and my cock ache with a mixture of intense pleasure and indescribable pain.

Blinking back the flood of colour, I take a drunken step towards the sound, following it towards a dark alleyway caught between two tall brick buildings. My palm slaps against the rough brick as I force air into my lungs, bracing myself against the overwhelming desire to seek out the owner of such a voice. I sway on my feet. I become rock hard, brutally turned on, *mindless* with need, the need to seek out the owner of such an incredible voice, the need to paint, and more surprisingly, the sudden overwhelming need to fuck.

Never in my life have I had that kind of reaction, so uniquely sexual. It pulses low, a heady feeling that makes my cock ache. Around me, the colours are so bright, so vital, so vivid and pulsing and alive, and try as I might I can't find it within myself to search for my headphones and replace them back over my ears to block out the sound.

It's too late now anyway. I'm already too far gone.

With colours weaving and twisting at the corners of my vision, I stumble towards a red neon light blinking up ahead.

Smokey Joe's it says.

I don't know anything about the place, but I can guess well enough that it's an establishment on the seedier side given the hidden, tatty entrance, and rough-looking doorman who looks like he's just snorted several lines of coke.

"Evening," the doorman drawls as I approach, eyeing me with disdain, his sneer doing nothing to put me off from entering. Neither does the thick smoke that seems to roll out of the entrance like mist across the ocean.

Tethered as I am to an invisible force pulling me towards her, I'm helpless against the need to lay eyes on the woman whose voice is a leash of colour drawing me forwards.

"Evening," I mutter in response, my voice hoarse as my gaze flicks behind him and into the darkened hallway beyond. Pulses of colour gather motion as the faceless stranger with the voice of a fucking angel continues to sing somewhere deep inside the club.

The doorman lifts a brow, his sneer turning into a knowing smile. "You high?" he asks.

I shake my head. "Are you?"

"No," he scoffs, very clearly fucking high.

"Then neither am I."

Which is debatable, frankly. I might not have inhaled coke or downed Molly, but I sure as fuck feel as though I have. I'm wired. Alert in a way I haven't been in so long. The doorman nods, giving me another once over, before shrugging and stepping aside.

"Knock yourself out."

I don't bother to reply as I step over the threshold, shoving a twenty dollar bill at the woman seated behind the entrance kiosk as payment for entry. She eyes me with interest, but I barely take in her features let alone mumble a response as she grabs my hand and stamps it with black ink.

"Enjoy!" she trills, her voice lost beneath the pounding of my heart and the throbbing colour, pulsating all around me.

Ripping off my beanie hat, I cram it into the back pocket of my jeans and swipe a shaky hand through my rain-slicked hair, then stalk towards the top of the stairs that leads to the caverness well of noise. Even though her voice is fucking angelic, I feel as though I'm about to step into Hell despite the colour wrapping around me in ribbons of kaleidoscopic light. How can something so beautiful feel so deadly? My heart skips in warning. A voice somewhere deep inside tells me not to enter, to turn around, to leave, that whoever this voice belongs to is someone who'll be the death of me.

"Fuck," I mutter, barely able to hang on to my motor functions let alone my ability to think straight or make a cognisant decision.

I've never been more affected. Grossly overwhelmed. Utterly consumed. I know myself enough to know that this is going to end in one of two ways. A week from now, I'm either going to be covered head to toe in splatters of paint, a masterpiece on canvas before me, my body exhausted, my soul momentarily free, or I'm going to be surrounded by a mess of unfinished canvases, unable to capture what I see, frustrated, overwhelmed, trapped, fucking depressed.

Neither outcome prevents me from descending into the bowels of the club as I step into Hell, or perhaps it's Heaven, depending on how you look at it. Either way, my body makes the decision for me as I trip down the stairs and stumble into the club.

TWO

Gripping the mic, my fingers wrap around the cool metal as I stare out into the darkened club and prepare to sing the last song of my set. Aside from a couple making out in a booth at the back of the club, a group of obnoxious men chucking back shot after shot, and the bartender serving a lone man a drink at the bar, *Smokey Joe's* is decidedly empty.

Not that it matters.

I don't need a captive audience to sing. I'm not here for praise or recognition. In fact, I abhor it. It's why I use a pseudonym to hide behind. Right now I'm not Harlow Richards, daughter to the famous Hollywood actress Melody Richards, I'm *Friday Love*. A name inspired by my favourite song by The Cure.

It's why I sing in dingy backstreet clubs and bars with people more interested in making out and getting annihilated on alcohol and drugs than listening to me sing. I'm background noise, a brief soundtrack to their evening, forgotten by morning.

That's exactly the way I like it.

I sing for me. I sing because it makes me happy. It erases the monotony of my everyday life, of only being known as the daughter of one of Hollywood's elite. Which you'd think would be glamorous, but is as far from glamorous as you can imagine, at least for me. As Harlow I'm the perfect Hollywood offspring, well-educated, polite, and nowhere near as beautiful or as alluring as her famous mother. Just how she likes it.

She's the star. Not me. Something that she's reminded me of for the best part of my life. Not that she'd ever admit that to anyone, least of all the press that she flirts with every chance she gets. As far as the general public believe, she's a Hollywood icon, most famously known for her role in the iconic nineties TV series, *Through the Eyes of A Child.*

She can do no wrong.

And I'm fine with that.

As far as I'm concerned fame is a curse, and I've no intention of ever following in the footsteps of my *still* fame-hungry mother. Or at least, not anymore.

At one point, in my early twenties, I had considered trying to get a record deal, but after a year of being groped by various record executives who assumed I was more than willing to give up my self-respect and my body in exchange for the promise of worldwide fame, I decided that it wasn't worth the humiliation.

Instead, I spend my days as my mother's personal assistant, following her around the globe and doing her bidding. When I'm not completing an errand on her behalf, or filling her calendar with talk show appearances, magazine interviews, and red carpet events, I'm writing songs in every bit of free time I have. Occasionally, like tonight, I pluck up the courage to sing at some dive bar or club, my identity kept hidden beneath dim lighting, a black wig, clothes I don't normally wear, and carefully applied makeup.

I actually had no intention of singing tonight, but a friend of a friend offered me the gig, and I accepted, grasping at the opportunity if only to get out of my mother's presence.

We're only in New York City for a few days so she can make an appearance on a TV chat show, and tonight is my first night off in weeks. Call it serendipity, call it fate, but I couldn't turn the opportunity down. My mother has no idea, she thinks I'm crawling bars looking for a man to spend the night with, not entertaining my need to sing.

"Go out. Meet a nice man. Have fun," she'd told me, which is code for '*I don't want you around. You're cramping my style.*' '*Get a life*'. Which is ironic really, given she actively goes out of her way to prevent me from having a life of my own.

For a million different reasons, I've had very few relationships in my twenty-eight years of life, and even less one-night stands, something my mother finds incredibly hard to understand given her past marriages and long list of lovers. My father was one of the men she cast aside after a brief affair in her early twenties. He was so insignificant to her that she never bothered to tell him I existed, and when he did the maths many years later and tried to reach out to me, she blocked his attempts. I didn't try to argue. It's something I regret immensely, but I haven't plucked up the courage to reach out to him, too much time has passed, and well, I guess the fact he didn't try harder to be a part of my life told me all I needed to know.

And so, with a red lip-sticked smile, she'd ushered me out of our hotel suite a few hours ago so she could entertain a man she has purportedly fallen head over heels in love with after being introduced to him at a social event we'd both attended back home in LA a month or so ago. I don't even recall being introduced to him, partly because I'd got so buzzed on the free alcohol, and partly because I left after two hours knowing if I stayed any longer I'd end up telling my mother to go stick her fake Hollywood smile up her arse.

All I know is that his first name is Robert, he's English, and a billionaire. To be honest, I lost interest listening to her after she repeatedly mentioned how wealthy he was, how he was flying in to see her on his private jet *for just one night* because he couldn't wait a second longer to be with her.

With three divorces under her belt, a bank account filled with millions of pounds worth of alimony, my mother is nothing if not predictable. I wonder how long it will take for her to sink her claws into him. Not long, I suspect.

Shaking my head free of thoughts of my mother, I clear my throat, press my eyes shut, then begin to sing a cover of *Young and Beautiful* by Lana Del Ray. I'm immediately lost to the music, to the way it makes me feel.

Through music I can express who I am. I can sing my emotions, emotions I keep hidden beneath quiet obedience. Unlike some other children of Hollywood celebrities, I never rebelled as a teenager, I conformed. I smiled and was polite. I acted with grace and humility. Hyper aware of being the best daughter my mother could wish for. I never acted up. I hid in the shadow of her fame, content to let her shine so that I could quietly write lyrics and make music.

I know I have a better than average voice, but I don't sing for compliments, I sing because it's the only time I ever truly feel like me. There's a release when I sing, like the lifting of a burdensome mountain from my shoulders. I lose myself to the music, to the endorphins that flood my system and buzz through my veins.

Singing for me is bliss. It's home. It's as simple as that.

Halfway through the song, I'm aware of someone staring at me. Behind closed eyelids I feel the penetration of their interest, and I crack my eyes open, searching the darkened club.

The group of the men are still knocking back shots, completely oblivious to me. Opposite, the couple making out are still wrapped up in each other's arms, and the man who was standing at the bar has sunk onto a stool with his back to me, nursing his drink.

Yet still I feel the intense sensation of someone giving me their undivided attention. It's not something I'm used to, and it throws me. I stumble on the next line of the verse, the words tripping awkwardly off my tongue as I trace my gaze around the club searching for the source of my discomfort, until eventually my eyes fall on a man standing in the entranceway, his hand gripping the doorframe. He's cast in shadow, the smoke machine they insist on using, combined with the muted lighting, smothering him in a shroud of grey-hazed darkness.

My skin prickles, an uncomfortable feeling bubbling in my chest as he steps fully into the club, stumbling as he moves. I watch as he grips the backs of the chairs and traverses the empty tables, swaying like a drunken man toward me. All the while staring at *me*.

Drawing in a breath, I continue to sing despite being intimidated by his undivided attention, stripped bare by his intense scrutiny.

Eventually he falls sideways onto a chair at a table situated directly in front of the stage, his hands shaking, his focus solely on me. I swear he's not even breathing, or maybe it's me who's not breathing, because as he shifts into a circle of light I can see him clearly, and this man...

This man is *beautiful*.

Droplets of water fall from his dark brown, slicked back hair, and I watch transfixed as they slide down the sharp cut of his cheekbones, dripping from his stubbled chin onto his rain-soaked shirt. His plump lips are parted, eyes a piercing blue as he quite literally drinks me in.

I've never felt this way before. So... so scrutinised.

His attention makes me want to simultaneously curl into myself, and bloom like a flower who hasn't felt the sun for days. I suddenly feel seen in a way I've never felt before. I'm not my famous mother's daughter. I'm not Harlow Richards, not even *Friday Love*. I'm simply the centre of someone's universe, the pinprick of sunlight on a darkened horizon, the lone star dazzling in a midnight sky.

My voice wobbles, and to the undiscerning ear, it's an unnoticeable mistake. Yet, his gaze flickers, a strange irrepressible connection snapping to life between us as his dark lashes blink slowly, and my heart stutters in my chest.

I recover as best I can, wanting... No, *needing* him to stay focussed on me despite the uncomfortable way he makes me feel, and as moments pass I'm no longer consumed by the song, but by this man who has caught my attention so thoroughly.

When he blows out a shuddering, shaky breath, there's a sharp flood of pain slashing across his features, and inexplicably I feel his pain stabbing in *my* chest, as though I bare it as much as he does.

It's not a physical pain he's suffering from, not as far as I can tell from my brief glance over his lean body. It seems deeper than that, an internal pain. I see it etched into the grooves between his brows, the dark circles beneath his piercing blue eyes that only seem to make them stand out more, and the muscle in his jaw that jumps and leaps as though he's trying desperately to hold on to his inner turmoil.

No, not turmoil. *Grief.*

He seems debilitated by it, and the utter devastation he appears to be wrapped in makes me wonder what his story is.

Am I singing a song that someone he once loved and lost, adored? Is he being bombarded with memories of a relationship that he's no longer a part of? Is he heartbroken? Is he high? Is he dangerous? Is he just a lonely man out late at night passing the time? Does he have family, friends? Do they know how much he hurts?

All those questions swirl around my mind as I continue to sing. As I continue to sing to *him*.

Because at this moment no one else exists.

It's just us, two strangers. A seemingly troubled, beautiful man, and a lonely woman connected by this song. I allow my eyes to fully take him in. Dressed in jeans, hoodie and brown boots, he's just like every other man I've passed by in the street. Except he isn't. He's so much more. It isn't just his beautiful face, broad shoulders and tall frame, it's... I can't even pinpoint what *it* even is. All I know is that I am caught up in the heat of his stare, lost to the painful rapture on his face, confounded by the intense attention he's paying me.

My brows pull together as I tip my head to the side studying him, and he presses his palms against his thighs, his fingers curling into the material of his jeans. That simple act, as though he needs to hold on to something to prevent him from rushing towards me, is both strangely attractive and incredibly over-whelming.

My heart pounds, his eyes flare. My pulse thumps, his lips part. I sway towards him, enraptured, he leans forward in his seat, trembling.

Each word, each note that passes through my lips seem suddenly provocative, filled with double-meaning. The pain in his face transforms into longing, and I feel that longing like a soft caress of a lover.

A feeling I haven't felt in a long, long time.

It makes heat crawl down my spine and gather between my legs. I gasp on the next note, my cheeks heating as my clit throbs. He bites down on his bottom lip, eyes flaring with an intense heat, a heat I feel scorching every inch of my skin.

I almost don't want to stop singing, knowing instinctively that this sudden, fraught, intense connection will end as soon as I do, but as the last word passes my lips, the elongated note hovering in the air between us, we continue to stare at one another long after the music fades.

Then as the bartender claps half-heartedly, the stranger's eyes flutter shut, his body goes limp and he slides to the floor with a violent thud.

THREE

"Hey, are you okay?"

Her voice.

The sweet, lyrical softness, the perfect rise and fall in pitch, the kindness imbued into every word tugs at my dulled senses, drawing me back out of the darkness and into stunning technicolour that continues to weave behind my closed eyelids, despite my body's attempts at blotting it out. She's American. I'm not sure why that surprises me, but it does.

"Can you hear me?" she continues, and I feel the soothing touch of her finger against my cheek like an electric current zipping through my bloodstream, my body reacting to her touch way before my mind can catch up. "Should I call an ambulance?"

Her warm breath cascades over my cheek as she leans in close, causing another eruption of goosebumps to scatter across my skin, igniting that electric current into a blazing inferno.

"No ambulance," I manage to mumble, groaning as I lift my

hand to my face to cover my eyes, acutely aware that I need a moment to gather myself, to regain a modicum of control.

It's been a long time since the overstimulation from my synesthesia has caused me to pass out. As a kid it would happen often, but these days it has become less common. Over the years I've been able to pick up on the warning signs and take action. Warning signs that I chose to thoroughly ignore tonight.

"Are you sure? You don't look too good," she says, worry threading through her singsong voice.

"I'm fine," I snap, my eyes still pressed shut as I force myself upright and draw up my knees. Who am I trying to kid? I'm far from fine. She huffs out a breath, about as convinced by my strained response as I am.

"Maybe you should get yourself checked out to be on the safe side?"

"It's been a long day," I hedge, hoping that's enough to allay her concerns. The last thing I need is a trip to the emergency room.

She shifts beside me, her arm wrapping around my back. Her scent wafts under my nose, and *fuck*, if a rainbow had a scent, it would be hers. Every hue becomes a perfumed aroma. There's sweet rose red, citrus lemon yellow, freshly cut grass green, ocean breeze blue, ripe plum purple.

Christ, everything about her overwhelms my senses. Her perfumed scent, the sound of her voice, the touch of her skin, the colours she brings to life before my very eyes. I briefly wonder if she would taste as heady as I imagine.

"Must've been one hell of a day," she replies, a soft laugh breaking free as her hand rubs up and down my spine. It's a comforting gesture, and one that makes my bastard cock twitch.

"You could say that," I reply, finally forcing my eyelids open as I blink up at her kneeling beside me.

She gives me a soft smile, and I find her molten brown eyes, flecked with green and amber and lined with dark kohl, staring back at me. I swallow hard, dragging in a much needed breath. God damn, have I died and gone to heaven? This woman is beautiful, made even more so by the colours still ebbing and flowing around her like a halo.

"Hey there," she whispers, her gaze locking with mine as her short black hair falls around her face in a bob, the blunt fridge offsetting her sun-kissed skin perfectly. "I'm... My name is Friday."

"Nice to meet you, Friday," I reply, weak-kneed. It's just as well I'm sitting down, because this woman is doing strange fucking things to me. Well, stranger than usual, at least. "Sterling," I add.

"Sterling," she whispers, cocking her head to the side, another smile tugging on her perfect lips as she ruminates on my unusual name. I mean, hers is hardly common either.

"That's my name, don't wear it out," I retort foolishly.

Way to go Casanova. Could I be any more awkward?

"You're English," she murmurs, clearly an afterthought or a delayed reaction given we've been conversing for a little while now.

"I'm afraid so," I reply, not sure if that was a compliment or simply an observation.

"Want to try standing?" she asks with a soft chuckle.

"I guess staying down here isn't the best idea, might catch something... From the floor, I mean," I quickly add, smiling a little. But even that is an effort.

"I know what you mean," she laughs, the soft tinkle making the colour wrapped around her tumble and twirl. "This place is disgusting."

But you make it paradise, I almost say. Thank fuck I don't.

"Jesus," I mutter instead, clearing my throat as I try in vain to suppress the unsuppressable.

My fingers curl into fists as I try to regain control once more. I'm itching to paint, but more than that... Fuck, I'm itching to pull her into my arms and lose myself in *her*.

That's never happened before, this sudden intense desire to claim the object of my attention. This almost feral need is just as forceful as my need to paint. And, yes, whilst it might be true that when I'm under the influence of my condition, I fall for the voice, no matter who's singing, my focus has only ever been on the process of bringing my art to life. It's a feeling I can only describe as being akin to love, but it's brief, and that feeling is always so tightly bound to the colours I see and the piece I eventually produce that it leaves me the moment I've finished painting. It has always been a brief love affair that culminates in a work of art.

Yet this unexplainable, immediate, overwhelming *connection* I feel for this woman is *more*. It's sexual, I can admit that. Who wouldn't be attracted to her, she's fucking stunning? Christ knows it's been too long since I've been with a woman, but it's also... Fuck, I don't know why it's different, I just know that it is. Right now I don't have the wherewithal to figure it out.

"Sterling? Do you need some water or—"

"I *knew* you were on something," a familiar voice says, interrupting Friday, the bouncer's looming presence hovering in my periphery.

"I'm not on anything," I grind out through gritted teeth.

"Yeah and I'm the fucking President. Up you go, it's time you get the fuck out," he retorts briskly, reaching down to yank at my arm.

"Get your hands off him!" Friday shouts, the sweetness in

her voice turning steely, her outburst as shocking as the sudden protectiveness glinting in her eyes. "Can't you see he's unwell."

"I'm not unwell... I'm just..." I mumble, not finishing my sentence, not wanting to explain what is actually happening to me or why for that matter. It's too complicated, too personal, too fucking humiliating.

"Unwell?" the bouncer snorts. "More like *high*. GET.UP!"

Friday jumps to her feet, shoving her palms against the arsehole's chest. "Back off!"

Her anger blazes brightly, catching me off-guard with her show of solidarity. There have been too many times my own father has told me to get my shit together when I fainted as a kid. To have someone care enough to face up to this arsehole is not something I'm used to, and I appreciate it. It also reminds me that I'm not usually like this. I've been in many brawls over the years, and can look after myself well enough. Just, apparently, not tonight.

"Fuck, don't. It's all good," I groan, shifting my weight forwards as I reach for the chair I slid off and haul myself to my feet on shaky legs. I stumble a little, and Friday reaches for me, placing a steadying hand on my arm. I feel the heat of her touch through my damp sweater and it takes everything in me not to moan, to give in to this intensity between us.

"Take it easy," she demands softly, despite her hard expression still aimed at the fucker watching this all play out.

"He needs to leave. NOW!" the bouncer insists.

"I'll go. It's all good," I mutter, forcing strength into my spine, but finding myself leaning into Friday more than I should.

"You're not going anywhere, not on your own," Friday insists.

"Either he leaves now, or I throw you both out," the dick-head snaps.

"Fine. I'll just grab my bag," she replies coldly, turning her attention to me, her voice softening. "Can you stand on your own for a moment?"

I give her a brief dip of my head. "I'm good."

It's a lie of course, I'm positively fucked, but I'm not about to admit that now. She nods, withdrawing her hand from my arm, and throws one last look at the bouncer.

"Do not touch him!" she warns, her finger jabbing into his chest.

The bouncer grumbles something cutting under his breath, but he doesn't try to manhandle me again. With a brief, concerned look in my direction, Friday twists on her heel and rushes towards the stage, grabbing a bag and coat concealed behind a swathe of moth-eaten velvet curtain, returning within moments.

"Off you go," the bouncer says, folding his arms across his chest as Friday reaches for me once more, her arm threading through mine.

She doesn't even blink, so caught up in helping a stranger stagger across the club that she forgoes all sense of concern for herself. I could be a psychopath praying on women for all she knows. I'm not of course, but that doesn't stop me from worrying about her sense of self-preservation. Is she always so... so *kind*, so unfazed by a stranger in need?

"What an asshole!" she exclaims as I walk unsteadily towards the exit. "What happened to a little human decency?"

"You seem to have it in spades," I reply, gripping the handrail and hauling myself up the stairs with her assistance.

"In spades?" she questions, a confused look on her face.

"It means you have a lot of something. In your case, human decency."

She nods, her lips quirking up in a smile. "You need help, I'm helping. I'd do that for anyone in the same predicament."

"I could be dangerous."

"Are you?" she asks, side-eyeing me as we reach the top of the stairs, the air isn't as thick up here, thank fuck, because believe me, I'm an inferno of blazing heat and unequivocal fucked-upness.

"No."

"Didn't think so," she murmurs.

"Pretty sure most dangerous men would say that," I reply.

"I trust you," she says as we step outside of the club, and I lean against the brick wall, dragging in deep lungfuls of air.

It's stopped raining now, the alleyway glistening with puddles from the recent downpour, the reflection of the red neon light of *Smokey Joe's* rippling in the nearest puddle.

"Why?" I eventually ask, flicking my gaze her way.

"Why what?"

She steps back, giving me space. Space I could easily eat up with one step toward her.

It gives me a moment to study her. I'm guessing she's around five foot eight, and whilst I'm making huge assumptions here, she's unlikely to be able to fend me off if I was a psychopath, hence the question. Then again she could be a black belt in karate, and more than capable of defending herself should the need arise.

Not that it would, I don't want to hurt her. I want to sink my cock inside of her and then I want to paint her on canvas. Not just the colours she entices within me, but *her*.

Fuck. Fuck. Fuck.

I really need to get my shit together.

"*Why* do you trust me?"

"Call it a hunch," she shrugs, pulling on her light denim jacket, the action causing her belly-coasting band tee to lift higher.

I rip my gaze away from that smooth expanse of skin and her gently rounded hips, my throat dry, my cock aching. I really fucking hope she doesn't look too closely at my crotch, because right now I'm sporting a very painful erection.

"Seems unwise to rely on a hunch," I comment, my head spinning momentarily, causing the ground to tilt beneath my feet.

"I'm not afraid of you. "

"I'm no more than a stranger," I counter.

She frowns at that, something I can't interpret flicking in her eyes. "Apparently so."

Her response is strange, bulging with hidden meaning, and I can't help but wonder if she feels this connection too, or am I so caught up in the barrage of my overloaded senses that I'm imagining things that aren't real?

"Get a grip," I mutter under my breath as I lean my head back against the wall and press my eyes shut.

"So, I know you said you didn't want to go to the hospital…" she says after a beat, her voice trailing off as I shake my head then push off the wall and begin walking down the alleyway towards the main road. I need to move, to force my body to act before I crumble again.

"I should get home," I croak out, forcing my hands into my pockets so I don't reach for her and do something rash like kiss her.

"Can I at least grab you a cab?" she offers when we reach the pavement and turn to face each other.

A breeze whips up her hair, and for the first time this evening I notice that it doesn't quite move in the same way natural hair does. It's stiff almost, coarser than I'd realised.

She must notice me staring because she reaches up and tugs, pulling off a wig to reveal silky honey blonde hair pulled back in a low bun. If I thought she couldn't be any more stunning, I was wrong.

"You're blonde," I say inanely.

"It's just something I wear when I sing. Part of the..." she frowns, then clears her throat as she runs a hand over her natural hair, smoothing down the wayward strands "Act, I suppose."

"You shouldn't hide yourself. I like it."

"Thanks..."

Her voice trails off as she stuffs her wig into her bag, and I can't help but notice that her hands are trembling a little. It makes me wonder if talk of me being a psychopath has scared her, that whatever snapped to life between us in the club has dispersed alongside the clammy late night air the city has been shrouded in of late.

"Can I have your number?" I blurt out, realising that I'm staring, staring at her beauty, at the colour that still twines around her, at the way her purple lipsticked mouth parts on a soft breath and a deep blush rushes across her cheeks.

She hesitates, considering my request, then nods. "Sure, let me have your phone."

Reaching into my pocket, I pull it out and hand it to her. She takes it from me, chewing on her lip as she types in her number. "There," she replies, passing me the phone back.

"Well, I should go," I say, pocketing my phone once more, finding this whole exchange excruciating. I'm not even sure why

I asked for her number other than to cover up the fact that I was staring at her like a creep.

"Sure. I guess I should get going too," she replies, obviously coming to her senses.

I can't help but feel disappointed. Not that it's her fault. I'm not a smooth talker like my best friends back home are when it comes to women. I've always been socially awkward, abrupt with people I don't know well. Growing up being different means I've had to adapt to the people around me, always trying to fit in. It's not been easy. Back home people know me as the heir to a multi-billion pound fortune, a man who, on the surface, is as polished and as good-looking as his father. Yet, that's just a front, a camouflage to hide the real me, the person who stumbles through each day trying to hide his differences, his awkwardness, all in an effort to make other people comfortable. Tonight she's seen a side to me very few people have, and honestly, I feel vulnerable. It's not a feeling I enjoy.

"I'm still happy to grab you a cab before I leave. There's plenty around."

"I only live a block away. I'll walk," I reply, shoving my hands into my jean pockets.

"You do? Okay... Well, I guess this is goodbye?"

She chews on her lip, a sudden nervousness slipping through, telling me she's not quite at ease in my company as she'd like me to believe.

"I guess it is," I reply, swallowing hard at the prospect of her departure, that chord I felt connecting myself to her earlier, tugging at my insides as she gives me a soft smile.

"Goodnight, Sterling," she says, pulling her bag across her front, hugging it to her chest as she twists on her heel and takes a step away from me. "I hope you feel better soon."

Inexplicably, the colour that has been hovering around her

begins to fade, and it guts me. It's as though the magic is wearing off, her departure cutting the connection with one fell swoop.

Fuck.

Before I can even contemplate what I'm doing, I'm striding after her, my fingers curling around her arm. "Don't," I bite out as she turns to face me.

"Don't?" she whispers, her eyes wide.

Don't go, I can't fucking bare it.

"Would you like a coffee?" I blurt out instead.

"A coffee?"

"Or tea?" I ask, internally cursing myself.

"Most places that sell coffee... and tea," she adds with a soft laugh, "Are closed."

"Yeah," I say, raking a hand through my hair, wishing the ground would swallow me up. "What I meant to say was, would you like to come back to my place, for coffee... or tea?"

There, *fuck*, I've said it.

I stare at her for long moments. Far longer than would be deemed socially acceptable, and being the awkward fuck that I am, I don't try to fill the silence, or say something charming to persuade her to come back home with me, I just wait.

"Sterling, are you propositioning me?" she eventually replies, her eyes dancing with a tentative kind of humour.

I baulk at her question. "No. Fuck... I... Shit... This isn't... I didn't mean..."

Yes, yes you absolutely fucking did, my inner voice needles me.

Because that's exactly what I'm doing. I'm asking her back to my place under the pretence of a coffee when all I want to do is strip her bare, worship her body and sink deep inside of her just so she can feel a fraction of what I'm feeling now. That is, totally and utterly out of control.

Her laughter fades, her smile turns serious, and just when I think she's going to walk away for good, she does something inexplicable.

She rests her hand on my arm before murmuring, "Yes, I want to go home with you."

FOUR

"Yes, I want to go home with you."

Did I actually say that out loud? Who am I?

Seriously, this isn't like me, I *don't* do these kinds of things.

I never go home with anyone for a one night stand. Actually, that's a lie. I did, *once.* It was back when I was in college under the influence of a steady stream of cheap beer, and false confidence. I regretted it the second I slept with the douchebag, whose name I can't remember. Pretty sure he only wanted me because I let slip who my mother was.

And that's generally the problem with the men I've been surrounded with my whole life, they're interest in me only extends to their fascination with my beautiful, gregarious, *famous* mother. There have been countless times that I've been taken out on a date by men who only feigned interest in me until they met my mother, then it was as if I no longer existed. Once my mother got her claws into them, I was long forgotten.

But this time it's different. *He's* different.

I also don't have the buzz of cheap alcohol running through my veins as an excuse to do something this reckless. Right now, there's just this strange kind of *wanting*. I want to get to know Sterling more. I want to know why he seems so in pain, why he fainted. I want to explore what this strange feeling is in my chest. Is it purely lust? Is it sympathy? Is it a culmination of my own loneliness? Is it simply the need to escape for a while in the arms of a beautiful, albeit troubled man who looked at me like *I* was someone worthy of their attention?

As we step into his exposed brick apartment, I don't regret my decision, not in the slightest. People do this all the time, right? Go back to someone's place for 'coffee', which everyone knows is a euphemism for sex. I can't deny the magnetism between us, and for once in my life I'm throwing caution to the wind and acting on instinct. All I know is that I don't want coffee, or tea, I want to get lost in him, even if it is for just one night. At least I hope it will be.

"I'm sorry my place is a mess," he apologises, grabbing some clothes thrown over the back of his battered, brown leather sofa and shoving them into a closet across the room. "I wasn't expecting visitors."

"And I wasn't expecting to end up back at a stranger's place this evening either," I reply honestly, biting down on my lip as I watch him stride around his spacious apartment, gathering empty glasses and dirty plates, and dropping them into the sink.

Whilst there are a lot of his belongings strewn around the place, there isn't much by way of furniture. Just the beat up leather sofa, a wooden island separating the living space from the kitchen, and a bed raised off the floor by a platform and several steps. I can see a door ajar in the far corner of the apartment, and a bathroom beyond.

"You want to leave?" he asks, his startling blue eyes drilling into me as he stills, a frown creasing his brows.

"Not at all."

"You don't seem certain," he continues.

"I don't want to leave, not even a little bit," I admit, then bark out a strained laugh, shaking my head at this woman I've suddenly become.

He cocks his head studying me. "Are you okay?"

"I'm... I don't..." Dragging in a breath, I puff out my cheeks. "I don't normally do this."

"Drink coffee?" he deadpans, and I've no idea if he's trying to make a joke or if it's an honest to goodness question.

His lack of, I don't know, seductiveness is surprising, and I'm honestly not sure how a man who looks like him could be the exact opposite of what I'd expect. It's kind of judgemental to assume that just because he's good-looking he would know how to charm a woman into bed, but I can't seem to help it. Maybe I'm more like my mother than I'd care to admit. She's the queen of judgy.

"Go back to a man's house for..." I clear my throat. "*Sex.*"

"You want to have sex with me?" he asks, and I suddenly feel as though I've read the situation wrong. God, what am I doing?

"You *want* to have coffee?" I counter, cheeks blazing with heat as he stares, and stares, and stares. I don't know where to look. Why does the way he looks at me make me feel so... exposed? "Oh my God, I've read this so wrong. I should probably–"

"I don't want to have coffee," he interrupts, swiping a hand through his hair, the silver striations in his eyes glinting with a sudden smouldering heat that resonates deep inside my chest.

"And the sex?" I squeak.

Why the hell am I pushing the subject? This is so damn reckless. Perhaps I'm more lonely than I'd thought? It's been over a year since I've slept with a man, and whilst that's never really bothered me, tonight I just need... Christ, I don't know. I guess I just need to be someone else for a few hours. Harlow Richards would never, *ever*, do something like this. But my alter ego, Friday Love? I guess she would. She *is*.

He hauls in a breath, rounding the kitchen island and steps towards me. "It's been a long time."

"Since you've drank coffee or had sex?" I ask, my mouth running away with me once again.

"Both," he replies, and it's strained, his response. In fact, his whole body is.

I see it in the way he holds himself. I see it in the tightness in his shoulders, the tenseness around his jaw, and the way his fingers flex and curl into fists.

"Yet here I am," I murmur, my arms falling to my side, my bag slipping from my shoulder and onto the floor as he approaches. I'm completely bewildered, uncertain of myself, yet willing to step into whatever's happening, despite his tension and my very apparent lack of sexual history. As a woman heading towards her thirties I should be more experienced, but I'm not, and I guess it shows.

My palms press against my jeans, the humid air still clinging to the material as I watch him approach. As he steps closer, there's a fierce kind of control in the way he moves his body, how he zeroes in on me. It's not in a way that scares me, but in a way that makes my pulse spike and my skin heat.

"Here you are," he agrees, that same intense look on his face as he reaches up and grazes the pad of his thumb across my bottom lip. My breath stills, his hands are surprisingly warm, his touch gentle, and so different to his intense demeanour. "Cotton candy pink."

"Sorry?" I ask, blinking up at him as a tentative smile softens his angular features with two sexy dimples. I imagine kissing them, and heat rises up my neck.

"Your lips, they're cotton candy pink," he murmurs, serious once more. Which seems an odd thing to say given I'm wearing purple lipstick.

"I–"

"I'm going to kiss you now?" he says, a question more than a statement as he palms my cheek with one hand, whilst the other reaches behind my back and tugs me close, waiting for my approval.

"Okay." I nod, giving him permission.

"Okay," he mutters, edging closer until his lips hover over mine, tentative.

I feel the warmth radiating off his skin, and that strange pull between us tightening as the tip of his nose brushes against mine. He angles his head to the side, his breath soft as his lips trail over my cheek. My heart thunders, racing to a beat that appears to match his own as I press my palm against his chest.

"You're wet," I say, the dampness of his hoodie seeping into my skin. It's a stupid statement, and it's not as if I hadn't already noticed.

"Got caught in the rain," he explains, his lips lingering on my cheek.

"Shouldn't you take it off... So you don't catch a chill?" I add quickly, likely ruining the moment.

He nods, then pulls back, eyeing me as he reaches for the hem of his hoodie pulling it, and the t-shirt he's wearing, off in one go. "There," he says, dropping them both to the floor with a wet slap.

My eyes drop to his chest, to his sculpted pecs and six pack, and his smooth, lightly tanned skin. God, he's even more beautiful naked. Well, almost naked. It has me wondering just what the rest of him looks like. Without even thinking about what I'm doing, I press my hand against the centre of his chest, and say, "Wow."

"You like what you see?" he asks, and there isn't an ounce of flirting as he says the words. It's simply a question, as though he doesn't realise just how attractive he is.

"From where I'm standing, you're pretty perfect."

He frowns as he steps back into my space, placing his hands where they were moments before stripping off. "Pretty sure I'm not."

I open my mouth to protest, but his thumb captures my bottom lip as his fingers caress my cheek once more. Warmth coils deep and low in my stomach, arousal blooming outwards. I have to bite down on a whimper.

"So this is happening," I blurt out instead, feeling like a teenager who's never been kissed before, let alone fucked. I really should shut up now.

"Yes," he mutters, and moments later his lips meet mine.

I expect softness, a kiss that's exploratory even, but what I get instead is a knee-trembling intensity. His lips are firm, his kiss verging on desperate, and I fall into it headfirst as my lips part and his tongue licks brazenly into my mouth.

Oh...

Damn...

I feel his desire and lust resonating deep within my chest as he plunders my mouth with his tongue. His kiss is passionate, commanding, and sexy. Yet I feel his damage, a strange kind of brokenness too. Is that weird? That I can feel his pain as much as his lust? I don't get to linger on that thought for long, because my body is reacting in a way I've never truly experienced before, and I'm lost to the taste of him, the feel of him, his... I don't know. His essence, his aura? Something undefinable.

Christ, whatever it is, all I know is that Sterling can kiss. I feel his need, and my own intense desire, scattering down my spine as our tongues twine. It spreads out to all my extremities, pulsing through my veins, zoning in on my clit.

Throb.

Throb.

Throb.

My panties are drenched in seconds.

A guttural moan rises up his chest as his fingers dig into my hair, yanking at the strands still caught in my hair tie. There's this potent kind of electricity snapping between us as he crowds my body with his and we stumble backwards against the wall, or at least that's how it feels to me.

I imagine sparks flying in the air between us, zipping and zapping as we kiss and kiss and kiss.

Is this what being kissed should feel like? Because I can with certainty say that I have never been kissed like this before. Everything feels heightened, and I can't seem to fathom why that is. He's a stranger. I don't know this man, and he doesn't know me, and yet this energy between us, this attraction, feels extraordinary. Maybe that's the point of one night stands, the not knowing a person, just acting on instinct, on basic human needs, pushing aside all rational thought and just *feeling*.

All I know is that I don't want him to stop. I *need* to see this through.

I'm a puddle of lust, moaning into his mouth as he grinds his hips against mine. I don't recognise myself as I grasp at him, my palm sliding upwards, cupping his face before sliding my fingers into his hair, pulling him closer.

Who the hell am I?

Oh, that's right, tonight I'm Friday Love, and I'm doing something reckless, something Harlow Richards would never do. It makes me feel empowered, and I ignore that nagging voice in my head to push him away and return to my monotonous life as Harlow, living in the shadow of her mother's spotlight.

We kiss for what seems like an eternity, and God, it's like lightning and starlight bursting behind my eyes. It's overwhelming, exhilarating. My mind is a whirl of random, disjointed thoughts, but my body? My body is definitely leading the way, ignoring every warning that rushes through my mind and fizzles out before I can even make sense of them.

"Off," he growls against my mouth, his hands sliding between us as he tugs at the buttons of my jacket. "Now."

"Yes," I respond, panting at the burning lust, at the frantic way our breaths mingle.

We're both trembling, fumbling with my buttons, and our heads bump in our haste to remove my jacket. I let out a soft, gasping laugh.

"Shit, sorry."

"Fuck," he mutters, stepping back, eyes widening as I reach up and rub my forehead. "Did I hurt you?"

"No. Not at all—"

But as I reach for him again, he abruptly turns on his heel and strides towards the sofa, leaving me quaking, reeling from his absence. My knees buckle, and my hands slap against the wall to steady myself. What is he doing now? I breathe heavily as he takes another step away from me, and another until he twists on his feet, and his arse hits the sofa.

"We should talk first. Get to know each other, yeah?" he offers, flicking his gaze away, looking as overwhelmed as I feel.

Truthfully, I want to say no, that I want to continue kissing him. I want to explain that if we stop now I might lose my courage, but I don't. Instead I clear my throat.

"Sure, okay. Let's talk. I can do that."

Really though, can I? I'm not sure I can string a sensible sentence together right at this moment. I'm a ball of fizzing energy, of trembling lust, and I have to take a steadying breath to centre myself a little.

"Make yourself comfortable," he says, jerking his chin towards me, indicating I should remove my jacket.

"Sure," I agree, slipping it off and draping it over the arm of the sofa as I approach him.

I'm pretty sure that someone with more experience with one night stands would handle this with far more grace than me. Perhaps they'd even ignore his desire to talk and strip seductively. I briefly consider doing just that, but a sudden shyness overcomes me, and I plop down onto the sofa instead. "Do you want to talk about what happened in the club?"

"No," he replies sharply, tensing up before quickly adding. "I apologise, that came out wrong."

"That's okay. I get it. Some things you just want to keep to yourself, right? Are you sure you're okay?"

He nods. "I appreciate your concern, but I'm good. Can we just concentrate on the here and now?"

"Of course." I don't question him further, understanding that when all is said and done I'm someone he's just met, and whatever caused him to faint, and the pain he seems to carry around, is a conversation that should probably happen when more trust is gained. I'm not even sure if I'll ever see him again, so why would he open up to me? "What do you want to talk about?" I add.

"You."

"Oh, okay. So what do you want to know?" I ask tentatively,

not sure why, given I already know that there are plenty of things I'm not going to share with him tonight, namely my relation to a famous Hollywood starlet or my real name. The last thing I want to do is think about my mother, let alone speak about her, and if I give him my real name it will lead to a conversation I don't want to have right now.

I want to remain Friday Love, I don't want to be Harlow Richards.

"Your voice is incredible," he says, tipping his head to the side as he turns his body to face me, his muscles tightening and releasing with the movement. He's cut to perfection, a veritable Adonis, and yet again I find myself wondering why this man isn't as arrogant or as self-assured as the men who I've met over the years appear to be.

"Thank you," I reply, pressing my palms against my thighs, not sure what else to say, not sure what to do, even.

"I heard you from the street. I *needed* to see who was singing," he adds, and the way he puts emphasis on the word needed, makes my cheeks flame. "Where did you learn to sing like that?"

"Nowhere in particular. I've never taken singing lessons. I just like to sing. It makes me feel..."

I shrug, not sure how I can explain what singing means to me, and my gaze drops to my hands as I try to untangle all these feelings and thoughts he's evoking in me.

"Alive?" he questions softly.

"Yes." I lift my gaze back to his, understanding passing between us. "But more than that, at *peace*. Singing is an escape for me."

"I felt that," he agrees with a nod, then whispers, "I felt more than that too. So much more."

I honestly don't know how to respond to that statement. So I don't.

Reaching for me, he curls his large palm around one of my hands and squeezes gently. "I told you it's been a long time. I'm sorry if this is awkward."

"No, please don't apologize. I'm not very good at this kind of thing either. I don't normally–"

"Go back to a strange man's place to have sex?" he asks, and despite the lightness of his tone, he remains as tense as ever.

"Exactly."

"I don't ask women back to my place to have sex very often."

"Very often?" So he *has* done this before.

"Well, ever, actually. You're the first."

"The first? You're not a virgin, surely?" There I go again. Why can't I shut the hell up?! He doesn't baulk at my question, he simply shakes his head.

"I'm not a virgin, no. But you are the first woman I've ever invited into my personal space."

For some reason that makes my heart squeeze. His truthfulness is extremely attractive.

"Then I'm honoured to be the first."

"You might change your mind after."

"So sex is still on the cards?" I blurt out.

"After I just head butted you, I wasn't entirely sure you still wanted to have sex with me," he admits, his thumb swirling circles over the back of my hand.

"You mean after *I* head butted *you*," I reply, heat radiating through me at our mutual frankness, at the way he's touching me.

"Looks like we're both out of practice."

"You've no idea," I say, meeting his gaze as he cocks his head to the side, studying me.

For long moments we just stare at one another, neither of us moving the conversation along, and despite normally hating to be the centre of attention, I just let him absorb me as our chests rise and fall in sync, and he shifts closer. His hand trails up the bare skin of my arm, coasting over the sleeve of my t-shirt, feathering along the collar before he presses his palm over my breast and I let out a soft, stuttering sigh. My nipples are hard, my ability to speak silenced by his warm, yet possessive touch.

"Is this okay?"

"Yes," I reply on a soft exhale.

"I want to fuck you," he adds after a beat, a frown appearing between his eyes.

"I thought you wanted to talk?" I squeak, squirming at how turned on I am, how I'm reeling from the whiplash of his remark.

"I do... but more than that, I want you to feel what I feel," he continues, zoning in on my lips.

"And what do you feel?" I whisper, gasping as he gently squeezes my breast whilst his free hand slides up my thigh, his fingers reaching beneath the bottom of my t-shirt, coasting over my belly. My stomach muscles tighten, not from stress or fear, but from anticipation, longing.

"Out of control."

I drag in another ragged breath. "You seem very in control right at this moment."

"Believe me, I'm not."

"So what now?" I ask, because despite his statement, despite palming my breast and running his fingers beneath the waistband of my jeans, he still doesn't bridge the gap and kiss me again. "Maybe you should eat something? You fainted after all," I add lamely.

"I don't want to eat," he says, the words rumbling up his

chest. "But I do want to hear you sing again. Will you sing for me, Friday?"

"You want me to sing for you, *right now?*" I ask, thrown a little, if I'm being honest.

"Please?"

I blink up at him, and before I can even contemplate his question, I find myself saying, "At this point, I'm pretty sure that I'll do anything you ask."

FIVE

My dick strains against the zipper of my jeans as I graze my thumb over Friday's nipple and she arches into my hand. Believe me, it's taking every last ounce of self-restraint not to rip her clothes from her body, sink inside of her, and give into this attraction between us, an attraction I've *never* felt before.

I'm also fully aware that my request for her to sing for me whilst we're on the verge of having sex might seem a little odd, but I *need* to hear her sing again. I need to see the vibrant colours that her beautiful voice evokes within me. I want to sink into her with those colours wrapping around us both and fully immerse myself in all that she is. I've never wanted anything more in my entire life.

"Will you?" I repeat.

"I can't promise I'll be any good," she says, her chest heaving as I continue to palm her breast.

"Any good?" I ask, my gaze dropping to the skin of her lower stomach where my fingers still graze her, making her shudder.

"I'm a little nervous." She lets out a shy laugh as my gaze

flicks back up to meet hers. "And entirely turned on. I might mess up."

"I'm nervous too," I admit, but not, perhaps, for the reason she might assume.

I'm not inexperienced when it comes to sex, but I wasn't lying when I said that I haven't ever brought a woman back to my sanctuary. This is completely out of the ordinary for me. I'm very protective of my personal space and who I allow into it.

"You are?"

"Like I said, you're the first woman I've brought back to my place. I'm..." I heave out a breath. "I'm not a particularly social person, more of a hermit to be honest," I admit, revealing something so fucking personal to me, that I surprise even myself. "Does that turn you off?"

"Not at all. It's a relief."

"How so?"

"Firstly, the fact that you're not afraid to be honest with me, is attractive. Secondly, I've spent my whole life around people who pretend to be someone they're not, with huge personalities and even bigger egos. It's exhausting being around people like that," she adds, slamming her mouth shut as though she's said too much.

I don't push her on the subject, or ask her who she's talking about. Instead I ask, "Do you think it's odd that I'm asking you to sing instead of taking you to bed?"

She reaches up and cups my cheek, her fingers stroking my skin as she contemplates my question. "Admittedly, your request is *unusual*, given the current circumstances," she replies, letting out another soft moan as I gently tease her nipple with the pad of my thumb, "But no, I don't think it's odd–" She pauses, gasping, as I lean forward and dip my head to her stomach, brushing a kiss there.

"That's good to know," I mumble against her skin.

"I'm actually flattered that you want to hear me sing again," she continues, her fingers stroking through my hair. "It will make this night even more memorable, I'm sure."

"It will," I agree, resting my cheek against her stomach, loving how gentle she caresses me. I've never felt more wired, more tense, yet inexplicably comfortable in another person's presence. That comfortableness is new to me. I like it.

"Your skin is so fucking soft," I murmur, the tip of my nose gliding upwards, wishing there wasn't any clothes between us. Reluctantly, I lean back, but not before I press another soft kiss against her lips.

"You *really* want me to sing right now?" she murmurs against my mouth.

"More than I've wanted anything," I reply hoarsely, forcing myself away from her, giving us both space to breathe.

She swallows hard, her throat bobbing as she gets to her feet. "What song?"

"Surprise me," I reply, my fingers pressing into my still damp jeans as I watch her chew on her lip as she decides, so fucking thankful she's willing to do this for me.

"I think I have the perfect song," she says after a beat, stepping back and blowing out a long, slow breath. "Just bare with me, okay?"

"I'm not going anywhere," I say, wanting to reach out and pull her close, but knowing that if I do I won't be able to stop there. I'll want to bury my head between her legs and feast on her pussy. I'll want to kiss every single inch of her body. I'll want to find nirvana inside of her. Instead, I grit my jaw, ignore my throbbing cock, and wait.

With one last soft smile, she closes her eyes, presses her palm against the centre of her chest and begins to sing.

"*My God,*" I mutter, as colour immediately forms at the edges of my vision, flowing inwards, twisting and tumbling, merging and shimmering, encasing Friday in so much colour.

My whole body is covered in goosebumps, the uniqueness of her voice tapping into something deep inside of me as I *feel* her voice coasting along my skin. It's like an invisible caress that simultaneously turns me on, and ignites another cascade of colour that ebbs and flows with every beautiful, enchanting note that leaves her parted lips.

It takes me long moments to even hear the words she's singing, but when I do, I gasp. She's singing *Iris* by the Goo Goo Dolls in her own inimitable style, and every word is like a declaration of her intentions tonight, and maybe even an insight into the woman she is. She sings softly, the pitch perfectly emotional, and there's a wistfulness that washes over her as she sways her body.

Enraptured, I notice how she begins to relax as she shares such an intimate part of herself with me, because that's exactly what she's doing. Every heartfelt word, every perfect note is a gift bestowed upon me, and I can do nothing more than absorb all that she is. Each colour becomes more intense with every second that passes, so startlingly bright that my heart beats faster and my fingers grasp at an invisible brush, painting imaginary strokes as I watch her.

A familiar magic rushes through my veins as she continues to sing, igniting my creativity. A large part of me wants to rush to my studio to paint, but an even bigger part wants to pull this expressive woman into my arms and lose myself so completely in *her*.

There's something so enchanting about Friday. She's beautiful in a way that's understated, as though she's hiding her true self from the world, and fuck knows that someone with a voice like hers should be centre stage singing to thousands of screaming fans, not performing in some dingy club hidden in the back streets of Brooklyn.

"You're incredible," I choke out. My need to paint, and my need to bury myself inside of her is tangling up inside of me, making me fucking tremble, making me so god damn hard.

As she sings the last line, slowly opening her eyes to meet mine, the notes quiver in the air between us, thick and potent, and before I can even contemplate what I'm about to do, I'm on my feet. I simply act on instinct as I rush towards her, ducking a little as I place my hands on her hips and lift her upwards. She lets out a surprised gasp as she wraps her legs around my waist.

"Sterling!" She laughs, and the joy she expresses, and the colour that feathers around her is so fucking exquisite that all I can do is be brutally, truthfully honest.

"You're a work of art, and damn, Friday, I want you. I want you so bad I think I might fucking die if I don't," I say, my words harsh, breathless, as I twist on my feet and carry her towards my bed.

She clings onto me, her cheeks blazing, her eyes smiling as I carry her up the few steps to the raised platform my bed sits on, and lower her onto the mattress.

"I need to see you naked. I want to see all of you, every single part."

What I don't say is that I want her naked not just because I want to bury myself inside of her, but so that I can imprint the form of her body into my memory, and later, paint her every curve into a vibrant masterpiece on canvas, because she deserves nothing less.

"Then I guess this will be another first for me," she replies, lifting her arms upwards so that I can pull her t-shirt over her head.

"Another first?" I question, confused a little by her response.

"On the few occasions I've had sex before, I've never actually been fully naked," she explains, wincing.

What the actual fuck? I think.

"You're joking?" I question instead.

She shakes her head as I drop her t-shirt to the floor.

"Let's just say, the men I've slept with have only ever really been interested in their own pleasure, and I guess seeing me completely naked hasn't ever really been that high on their list of things to do."

"Damn," I mutter, my gaze dropping to the plain black cotton bra covering her beautiful breasts. There's nothing fancy or seductive about it, and yet that piece of material is as alluring as she is. Perhaps because she's the one wearing it. "How could anyone not want to see you naked? Those men were fools."

"This isn't exactly sexy. I haven't dressed for the occasion. Sorry about that," she says with a depreciating laugh, shrugging off my remark as I finger the strap of her bra.

"Well, I want to see *you*. All of you. Take it off," I grind out, blinking back the fog of lust that seems to shroud me every time I look at her.

She nods, reaching behind her back and unclipping the fastening with shaking fingers. The straps loosen around her shoulders, and I reach forward, sliding them off her arms until she's bare. Her breasts are a perfect handful, with pink, rosy buds that make my cock leak and my mouth water to taste.

"You're exquisite."

"I'm not even fully undressed yet," she retorts softly.

"Then please do me the honour of showing me everything that you are," I say, meeting her soft brown gaze once more. "Stand up."

She laughs, taking my proffered hand and moving to her feet, standing before me. "You're kind of bossy."

"Not usually. I apologise."

"Don't. I like it."

"Good," I say, releasing her hand and dropping to my knees, my eyes level with her navel.

Pressing a kiss against her stomach, I duck lower, reaching for the hem of her jeans, urging her to lift her foot so I can remove her boots. She rests her hand on my shoulder, quiet as I unzip them. Pulling each foot free, I cast the boots aside, then slip my fingers under the hem of her jeans once more as I graze her ankles. She lets out a small whimper as I remove each sock in turn, the palms of my hands pressing against the bridge of her feet momentarily.

"You also have a gentle touch," she whispers.

"I almost feel as though you might disappear," I reply, sucking in a ragged breath as I slowly lift my gaze to meet hers. She's a fucking mirage of colour, a vision of inspiration, a feast for my very soul.

Cocking her head to the side, she regards me. "I'm right here. I'm not going anywhere."

I nod, reaching for the waistband of her jeans, unzipping them before my fingers curl over the material. Inch by tantalising inch, I slowly reveal her shapely legs, they're muscular yet feminine and soft.

"Look at you, so fucking beautiful," I mutter.

"There you go again, flattering me," she whispers, leaning forward, her hands resting on my shoulders once more as she lifts one foot, then the other.

"Can I?" I ask, discarding her jeans and looking up at her as her hands fall away from my shoulders.

She nods, her eyelids at half-mast as my fingers glide up the front of her thighs, resting on her hips and the tiny stretch marks that are scattered across them. My attention hones in on those pretty silver lines, how they seem to shimmer. So fucking beautiful.

"I– I've been heavier," she mutters, her voice laced with something close to shame as her eyes flit away, but it's the way her voice trembles that tells me these marks are more than skin deep for her, that there is a story here, a trauma.

"We all have scars, Friday. Mine just happen to be on the inside," I reply, and she snaps her gaze back to mine, understanding passing between us even if we don't voice our trauma out loud.

I'm trembling as much as she is, in utter adoration of this woman as I slowly remove her knickers, revealing a strip of neatly trimmed hair, the colour a darker shade of blonde.

"Fuck," I groan as she steps out of her knickers, baring herself fully to me.

"I'm not sure what to do with my hands," she blurts out, running her palms over her hips as I stare up at her, utterly transfixed. "I'm not very good at this."

Her candidness is comforting, it gives me the courage to take the lead.

"Let your hair down," I instruct, gazing up at her, my face inches from her pussy. Her musky yet sweet scent, making me want to tip my head back and roar like some feral fucking beast.

"Sure," she whispers, and moments later her hair is free, framing her face in a halo of honey-blonde, the tips hanging a couple of inches below her chin and churning up a topaz blue that only I can see within the strands.

"How's that?"

"Perfect. *You're perfect.*"

"Pretty sure I'm not," she replies, throwing my earlier statement back at me with a smile.

"Then perhaps we can be imperfect together?" I offer.

"That I can do," she murmurs in response.

I know if my friend Dalton could see me now he'd be telling me to stop messing about and fuck this beautiful woman into oblivion. But I want to savour the moment. I want to taste her pussy. I want to stroke her glorious skin, and feel how she reacts to my touch. I want to make her come first before I allow myself the gift of sinking inside of her.

"Lie back on the bed, prop your head up on a pillow and spread your legs for me, Friday," I command, my voice rough.

She chews on her lip, her hair fanning out across the pillow as she lies back on the bed, parting her legs a little. Not nearly enough.

"Wider. Put your feet on the mattress. Let me see you."

"I feel so exposed," she whispers, her chest heaving as her cheeks flush. Yet, despite her coyness, she does exactly as I ask, giving me her trust.

"Berry red, my favourite colour," I say, my gaze focusing on her glistening slit, a shudder running through me at how fucking spectacular she looks baring herself to me like this.

"Oh my," she whispers, her fingers curling around my deep blue sheets as I kick off my boots and remove my socks before I reach for the zipper of my jeans, sliding them off alongside my boxer shorts. My dick springs free, the tip glistening with pre-cum as I fist my cock, palming the firm length as her gaze drops to my dick.

"Thought so," she mutters, biting on her lip as she flicks her gaze back up.

I cock my head to the side, a questioning look on my face.

"It's as though you've been carved out of stone," she explains.

"I'm certainly rock hard for you, Friday," I blurt out, heat rising up my cheeks.

Fuck, she must think I'm a fool.

"There's no denying that," she replies with a soft laugh, not an ounce of judgement in her voice at my stupid remark as she shifts on the bed, moving to reach for me. I shake my head.

"Stay right where you are, I need to taste you first," I say, pressing my knees against the edge of the mattress as I adjust myself between her legs and kiss her inner thigh.

"Are you sure?"

I lift my head, frowning. "You don't want me to?"

"Yes, *please*, more than anything. It's just..." She brings her hands up to cover her face, but not before I see her blush deeply.

"Just what?" I ask, pressing more kisses against her inner thighs, rising up her stomach until my mouth latches on to her nipple and I suck her beautiful tit into my mouth.

She moans, forgetting my question as I lave her nipple with my tongue, swirling around the tight bud, moving from one breast to the other, sucking and licking.

"Just what, Friday?" I persist, brushing my cheek against her breast, pressing kisses down her sternum, dragging my lips over her stomach towards the place I want to taste the most.

"I've only had one person go down on me before," she admits, "And, honestly, I don't think he enjoyed it very much. He gave up after a minute. I always wanted to try again..."

"Please tell me you're lying," I say, settling between her legs once more.

"I wish I were," she murmurs, peeking through her hands,

her voice trailing off as I press a kiss against her mound unashamedly, the soft curls tickling my skin.

I shake my head. "Whoever that prick was, he clearly has no idea that your pussy is fucking delectable."

"I'll take your word for it."

"His loss is my gain," I say, swiping my nose along her slit, breathing her in, shuddering from her scent.

She gasps and I look up at her, the view fucking perfect as I gaze up and over her stomach, meeting her eyes.

"Did you just smell me?"

"Fuck, yes I did."

She giggles then, and I already know that it's a nervous kind of laughter, that she isn't laughing at me but the fact she hasn't ever had a man do something so fucking feral. Believe me, this isn't usually part of my repertoire. Usually I forgo talking, given I'm not particularly good at it, and fuck, *hard*. But there's something so refreshing about Friday's reactions to my words, my touch, and I vow there and then that I'm going to show her just what it means to be adored. Selfishly, I'm glad she's had sub-par sex, because tonight I'm going to show her just what it means to truly feel wanted, and fuck, *I want her*.

"Do you always say what's on your mind?" she asks, resting her hands by her side.

"I try not to most of the time," I reply. "You seem to bring out the worst in me."

"Not the worst, not at all. Keep doing what you're doing, I like it," she mutters, and I reward her with a swipe of my tongue up her slit, her musky taste exploding on my tongue. She shudders, her whole body reacting beautifully.

"Your scent is the perfect mixture of feminine musk and sweet, *sweet* arousal," I say, refusing to curb my thoughts given how much she seems to like them.

"You really do have a way with words," she replies breathily.

I can't ever say that anyone has said that to me before, and I reward her with another swipe of my tongue, this time dragging the flat of my tongue slowly from crack to slit, swirling her clit before sucking on the tiny nub gently. She gasps, and I groan against her skin, my dick pressing against the mattress as I rock my hips for some relief.

"And you taste delicious, Friday," I say, lifting my head, and grasping her breast, squeezing gently. "I'm going to eat you out now, then I'm going to kiss you so you can taste yourself, so you know that I'm telling you the truth."

"Please," she moans, her hands flying to my head, her fingers curling into my hair, displacing the colour wrapped around her into a plume of jewel-coloured tones of sapphire blue, amethyst purple and rich, emerald green. The more turned on she is, that I am, the deeper, more vibrant the colours appear to be until she's glimmering in opalescent, iridescent colour.

Fuck, if only she could see what I see; the absolute gut-punching, soul-blinding beauty that ebbs and flows around her, that's a part of her as much as me.

"Say that again," I mutter, before burying my face between her legs.

"Oh. God. *Please*," she mewls, her soft pants and slick pussy driving me wild.

I give her everything she begs for. I tease her clit, circling and flicking the tiny nub rhythmically over and over again until she undulates her hips beneath me, moaning in abandonment.

Time seems to still as I plunge my tongue into her quaking cunt, and fuck her beautiful pussy like a man bent on causing havoc, in her, in me. I could stay here forever, tasting her essence, sucking her clit, licking her pussy. I don't care how long it takes, I'm going to be the first man to ever make her come this way.

So that's what I do. I work her body, giving in to this complicated, euphoric feeling unfurling in my chest. My synesthesia is potent, and there's so much colour that I'm almost blinded by the vividity, but I'm not just affected that way. Like earlier at the club, all my senses are heightened. Her scent and taste is intoxicating, the sound of her moans is music to my ears, her touch like electric currents ripping through my bloodstream. I'm wired, bound tight, desperate to fuck her, but I ignore my base needs and concentrate only on hers.

An indefinable amount of time passes, and then like an oncoming storm, her breaths come hard and fast, and her fingers grip the strands of my hair even tighter as she stiffens beneath me.

"I'm going to come, Sterling. Oh my God, I'm going to come!" she yells, entirely overtaken by feeling, lost to sensation. My cock jerks violently, begging me for release, but I refuse to satiate my own indescribable needs before I satiate hers.

Instead, I slip my hand between her legs, and insert two fingers inside of her quaking cunt reaching for that soft, spongy spot deep inside, then flick my tongue over her clit as fast as I can. My tongue aches, my cock is so hard I fear it might snap off, but I need her release. I need to see what happens to the colours that tumble and twist, that fucking *soar* into the air with every pulsing heartbeat as she climbs higher and higher and higher.

"Sterling!" she cries, her back arching, her body taut like a string as her orgasm hits like a wrecking ball, splattering colour against the headboard, the sheets, the walls, over us both.

Fuck, I have never witnessed anything so fucking vital, so visceral as witnessing Friday come. She's fine art. She's an abstract painting personified. She's so impossibly stunning as her body finally releases, shuddering, shaking, coating in a flush of pink as she orgasms.

I'm so damn close to coming myself, so utterly consumed that I have to push upwards onto my knees and grip my cock, giving it two firm tugs.

"I need to be inside of you," I stutter out, bending over her body, one hand pressed into the mattress by her head, the other still fisting my cock as I look down at her, mouth parted, chest heaving.

She blinks up at me, her pupils blown wide, her cheeks flush, her thoughts rushing behind her eyes right before her mouth parts. "C–condom?" she manages to stutter. "I mean, I'm on the pill, but..."

"Give me a second," I grit out, my voice strained, not because of her request, but because my balls are so high and so tight against my body that it's verging on painful.

Somehow I manage to climb off her and stagger to the bedside cabinet, pulling it open. With shaking hands I grab the pack of unopened condoms, and take one out. Traversing the bed, I rip open the foil, and sheath myself. As much as I'd like to fuck Friday bare, I don't want her to feel unprotected in anyway. I know I'm clean but now is not the time to be having a conversation about past sexual partners. So condom it is.

"I'm so turned on Friday, this might be quick," I apologise, climbing above her.

"I don't care. Please, Sterling, take me," she pants as she pulls me towards her and kisses me, groaning into my mouth, tasting her arousal on my tongue. My cock hits her mound, dropping heavily against her pussy, and I can't help but rock my hips, sliding the underside of my cock through her folds.

"You're certain?" I reply hoarsely, searching her gaze as she reaches between us and guides me to her entrance, the tip of my cock dipping inside of her just an inch.

"Yes," she whispers, and that's all the encouragement I need.

"Friday," I groan, her pussy fisting the head of my cock so tightly that I'm already seeing another wild explosion of colour as I squeeze my eyes shut and just absorb what it means to be joined to her.

"Sterling," she whimpers back, pleading with me as her fingernails dig into my arse and her lips slide across my cheek, searching for my mouth once more.

Then she kisses me again, rough and hard, her tongue searching, her legs tightening around my waist until I'm pressed right up to the hilt, the tip of my cock hitting her cervix.

"Ahhh," she cries, adjusting her body to accommodate mine as I edge in a further inch.

"I'll go slow," I say hoarsely, my nostrils flaring as I squeeze my eyes shut, trying to regain control. "I don't want to hurt you."

"No! Don't do that. Please, look at me," she pants, her voice cracking as she grasps my face, the golden flecks in her eyes like wildfire burning brightly as I snap my eyes open. "I want to know what it feels like to have someone fuck me because they're here in this moment, *with me*. I want to feel connected, just this once, *please*."

"God damn it, Friday," I reply, angry at the men who've fucked her before, who've made her feel this way. "I *am* here with you. I *see* you. "

Fuck, how I see you.

Colours continue to swirl in a vortex around us both, and they're so unbelievably stunning that I almost cry out in pure joy, but I don't. I don't because *she's* my focus right now. I want to give her that.

"Keep eye contact with me, okay?"

"*Please*, Sterling," she begs, and there's something vulnerable in her tone that speaks of a deep wound inside of her.

"Then relax, let me in," I say, overwhelmed by how tightly her pussy grips my dick.

She nods, her mouth parting as she relaxes.

My restraint snaps, and I slam into her with one hard thrust.

She cries out, eyes fixed on mine as her arms fly above her head and she presses her palms into the headboard to prevent her body being shunted upwards.

I pound into her over and over and over again, desperate to ease the ache in my chest, and heal the wound in hers.

Hard. Fast. Feral. Mindless.

I let it all go. I give in.

My fingers curl into her hair, my elbows pressing into the mattress either side of her head as I give her what she needs, never once unlocking my gaze from hers, and with every thrust of my hips, colour billows outwards like an angry storm cloud begging for my attention.

We're bathed in colour, she and I.

It licks over our skin, seeps into our flesh, coats us in arousal.

Yet, despite the incredible display of colour, I'm wholeheartedly focused on Friday.

I feel her *everywhere.*

Beneath my body. Pulsing in my veins. Clenching me tight as I fuck her.

Sensation heightens with every slip and slide of our bodies, with the tightening and loosening of our muscles. Every moan of ecstasy is tormented bliss, and there isn't a single part of me that isn't overwhelmed by Friday. Her soft pants, her skin hot against mine, the perfect velvet fist of her pussy clutching me tight, the way she stares deep into my eyes as though she can see into the very depths of my soul.

I'm anchored to her in a way I've never felt before, my body a willing prisoner to hers. I don't know if it's because I've never fucked a woman whilst in the midst of a synesthesia episode, if this is just pure, undiluted physical attraction to Friday, or a recognition of mutual pain, all I know is that I don't want this to end.

"Fuck!" I groan, pulling back a little so I can grip one of her thighs and throw it over my shoulder, needing to go deeper, needing to feel her come around my cock.

"Sterling, I... Oh, GOD!" she cries as I slam my mouth against hers, devouring her cries of pleasure, absorbing everything about her, tattooing this moment into my memory.

She doesn't realise it, but she's drawing something out of me, a part of me that I only allow to take control in the midst of creating my art.

It's the feeling of complete and utter *obsession*.

And as that thought buries itself deep into my psyche, another orgasm wracks her body. Her internal muscles ripple then grip me so tightly it's as though she's claiming me as much as I'm claiming her.

"FRIDAY!" I roar, unable to hold back a second longer as my own orgasm fires through me, rushing upwards from the base of my spine, and surging through my dick as I empty myself inside of her.

I come so damn hard that for a moment there is nothing but the feeling of bliss as her body wrings out every last drop of cum, her leg on my shoulder falling beneath us.

In that moment, as my body collapses on top of hers, utterly spent, my mind drifts off to some faraway place before I can stop it. It's a place filled with colour that shifts and reforms into shadow and light, into sharp edges and soft curves as images slowly begin to form.

I see the crook of Friday's elbow, the soft curve of her stomach, the mound of her breasts, her rounded hips where a few silver stretch marks pattern her skin, the shell of her ear, the arch of her foot, the sharp line of her jaw, the shape of her mouth opened in an expressive 'o'.

I *see* Friday, every intricate, detailed part. She's the most beautiful woman I've ever laid eyes on.

"Sterling?" Friday whispers, her faraway voice dragging me back to reality.

"Sorry," I mumble, my mouth pressed against the fluttering pulse in her neck as I drag myself back into the present moment and lift upwards onto my elbows.

"Are you okay?" she asks, gently running her fingers up and down my spine, her touch soothing me as I bow my head and press my forehead against hers.

"Yes," I manage to croak, then with great effort, I gently pull out of her, settling onto my side.

"You spaced out there for a bit," she says, turning to face me, strands of her hair falling across her face as she moves.

I reach up, brushing my knuckles across her cheekbone as I push her hair behind her ear, tracing the shape with the pad of my thumb. For a moment my attention is on my forefinger and thumb as I gently massage the lobe of her ear. It takes me a few, deep, even breaths before I can meet her gaze once more.

"Sterling, you seem... Are you sure you're okay?" she asks, frowning a little.

"I'm good," I lie, because I'm far from good, I'm fucking wrecked in all the best and all the worst possible ways.

"That was intense," she whispers, shifting closer, brushing her lips against mine.

"It was..." I agree, my muscles liquify, my body becomes heavy as an overwhelming exhaustion pulls at my consciousness, but I refuse to let it drag me under. I don't want to sleep just yet.

"Was it okay for you?" she asks quietly, looking up at me from beneath her lashes.

"It was more than okay, Friday. It was..." I pause, unable to find the right words.

She smiles softly, nodding in understanding. "It was the same for me too."

Because we both know that this was more than two strangers seeking release in each other's arms. This was more than just sex. This is the start of something.

"What's your full name, Friday?" I murmur after a while, realising that I don't actually know.

"Love. My name is Friday Love."

"Friday Love," I repeat with a smile, my eyes drifting shut as my body finally relents, and I fall into a deep, dreamless sleep, her name echoing in my mind.

A sleep that I wake up from hours later, alone, with a note left on my pillow that simply says: "Thank you for seeing me. Goodbye, Sterling."

SIX

One month later

"Take a seat, Harlow. Robert and I have something we wish to discuss with you," my mother instructs as she reaches for Robert's hand, curling her perfectly manicured fingers around his.

He's been staying at our home in Beverly Hills for the past week, and their laughter, overt displays of affection, and very loud fucking has made my stomach roil on more than one occasion. To be fair, Robert's a good looking man, tall and broad, with silver streaks in his dark brown hair, and penetrating steel grey eyes, so I can see why my mother's attracted to him, but as much as I want my mother to be happy, I know where this is heading. It'll only end in another nasty separation, and given the sizeable engagement ring now glinting on my mother's finger, divorce number four, no doubt.

I sure hope Robert has a prenup in place.

Grabbing my glass of freshly squeezed orange juice, I traverse the kitchen island, and take a seat at the table, flicking my gaze to Robert who smiles at my mother adoringly. He's got it bad. Maybe I'm just jaded when it comes to love, or rather when it comes to my mother being in love. I'm honestly not sure she understands the concept.

"What is it?" I ask, feigning ignorance as I take a sip of my drink before placing it onto the table. My gaze flits to the view out of the french doors behind them, fat droplets of rain hit the manicured garden beyond as thunder rumbles overhead, and I have the sudden urge to rush outside and let the September rain wash away the anxiety bubbling in my chest. Of course, I remain seated.

"Robert and I are very much in love. He's my soulmate, darling," my mother begins, giggling as he nuzzles his face in her hair.

"I see," I reply evenly. I realise my response isn't what she wants to hear, but this isn't the first time my mother has made such a statement, and I doubt it will be the last.

"And we've decided to get married," she adds, eyeing me as she flashes me her engagement ring.

There's caution in her stare, a warning if you will. I know that look, it's the 'keep your opinion to yourself' look that she's given me on countless occasions in the past when she knows I disagree with her choices, but doesn't want to listen to reason.

"When?" I ask, deciding that I don't have the energy to give her my opinion, knowing this will happen whether I like it or not.

"Aren't you going to congratulate us?" she questions, her eyes narrowing at me.

"Congratulations."

"Harlow..." she warns, and Robert, picking up on her tone of voice, decides to pitch in.

"I love your mother. I want her to be my wife. Will you give us your blessing?" he asks.

"You're adults, you don't need my blessing," I reply, wincing at how awful that sounds. I can see that he's trying here.

"Well, that is very true," my mother points out. "But it *would* be nice."

I momentarily consider laying my thoughts bare, then decide against it as I force a smile on my face. "I hope you'll be very happy together."

My mother nods, and Robert's smile widens. "Well, I think we should celebrate our engagement. How about dinner tonight, just the three of us?"

"Oh Robert, I was hoping we'd spend our last night together... *alone*," my mother says, cutting a look my way.

"I have plans tonight anyway," I reply, getting the hint loud and clear.

I try not to let the disappointment settle inside of me, but it happens anyway. It's not as if I want to spend time with them both fawning over each other, it's just... I just wish she'd at least talked to me about it first, or had considered how I'd feel about having yet another step-dad. Then again, what did I expect? My feelings never factor into my mother's decisions about anything, least of all something as important as a new husband.

Besides, I don't have any plans. I never have plans outside of spending time in my room, writing songs when I'm not organising the minutiae of her life. She's the sociable one with lots of friends. Any friends I had have long since given up on me, my mother's unreasonable requests often preventing me from having a life of my own.

For a brief moment, I remember that night I'd spent in the arms of Sterling, a man I've thought about every day since. There's a dull ache in my chest, and I absentmindedly press the palm of my hand there, trying to soothe it. I made the choice to slip away whilst he was sleeping, knowing that whatever passed between us would be better remembered with fondness, than tainted with the possibility of my mother ruining any chance of happiness. It's why I gave him a false number, because I knew even before I agreed to spend the night with him that there could never be a future between us. My mother would make that impossible despite her constantly needling me about being a 'spinster'.

"That's a shame. Next time I visit then?" Robert adds, cocking his head to the side as his gaze flits over me.

"Sure. Next time... Will that be all?" I ask, itching to get away.

"There is one more thing," my mother says, smiling sweetly.

"Yes?" I ask, my heart plummeting into my stomach.

"I need your help planning the wedding."

Help? I know my mother well enough to know that she won't be lifting a finger, that it'll be me organising everything. It's my job after all. Another well of sadness rises inside of me. If she were different, if our relationship were different, then perhaps arranging this wedding would be fun, something to bring us closer together as mother and daughter rather than employer and employee.

"We have lots to arrange since we've decided on a New Year's wedding," she continues, "And there isn't anyone in the world that I trust more than you."

"New Year's Eve, but that's in three months' time?!" I point out, ignoring her attempt at stroking my ego.

She might trust me, but she doesn't appreciate me. Asking me to organise their wedding is just another way to keep me so busy that I don't have time to live my own life. I've been trying, and failing, to extract myself from her grasp for a couple of years now. Every time I get close, something *pressing* comes up and I'm reeled back in, doing her bidding once again.

Could I choose to get away from her by giving up my position as her personal assistant? Yes, but would that mean a lifetime of listening to my mother guilt-tripping me? Most definitely. Maybe her marrying Robert will finally give me the way out I need. That gives me hope, and it's the only reason I entertain the thought of pulling off this wedding.

"Yes, we didn't want to wait," my mother explains.

"Three months to organise a wedding isn't a lot of time, but I think I could do it," I reply.

"Excellent!" Robert grins. "And I, of course, have the funds and the contacts to ensure that this wedding will be the best Princetown has seen. Whatever you need, you contact me, and I will make it happen."

"*Princetown?* So you're getting married in England?"

"Of course we are. It's Robert's home, and soon to be ours," my mother adds.

"Ours?" I flinch, cold dread skirting down my spine. "Yours, you mean?"

"*Ours,*" she insists. "You're my personal assistant, Harlow. Of course you'll be moving in with us. I need you by my side, darling."

"I'm your daughter," I remind her, my voice rising in pitch no matter how much I try to remain calm. "Don't I have a say in where I live?"

She glares at me. "Perhaps this is a discussion we'll pick up once Robert has returned home, yes?"

In other words, do not embarrass me, and do what you're told. I blow out a breath, forcing myself to stay calm. I'm twenty-eight years old, not a goddamn child for Christ's sake, but try as I might, I can't seem to extract myself from her controlling ways. I also can't blame my mother for everything that's wrong between us. I've allowed her to treat me as no more than an employee. I've let her walk all over me for the last seven years since I've been her personal assistant, and this toxic relationship we share is as much my fault as it is hers. It's unhealthy, bordering on abusive, and deep down I know the real reason that I've put up with her shit. I had once believed that being her assistant would bring us closer together, that she'd actually appreciate me as a person, see me as an individual, as her *goddamn daughter.* So far she's always disappointed me, and it has to end.

"*This* is my home," I say forcefully, trying to claw back some self-respect.

She huffs out a breath. "A home is somewhere that you *belong,* Harlow. You don't have friends here. You work for me. Whatever it is that you do in your spare time, you can continue to do it in England by my side. There's no reason for you to stay in LA."

God, I could wring her neck.

Of course this is all about her. Her marriage. Her happiness. Her future. Her life. Why did I ever think that my needs and wants would ever register in her brain for once? My happiness has always come second to her needs, and even though she might be right in saying that I don't have friends here, that doesn't mean to say that I can't make some once she's out of the way. Long term friends are hard to come by when your famous, self-absorbed, mother takes great pleasure in scaring them all away. As far as she's concerned my attention should be on her at all times. Frankly, I'm more her property than her daughter.

How the hell did I allow myself to get to this place?

"There is plenty of room at Adaga Hall for you, Harlow. My home is your home now. I will do anything to make my beautiful wife-to-be happy, and that extends to you too," Robert says, oblivious, or perhaps unwilling to see just how selfish his *beautiful wife-to-be* really is.

"Darling, you really are incredibly generous," my mother simpers, a gleeful look on her face. "I can't wait to see Princetown. God knows I've had quite enough of Hollywood for one lifetime. Truly, it's getting more and more difficult to breathe without all the paparazzi buzzing around me all the time."

The paparazzi that she loves to entertain more like.

"Don't worry about the paparazzi, their obedience can be bought. I promise, you'll have your privacy, and you will be quite the lady of the manor. Adaga Hall is a palace fit for a queen, " Robert says, dropping a kiss to the top of her head.

"Oh, that's such a relief. As you know, I've always wanted to live in England. Do you have horses?" she asks him.

She has? That's news to me.

"We have a stable, yes. If you'd like, I could purchase you your very own horse?"

"Oh, yes, darling. I would love a horse!" My mother squeals in excitement, clapping her hands together.

I heard once that it's almost impossible to spend a billion pounds because of the amount of money earned daily on interest alone, and according to the Forbes list of billionaires, Robert has *several* billions. Though, I'm pretty sure my mother would only see that as a challenge. She'll make a dent in his fortune in no time at all.

"See, Harlow, it's going to be so much fun!" she screeches, the excitement in her voice grating. "Haven't you always said that you wanted to holiday in England? Now you can live there!"

She's right, I have always wanted to visit England, but on my terms, not hers. She's taken my dream and twisted it into something I don't recognise.

"What about your family, Robert? How do they feel about all of this?" I ask pointedly. I know he has a son, my mother mentioned him in passing, surely he has a say?

"You and Melody are my family now," he says firmly. "Besides, it's *my* home, and who I invite to live in it is of no concern to my son so long as he continues to defy me."

Defy him? I open my mouth to ask what he means by that, but my mother glares at me, and I slam my mouth shut instead.

"Well, that's settled then. You will arrange our wedding, and move into Adaga Hall with me and Robert after the wedding takes place. It's going to be so wonderful. Thank you, Robert," my mother adds, turning her attention to him as she palms his face and pulls him in for a kiss that I have no desire to witness.

"I'm going to take a walk," I say, pushing up from the table, and heading towards the door.

"Before you go, darling, I've sent you an email with a list of things to start working on for the wedding. Perhaps you should get a head start now and we can discuss it further in the morning? No point in going out in this weather, you'll catch a cold and we can't afford for you to be lying in bed for days when there's so much to do," my mother calls after me.

"Chance would be a fine thing," I mutter.

As the sun slips past the horizon, and the sky turns an inky-black, I place my laptop on my bedside table and stretch my arms above my head, pleased with the progress I've already made on the wedding plans. My mother and Robert left for an early dinner a couple of hours ago, and I'm looking forward to making a grilled cheese sandwich and taking a long hot shower before they return.

I didn't go for that walk, not because of my mother's concern for me catching a cold–which I know wasn't concern at all but a big fat fuck you to me doing anything that's remotely enjoyable–but because I figured if I'm going to have any chance at finally loosening her grip on me, then getting their wedding arranged has to be a priority. I can only hope that she'll be so distracted by Robert and the extravagant lifestyle his money can afford that she won't care about what I choose to do with my life. Picking up my phone, I scroll through my Pinterest board, smiling at the photos of the life I'm hoping to manifest, one where I'm living in a small cottage by the sea penning songs and writing lyrics for other artists somewhere far, far away from my mother.

"One day this will be my life," I tell myself, already feeling a little bit lighter.

As I'm about to discard my phone it vibrates, making that little buzzing sound when a notification is received. I groan, expecting to see a message from my mother but when I glance at the screen, I notice a notification from Instagram instead, informing me I've received a direct message.

"Weird, I haven't used that account in years," I mutter, clicking the app open.

For a brief moment, I look over my old posts. The last recording of my voice was uploaded over two years ago. In an attempt to keep my identity hidden, I chose *@FridayI'mInLove* as my account name, a nod to my favourite song, and of course my stage name. Then I posted footage of something scenic with my music playing over the top, hoping that the viewer's focus would be drawn to my voice and nothing else. At one point, I'd had the grand idea that one of my videos would go viral, but they never did, and I guess I just didn't have it in me to keep posting.

It's been a while since I've checked the account, and I can see that since I last checked I've had quite a few messages which I haven't been notified about before now.

"There must've been some kind of update and these are just a load of spam, or perverts sending dick pics," I mumble, clicking on the first message.

"Do I want help with social media advertising?" I read, rolling my eyes, then deleting the message and moving onto the next.

Want more followers, the next one reads and I groan, deleting that too. I keep opening the messages finding nothing more than sales pitches or marketing companies offering me help.

When I open the next message on the list, I'm surprised to find something altogether different.

> Your voice is stunning. Why haven't
> you posted in such a long time?

Stunning? I stare at the screen, the message blinking back at me as I frown. A surprising feeling of warmth unfurls in my chest at the compliment, and I consider responding to the message that was only sent a few days back, but what would be the use? I don't use this account anymore, and frankly I should've deleted it ages ago. Still, I chew on my lip, debating whether to reply. In the end I simply respond with a thank you, then click out of the app, throw my phone onto the bed and head into the shower.

Twenty minutes later I'm clean and wearing a pair of soft

cashmere joggers and hoodie, standing barefoot in the kitchen, eating the last bite of my grilled cheese sandwich. My still damp hair is hanging loosely around my face as I pick up my generous glass of chilled white wine and head into our living area, wandering over to the record player in the corner of the room.

I've always loved the scratchy sound that a track makes when played through a record player. It reminds me of the days when my mother showered me with affection, singing and dancing with me in the living room when I was a kid. It's those memories that I cling on to every time she does something to disappoint me.

We loved each other fiercely once.

That seems like a lifetime ago now. When I look at her now, I don't even recognise the person staring back at me. Where has the woman gone who used to care about my happiness, who would watch me dance and sing, often joining in as we pranced around our living room, filled with joy and love for one another?

My fingers linger on the LP of *You Are The Sunshine Of My Life* by Stevie Wonder, and the memory of us singing this song to each other fills me with a hopeless kind of longing. Taking a sip of my wine, I place the glass on the side cabinet, pull the LP from the sleeve and place it on the turntable, hovering the needle above it, before pressing the play button. Within moments the music begins to sound through the speakers, and I close my eyes letting the memories of that time wash over me.

I don't even realise that I've been singing along to the track until I hear someone behind me clear their throat. Heat rises up my chest as my hands drop to my sides, and I turn to find Robert and my mother standing in the entranceway staring at me. My mother is scowling, but Robert...? His eyes are wide, mouth open in... Shock? Surprise? Appreciation?

"Harlow, what on earth are you doing? We could hear you halfway down the drive!" my mother admonishes, flicking her gaze to Robert who is still gaping at me.

"Just remembering," I reply softly, my heart pounding in my chest.

Please mom, just remember who we were, I find myself thinking.

"Remembering?" Robert asks, swallowing hard, his throat bobbing up and down as he looks between us, sensing the tension, not understanding it.

I'm not sure I do either. When did it all go so wrong?

"Mom and I used to–" I begin, but my mother interrupts.

"Harlow fancies herself a singer, don't you? I've told her time and again that her voice isn't up to scratch," she says, her nasty comment like a knife straight to my gut.

I reach for my glass of wine, gulping back a mouthful before shaking my head. "I don't fancy myself as anything. I just sing sometimes, that's all."

"Your efforts would be far better focused on organising my wedding. I take it you've not even read the email I sent you?"

"I have actually–"

"Focus on that, not this..." she waves her hand in the air, "This *fantasy* of yours."

"That's enough, Melody," Robert scolds, his voice cold as he glances down at my mother.

If she's taken aback by his remark, then I'm even more so.

"I just meant–" she begins, but he cuts her off.

"Harlow, you have a *beautiful* voice," he says, and I hear his sincerity, see it in the warmth of his eyes.

"Th-thank you," I stammer, not sure how I feel about his compliment if I'm honest.

Part of me is grateful for his kindness, the other part knows only too well that my mother will hate me for it. I glance at her, and she narrows her eyes at me. God, I'll never live this down. "I should go to bed, leave you both to continue with your celebrations."

"Why didn't you tell me that Harlow could sing?" Robert asks, casting a look over his shoulder at my mother as he strides into the living room and takes a seat on the sofa. I watch as he unbuttons his suit jacket, flipping the material aside to make himself comfortable.

"It never occurred to me," she replies, still very obviously annoyed by the whole situation.

"Harlow, will you stay a while? I'd love to hear you sing some more," Robert offers, and it feels like an olive branch, one my mother will expect me to ignore.

I shift on my feet awkwardly, lifting my gaze from Robert to my mother as she approaches, settling beside him on the sofa. Her mouth is pressed into a hard line, her eyes screaming at me to deny him.

"I was just heading to bed. Maybe another time?"

He nods, disappointment skirting across his features.

"Goodnight then," I say, stepping away from them both.

"Wait a moment," Robert says, reaching for me. His fingers curl around my wrist and I pause, hating the way my mother's eyes fix on the spot where he's touching me. I gently pull my arm from his grasp.

"Yes?"

"How would you feel about singing at our wedding?" he asks.

"You want Harlow to sing at our wedding? I've already made a shortlist of musicians that I'd like to perform at our reception," my mother says quickly, not quite able to hide the surprise in her voice.

"Not at the reception, but perhaps Harlow could sing at the ceremony?" he suggests.

"Harlow has no experience performing in front of an audience. I'm sure she would find it overwhelming, wouldn't you, darling?" she says, hiding her annoyance behind a sickly sweet smile, incorrect in her belief that I've never performed for an audience before, but wholly correct in her assumptions that I would find it overwhelming. Performing as Friday Love is one thing, but as myself, quite another.

"You'll be amongst friends, *family*," Robert continues. "I think it would add such a personal touch to the ceremony. Not to mention, a voice as beautiful as yours should be enjoyed."

"I don't think so, but *thank you* for asking. It means a lot," I reply pointedly.

I don't know Robert well, but I do appreciate his kind words. It's more than I've ever received from my own mother, and that alone makes me warm to him a little more.

"That's a real shame, Harlow. I do want you to feel involved in this wedding, as I'm sure your mother does too. Why not sleep on it?"

"She said she doesn't want to, Robert. Harlow isn't one to be center stage, she just doesn't have it in her," my mother says, eyeing me.

What she really means is that she doesn't want anyone else to take away from her on her big day, and even though I would never want to do that, her cruel remark just makes me want to defy her.

"You know what, I'd love to," I reply, and before my mother can say anything to the contrary, I turn on my heel and leave.

SEVEN

"How are you?" my mother asks, resting her hand on mine as we sit together in a quiet corner of a café overlooking Central Park, the scent of percolating coffee and freshly baked bread only adding to the comforting atmosphere. Outside the leaves on the trees have already begun to change to burnt orange, deep maroon, and ochre as the season slowly transforms from summer into autumn.

"Shouldn't I be asking you that?" I reply, squeezing her fingers as I take in her gentle smile. Despite her almost serene appearance, her pretty ice-blue eyes, that are so similar to mine, are tinged with a lingering sadness that she can't hide from me.

"You know I'm fine," she says, gently patting my hand.

"Fine is not the same as good," I argue, frowning a little.

"Then I'm good. *Truly.* You need to stop worrying about me. It's my job to worry about you, not the other way around. How are you enjoying New York City? Have you made any friends? Are you happy?" Her voice trails off as I sigh heavily.

"Stop changing the subject. I know you've heard about

dad's upcoming wedding. Christ knows he's called me often enough to gloat about it. I imagine he's taken great pleasure rubbing it in your face too. God, I fucking hate that man."

"Firstly, I'm not changing the subject, I'm simply interested in my handsome, talented son's life," she insists, reaching up and briefly cupping my cheek. "Secondly, yes, your father has informed me of his plans to marry again. I'm happy for him."

"You are? *Why?* He hurt you, Mum."

"He did, you're right, but I prefer to live in the present with forgiveness than wallow in the past with bitterness," she says, tucking a strand of silver-blonde hair behind her ear. "Nothing good ever comes from holding hate in your heart, Sterling. It was important to me to move on from my marriage to your father with grace and humility. Besides, I *am* happy. I have a good life. I get to travel the world and see all the places I always wanted to visit before I met and fell in love with your father. I also get to see you doing what you love. Your art is... My gosh, Sterling. It's *extraordinary*. I'm so very proud of you."

"Thank you," I murmur, letting her words of love permeate the anger I feel at my dad for breaking her heart. Despite his flaws, of which he has many, she loved him, and she was devastated when he ended their marriage.

"So, *have* you made friends? *Are* you happy here?" she persists, lifting her cup of chai latte to her lips and taking a sip.

"I'm happy," I reply, not wanting to tell her the truth, or give her any reason to be worried about me, because despite being able to work on my art freely without my father's constant disapproval, I'm lonely. So fucking lonely.

"Sterling," she warns softly, knowing me only too well, "Please don't try to protect my feelings. I know you. Tell me how you really feel."

I could lie to her.

I could tell her I've made lots of friends who accept all that I am. I could say that I'm not tormented every day by the vision of a woman who I spent a few incredible hours with, and who is forever immortalised in my best pieces of art to date. I could pretend that I'm as happy as she tells me she is, that I'm thriving in this incredible city so bustling with life, but it would all be a lie.

Instead, I scrape a hand over my face, and heave out a sigh, needing a moment to just sit with the truth. I still hold so much anger and hate towards my father, not just for hurting my mother, but for hurting *me*. I'm not sure that I'll ever be able to let that go, to forgive as easily as my mother seemingly has.

No matter how much I've tried, I can't seem to shake the gut-wrenching rejection I've always felt from my father. He's a selfish, cruel man who only cares about himself and the billions that line his pockets. I'm not sure what's worse, not having a father at all, or having a father who hates my guts. Not only that, I'm constantly afraid that I will feel this lonely for the rest of my life, and that I'll never experience what it means to truly belong to someone, without fear of being rejected. But mostly I just feel a desperate kind of longing for a woman who walked away from me over a month ago, a woman who gave me a false name and number, and who has become my muse and my complete and utter obsession.

"Talk to me, Sterling. Let me comfort you, like you've comforted me this past year since my divorce."

"This city is incredible," I begin, giving her a half-hearted smile.

"But...?"

"But I haven't made any friends. I spend my days and nights alone. The only thing that has kept the loneliness at bay is my art, and even then..." I grit my jaw, hating how fucking pathetic I sound.

"Even then?" she gently prods.

"It's not enough. I thought it would be, but it isn't."

"Oh, Sterling." She takes my hand in hers, her warm touch, soothing.

"Don't get me wrong, I love the freedom of being able to paint without dad's constant disapproval, but it doesn't seem to matter where I go, I can't hide from the fact that I'm still *different*, despite all the years dad spent trying to change me into his view of the perfect son."

"Your uniqueness is a *good* thing, Sterling," she says fiercely.

"He doesn't think so," I argue.

"You are incredible just the way you are. Your art is utterly captivating, and your father is a fool for not realising that, for not seeing what I see, what other people will see if you gave them the chance."

"I appreciate you saying that, but–"

"No buts. Not only are you a gifted artist, you are a *good* man. You are thoughtful, kind, intelligent, tenacious, hilarious when you allow yourself to be," she adds with a wink, that softens into another smile, "And you have so much to offer the world. Do not give up hope. Good things are coming, I promise you that."

I laugh, shaking my head. "How can you be so sure?"

"I'm a mother, we tend to know things about our children."

"And what is it that you think you know?" I ask, humouring her.

"I know that you will attend your father's wedding–"

"I'm not going. I fucking refuse," I bite out, interrupting her.

"You will go, and I'll tell you why. It won't be because your father demanded that you attend, but because it's time to face him as the man I've always known you could be: strong, independent, *formidable.* This is your opportunity to prove to *yourself* that you are worthy of the Blade family name, not because you are anything like him, but because you are so uniquely you."

"You have a lot of faith in me," I mutter.

"Of course I do, and that isn't just because you're my son, but because I've seen with my own eyes how you've traversed a world that can be unutterably cruel with spirit, and enduring strength."

"I don't feel particularly strong," I admit, and as difficult as it is for me to voice that out loud, it's the truth.

"I know that, but I also know this is just a season you're passing through. It won't always be this way. You will continue to grow, evolve and flourish, and that loneliness you feel will someday be filled with contentment, happiness, and so much love. I know it, as sure as I know that I will never stop loving you."

And that's what *I* love the most about my mother, her unwavering positivity. Fuck knows I could use some of it because I *want* to be happy. I want to be this man she sees. I mull over her words, ruminating on them as I sip on my coffee, barely tasting it.

"Do you want to talk about that beautiful woman in your paintings?" she finally asks, filling the silence.

"She's just someone I passed on the street. I thought she had an interesting face," I say, the lie slipping from my mouth far too easily.

Fuck, if only Friday were just someone I'd seen in passing and been inspired by, but she isn't. She plagues my every waking moment, she's all I dream about at night. Somehow she's buried herself beneath my skin and settled into every goddamn cell. She's my utter obsession, and I've spent my nights searching every backstreet bar and club just to hear her voice, to see her again, but it's as though she's disappeared off the face of the earth. I even returned to *Smokey Joe's* to see if they could give me some more information about Friday, but they had nothing. I can't find her, and as each day passes it's as though she wasn't even real, that she was a figment of my imagination.

My mother lifts a brow. "That is not a painting of someone you passed on the street, Sterling."

I huff out a breath. "There's no keeping anything from you, is there?"

She grins. "So, are you going to tell me who she is?"

"Will I ever hear the end of it if I don't?" I counter.

"Absolutely not."

We both laugh then, but my smile slowly fades as I recall the night I met Friday. "I heard her singing in a club in Brooklyn just over a month ago now. It was late, and I was on my way home when some arsehole bumped into me in the street. Somehow my headphones got knocked off and..." I blow out a breath, even the memory of that night has me itching to head back to my studio to paint.

"And?" she persists softly.

"And I was completely overwhelmed with colour, Mum. It was like I was standing inside a fucking rainbow. Everything was so bright, so vibrant, and my whole body reacted in a way I've never experienced before..." I clear my throat, glancing her way, wondering whether she's picking up on what I'm implying, but she just nods, listening intently. "All I could do was follow the sound of her voice... Fuck, it was incredible, like nothing I've heard before or since. I have never reacted so intensely."

"That good, huh?" she asks, eyeing me with interest.

"Yeah," I agree, swiping a shaky hand through my hair. She

notices me trembling and the interest in her gaze turns to concern.

"Sterling?" she questions. "Did something bad happen?"

"No, I mean, I did pass out, but she helped me."

"You fainted? That hasn't happened since–"

"I was a kid, I know," I reply.

"So you fainted on the street? How did she help you if she was inside the club?"

"Not then, I passed out later," I explain.

"Okay, go on," she urges.

"Drawn to her voice, I acted on autopilot," I continue, "And I ended up stumbling into the club, and sitting at a table right in front of the stage. I couldn't keep my eyes off her. Every note just exploded into colour, it was like looking through a kaleidoscope, the colour shifting and changing form."

"That sounds incredibly intense, Sterling."

"It was," I agree. "But it was more than that. As she was singing, I felt this connection."

"A connection?"

"Yes, a physical one that went beyond my synesthesia, I was..." I wince, not sure that I'm comfortable having a conversation with my mother about my sexual attraction to Friday, or whatever her name really is.

"Sterling, I may be a mother, but I'm a woman too, I understand what you're getting at here," she says, quirking her lips into a smile.

"She was beautiful, not just because of the colours she conjured within me. Yes, I was initially drawn to her by the sound of her voice, inspired by it, but something about *her* called to me too. It went deeper than my synesthesia. I can't even explain it, to be honest."

"Some things are just unexplainable," she says, patting my hand. "So what happened next?"

"My brain short-circuited from the over-stimulation, and I passed out," I say, with a shrug. "When I came to she was crouched beside me. She wanted to call an ambulance."

My mother gives me a knowing look. "I'm guessing you didn't end up in A&E?"

"No."

"Sterling!" she scolds.

"You know as well as I do that there isn't anything they could've done," I say in an attempt to placate her. "Anyway, the bouncer kicked us both out. He thought I was high, Friday helped me to my feet and kept me steady as we left the club."

"She sounds like a good person," my mother says.

"She is, at least I *thought* she was," I reply, swiping a hand over my face, feeling the sting of Friday's rejection still.

"What do you mean by that?"

I wince. "Let's just say I invited her back to my place, we spent the night together but when I woke up she was gone."

"Ah, I see."

"She left a note, gave me a false number, and I haven't seen her since."

Though not for lack of trying.

"That must've stung."

"It did. It *does*. I thought she'd felt what I'd felt too, which is fucking stupid, right? How could she possibly? It was just a one night stand for her, just sex, but for me..."

"It was more?"

"So much more. I can't get her out of my head," I say, reaching up and tapping my temple. She frowns at that, but keeps her thoughts to herself.

"Because you felt connected to her in a deeper way?"

"Exactly. I can't stop thinking about her, and it's messing with my head. No matter how many times I paint her, this feeling remains. In fact, it just deepens."

"And what exactly is it that you're feeling?" my mother questions softly, cautiously almost.

"I honestly don't know," I lie, because I *do* know, and this obsession is getting worse every day. Most nights I can't fall asleep, so consumed by the memory of Friday's body beneath mine, how it felt to be inside of her, to kiss her, to taste her. Fuck, I can barely remember to eat most days because all I'm doing is painting her image over and over and over again. If I didn't leave my apartment much before, then it's even worse now, only venturing out late at night to search another club or bar in my attempt to find her. The only reason I'm sitting in this café freshly showered and wearing a different set of clothes, instead of the same jogging bottoms and t-shirt I've been wearing for fucking weeks, is because of my mother's visit. *I'm a fucking mess.*

"Have you tried to find her?"

"Yes. I've searched every bar and club in New York City. She's disappeared. It was like I imagined her or something..."

"Oh Sterling, I am so sorry. I wish I could help."

"There's nothing you can do. She clearly doesn't want to be found, and I've just got to find a way to get her out of my system once and for all. This will pass in time."

But even as I say those words, I know it's bullshit, that I won't rest until I find her, until I make her mine.

My mother nods. "Well, now that I'm here visiting for a while, I can help to take your mind off things, yes?"

"That'd be good," I reply, plastering on a smile as I reach for the bill and move to stand so I can pay it.

"Sterling," she says, grasping my arm.

"Yes?"

"I know you said that you don't want to return to Princetown for your father's wedding, but perhaps it'll be a good thing?"

"Mum, you know how strained things are between me and dad."

"Like I said before, it's time to be the man that I know you are, but I'm not just talking about that. I'm sure Benedict would love to see you, Dalton and Drix too. You might not have made any friends here, but those men *are* your friends, and it looks like you could use their support now more than ever, yes?"

"I'm not going back home to live with dad in Princetown. No way."

"I'm not suggesting that, but a short visit can't hurt, can it? Go home, attend your father's wedding, spend some time with your friends."

"Maybe," I reply, but a couple of months later I find myself back in Princetown with no idea that my short visit will become a more permanent stay.

EIGHT

Present day

"Darling, have you heard from Julian? I need to make sure that I'm looking my absolute best tomorrow, and Julian is the *only* person I trust to do my hair. If he's delayed it will ruin every-thing and there won't be time to replace him. I can't be expected to do my own hair on my wedding day!" my mother trills, her voice rising as her unwarranted panic sets in.

"He's currently on a flight from Paris, and will be arriving at the hotel later this afternoon," I remind her for the tenth time this morning, more than a little exasperated. Her makeup artist, Stephanie, flits me a small grin as she applies my mother's makeup. She knows only too well how trying my mother can be.

Jorge Visagé is the hairdresser to the stars, and has cost a cool three hundred thousand pounds to hire for the weekend, expenses on top, *of course*. But to a billionaire like Robert Blade, that kind of money is, apparently, small change.

"Only the best for my darling fiancé," he'd responded when I'd emailed him my mother's list of requirements and the corresponding fees, totalling to just over one million pounds. Robert has more money than sense in my opinion, but despite my initial reservations, he genuinely seems to love my mother and has made a huge effort to include me in this wedding. His genuine appreciation for my singing ability has worn my mother down, and she has done a three-sixty turn about the whole idea of me singing at the ceremony. But honestly her approval is the least of my worries right now.

Because I have a *stalker*.

Or at least that's what I'm beginning to think, given the escalation of the messages I've been getting over the last few months on Instagram since I responded with a simple *thank you* to that first message I'd received. After that they've become more frequent, starting out almost like fan mail. At first I wasn't sure if it was a man or a woman messaging me, but the latest message I received confirmed he's male. He started off complimenting me on my singing ability, asking when I'd be posting another song, whether I had a Spotify account for my music. But over the last few months, each message has become increasingly more personal, more insistent, more intrusive, and now *sexual*.

I received the latest message just this morning.

> When I listen to your voice I can't help
> but touch myself. You taunt me. I
> can't eat. I can't sleep. I can't stop
> thinking about you. I'm gripping my
> dick now, listening to you sing.

I should probably just delete the account or block this person, but there's a small part of me that thinks if this escalates any further then at least I'd have evidence. I've received other messages from different accounts too, but I've been too afraid to open them in case it's this person trying to reach me from another account, given I haven't responded to any of his messages since that first time.

I honestly don't know what to do, and it's messing with my head. I've considered telling my mother, hoping she'd have some advice, that she would try to help, but then I would have to explain to her about my Instagram account, and that I've been performing in secret as Friday Love. I just know she wouldn't understand. So I've kept quiet, concentrating on organising her upcoming wedding and vowing to file a report once the wedding's over.

"Harlow, are you even listening to a word I'm saying?" my mother scolds, forcing me back to the present moment.

"You really need to stop questioning everything that I do," I reply sharply, frustrated with her self-absorption, and lack of emotional intelligence. Surely someone who truly cared about their daughter's happiness and well-being would *see* that something is up, would notice how jumpy they were, and would question it? Not my mother.

"I'm just checking," she snaps, looking up at me. "Robert and I just want to make sure that everything goes smoothly for our special day."

I heave out a sigh, pushing my own worries, and feelings aside. "I know, but everything is covered. I promise."

"So you keep telling me, darling, but I just worry. Don't take it to heart, I'm just a woman in love wanting to make sure everything is perfect, and you do have a habit of getting distracted with your..." She waves her hand in the air between us, her eyes dropping to my notebook that I use to write lyrics in, "*Other* interests."

Distracted? I've only spent the last few months since Robert proposed working my arse off organising this over-the-top, extravagant-as-fuck wedding, but that doesn't seem to register with my mother. Though I shouldn't be surprised, we've already established that she doesn't notice much unless it directly affects her.

"It *will* be perfect," I reply tightly, then add, "And how I spend my free time has no reflection on my job. Have I ever let you down before?"

She arches her brow. "Darling, are you forgetting that time when you failed to arrange for a chauffeur to pick me up, and get me to my final interview in New York after you spent the night God knows where. I had to call the hotel's Maitre'd to organise it for me. It was so humiliating."

"It was my first night off in months, and I didn't fail to organise anything, the driver *failed* to arrive," I remind her, my cheeks heating, not at her complaint, but at the memory of that night in Sterling's arms.

That one night of escape is the *only* thing that has gotten me through these past few months. I've done little else but organise this damn wedding, pushing my own wants and needs aside, not to mention my safety. Admittedly, for a while I'd considered that Sterling was the one sending the messages, that he'd somehow found my Instagram account, had recognised my voice, and he's been sending them as punishment for sneaking out on him that night. But I refuse to believe that's the case, and maybe it's foolish to think this, but he didn't seem like the stalking, creepy type. There have been many people who I've met over the years who fit that bill perfectly, but not Sterling.

He was intense, sure, but he was also... *wonderful*.

Then again, what do I know? No matter how incredible that night was, how connected I felt to him, I don't know him. I don't even know his full name, let alone whether he could be capable of sending those messages.

"Well, if you'd been available, instead of doing whatever it was that you were doing, then I wouldn't have been so inconvenienced. It was extremely embarrassing for me to arrive late for my interview. You must understand that?"

I almost remind her that she practically chucked me out of the hotel room that evening so that I wouldn't inconvenience her when Robert came to visit, but I don't. Instead, I swallow my anger and say, "Your lunch will be arriving shortly. I'm going back to my room to check my emails and make some calls, okay?"

"Very well..."

Her voice trails off as she gives me a rare smile, a smile that isn't practised or plastered on for the press, a smile that I see very little off these days. It makes me feel momentarily guilty, but I shouldn't. As much as I love my mother, I know her better than I know myself, and this smile, though true, isn't heartfelt. She knows she's pissed me off and she's trying to placate me.

Too bad I can see right through her.

Pushing to my feet, I gather up my notebook, phone, laptop and room key. "I'll see you in the morning."

"You're not coming to dinner tonight? I'm having a little get together in the bar with my close girlfriends who arrived this morning. It's a bachelorette party if you will."

"Would you like some strippers to entertain you?" I ask, my face straight, my voice saccharine.

Stephanie smothers a smirk as my mother bats her hand away and leans forward in her seat. "Don't be so obtuse. Of course I don't want a stripper! This is just me and my girlfriends spending some time together. God knows I'm so busy that I barely have time for myself. Something Robert insists on changing as soon as we're married. I will finally be a lady who lunches," she adds with a simpering laugh.

Oh, give me strength! Sometimes I wonder how I could be so very different from my mother. She wouldn't know a day's hard work if it slapped her around the face. She's spent the best part of almost a decade since I've been her personal assistant being chauffeur-driven from one interview to the next, waited on hand and foot whilst I've run around making sure all her ridiculous needs are met. The woman has so many *self-care* spa days that it's almost impossible to squeeze in an interview or press junket to keep her relevant.

"Well, it sounds *positively* lovely," I say with more than a little sarcasm, "But I have some last minute things to finalise–"

"I thought you just said everything is in hand?! What last minute things?" she asks with a scowl, her voice rising in pitch, that smile from a few moments ago replaced with an expression I know all too well.

"Everything *is* in hand. I just need to make sure the security detail has the final schedule for this evening's late arrivals. There's been some changes to our requirements given that Councillor John Hoxton and his wife, Elodie's, flight from Europe was slightly delayed. It's nothing that I can't manage."

"Oh well. Yes, that's important," she nods, appeased, then adds, "I shall see you in the morning then?"

"In the morning," I agree, dropping a kiss to her cheek. "Have a lovely evening, Mom."

"I will," she replies before adding, "Make sure to order something from room service. The food is delicious."

"I've noticed. The Wagyu burger, and truffle chips I had last night was so tasty," I reply, my stomach rumbling at the memory. I skipped breakfast this morning as well as lunch because I've been so busy, and I'm suddenly starving.

"You might want to order a salad then, hmm? You don't want to be bloated tomorrow, that silk dress will show every flaw. You know how easy it is for you to put on weight."

Bloated? Flaw? Put on weight? Urgh!

My mother thinks being a US size six is too big, and I've fluctuated between a size six and ten for most of my adult life. Admittedly, there was a time when I'd force myself to throw up just so I could keep my weight down all in order to conform to my mother's ideal of beauty. It was a time of my life when I'd felt my lowest, and I've clawed my way back to a healthy weight. But if my mother had her way I'd be a tiny size two like her. It's unrealistic, not to mention unhealthy for my frame. Blowing out a breath, I don't bother to respond to her parting dig, instead I stride across the room and leave.

An hour later I'm sitting at the dining table of my suite, surrounded by a veritable feast. I decided to order macaroni and cheese, which they serve here as a main dish rather than a side, a bowl full of vegetables smothered in garlic butter, some mouth-watering bread, and a slice of the most decadent chocolate cake. I've already devoured the macaroni and cheese, half of the vegetables and all of the bread, and I'm just about to take my first bite of my chocolate cake when my phone buzzes with an incoming call.

Grabbing my phone I look at the screen. It's Robert.

"Robert, what can I do for you?" I ask, dropping my fork to the plate, internally groaning.

If it isn't my mother harassing me every five minutes making sure that *everything's in hand*, it's Robert making sure all my mother's needs are met. I can't fault him for it, but I just want this wedding to be over, and my mother distracted by her new husband, so that I can finally start my own life.

"Just checking in," he replies. "How are you, Harlow?"

"I'm fine," I respond, a little flatly to be honest.

"Really? You sound stressed."

"It's been a long few months," I admit.

"I see..." his voice trails off for a moment.

"Robert, I don't mean to cut this call short, but I've got to send some more emails to the security team and I–"

"Harlow, I just want to let you know that I appreciate everything you're doing. This wedding wouldn't have happened without you. I'm honoured to welcome you into my family."

"I... Thank you," I reply softly, feeling a sudden well of tears burn my eyes. It's been a long time since anyone, namely my mother, has thanked me for anything.

"Credit where credit's due," he replies, clearing his throat. "Is your suite to your taste?"

"It's beautiful." The suite is stunning, and far too grand for my needs, but I appreciate it nethertheless.

"Only the best for you."

"It's very generous of you. I would've been happy to have a standard room. This wedding is already costing you quite a substantial amount of money."

He barks out a laugh. "I'm a billionaire, Harlow. I can afford it."

"Even so..."

"Whatever you need, you just ask and I'm sure I'll be able to accommodate you."

Accommodate me? Why does that phrase seem so *loaded?*

"I don't need anything, but thank you, that's very... kind," I reply, glad we're on the phone and he can't see how uncomfortable I'm suddenly beginning to feel.

"You're going to be my daughter very soon–"

"Step-daughter," I interject.

"Semantics," he replies, before adding, "And I want you to

feel part of the Blade family. Making sure you're comfortable, that you have everything you need, is the least I can do."

"Was there anything else?" I ask, wincing at how abrupt I sound. It must be the stress of organising the wedding, my mother's constant digs, and the anxiety building inside of me from these messages I keep receiving. It's not Robert's fault I'm projecting. "Sorry, I'm a little tired, that's all," I add.

"That's understandable, but there was *one* more thing."

"Okay, shoot," I say, aiming for lightheartedness to try and dispel this uncomfortable feeling brewing inside of me.

"My son..." His voice trails off, and I can practically see the scowl he must be wearing at the mention of his elusive child.

"Yes?"

"He's decided that, in fact, he would like to be my Best Man."

"He does?" That's news to me, I hadn't even realised he was attending the wedding given his name wasn't on the guest list.

"He's been home for a couple of weeks now, and let's just say he's seen sense."

"A couple of weeks? I didn't realise."

"Perhaps it was remiss of me for not introducing the two of you earlier, but you've been so busy with the wedding and arranging your mother's schedule, and given you both only arrived in Princetown a few days ago, I didn't want to add any more pressure by introducing you to my son who can be... *difficult.*"

Difficult? Great, that's all I need.

"I guess I'll meet him tomorrow then?"

"Indeed, and given he's had a change of heart, I'll need you to arrange a boutonniere for him. Can you do that in time?"

"Of course, I will call the florist directly, and get them to deliver an identical one to yours tomorrow morning. That should be manageable."

"Excellent, well, I shall see you in the morning then."

"Of course... Oh, and Robert, you've never actually mentioned your son's name. I'd feel awkward not knowing it given we're meeting tomorrow for the first time."

"I've not?" he asks.

"No, you haven't," I reply.

"His name is Sterling," Robert says, before abruptly hanging up.

Sterling?

Wait? His son's name is *Sterling*?

No. It can't be.

I stare at my phone, mouth agape, a sudden rush of goosebumps covering my skin.

"Absolutely not," I mutter to myself. "It's just a coincidence."

But that doesn't stop me from reaching for my laptop, and doing a quick search. It takes me a while, because apparently Robert's son avoids being in the spotlight as much as I do, but eventually I click on a link with a grainy photo attached to it.

"Oh fuck!" I exclaim, because staring back at me is the man I had the best sex of my life with just four months ago, the very same man that I left sleeping with nothing but a note to say goodbye.

NINE

"You have the rings?" my father asks me as we take our spot at the head of the aisle, his guests seated behind us talking in low voices whilst we wait for his bride to enter. I've spent the morning plastering on a smile and stumbling through conversations to keep up appearances. I'm already fucking drained.

"I have them," I reply, eyeing my father who nods.

"Good," he says under his breath, his gaze flicking to the harpist who is playing a beautiful melody that has my synesthesia sparking to life.

It's taking everything in me not to react to the music, but I'm just thankful that no one is singing, I'm not sure I have the energy to battle the effect that would have on me. I'm barely keeping my shit together as it is.

"Have you got yourself under control?" he adds, clearly noticing my discomfort. "I don't need you acting up on my wedding day."

Acting up? *Motherfucker.* If he had any concern for me, he'd have made sure that my synesthesia wasn't triggered in any way.

"Would you rather I leave right now? Because believe me, I'm more than willing to oblige," I bite back.

"You do that and you can forget about your inheritance, *son*," he adds with a snarl.

"I don't give a fuck about my inheritance," I hiss back.

He laughs, angling his body towards me as he throws his arm around my shoulder, no doubt to hide the vitriol that's about to pour out of his mouth. "So you want to live the rest of your life as a starving artist, is that it? How's that panning out for you?"

Fully aware we have an audience, who at the present moment think we're having a father and son heart-to-heart given the fake smile plastered all over my father's face, I grin, keeping up the charade. "You'd love that wouldn't you, to see me struggle?"

"I've spent my whole life watching you flail like a fish out of water, makes no difference to me," he replies, his smile widening as he removes his arm.

I don't bother to respond, what would be the point? He wants to see me fail, it would mean every thought he's ever had about me would be validated. Except he's so fucking wrong. I'm far from the starving artist he thinks I am. In fact, my paintings have sold for hundreds of thousands of pounds each, and right now I have a very tidy sum in my bank account. It might not be the billions he's used to, but I'm a relatively wealthy man all on my own.

"Enough of this. It's my wedding day," he says, ending the conversation I didn't want to have in the first place. "We'll discuss your future after Melody and I return from our honeymoon."

He fucking wishes.

I'll be long gone by then. I have no intention of sticking

around, and I already have my return flight booked to New York the day after tomorrow. The *only* thing that has got me through these past few weeks since I returned home is painting in my studio on the grounds of Adaga Hall. I've barely seen my friends, choosing instead to lock myself away. The only silver lining is that there are five more paintings, and all of them are of Friday.

Shifting on my feet, I drag in a long, steadying breath, trying to calm my fraying nerves. The sooner I get through this farce of a wedding, the sooner I can get out of here. Frankly, I'm fucking glad my father has kept me away from his new wife and her daughter, I'm not sure I could've remained polite, least of all hospitable. Despite my mother's faith in me, I've reverted to the man I've always been in my father's presence. Angry, frustrated, bitter.

I fucking hate the person I become around him.

The minutes tick by slowly, and with every passing second my anxiety builds. I just need to get through the next forty-eight hours, and then I'll be free to live my life the way I choose, but more importantly, free to continue my search for Friday.

Because here's the thing. I have a lead on finding her.

A week or so after my mother's visit, I decided to open an account on Instagram just so I could see whether Friday had ever posted there. Honestly, I've avoided the app like the plague just because music is so pervasive in the app, but I was beginning to get desperate after my physical searches for her were coming up empty.

After punching in her name, a raft of variations came up with accounts. There were hundreds, but determined I looked through each of them until I *finally* came across an account called *@FridayI'mInLove*. I'd almost passed it by because all the videos were scenes of nature, but something told me to click on the first video. You can imagine my surprise when it was *her* voice that I heard.

Truth be known, it'd sent me into a tailspin, and for the next few days I didn't eat or sleep. I was so fucking overcome with inspiration that all I could do was paint, and when I'd finally satiated my synesthesia enough to think straight, I did a little digging.

Apart from her very distinctive voice, there was nothing to correlate the random account name to Friday. Neither was there anything in the content of the posts apart from the title of the song to give me a lead on finding her, and the last time she'd posted was over two years ago, so I figured she no longer used the account. Didn't stop me from messaging her though.

"You embarrass me, and we'll have a problem," my father suddenly says, dragging me back into the present moment.

"What the fuck do you mean by–" I hiss, but the rest of my reply is abruptly cut off by the sound of someone singing.

What.

The.

Actual.

Fuck.

A bomb goes off in my head.

Purple explodes into red, ripping outwards into deep blue, as I blink and gasp trying to make sense of what I'm hearing.

It can't be.

Green pillows and blooms like a dust cloud, curling into a deep brown and then coral as I shake my head, forcing my eyes to blink.

Is that...?

Silver sparkles against black, as lightning strikes of yellow burst across my vision.

I gasp, dragging in a tremulous breath.

She's here?

White splinters the colours tumbling around me, merging with grey then twisting into cerise pink as my stomach curls with nausea.

How the hell is she here?

FUCK!

"No!" I mutter as my body stiffens and my skin covers in a cascade of painful goosebumps.

"Sterling!" My father warns, but his voice is lost beneath the pounding of my heart, so loud that I stumble into him.

"Get a fucking grip!" he snarls under his breath.

"It *can't* be," I groan, righting myself on unsteady legs as *her* voice, the voice of the woman I've longed for these past few months, who I've listened to obsessively, washes over me.

I'm immediately thrown into a cyclone of more colour that's so fucking vibrant that the ground beneath my feet undulates with a tidal wave of feeling.

Elation. Joy. Anger. Confusion. Fear. Bliss. Lust. Pain.

Emotions rise up, making me tilt sideways again, and if it wasn't for my father's painful grip on my arm, I'd have collapsed to the floor. His grip is the only thing keeping me upright as my brain tries to contend with the onslaught of colour.

Deep reds tumble into velvety purple. Vibrant greens roll into decadent blues. Golden hues of orange and sunburst yellow morph into deep browns and indigo, coal black and star-glittering silver.

All whilst she sings.

The woman I've been so desperate to find is here, at my father's goddamn wedding.

I can't fucking breathe.

I

Can't.

Fucking.

Breathe.

And to make matters infinitely worse, she's singing *The Rose* by Bette Midler, my *mother's* favourite song.

"You piece of shit," I growl, digging into the anger roaring inside of me, holding on to it with all my might, because without it I'm done. I can already feel the darkness setting in, and I grind my teeth, willing myself not to pass the fuck out.

"Her voice is beautiful, isn't it," my father says, leaning in close, his breath cloying against my face.

"*Whose* voice?" I manage to grind out as a bead of sweat trails down my temple, fighting against my body's desire to end the torment.

"Melody's daughter, *Harlow,*" he smirks, before dropping my arm and turning to greet his bride.

And at that moment, as I glance past my father and his bride, my eyes settle on the cause of my pain, the reason for my torment, my inspiration and my obsession.

Friday Love is Harlow Richards, and in just a few minutes she's about to become my fucking step-sister.

Somehow I make it through the ceremony, my attention focussed on Friday, or should I say, Harlow, as sweat glides down my spine and sticks my shirt to my back. I function on autopilot, passing the rings to my father when asked, nodding in all the right places, barely fucking breathing.

She's even more beautiful than I remember.

Different somehow, but still just as beautiful.

Her hair is hanging loosely in soft waves just above her shoulders, and this time a decadent purple floats within the strands, a colour my brain has concocted to match her strappy silk dress that clings to her figure in all the right places. Her shoulders and arms are bare, the sheen of her skin sparkling as though doused in glitter. She looks thinner than I remember, and I can't help but notice the stress around her eyes.

My gaze dusts over her profile that I've painted dozens of times over the past few months. Long dark lashes fan against her cheeks as she casts her gaze downwards momentarily, the bridge of her nose, turned up at the tip, already embedded into my memory. Her glossy lips are parted slightly, the colour a deep pink, and only serving to remind me of all the kisses we shared that night in my apartment.

Utterly captivated, I watch as she smiles softly at something my father says, and a mixture of anger, jealousy, and lust fires through my blood, making my pulse pound in my ears, and my cock harden.

Did she know who my father was when we fucked? Of course she must have, otherwise she'd be as shocked as I am. What the fuck is going on?

But despite feeling like the ground has been ripped out from beneath me, despite feeling anger and sharp disappointment curling inside my chest, I can do nothing but stare at the gentle slope of Harlow's shoulders, the soft curve of her breasts and stomach, at her shapely legs, the hem of her dress gently floating across her knees.

She's so fucking beautiful.

I want to stride across the aisle, pull her into my arms and kiss the breath from her body. I want to shout and rage about the unfairness of it all. I want to punch the air and shout *I've found you.*

Yet, I do none of those things. Instead I fight the lingering effects her voice has had on my body. Forcing myself to breathe,

I remain rigid, my jaw muscles screaming at me from gritting my teeth so hard.

Her cheeks pink up, aware of my intense stare but refusing to acknowledge it as her slim fingers fiddle with the white ribbon hanging from her bouquet. If I didn't know her better, I would assume that she's just enjoying the moment, but I can see how tensely she holds her body, how her breath is slightly laboured, snagging the material of her dress over her pert nipples as she takes each breath.

She's as aware of me as I am of her, and I've no idea if that's a good or a bad thing.

How the fuck can this be my reality?

She's the daughter of my dad's new wife.

She's family now, albeit by marriage.

Fuck. Fuck. FUCK!

How impossibly cruel is this twist of fate?

I've longed to see her again, and now here she is standing right in front of me. It's torturous, yes, but somehow I've managed to keep a hold of myself. My synesthesia is still potent, colours still taunt me with the desire to paint, and yet I've not passed out from the overstimulation. The utter shock at seeing her again, here of all places, has kept me in check. I can only hope that I can hold it together long enough to get some answers.

"I now pronounce you husband and wife," the officiant says, dragging me back to the present moment as the guests begin to clap, and my father pulls Melody into his arms, sealing their marriage vows with a kiss.

Moments later they turn to walk down the aisle, and as is tradition, I fall into step behind them, Harlow at my side. For the briefest of moments our eyes meet, and I'm struck dumb by the emotion in her gaze as her pupils dilate and her eyes widen a fraction.

"Sterling," she whispers, her soft smile hesitant, unsure.

Her fingers briefly brush the back of my hand, sending a spike of need through my whole body.

Fuck, her voice, her touch make me *ache*.

"Don't," I cut out, yanking my hand away and regretting the harshness of my tone the second the word leaves my lips, but I *can't* do this right now.

Instead, I nod at the guests who throw their congratulations our way. Everyone is smiling, happy for my father and his new wife, for this joining of two families, but the thought makes me sick to my stomach. How the fuck can I make her mine now? That's one of many thoughts that tumble through my head as we exit the room and into the reception hall beyond.

Harlow steps away from me, greeted by some friends of my fathers, and I head towards the table of drinks at the back of the room, needing some alcohol to steady my fraying nerves. Grabbing a glass of champagne, I gulp it back, the bubbles fizzing on my tongue as my childhood friend Benedict approaches.

He gives me a tight nod, his green eyes assessing me. "You good?" he asks, taking the empty glass from me and handing me another.

"Could be better," I admit, loosening the tie around my throat, feeling as though I'm being fucking strangled.

He frowns, but doesn't say anything. One of the few people in my life who's aware of my synesthesia, Benedict understands how difficult hearing Harlow sing would've been for me. He doesn't yet know about our history, however. That's a conversation for another day.

"I feel you, can't say it's been easy for me to see Elodie here with her slimy cunt of a husband, either," he grumbles, his attention straying to the other side of the room, and to the only woman he's ever truly loved, the woman who dumped him a couple of years ago then promptly married a guy twice her age.

"Fuck, mate. I'm sorry," I reply. Looks like I'm not the only one struggling today.

He grimaces, picking up some champagne, and sips it. "She has barely glanced my way. Nice to know that I meant so fucking much to her. Still," he adds, plastering on a smile as fake as the one I've been wearing all morning. "Plenty of alternatives available to take away the sting. Harlow's fucking stunning."

"Don't even think about it!" I snap, scowling at him as he casts an appreciative gaze over my woman.

My woman? Fuck, I'm delusional.

"Woah!" he retorts, holding his hands up. "I'm just kidding. I'm not like Dalton who will fuck any woman regardless of whether they're married, related to his friends, or just simply has a vagina."

"Well, don't. The last thing I need is my best friend making a pass at my..." My voice trails off. I can't even bear to say the words stepsister. "At Harlow."

"You might want to make that clear to him then too," he says, jerking his chin towards Dalton who's currently deep in conversation with Harlow right as we speak.

"God-fucking-damn-it," I growl, tensing at the way she laughs at something he says.

Dalton is the son of Carl Gunn, who happens to be best friends with my father, and who owns the hotel we're standing in. We all grew up together. Me, Benedict, and Drix, brought together by our father's friendships, making ones of our own. Over the years Dalton has formed quite a reputation for himself as the self-proclaimed billionaire playboy, and seeing him flirting with Harlow makes my teeth itch, and my blood turn to acid in my veins.

"I'll fucking kill him if he makes a pass at her."

"I see you've already got that protective brother streak down," Benedict says, nudging me with his shoulder. "But I wouldn't worry too much, Drix and Lia have come to your sister's rescue."

"She's not my fucking sister," I cut back, eyeing Drix across the room. He dips his head in acknowledgement, and I know I can rely on him to keep Dalton away from Harlow.

"Want to talk about it?"

"Talk about what?" I reply, chucking back my second glass of champagne.

"Whatever the fuck is wrong, of course. You've been home for weeks now, Sterling, and I've barely seen you. We've missed you, all of us. What's going on? I mean, apart from the obvious."

"Where do I start?" I throw back.

"I know you're still pissed at your dad for divorcing your mum, and I get that you're on edge from having to listen to Harlow sing... But, I know you, something else is up. What gives?"

"Now's not the time. I need to get through this shitshow first."

He shrugs. "Fine, then I'll join you in getting fucked on all the Veuve Cliquot," he offers, his green eyes sparkling with mischief. "You're dad's spent a small fortune on this wedding, and I'm more than happy to sink a few bottles. We can have that chat later, yes?"

"Later," I agree.

"Uh oh," Benedict says, pulling a face.

"What now?"

"Your dad's eyeing us up. Looks like you're needed."

"Sterling, come here."

I tense up hearing my dad's voice.

"Fuck sake," I grumble.

"Good luck, mate," Benedict offers, removing the empty glass from my hands, and passing me another glass of champagne.

"I'm going to fucking need it," I reply, turning on my heel and heading towards my arsehole dad and his new bride.

"Sterling, I'd like you to officially meet my wife, Melody," my father says proudly.

I ignore the surprised glances thrown our way from the guests mingling around us, because fuck him and his manipulative ways. He's always been so adept at spinning a story to suit his needs to make him look like a fucking martyr, and me the *difficult* son. This is no different, and honestly, I don't give a fuck about what anyone thinks.

"Melody," I say with about as much enthusiasm as a criminal on death row heading towards the electric chair.

She smiles at me and her eyes, so similar to Harlow's, sparkle with happiness. Knowing my father, that happiness will be short lived. If I had it in me to feel sorry for her, I would, but I don't. She's my mother's replacement after all.

"I'm so glad you decided to come to our wedding," she exclaims, her gaze roving over me before she leans in and presses a kiss against my cheek. "It wouldn't have been the same without you."

Swallowing my cutting retort, I simply nod. I'm not one for small talk with strangers at the best of times, and right now the last thing I want to do is exchange niceties with my dad's new wife. I don't give a fuck if that makes her uncomfortable.

"Well, I suppose I ought to introduce you to my daughter," Melody adds after a prolonged, and very awkward, silence. "She's been dying to meet you."

"Has she?" I question, meeting my father's hard gaze as he glares at me, my flippant response needling him.

Part of me wants to inform them that we're already very well acquainted, the spitefulness my father so easily draws out of me rising to the surface, but I reign myself in. Now's not the right time. It'll never be the right time to tell them both that their children have fucked.

"Harlow, come here will you?" Melody calls, waving her over.

My whole body stiffens. I'm not nearly ready to have her in such close proximity again. I need a lot more alcohol than a couple of glasses of champagne to get through this fucking nightmare.

"Congratulations, Mom, Robert," Harlow says softly as she steps into my periphery, her familiar scent wafting under my nose. I swallow a moan, forcing myself not to react.

"Thank you, darling. We're so unbelievably happy," Melody replies, her gaze flicking between us both. A small frown appears between her brows as she senses the tension, assuming it's because we've only just been introduced.

"You sang beautifully," my father adds, dropping a kiss to Harlow's cheek, before glancing at me pointedly, unable to hide his fucking delight. "Didn't she, Sterling?"

"Yes," I grind out, vibrating with the very real need to get the fuck out of this place.

The truth is, she sang like an angel. It was torturous, and he fucking knows it.

"The song choice was *perfect*," he adds, knowing full well what he's doing.

It's as though he wants me to fucking punch him. God, if my mum finds out that they chose her favourite song to usher in his new bride it will break her heart.

Gritting my jaw even tighter, my gaze drops to his hand still lingering on Harlow's arm, and a sudden rash of possessiveness rushes through my body. I'm going to give him five seconds to remove his fucking hand before I remove it for him.

One, I count inside my head, my body trembling from the effort not to deck him right this second.

Two.

Three.

Four.

Luckily for him, his hand falls away.

"Harlow, meet Sterling. Sterling, meet Harlow," Melody says, oblivious to the close call, and the rage gaining traction inside of me.

"Nice to meet you, Sterling," Harlow says evenly, turning her body towards me as she holds out her hand.

My eyes flit from the pleading look in her gaze, to her hand stretched out towards me, the remnants of lilac and gold, peach and crimson, still floating around her body.

Take her hand, Sterling. Just take her fucking hand, I yell at myself.

I know it's the right thing to do, the expected thing, but if I touch her...

Fuck, if I touch her all bets are off.

Agonising seconds tick by, my breath leaving my body in harsh pants as my fingers curl tighter around the champagne flute. I feel as though I'm underwater, the muffled sound of the wedding guests' conversations drowned out by the rush of blood pounding in my ears.

I'm vaguely aware of my father's gaze drilling into the side of my face. He thinks I'm behaving this way because of my synesthesia, and he'd be right to an extent, but I'm trying my best not to do what my body, my fucking *soul* is yelling at me to do despite *still* feeling the sting of her rejection, and that is take Harlow in my arms and claim her as mine.

Right here, right now.

"Greet your step-sister, Sterling," my father demands.

Step-sister.

I snap, my fingers crushing the glass in my hand, shattering it.

"Oh my God, you're bleeding," Harlow cries, reaching for me.

I snatch my hand away, unfurling my fingers as blood trickles from my palm. A shard of glass is embedded in the surface, the rest scattering to the floor at my feet.

"Get yourself cleaned up," my dad hisses as Melody gasps in shock.

Gritting my jaw, I turn on my heel and stride away, the pain in my hand nothing to the agony I feel inside.

TEN

"Do you think I should check on him?" I ask, my heart thundering in my chest as I watch Sterling stride across the room, a trail of blood dripping from his hand onto the pristine marble floor.

Drix, the man who I was introduced to a few minutes ago, follows him, a worried expression on his face. Apparently they're friends, and have known each other for years, so I'm glad he has someone looking out for him. Even still, *I* caused this. *I* should be the one checking on him, to make things better.

Better?

How on earth can I make this situation better? Our parents have just got married for crying out loud, and despite the way my pulse spiked the second I laid eyes on him, how my skin heated with the intensity of his stare, despite the way I was thrown back to that wonderful night we spent together, *nothing* can happen between us again. It just *can't*.

"Leave him, he clearly doesn't have any respect for me or your mother given the disgusting way he's just behaved," Robert says, anger blazing across his face as my mother continues to blink away her shock.

"I think he was just caught off guard," I mumble, trying to appease Robert, and calm my own frayed nerves. The truth is, I should've reached out to him the second I realised who he was. It was cowardly of me.

"His behaviour is inexcusable, Harlow. I warned you he was difficult," Robert continues, shaking his head. "I should never have allowed him to attend our wedding."

Guilt climbs up my throat. *None* of this is Sterling's fault.

I was the one who left him with just a note to say goodbye. I was the one who was too terrified to reach out last night when I found out who he was. God, the shock on his face when he heard me singing, and the way he seemed to fall into his father was hard enough to witness, but to see him struggle to hold back his very warranted anger just now, that was painful.

I did this, it's all *my* fault.

"Oh, darling, don't blame yourself," my mother interjects, patting Robert's arm. "I'm sure once he's gotten used to the idea, things will be better, yes?"

Robert scowls, his response cut off by a couple approaching us.

"Robert, Melody, what a beautiful ceremony," the man says, holding his hand out for Robert to shake.

"Thank you, John. I heard you had a delayed flight. I'm glad that you and Elodie were able to make it to our wedding on time," Robert replies, greeting John's wife with a kiss to her cheek. "You look stunning as always, Elodie."

"Thank you, Robert," she replies softly.

My mother stiffens, jealousy flaring in her eyes momentarily before she covers it up with a smile, her ability to hide her true emotions, a sign of how good an actress she is. I can see why she might feel threatened. Elodie's a gorgeous woman, with long, curly brown hair, deep blue eyes and an incredible, hourglass figure, but more noticeably, many decades younger than her somewhat stout husband. Not that I'm judging either of them in any way–though I'm sure my mother is–just making an observation. I know from the guest list, and my mother's tendency to boast about the very rich and influential friends of Robert's, that John is a member of the British parliament, a role that's similar to the US members of Congress.

"Your security team made sure we got here in good time. I hear we have you to thank for that," he says, turning his attention to me as he holds out his hand to shake. "Harlow, isn't it?"

"Yes, and it was no trouble," I reply, taking his proffered hand.

He grips my fingers, his thumb rubbing against the back of my hand, making my skin prickle with warning. I don't like the way he's looking at me, nor do I like the fact that as I try to pull my hand away, his grip just tightens.

"I was very impressed with your singing ability. Quite the voice you have," he states, his black gaze uncomfortably penetrating as he leans in and presses a lingering kiss against my cheek.

"Thank you," I reply, pulling my hand back with a sharp tug, and stepping back, heat rising up my chest as I flick my gaze to his wife.

Her eyes widen a little, and she gives me a look that tells me she's as uncomfortable by her husband's behaviour as I am.

"It was nice to meet you both," I say quickly, "But I hope you don't mind, I just need to ensure everything is running as planned. We should be entering the dining suite shortly, and I want to see whether the staff are ready for us."

"Of course, perhaps we can talk more later?" John offers.

"Perhaps," I reply.

Hell no, I think, as I turn on my heel and head towards the door Sterling left through just minutes before, needing to apologise, to try and fix things somehow.

"Is there anything I can do?"

Drix's deep baritone voice makes my feet still as I exit the room, the door clicking shut behind me. He's standing with Sterling in an alcove halfway down the corridor.

"You have your own problems to deal with. I'm not adding to them, Drix," Sterling replies, tightening a piece of material around his hand, spots of crimson seeping through the white.

"You're my friend. Your problem *is* my problem," Drix counters.

So that's what I am, *a problem?*

I guess I deserve that.

Swallowing my nerves, I walk towards them both, the sound of my heels clicking against the marble floor informing them of my presence.

"Could I have a moment with Sterling, please?" I ask as Drix flicks me a look, before glancing at Sterling who nods.

"Sure," Drix replies, giving Sterling's shoulder a squeeze before saying, "Talk later?"

"Later," he agrees.

"You've organised a beautiful wedding," Drix says politely, giving me a warm smile.

"Thank you."

"See you then," Drix adds with one final glance at Sterling, before striding down the hall.

As soon as I hear the door shut behind him, I blow out a

breath and reach for Sterling, resting my hand on his arm. "Sterling, I'm *so* sorry," I begin. "This is… I think we should talk."

He shakes his head, barely able to look at me as he grinds out, "Not here. Not now."

"Please, Sterling, I need to explain a few things," I respond, not wanting to put this conversation off any longer. It'll only be harder if we do. He stares at me, his eyes glistening with a mix of emotions that I feel only too keenly myself.

"We'll go to Dalton's office."

"Dalton's office?" I question, quickening my pace as I try to keep up with him.

"Dalton manages this hotel for his father, Carl. His office is this way. I'm surprised he didn't tell you that already given you seemed *very* interested in everything he had to say when you were talking with him a moment ago," he bites out, and the implication is clear. He thinks I was flirting with him.

"It wasn't like that," I respond, confused and a little hurt to be honest.

"Sure it wasn't."

"What's that supposed to mean?" I reply, my steps halting, hating that he thinks so little of me, but what did I expect? Of course he'd assume that I'm able to move on so easily, that I'm not as affected by this whole situation as he so obviously is.

"Exactly what you think it does," he snaps.

"Sterling, he's a guest at my mother's wedding. We were just getting to know each other."

"And does he know that you're also a damn liar?" he bites back, turning to face me, his chest heaving, his eyes flashing with anger, and undeniable pain.

"I never meant to–"

"What, hide who you really were? Sleep with me? Leave

me a note to wake up to after we fucked? What did you never mean to do, *Friday*?" he hisses.

"I–" My response is cut off as a member of hotel staff walks towards us.

Noticing them, Sterling grabs my wrist and tugs me along the corridor, pushing open a door a bit further along and dragging me in behind him. The second we're inside what I'm assuming is Dalton's office, he slams the door, dropping my wrist as though burnt.

"You lied to me. You lied to me about who you were. You gave me a false number. You fucking left without saying goodbye. You fucking *used* me. I've spent months trying to find you, so you can imagine my surprise when you turn up here at my dad's wedding, *Friday*!" he shouts, pacing back and forth.

He spent months trying to find me? Oh God. A flood of guilt swarms in my stomach, but more than that, a dangerous kind of warmth that I cannot entertain.

"It's Harlow," I reply, tears pricking my eyes. "And she's my mom, Sterling. This is our parents' wedding, I have to be here."

"Don't you think I know that?!" he explodes, raking a hand through his hair, breathing heavily as he tries to control his anger. He's so beautiful, so hurt, and guilt makes those threatening tears tremble on my lashes.

I don't blame him for it, because he's right in a lot of ways. I should never have hidden who I was. I should've been honest, and even though I started out just wanting a night of mindless sex, I didn't use him, I just didn't want my mother to ruin the beautiful connection we shared, because she would've found a way to do that if I'd welcomed him into my life. Now there's no chance of anything further developing between us.

"I didn't use you," I say, a little helplessly, blinking the tears back.

"What do you call sleeping with me and then disappearing, huh?" he persists.

"It's difficult to explain," I mutter.

"*Try.*"

"My mother..."

"What about her?"

"She's famous," I say, wincing at how ridiculous I sound.

"What the hell has that got to do with anything?"

"It has made her self-absorbed. Selfish. Controlling in a lot of ways," I admit, glancing up at him.

Sterling frowns, folding his arms across his chest. "Go on."

"That night we met, Robert was visiting. It was the early days of their relationship, and she wanted me out of the way. I called a friend of a friend and he got me the gig at *Smokey Joe's*. Like I told you that night, singing is an escape for me. I wanted to be someone else for a while. Not Harlow, the daughter of my famous mother, a woman who has spent the last seven years being her personal assistant and putting her own needs and wants aside. As much as it is embarrassing for me to admit, I've barely lived my own life, and on the occasions I've tried, my mother has always found a way to ruin whatever plans I've made," I explain.

"What do you mean she ruins your plans to live your own life?" Sterling asks, a muscle feathering in his jaw as he stares at me.

I press my eyes shut briefly, willing myself not to cry. It's humiliating enough to admit that I'm still very much under the control of my mother, let alone that I'm not strong enough to walk away.

"Harlow," Sterling insists, not letting this go.

"We have a complicated relationship," I continue shakily, "And if I'm honest with myself it's unhealthy. My mother doesn't want to see me happy with anyone because I think she believes deep down that I would abandon her. So in the past whenever I've gotten close to someone, friend or lover, she's found a way to ruin my relationship with them. And the worst part is that I've let her because in really twisted, fucked up way it makes me feel loved by her when most of the time I just feel like her employee," I heave out a breath, not feeling any lighter despite sharing the truth. "On occasions, to escape our messed up relationship, I become Friday Love, just like I did the night we met. My mother has no idea."

"I still don't understand why that would make you lie to me. I thought we had a connection, but it was just sex for you, wasn't it? Like you said, a chance to escape."

"Yes and no," I admit.

"Which was it, Harlow?"

"I guess in the beginning it was about sex. You were so..." I heave out a breath. "So different from other men I'd met before, intense, interesting, but more than that, apparently interested in *me*, and I wanted to throw caution to the wind, to just do something I wanted to do for once. I admit that I wanted to feel a man's hands on me knowing that *I* was the object of his desire."

"I see."

"But please believe me when I say that I felt that connection too," I pause, chewing on my lip. "I felt it, Sterling."

He folds his arms across his chest, closing himself off from me, and the way the material of his suit jacket stretches around his arm muscles makes my throat dry. Jesus, why does he have to be so handsome? Why does my body tingle every time he lays his eyes on me? Why does the man I've thought about ever since we met have to be my step-brother?

"Despite what I felt," I continue, forcing strength into my spine, holding myself rigid so I don't throw myself into his arms.

"I knew that any kind of relationship with you would be impossible. My mother would go out of her way to ruin it like she's ruined every other relationship I've tried to form. I wanted to remember that night fondly, and not taint it in any way."

"So you kept your identity a secret because you knew our parents were together, is that it? You slept with me knowing my father was pursuing your mum. That's fucked up, Harlow."

"No! I didn't know you were his son then, Sterling. You never told me your last name, remember?" I reply, shaking my head. "I didn't find out who you were until last night. I left you a note that night we met not because I knew you were Robert's son, but for all the reasons I've just explained."

He blanches. "You really *didn't* know?"

"Once things began to get serious between my mother and Robert I found out he had a son after my mother mentioned it, but whenever I brought you up, Robert shut the conversations down. He implied you were–"

"Let me guess, *difficult?*" Sterling interjects, with a shake of his head.

"Yes, and I assumed you were estranged. I didn't push the subject. I wish I had now, truly. As the weeks wore on, all my time was taken up organising this wedding, not to mention..." My voice trails off, he doesn't need to know about the messages I've been receiving.

"Not to mention?"

"Nothing, I've just had a lot going on," I say, clearing my throat. "Anyway, last night I was on the phone to your father, he explained that you wanted to be his Best Man after all. That you were, in fact, coming to the wedding, and have been in Princetown for weeks now. I asked him your name and he gave it to me. I thought it was just a coincidence. What were the chances that Robert's son had the same name as the man I'd slept with? So I looked you up on the internet, and found a photo of you."

"Fuck," Sterling exclaims, all the fight leaving his body as his shoulders slump, and he drops his arse onto the desk behind him. I can't help but notice how his fingers curl around the edge of the desk, how his knuckles turn bone-white from gripping so hard.

"I should've reached out to you the second I found out," I say, blinking back another sudden sting of tears forming in my eyes.

"Then why didn't you?"

"Because I'm a coward," I whisper, dropping my gaze.

He makes a noise in his throat, and I force myself to look up at him again. "Sterling, I wish…"

"If your relationship with your mother was different, and you didn't have to fear that she would try and ruin something between us, would you have stayed until morning? Would you have wanted to explore something with me?" he asks, pushing up from the table and taking a couple of steps towards me.

"It doesn't matter now," I say, shaking my head, glancing away so as not to see the hunger in his gaze, worse still, the *hope*.

"It matters to me, Harlow," he counters, reaching for me.

I back up again, my back hitting the door as his warm hand cups my arm sending tremors throughout my body. "Don't."

"I have thought about you every second of every day. Every night since we met, I searched for you in all the nightclubs and bars across New York City."

"Please, Sterling. Don't make this any harder than it already is. This is our parents' wedding day," I whisper.

"I don't give a fuck about them. I care about *us*."

"There is no us. There can't ever be an us. You have to know that," I plead.

"I know that I can't look at you without wanting to kiss you. I know that it's been fucking torture these past few months not knowing if I'd ever see you again. I know that when I heard you singing just now, despite my anger and shock, all I wanted was to yell that I'd finally found you," he says vehemently, his hand reaching up to cup my face as he steps closer, the heat of his body penetrating mine.

"How can we be together now? It's an impossibility."

"Nothing is impossible when it comes to us."

"Please don't do this," I beg as his fingers slide across my cheek and dig into my hair.

"You have plagued my thoughts, Harlow. That night meant something to me. *You* mean something to me."

"We barely know each other," I counter, pressing my hands against his chest in an attempt to keep some distance between us. His heart thunders beneath my palms, matching the frantic beat of my own.

"And now we have the chance to do exactly that."

"But we're family now," I protest.

"By marriage only," he insists, but I hear the note of desperation in his voice, as though he's trying to convince himself that it doesn't matter, as much as he's trying to convince me.

"We can't," I whimper, but he leans in, his nose brushing mine gently.

"Tell me you don't want this," he whispers roughly. "Tell me you're not as affected by me as I'm affected by you. Tell me right now, and I will walk away. Tell me, Harlow."

But I don't. *I can't.*

Closing the last few inches between us, he presses the length of his body against mine, and I can feel the swell of his cock hardening against my stomach. I let out another whimper, every part of me wanting to fall into his arms, to kiss him, to explore this undeniable attraction, this fierce lust, this violent connection that has snapped back to life in his presence.

He brushes his lips against mine, so softly, so reverently, that my fingers curl into his shirt, holding on instead of pushing him away. "This is wrong."

"It doesn't feel wrong to me," he replies, pressing a kiss against the corner of my mouth. "Fuck, Harlow, can't you *feel* that?"

And I do feel it, my body reacting before my mind can even catch up as Sterling's tongue pushes past my lips and sweeps into my mouth in a desperate, toe-curling kiss.

And that's all it takes.

We fall into each other.

Teeth clashing, fingers grasping, chests heaving.

It's as though the last few months apart were just an insignificant moment in time, as though we're not at our parents wedding, and aren't two people very recently bound together by their marriage. I'm vaguely aware of the desperate moans emanating from my chest as his hand grips my hip and he rocks against me.

"Goddamn it, Harlow, *why?*" he groans, briefly breaking our kiss as we both try to gather ourselves, but it's no use, I don't want to stop anymore than he does, and he smashes his lips against mine once more.

I know what he's asking, why have our parents fallen in love? Why can something that feels so good be an impossibility?

We're family now.

This shouldn't be happening.

"This is wrong," I repeat helplessly.

Yet that doesn't stop us. It doesn't stop Sterling from reaching for the hem of my dress, from dragging his fingers up my thigh, from coasting his fingers over my panties as I part my legs and allow him access.

It doesn't stop him from saying, "You're drenched, Harlow. How can this be wrong when your body knows it's right?"

His words penetrate the fog of lust, only making me want him more, and despite my weak attempt of putting a stop to this, it doesn't prevent me from rocking against his hand, already so close to coming, so tightly bound and needy that I gasp and whimper into his mouth as he slips his finger past the material of my panties and pushes deep inside of me, into my soaked core.

Oh God.

We shouldn't be doing this.

But no matter how much my conscience tries to convince me to push him away, to stop this, I can't. I don't. Instead I ride his fingers as he kisses me roughly, meeting his passion with my own. He pumps his finger inside of me, adding another, stretching me as my body welcomes him.

"Please," I whimper, desperate for the pinnacle, a moment of utter bliss as I grind against his hand unashamedly.

In response Sterling bites my bottom lip, the sharp sting making me gasp as he drops to his knees and shoves up the material of my skirt, bunching it in one fist while he reaches for the thin strap of my g-string.

"Y-you *bit* me," I reply in shock, but unexpectedly turned on.

My chest heaves at the feral look in his eyes as I raise a shaky hand to my mouth. I didn't know he could be so possessive, and even though I shouldn't, I like it. I like that he wants me, that he was so hurt by what I did that he shows me that.

"That was for walking out on me, to make you feel just a fraction of the pain I've felt ever since you left," he says, before ripping at the elastic of my panties, the sting from the action making me gasp. "But this is for walking back into my life," he adds, then buries his head between my parted thighs and sucks my clit into his mouth, roughly, possessively, still pumping his fingers inside of me.

I can't stop falling into this moment, as I arch my back giving him more access.

I can't stop rocking against his face, or gripping his hair as he laves his tongue against my clit.

I can't stop the intense heat building deep inside of me as my mind falls blissfully blank.

And I certainly can't stop as a powerful orgasm rips outwards from my core, forcing a startled scream to erupt from my lips.

It fires through me, making me jerk and shake as I fall forward, my body curling over Sterling, my palms slapping against his broad shoulders. I'm so caught up in the moment that I don't immediately notice the door handle rattling.

"Sterling, are you in there?" a muffled voice asks, the handle rattling in earnest now as the person behind it tries to open the door.

Startled, I push upright as Sterling stands, stumbling a little as his face flushes and he swipes a hand across his mouth, erasing my cum glistening on his face.

"Fuck, it's Dalton."

"Do you think he heard us?" I ask, pushing away from the door on shaky legs as my skirt drifts back over my knees, and my torn panties slip down my leg and puddle over my foot.

Sterling ducks, snatching my panties up as I step out of them. He pockets them, but not before he presses them against his nose and breathes in deep.

"Did you just–?"

"Fuck, yes I did," he responds, his voice gravelly, potent

with lust, only serving to remind me of the time when he ran his nose through my pussy all those months ago.

"What about Dalton?" I ask shakily.

I'm terrified now, of how I feel, at what we've just done, but more than that, how much I wish we could continue. I shake my head, trying to force myself to think straight.

"He won't say anything," Sterling replies.

"But–"

"Trust me, okay?" he adds, before blowing out a rough breath to regain some composure. "I need to let him in."

"Okay." I nod, pressing my palms against my skirt, trying to flatten out the creases as he unlocks the door.

"Come in," Sterling says, briefly coasting his fingers over my hip as I move aside.

Dalton enters, his brows lifting as he takes in our appearance and we both try, and evidently fail, to hide what's just occurred between us.

"Your parents are looking for you both," he says, eyeing us with barely veiled amusement.

"We were just talking," I mumble.

Dalton's gaze falls to Sterling's crotch and the very noticeable erection forming a tent of his trousers. Sterling doesn't even try to hide it, he just glares at his friend in challenge.

"Of course you were," Dalton smirks.

"Don't start with me today, Dalton," Sterling grinds out. "You are in no position to judge."

"My lips are sealed," he replies, holding his hands up in mock surrender.

"Oh God," I murmur.

"Though I should warn you," he continues, looking pointedly at us both, "Everyone's about to sit down to eat. If you don't show your faces soon, people will start to talk."

"I should go," I say, my heart pounding as I step towards the door and avoid Dalton's gaze.

"You might want to clean up first," Dalton says, resting his hand briefly against my arm as his gaze falls to my neck.

"Clean up what?" I murmur, reaching up to press my fingers against the spot he's staring at. When I pull my fingers away, there's blood. I glance at Sterling's hand and the blood seeping through the material he'd wrapped around it. "Shit."

"Let me deal with that," Sterling says, his eyes flickering with an intense kind of heat as he steps towards me.

"I can manage," I whisper, as he grasps my hand and shakes his head.

"It's my blood. Let *me* deal with it," he insists, his voice hoarse as he lifts my fingers to his mouth and draws them between his lips, sucking his blood from my skin.

I gasp as desire licks down my spine in a dangerous caress.

"Fuuuuccckkk, Sterling," Dalton mutters, and my gaze ping-pongs from Sterling to Dalton and back again. "That was actually kind of hot."

"Shut the fuck up, Dalton," he grinds out, his eyes still fixed on mine.

Heat blazes between us, and I honestly don't know what to say. I'm not even sure I could find the right words. I feel so tongue-tied. He just licked his blood from my fingers, and I am... *turned on*.

"You should let me go," I whisper, my chest heaving as Sterling licks his lips, stepping closer as he releases my hand.

"I'm not done."

"But—"

The rest of my protest is caught in my throat as he gently sweeps my hair over my shoulder, then leans in. As Sterling angles his body towards mine and presses the flat of his tongue against my skin, I'm too stunned to do anything other than remain perfectly still. Red hot lust fires through my body, and for the briefest of moments my eyes flutter shut.

"Oh," I breathe out, completely forgetting Dalton is still in the same room as Sterling licks his blood right off my skin, his free hand squeezing my hip possessively.

"There," he hums against my neck, pressing a brief kiss against my thready pulse before leaning back. "All better now."

"I should..." I mumble, my cheeks flaming with heat as Dalton whistles low. "This isn't... You shouldn't have... Oh, God..." I take two shaky steps back, holding my hands up towards Sterling to try and fend off any more advances. Right now, I don't think I have the strength to keep him at bay. "I have to go."

"Harlow, just wait a minute," Sterling begins, that damned muscle in his jaw jumping as he grits his teeth. I don't know why I find that so attractive, I just do. I pause in the doorway, dragging in a shuddering breath.

"Please, Sterling..."

"*I* see you, Harlow."

"Don't," I bite out, regret for what can never be, opening up a well of pain inside my chest.

"This *isn't* over," he counters.

"It has to be," I whisper as reality comes crashing back full force, and I flee the room.

ELEVEN

The next couple of hours pass in a blur.

I eat just enough to try to fend off what I know will be a god awful hangover, chasing down the few mouthfuls of food I managed to consume with the free-flowing alcohol. I know I'm on dangerous ground, that getting drunk is a stupid thing to do, but I need to dull my senses, and the constant bombardment of conversation, laughter and background music is making my head spin far more than the alcohol. Not to mention sitting in such close proximity to Harlow and not being able to continue what we started in Dalton's office.

Fuck.

I can still taste her on my tongue.

Perhaps I should feel guilty, but I don't, because I know that she couldn't stop herself any more than I could. The attraction between us blazed to life the moment we were alone together, and whilst a part of me wanted to remain angry at her for walking out that night the way she did, that anger dissolved as soon as she explained why. I just couldn't hold on any longer, my need to claim her far outweighing every feeling of hurt that she'd caused.

Fuck, the way it had felt to hold her in my arms again, to kiss her, to taste her, knowing that she didn't use me, that she'd felt what I'd felt too, was a fucking relief. She might've walked away from me again when Dalton caught us alone together, but I meant it when I said it wasn't over, despite her arguing otherwise. There isn't a chance in hell that I'm letting her go, not now that I've found her again.

Sitting three seats to my left, Harlow is currently in conversation with Walter Pike, Ben's father. He's one of the few people in attendance that I actually like. Whilst an extremely wealthy man in his own right, he isn't as pompous or arrogant as my dad, far from it in fact. I always envied Ben and his relationship. So easy, so loving, so *normal*.

I spent hours at their home, Wildridge Estate, growing up, and even though it is as palatial as Adaga Hall, it always felt like a home should, filled with laughter and so much love. In contrast, Adaga Hall is bland in its finery, built to impress, and filled with expensive furniture and works of art that have little meaning other than my father's desire to show off his wealth.

Perfect home. Perfect life.

Imperfect son.

And just as those thoughts pinball around my head, the fucking universe decides it's time to test my limits again as music begins to play. My spine stiffens as my father and Melody head to the dancefloor for their first dance.

"I need to get the fuck out of here," I mutter under my breath, and with a shaky hand I knock back the last dregs of my red wine, grateful that it's dulling my senses just enough to enable me to seek out an escape.

Flicking my gaze to the door, I get ready to flee whilst all eyes are on the couple, Harlow's included, but Walter rises from his seat and holds his hand up, microphone in hand.

"Ladies and Gentlemen. The bride and groom ask that you now join them on the dance floor. So gather your loved one and let's get this party underway!"

Fuck no.

Pushing to my feet, I traverse my seat, grabbing the back of the chair briefly as another rush of colour swamps me, causing my body to sway. My synesthesia is angry, as though it's forcing me to *see* after spending all day trying my fucking hardest to suppress it, to deny that part of myself so that I don't embarrass my father, his new wife, and their friends and family.

I've held on to my anger towards my father all day, pushing aside the colour over and over again. I've done everything I can to ignore it, to not react, to be normal, and all for what? To keep up appearances, to hide the real me?

But I *do* see.

I always have, and I know that repressing my feelings and ignoring the colour will catch up with me sooner or later. But I have to hold it off a little longer. I must.

Despite that, every shade and hue imaginable penetrates my tired brain, my wired body, my depleted soul. It's taking an enormous amount of effort not to fold, to let my synesthesia take hold of me as my fingers grip the chair, my grasp so tight that I swear any minute now my bones will pierce through the thin layer of skin on my knuckles.

Fuck. Fuck. Fuck.

I *can't* do this.

With great effort I drag in a shaky breath when I feel eyes on me. Lifting my head, I'm greeted with Walter's wide smile, oblivious to the fucking agony I'm in right now.

"Sterling, your father and stepmother would like you and Harlow to join them too."

No.

No!

I shake my head, but he doesn't seem to notice, and when he reaches down to cup Harlow's elbow, offering her to me, my body moves towards her before my brain can even catch up.

"Sterling?" Harlow murmurs as she stands, her gaze shifting to the table and the empty wine bottle positioned next to my also empty glass. "You don't look too good."

"I'm fine," I snap.

She nods, but I know she doesn't believe me as I take a wobbly step towards the dance floor. I don't know what's worse, having to dance with Harlow whilst battling an episode, or not being able to haul her against my chest and bury my nose in her hair just so I can breathe her in and find some peace in her arms.

"You're not fine," Harlow whispers, her tone gentle as I place one hand on the centre of her back, and grasp her hand with my other, my fingers curling over hers.

"I'm not drunk," I reply as we begin to sway to the music, music I'm desperately trying to ignore.

Gritting my jaw, I try my damndest not to pass out.

"You barely ate," she counters.

"I'm not particularly hungry."

She sighs, her fingers twitching in mine. "I'm sorry."

"For what?"

"For *everything*," she breathes. "We should never have–"

"Don't," I snap, my palm pressing against her lower back a little firmer, forcing our bodies closer so that I can lean in and press my lips against her ear.

"Don't what, Sterling, tell the truth?" she sighs, her voice soft, barely audible beneath the music as she presses her palm against my chest and attempts to put space between us.

"I swear to God, Harlow," I warn, my fingers flexing on her back. "If you're about to tell me that we shouldn't have kissed, that I shouldn't have fucked your pussy with my fingers and tongue, I will drop to my knees right here and now and finish what I started back in Dalton's office."

"But I *did* finish," she chokes out, her breath hitching, and just for a moment she gives me a glimpse of the woman I met that first night, the woman who said whatever's on her mind.

"You think that I'm okay with *just* one of your orgasms after searching for you for four fucking months? Believe me when I say, we've only just begun."

"Sterling, we're fam–"

"Do *not* say it," I respond, pressing my eyes shut as I battle everything.

My synesthesia.

My rage.

My burning need to kiss her again.

"Not saying it doesn't make it any less true," she whispers, as I slowly peel my eyes open, ignoring the colour swarming around us both, and the beat of the music pounding in my ears.

"We're adults, Harlow. We met four months ago. Just because our parents got married, that doesn't make us family. I *don't* want to fuck my sister. I want to fuck you."

"So this is just sex?" she snaps, *her* eyes blazing with anger now. "Just over an hour ago you were accusing me of the same thing."

"You know it isn't," I reply, my fingers digging into the bare skin of her back. "That's not what I meant."

"Either way, it doesn't matter."

"It matters–!"

"Can I cut in?"

We both still as Benedict appears to my left.

"Ben?" I question, cursing him internally for interrupting us.

He gives me a look, and I know he thinks I need a reasonable excuse to escape because of the music, but this time he's got it so fucking wrong. I don't want to escape this wedding unless it's *with* Harlow.

"Harlow and I haven't really had the chance to talk given your father stuck me at a table with a bunch of strangers," he explains as Harlow gives him a polite smile.

"Now's not the time," I bite out.

"Pretty sure that now is *exactly* the right time," Ben argues, looking at me pointedly before turning his attention back to Harlow. "I figured we should get to know each other because I know this arsehole hasn't told you I'm his best friend."

"Okay, um... Sure," Harlow replies, attempting to step back, but my palm just presses against her back firmer, pinning her to me. I do not want to let her go, despite the fucking colour, the loud music, and the overstimulation from just about everything.

Ben's gaze drops to my hand, then lifts back up to my face with an arched brow before looking at Harlow's flaming red cheeks. "Thought as much," he says.

"Later," I warn him before he could say anything more.

"This isn't what you think... We're not..." Harlow mumbles, understanding Ben's insinuations as I scowl at my best friend.

"Not my business," Ben shrugs amiably. "But I *would* appreciate a favour."

"A favour?" I ask, releasing my grip on Harlow a little, if only to let her breathe more freely.

"I may or may not have said something inappropriate to Elodie's husband just now," he explains, smirking ruefully,

"And whilst I'm pretty sure he's not going to make a scene, I think he's less likely to try and punch my lights out if I'm dancing with Robert's step-daughter."

"So you want to use me as a human shield, is that it?" Harlow asks with a quirk of her lips, bringing some much needed levity to the moment.

"Partly," Ben admits, then lowers his voice, "But if I'm being perfectly honest, this thing you got going on," he continues, wagging his finger between us, "Is starting to become noticeable. You're lucky that most of the people here are already drunk or are too busy stuffing their faces and getting drunk to wonder why you two are giving each other the stink-eye."

"The stink-eye would imply we hate each other," I argue.

"Not when you look like you want to rip each other's clothes off as well," he adds, humour sparkling in his eyes.

"Oh," Harlow murmurs, throwing a look to her mother and my father, who are currently too busy looking at each other to be interested in what's going on between us. Doesn't stop her from worrying her lip with her teeth though.

"Besides, you my friend, look like you could use some fresh air, yes?" Ben adds, giving my shoulder a firm squeeze.

In other words, *get the fuck out of here before you screw shit up.*

He's not wrong. I do need air, but I also don't want to let go of Harlow, and I can't help but pull her closer once again, angling my body between them as my possessiveness takes over.

"Sterling," Ben persists, his voice laced with concern.

"Fine," I grind out, reluctantly releasing Harlow, whilst he takes her in his arms and I try not to punch him. "I shouldn't need to tell you to be—"

"*Respectful?*" Ben throws back with a laugh. "I'm not

Dalton, and whilst Harlow is stunning, you and I both know there's only one woman for me."

"Let me guess, Councillor Hoxton's wife, Elodie?" Harlow says following Ben's gaze across the room.

"Very astute, Ms Richards," he responds. "Now let's dance."

With that he spins her away from me, and I make my escape.

TWELVE

"So, you and Sterling, huh?" Ben questions as he dances with me.

"There is nothing–" I start to protest, but he just grins.

"Listen, I make no judgement here," he soothes, his smile faltering when he notices my terrified expression. "Please don't worry, I won't out you both. Besides, Sterling's my best friend, I wouldn't betray his trust, and therefore I won't betray yours. Whatever's going on between you is your business, but tonight probably isn't the best time to get all up and personal with each other given your parents have literally just tied the knot."

I nod, he's right of course. "I appreciate you stepping in when you did. This is... difficult for me."

"For Sterling too, I imagine," he responds, cutting a look at our parents who are still dancing. "His father likes to make his life a misery. Robert's an arsehole."

"I understand that their relationship is strained," I reply, looking up at him with a question in my eyes. "Could you help me to understand why?"

Ben winces, casting Robert a disapproving look, his expression darkening. "If Sterling hasn't opened up to you about his relationship with his dad, then I'm not going to. You should probably ask him."

"That's fair," I agree softly.

"Just know that a friend of Sterling's is a friend of mine, okay?" he quickly adds, giving me a beaming smile that would no doubt melt the panties off most women, and likely some men.

"Thank you."

"So," he begins after a beat, swiftly changing the subject as we continue to dance. "Your voice is pretty spectacular."

"That's nice of you to say," I reply, my cheeks heating at his compliment.

"You sing professionally, I take it?"

"Actually, no. I work as my mother's personal assistant. Have done so for the last seven years."

"Well, that's a complete waste of talent. Ever considered getting a manager?"

"Never," I reply with a depreciating laugh.

"Why the fuck not?" he insists. "Surely it must've crossed your mind?"

"Back in my early twenties I reached out to a few people," I admit. "But it ended up with me getting propositioned by some dodgy record label executives, and I decided I didn't want to exchange my body for a record deal." I shrug, like it's no big deal, when really it made me feel like shit.

"That's fucked-up. If I was your manager I would've knocked their lights out," he retorts, scowling, and I warm to him even more as he tucks me tighter against his chest in a completely platonic, albeit protective embrace.

"It was fucked-up," I agree, huffing out a breath.

"So that put you off from pursuing a career as a singer?"

"Partly, but I'm not really one for all the attention."

"You gained the attention of a lot of people today. Pretty sure everyone was struck by your voice. It's a gift, Harlow."

"I hadn't intended on singing today, but Robert wanted me to."

"Not your mother?" he questions with a frown, picking up on the fact that I don't mention her.

"She doesn't think much of my singing," I explain, ignoring the hurt that blooms in my chest.

"Is she for real? Your voice is outstanding."

"So you've said," I reply, heat burning my cheeks. I'm not used to the compliments, and tonight I've had plenty of them. It feels nice, admittedly, but receiving compliments and accepting them as fact are two very different things.

"Do you want a manager?" he asks, easing me to the side when a drunken couple almost stumbles into us.

"Sorry, slippery floor," the guy replies, the woman in his arms giggling. I'm pretty sure she's an acquaintance of my mother. Both of them are drunk.

I laugh, partly because of the way the couple stumble off the dance floor, and partly because of Ben's question. Like I'll ever be able to make a career out of singing now.

"You know someone?" I ask, humouring him.

"Yeah, me."

"*You?*"

"Don't sound so surprised, I happen to be a bloody good manager. I manage Bandits Bar in town–"

"So you manage a *bar?*"

"Actually, I own the bar and manage the band that has made it famous. Princetown Bandits are going to be the next big thing, and they started out playing at my bar. They still do most nights. I'm in talks right now with a couple of well-known record labels who are currently in a battle over who's going to sign them and make a shitload of money, but keep that to your-self, it's kind of a secret," he says, winking at me.

"Well, that's impressive."

"I'm not *just* a pretty face," he retorts with a smirk, and to be fair he *is* very good looking with his curly brown, tousled hair, incredibly piercing green eyes, and taut body beneath his well-cut suit. As much as I appreciate his good looks, I happen to prefer his best friend, and Ben seems very interested in a married woman.

"I'll take your word for it," I joke back, and his grin widens.

"I rather like you, Harlow Richards. I think you'll be good for my surly, mostly awkward-as-fuck best friend."

"Not sure anyone else would agree," I reply, catching my mother's eye as she lifts a brow then whispers in Robert's ear. She steps out of his embrace, and heads towards our direction, but is stopped by another member of the wedding party, thank-fully. Still, I really don't want to talk to her right now, so I gently ease myself out of Ben's arms, and say, "It was nice talking with you, Ben. Hopefully we can catch up another time?"

"Absolutely, and if you ever decide you want a manager after all, then here's my card," he says, reaching into his inside pocket and handing me a black business card with green foiled writing. "This has my contact details. At the very least give me a buzz if you need a friend, yeah?"

I raise a brow. "A friend?"

"Purely platonic, I swear," he grins.

"I'll think about it," I reply, taking the card from him and giving him one last smile, hoping my mother doesn't follow me.

Thankfully when I cast my gaze over my shoulder, I find that Ben has snagged my mother for a dance. I catch his gaze and he winks, and I let out a sigh of relief.

Deciding that I need a moment to gather myself, I grab my bag from the table I left it at, tuck Ben's business card inside it and head towards the ladies room, giving polite smiles to some of the wedding guests as I pass them by in the hallway. It was sweet of Ben to offer me the opportunity to sing at his bar, but I'm not sure that would be a good idea, mostly because my mother would hate it.

Then again, what would be the harm? She agreed to me singing at her wedding, albeit reluctantly, would it be so bad to do it again in a more informal setting? I don't even have to hide behind my alter ego Friday Love, and the thought of being able to sing freely as myself is, admittedly, quite tempting.

Truth be known, singing today has given me some much needed confidence, and whilst I still don't particularly like the attention, I'm not immune to the compliments I've received over the course of the evening, even if I still find them difficult to accept.

Musing on the idea, I step into the ladies room and head to a stall. Closing the door, I take a seat on the toilet, not actually needing to relieve myself but needing a moment's peace.

I'm still reeling from my interaction with Sterling in Dalton's office, and despite everything, I can't just switch off my attraction towards him, or the connection I feel. I'm struggling with all the conflicting emotions, and honestly, it's a lot to deal with.

The worst thing is that I don't have anyone to talk to about it other than Sterling who is, apparently, more than willing to pursue a relationship despite the fact we are now, for all intents and purposes, family. I don't have any close girlfriends to discuss my predicament with, and even if I did have a better relationship with my mother, I can't talk to her for obvious reasons.

Right now I feel incredibly lonely, and this whole shitstorm has only highlighted just how alone I really am. Heaving out a sigh, I press my eyes shut willing the tears forming not to fall. Feeling sorry for myself isn't going to change anything. I need to think rationally and without emotion, and I can't do that if I'm constantly tempted by a man I cannot have, which will be awfully hard to do considering I have nowhere else to live. Living in Adaga Hall with Sterling is going to be challenging to say the least.

"These shoes are killing me," a female voice mutters, her footsteps clicking on the marble floor just beyond the closed door.

I know how she feels, I'm dying to head back to my room so that I can strip down and relax in a bubble bath. I'm about done with socialising for one day. Deciding it's about time I do that, I open the cubicle door and head for the sink to wash my hands even though I don't really need to.

Out of the corner of my eye I see a pretty, petite woman with striking strawberry blonde hair with pink streaks highlighted throughout. We haven't been introduced formally, but I believe she's called Daisy and is the younger sister of Drix. I only know that because Dalton had pointed her out in our brief conversation earlier when she'd looked our way and had thrown him a glare which he had returned with a wink.

I'd assumed that they know each other well, considering her relationship with Drix, and Dalton's friendship with him, but her responding scowl when he'd pointed her out threw me a little.

"You're Harlow, right?" Daisy asks, stepping towards me as I reach for a paper towel and dry my hands.

"I am," I confirm, dropping the paper towel into the trash

tucked beneath the vanity unit, before giving her a soft smile. "And you're Daisy?"

"That's right, how did you know?" she asks me, cocking her head to the side as she gives me a curious look, her pretty hair falling around her face in soft waves.

"I was talking to Dalton earlier—"

Her expression immediately changes from warm and welcoming to downright disgust as she wrinkles her nose. "Don't tell me, he tried to hit on you? That man has literally zero boundaries when it comes to pursuing women. I'm sorry you had to deal with that."

"No, he didn't hit on me at all. He was actually super friendly."

"I *bet* he was, Dalton can lay on the charm when he wants to," she replies, not at all convinced.

"You don't like him then?"

Daisy shakes her head. "He's an arse. An arrogant, egotistical, self-centred one at that. That man thinks with his dick more than his brain. I think he's slept with most of the single women in Princetown and quite a few of the married ones as well."

"I see," I laugh, unable to help myself. She's kind of fiery, and I like that.

"He's also my brother's best friend, and has been the bane of my life. Drix has terrible taste in friends."

"You don't like Ben or Sterling either?"

"Excluding them, of course. They're good guys, but Dalton? Urgh, I honestly don't know what Drix sees in him."

"I can't help you there, I'm afraid, I really don't know anyone very well at all. This is the first time I've met them," I explain, and even though it's only a little white lie, I still feel guilty for lying, given Sterling and I are already acquainted.

"What, this is the first time you've met Sterling?" she asks, mouth agape.

"My mother and I only arrived a couple of days ago, and well, Robert..." My voice trails off. I'm not sure how to explain why Robert only saw fit to introduce us at his wedding for the first time. Well, at least that's what he thought he was doing.

"Ah, yeah, that makes sense. Robert and Sterling do *not* get along," Daisy says, pulling a face that has me even more curious about their strained relationship. "In all honesty, I'm surprised Sterling agreed to be his Best Man."

"Can you tell me why? I seem to be a bit out of the loop here."

"Mostly because Robert is an arsehole—"

"Funny, you're not the first person to say as much," I reply.

"That's because it's true," she shrugs, giving me a rueful grin, but her smile drops when she sees my frown. "Sorry, he's just married your mum. I'm sure they'll be very happy together."

I get the distinct impression that she's telling me what I want to hear. Right now I just want the truth.

"He's only been welcoming to me," I insist, not in defence of Robert per se—there's clearly something I'm missing here—but because I don't understand *why* he's considered such an arsehole by others too. Admittedly, it's beginning to make me question the man Robert's portrayed himself to be.

"I'm glad, truly," she replies, wincing a little.

"So why?" I insist, wanting to get to the bottom of it.

"Why he's an arsehole or why Robert and Sterling don't get along?"

"Both, I guess."

"Well, Robert divorced Sterling's mum after thirty years of marriage and broke her heart, casting her aside like she meant nothing to him," she says. "It was devastating for her, and Sterling loves his mother deeply."

"That would explain some of the animosity between them, but people divorce all the time. Not that I'm saying that it wouldn't have been hurtful to Sterling and his mother, but it happens. Marriages break down, that's all I meant," I add quickly.

"I know that's what you meant, but..."

"But?"

"Well, Robert isn't well known for his kindness, let's put it that way. He's a ruthless businessman, and..." Daisy hesitates, chewing on her lip.

"And?"

"I think this is a conversation you need to have with Sterling," she replies, chewing on her lip.

"Okay," I reply, realising that she isn't going to say anything further, and I don't blame her, she probably feels a little cornered by my questioning. The last thing I want is for her to think I'm trying to go behind Sterling's back and dig for information. But my concern only deepens, given Ben had said something similar as well.

"So, your voice..." Daisy says, her face lighting up with a beaming smile. "It's pretty amazing."

"Thank you."

"Honestly, I don't think I've heard anything more beautiful."

My cheeks heat as I let the compliment sink beneath my skin and really settle inside of me, but after years of my mother putting me down, and ridiculing my dreams of becoming a singer-songwriter, it's still difficult to believe that my voice is as good as everyone appears to think it is. Not that I don't appreciate her kindness, because I do.

"So, what do you do for a living?" I ask, changing the subject.

"I work here at the hotel," she explains. "On reception. Have done so for a few years now."

"You work with Dalton then?" I ask.

She pulls another face. "Unfortunately, yes."

"You *really* don't like him very much do you?" I mean, she said as much just a moment ago, but there's disliking someone and there's hating someone, and I'm beginning to get the impression she very much despises Dalton.

"Is it that obvious?"

"I'm afraid so."

She reaches into her clutch, and pulls out a bright pink lipstick, taking off the cap as she begins to apply some to her lips. "I'm not the only one. I think most of the women he's fucked and then cast aside hate him a whole lot too."

"You've slept with him?" I blurt out, instantly cursing myself the moment the question leaves my lips when she snaps her head around to look at me.

"Oh, hell no!" she replies, making a gagging face. "I wouldn't touch him if he was the last man on earth. I just meant that I'm one of the many women who dislike him. I just have different reasons as to why."

"Ah, I see." I don't see, but I'm not in a position to delve any deeper given we've only just met.

She looks at me in the mirror, applying the last of her lipstick, before recapping it and placing it in her clutch. "Are you coming back outside, or do you need another minute?"

"I'm just going to stay in here for a bit," I reply, dropping my gaze. I should go back outside and join in on the celebrations, but I'm not ready to face my mother, let alone Sterling.

"Sure thing," she responds, turning to face me. "I get it.

Meeting everyone for the first time tonight must be over-whelming."

"It is," I admit.

"Well, it's been lovely chatting with you. If you ever need a friend, please don't hesitate to reach out to me. Sterling has my number, and I happen to know a lovely café in town. I'd be happy to meet you for a coffee or something..." she offers, giving me a genuine smile.

"That's really nice of you," I reply, not making any promises.

It's not that I don't like her, and from first impressions she seems really friendly and exactly the type of person I'd be friends with if I had the chance. It's just that I'm not planning on sticking around long enough to form any lasting friendships.

"Well, I hope to see you around, Harlow," she replies, leaving me to contemplate the true nature of Sterling and his father's hostility.

THIRTEEN

"Another drink?" Dalton asks as we sit in the bar of the hotel, his gaze flicking to the empty bottle of whisky we've shared between us.

Ben groans, leaning forward and pressing his forehead against the table, whilst Drix releases the tight bite of his jaw and shakes his head, the soft glow of the sun rising outside colouring the side of his face in dappled pinks and oranges.

"It's almost five am, I'm done," he grinds out, his jaw clamping down on the anger he's trying very hard to contain. I don't blame him for it, he's had a rough night.

"Me too," I mutter, puffing out my cheeks as I blow out a steady breath that does nothing to soothe my inner fucking turmoil.

Then again, I'm not the only one fucked-up over a woman tonight. Just a few hours ago Ben propositioned the husband of his ex, offering him a substantial amount of money for one month with her. If the bastard agrees it will only cause Ben even more heartache, and make Elodie despise him. Scratch that, she probably does already just for the sheer fact he had the gumption to offer such a deal. I mean who, in their right mind, makes an indecent proposal like that and expects it not to blow up in his face?

Not only that, Drix's girlfriend, Lia, found out about his position as the town's enforcer, and the violence that goes hand-in-hand with such a job. A job he's *reluctantly* doing for Carl, Dalton's father, to pay off a debt. The fact that she's only just escaped an abusive relationship with a violent man doesn't help matters. Despite Drix being the most honourable and decent man I know, she's understandably questioning the choices she's made getting involved with him.

To make matters infinitely worse, apparently a couple of hours ago Daisy accepted Carl's offer of relieving Drix of his duties, and writing off his debt so long as she marries Dalton, who can't keep his dick in his pants for longer than an hour. And let's not forget my own fucked-up situation to add to the mix. To put it bluntly, we're all screwed.

"Pretty sure I'm about to throw up," Ben mumbles, as he turns his head to the side and presses his cheek against the table.

"Pretty sure you're about to get into a shitload of trouble with that cunt John Hoxton," Dalton adds, leaning over the table to give him a shove.

"Ah, fuck off, Dalton. You're one to talk," Ben groans, batting his hand away. "Are you *really* going to marry Daisy?"

"Over my dead fucking body," Drix mutters.

"We've talked about this," Dalton counters, his smile dropping. "As much as I hate the fucking idea, there's no other way. We're helping you."

"First off, *you're* not fucking helping *me*. Second, there's always another way," Drix counters. "You'll speak with your dad and get him to change his fucking mind, and I'll talk some sense into Daisy. I'll be damned if I let her throw her happiness away for a decision I fucking made. My debt is mine and mine alone to deal with."

"Have you forgotten that you're in quite the predicament?" Ben says as he pushes up off the table. "As much as I hate to say it, Lia doesn't need more violence in her life. It's about time you got out from under that prick. No offence, Dalton," he adds.

"Oh, I'm not offended, my father *is* a prick," Dalton agrees.

"I am not a danger to Lia. I'll *never* hurt her or Toby. I fucking love them!" Drix cuts out.

Ben winces. "We know that, mate, but you've got to see her point of view."

"I do, but how the fuck can I let this selfish dick marry my sister just so that I can be happy?" Drix snaps, crossing his arms across his chest.

Dalton swipes a hand through his hair. "If it helps, I'm not all that happy about the situation either."

"I don't give a fuck about *your* happiness, arsehole," Drix snarls, slamming his curled fist against the table, causing the glasses and empty bottle of whisky to shake. "If you go through with this arranged marriage *you're* guaranteed to inherit a lot of fucking money, all my sister gets is a fucking divorce a couple years down the line, and a lifetime connection with your fucked-up family if she provides your cunting father with the heir he's so desperate for."

"Daisy agreed to it, and you know what she gets like. Stubborn little thing," Dalton adds with a scowl.

"Daisy is a fucking saint, and you'd do well to remember that," Drix strikes back in warning.

"Guys, damn it, do you *have* to do this now? My fucking head feels like it's been hit by a sledgehammer," Ben moans, his skin turning a dull shade of grey.

"Maybe you should sleep on it and talk again whilst this isn't so raw?" I suggest, looking between Dalton and Drix and wondering how the fuck they're going to navigate this.

No matter what either of them wants, or Daisy for that matter, Carl is just as much of a conniving bastard as my father, and he *will* make sure this arranged marriage takes place. It's why Carl and my dad are the best of friends, they both know how to fuck people's lives up to benefit them, and damn the consequences.

"Excellent suggestion," Ben mumbles, his bloodshot eyes only serving to make the green of his irises even more striking. "Now, which one of you bastards is going to help me back to my room, because right now I don't think my legs can carry me."

"Not before you explain why you thought it was a good idea to *buy* a month alone with Elodie," Dalton says, no doubt glad to move the focus of this conversation off him. "She's married."

"Never stopped you," he counters darkly.

"But *I* never have to pay to get women to spend time with me," Dalton says, clearly regretting his retort when Drix snaps his head around to glare at him. He definitely doesn't need another reminder of Dalton's philandering ways.

"It's my money, I can do what the fuck I want with it. Besides, why am I the one suddenly getting grilled, Sterling here fucked his step-sister," Ben replies.

"If you weren't about to die of alcohol poisoning, I'd fucking kill you myself," I snap, punching him none too lightly on his arm.

"Ow, fuck! I didn't mean it like that," he whines, turning puce as he gags.

"Like I already told you all, she wasn't my step-sister when we met. We were strangers."

"What's the big deal, it's not as if your blood related?" Dalton points out.

"Because, dicksplash, some people have integrity, unlike you," Drix grinds out.

"Tell that to Sterling who was getting all up and personal with Harlow in my office right after the wedding ceremony," Dalton replies, flicking Drix a glare of his own.

"That's what you were doing?" Drix asks, cutting me a look. "You're playing with fire, you know that right?"

"Give me a break, okay? It was the first time I saw her since we slept together. I couldn't–"

"Keep it in your pants?" Ben says, his joke falling flat as I glare at him. "Sorry, you know humour is my way of dealing with shit. I don't mean anything by it."

"There's nothing about my predicament with Harlow that I find amusing," I reply, pinching the bridge of my nose, the headache that's been threatening to develop into a full-blown migraine all damn night causing nausea to rise up my throat.

"Seriously though, Sterling, what the hell are you going to do?" Ben asks.

"Right now? I have no fucking clue," I reply.

With my paintbrush gripped tightly in my hand, I look at the huge six foot by six foot canvas before me, studying it through narrowed eyes. I ache all over, and for the last few hours every muscle in my body has screamed at me to stop, to rest. But I *can't* rest. I won't rest until the piece is done.

As soon as I got home this morning I headed straight to my studio on the edge of my father's property, knowing that I couldn't ignore my synesthesia a second longer. Trouble is, even after almost ten hours of painting nothing feels better. *Nothing.*

"Fuck, something's missing," I muse, scraping a hand through my tousled hair and ignoring my growling stomach as I take a few steps back, my bare feet stepping into flecks of wet paint that cover the floor.

I haven't eaten anything since last night at the wedding, despite it now being late afternoon the following day. The sandwich a member of staff brought to me a couple of hours ago is still sitting on the table where I left it, and the second lot of headache pills I took at midday are beginning to wear off. Yet despite the exhausted state my body is in, my cock hasn't got the damn memo and is *still* rock fucking hard.

The truth is, I've been perpetually turned on ever since that hot as fuck moment I shared with Harlow in Dalton's office last night. Fuck, the way she'd fallen into me, the way she'd tasted on my tongue, and her moans of pleasure have played over and over in my mind, keeping me hard for hours.

She's mine. She's mine. She's mine.

Those two words have been circling in my brain over and over, and over again. I feel this intense kind of ownership and possessiveness towards her. It's like nothing I've felt before. On top of all of that, I'm agitated as fuck.

This painting before me is a reflection of all the uncertainty that I'm feeling right now, though it's not about *my* feelings towards Harlow, or the fact that I want her. I truly couldn't give a flying fuck if my dad and Melody found out that we've been intimate, that we're attracted to one another. What I am uncertain about is Harlow's willingness to explore this connection between us now that we have parents in common. I don't know whether Harlow will ever be able to get over her belief that being together now is wrong, despite how right it felt to hold her in my arms.

All that uncertainty has bled out onto the canvas in a display of frustrated and passionate brushstrokes that whip across the canvas in a violent storm of striking scarlet, bright crimson, and deep blood red. They depict every tumultuous thought I've had since I've laid eyes on her again, and right at the heart of the painting is Harlow. Her face is in profile, her expression one of orgasmic bliss. But around her, all that red? It may as well be the raw bloody mess of my heart, every stroke and every drop of paint baring my emotions for all to see.

Yet, it's still *not* finished.

"Goddamn it!" I mutter, pulling up a chair, my tired body crumpling into the seat as my legs give way beneath me.

In sheer frustration I throw my paintbrush across my studio, causing more paint to scatter across the floor as it finds its resting place beneath a bench pushed up against the wall on the other side of the room. I'd hoped that painting would give me some relief.

It hasn't.

I'm still wound up, coiled like a fucking spring. My muscles ache, my eyes sting, my brain is wired from almost twenty-four hours of heightened emotions and overstimulation. I know that I should eat, that I should try to sleep, but I can't do either of those things until I've finished this damn painting.

My eyes trace over the paint strokes before me, lingering on Harlow's lips that are parted in pleasure, then move across her jaw and the slope of her neck as she tips her head back in ecstasy. Her eyes are pressed shut on a moan, and her face is surrounded by a mist of red. This painting is profoundly sexual and deeply personal, but despite my efforts, I'm still not satisfied.

Maybe *that's* the problem.

Harlow came on my tongue, but I've had no such relief.

My cock throbs against the zipper of my trousers, reminding me that my base desires have not been satisfied, and my hand falls to my crotch, giving it a tight squeeze.

"Harlow," I mutter, her name strained on my lips as my cock jerks from the contact.

I'm well aware that if I don't relieve some of the tension right now then I might do something stupid and drive back to the hotel to seek Harlow out. Which would be a bad fucking idea given how volatile I feel, and how uncertain she is about us. Instead, I widen my legs, unzip my trousers and pull my cock out through the opening of my boxers, grasping the base.

"Yes," I hiss, my hips thrusting up shamelessly as my eager cock slides through my fist.

I stare up at Harlow's expression, my cock growing in my hand as I tug on its length, the veins in the back of my hand and forearm thick beneath my paint-splattered skin as I jerk myself off.

"Fuck," I groan, white-hot pleasure gathering in my balls as they lift high and tight against my body. But without any lubrication the friction soon verges on painful, so I drop my chin to my chest whilst gathering spit into my mouth, then part my lips and watch as my saliva drops onto the engorged head of my cock imagining it's Harlow's cum making me slick.

Pressing the pad of my thumb over my slit, I drag the wetness down my shaft as I lift my gaze, focussing on Harlow's face before me, her captured pleasure matching mine.

"Damn it, Harlow," I groan, cork-screwing my fist up and down my length. "I want to fuck your beautiful mouth... I want to bury my cock deep inside your throat whilst you finger-fuck yourself... I want to watch you swallow my cum..."

My hips jerk as I thrust upwards into my fist, the wooden frame of the chair I'm sitting on digging into the stretch of muscle beneath my shoulder blades. "I want you to sit on my goddamn face until I can't fucking breathe!"

I'm fully aware how fucking crazy I sound jerking off over a painting and talking dirty to an empty fucking room, but that doesn't stop me, and before I know what the fuck I'm doing, I'm pushing down my boxers and trousers past my hips, kicking them off.

Completely naked, I fist my cock remembering the way Harlow had kissed me with abandon, with passion, with greed, clawing at me as she pulled me close. I recall how she'd rubbed her pretty cunt against my face in Dalton's office.

"Fuck, yes," I groan, my cock jerking in my hand, precum oozing from the slit as I press my eyes shut and remember how it felt to hold her in my arms back in my apartment all those months ago, how her cheeks had flushed pink when I complimented the taste of her pussy, how she'd cried out my name when she came. Every moment is etched into my memory as my eyes snap back open and I stagger to my feet, taking a few shaky steps towards the painting.

"You'll look so fucking pretty with my cum decorating your face," I grind out, slapping my hand against the brick wall beside the painting, my hips pistoning into my fist. "Yes, fuck. Yes."

Pinpricks of pleasure scatter over my skin and gather at the base of my spine as I drop my forehead against the canvas, not caring that the paint is still wet. I know I'm going to come hard, the oncoming violence of it matching the paint strokes surrounding Harlow's bliss-filled expression. God, how fucking pretty she'd looked in the throws of an orgasm, how beautiful when she'd begged me to fuck her that night we met.

"Please, Sterling, take me..."

The memory of her voice is all it takes to push me over the edge, and I feel my release racing up my cock, euphoria painting the canvas in thick ropes of white as I come hard and fast.

"Fuuuuuuuckkkk!" I groan, my chest heaving as I blink back the fog of my orgasm, and with each inhale of breath, I stare at my cum mixing with the differing shades of red, my agony and my ecstasy staining part of the canvas pink. I should probably remove every trace of it. Instead I release my cock, press my fingers against the canvas and paint my cum into her lips.

FOURTEEN

The wedding was over a week ago, and I've spent the whole time avoiding Sterling, which isn't as hard as it may seem given Adaga Hall is an enormous mansion with too many rooms to count.

When I imagined what Adaga Hall would look like, I had anticipated a grand brick building with ivy growing around the windows, wooden panelling, tapestry hanging from the walls, and a kind of ambience that speaks of fine brandy and cigars.

Instead Robert's home, whilst beautifully styled, is a modern building with huge glass windows, and nothing like what the name suggests. It has crisp modern furniture, white walls and marble floors throughout. There's also an indoor gym, outdoor pool, hot tub and sauna. On the first floor is a movie theatre situated next to a huge library which is the only space that seems to have a little character. The ground floor houses a parlour with a baby grand piano that I hope to be able to play at some point, as well as a huge kitchen, Robert's study, three sepa-rate living rooms, a massive dining room, and a den. Outside there are hundreds of acres of grounds housing a paddock and stable that is yet to be filled with the horse Robert promised my mother, a huge garage filled with expensive cars and even a helicopter pad. It reeks of wealth, and is stunning, but sadly lacks character.

The staff that work for Robert are seen but not heard, moving around like ghosts, barely making eye contact with me, let alone conversation, and honestly, I feel like a trespasser even though Robert tried his best to make me feel welcome, providing me with a substantial suite in the north wing of the house that is far too grand for my needs. This evening is the first time I've left my suite for an extended period of time, choosing instead to avoid any kind of interaction with Sterling. After Ben interrupted our conversation on the dance floor the night of the wedding, I haven't seen him. He wasn't around to say goodbye to our parents when they left for their honeymoon the day after the wedding, and despite what he'd said to me after Dalton found us alone together in his office, he hasn't even tried to seek me out.

It's probably for the best anyway.

Not probably, it *is* for the best.

My fingers curl around a mug of coffee as I stand in the kitchen, staring out the french doors that open out onto the huge heated swimming pool. It's early evening, and the sun has already dipped behind the horizon, but as the pool is lit up with underwater lighting, I can still see the steam lifting off the surface of the water, enticing me to enter, which is exactly what I'm going to do as soon as I've finished my drink.

For the past week I've spent a lot of time pacing back and forth in my room going over everything that's happened, and it's left me feeling anxious and wound-up, so I figured I'd make use of the pool to try and alleviate the mounting stress.

To make matters infinitely worse, I'm *still* getting creepy messages, and every day they're more and more sexual. The last one I received this morning had me chucking my phone across the room. I can't even think about it without feeling violated.

> I bet your pussy is as silky as your voice. Are you dripping for me? Will you scream when I force my dick inside of you? Will you enjoy it?

It was the use of the word 'force' that had my hackles rising even more. Whoever this arsehole is, he's doing a good job at getting into my head. I know I should tell someone, but there's a part of me that thinks I'm overreacting. It's not as if he knows who I really am. This is just some guy getting a kick out of sending me dirty, threatening messages, right?

But then again, what if he *is* dangerous? What if he somehow finds out who I really am and makes an attempt of following through on his threats...?

"What a creep," I mutter, taking a sip of my coffee as I push those thoughts aside and wonder what the hell I'm going to do about Sterling and this situation we've found ourselves in.

"Is there anything you need, Miss?"

I let out a yelp of surprise as a middle-aged woman enters the kitchen holding a tray loaded with dirty plates. She's dressed in the same uniform as the rest of the staff, a dark blue pinafore dress with the Blade family crest embroidered onto the sleeve.

"You startled me," I say, my hand flying to my chest as I turn to face her. I don't know her name, but as far as I've gathered she's the head housekeeper and has worked for the Blade family for over twenty years.

"Apologies," she replies, giving me a soft smile as she places the tray on the counter beside the sink. "I was just about to put supper together for Sterling, are you hungry too? Can I get you anything?"

"He's home?" I ask.

I mean, I was pretty certain he hadn't gone anywhere, but admittedly there was a small part of me that had convinced myself he'd returned to New York, hoping that would explain his absence and not the fact that he has been avoiding me as much as I've been avoiding him.

"He is, yes," she replies, frowning a little at my question.

"I've just not seen him around, that's all," I mumble, my cheeks heating.

She nods. "He prefers his own company."

"Oh, okay..." My voice trails off as I absorb that information. He'd told me he was a hermit the night we met, so I guess it shouldn't come as a huge surprise.

"So would you like something to eat?"

"Actually, I was going to take a swim," I explain, plucking at the strap of my one-piece bathing suit that I'm wearing beneath my joggers and hoodie.

"I can prepare something for you when you've finished," she offers.

"Are you sure? I was just going to make a sandwich anyway. I don't want to trouble you," I reply, finding this whole conversation uncomfortable, not because she's done anything wrong, but because I'm not used to having people catering to my every need. I've felt guilty every time one of the staff has brought food to my room.

"It's no trouble. Would you like anything in particular?"

"Chicken with salad?" I offer.

"Of course. Shall I bring it out to you so you can eat it after your swim?" she questions.

I shake my head. "If you don't mind just leaving it on a

plate, and I'll eat it here when I'm done. Thank you... Erm, sorry, I don't know your name?"

"It's Stephanie, Miss," she replies with a soft smile.

"Thank you, Stephanie, and please call me Harlow."

Half an hour later, I've swum enough laps of the pool to take the edge off my anxiety and am

lying on my back staring up at the sky, my hearing muffled by the water as I enjoy the cool winter air blowing across my cheeks. Steam rises upwards as I marvel at the smattering of stars glistening above me.

Even though I feel wholly out of place here, I know my mother will enjoy her life here, but me? I'd be happy with a small stone cottage, a log burning fire, and a cosy living space just big enough to house an upright piano. It's a dream I can't ever see coming true. Heaving out a breath, I flip over on my stomach and swim to the edge of the pool. As I swipe the water out of my eyes I hear the sound of splashing behind me, and turn around to catch Sterling breaking the surface.

Oh God.

I should get out of the pool. I should return to my suite and avoid all contact, but I can't seem to move, my gaze is drawn to his strong arms and shoulders as he cuts through the water with powerful strokes towards me. His muscles tense and release as he swims, and my body reacts instantly, heat blooming beneath my skin as I watch him swim. I can't help but squeeze my thighs together to try and alleviate the throb between my legs that his presence immediately conjures.

I really, *really* should leave.

Deciding that the best course of action is to do exactly

that, I reach for the edge of the pool and attempt to lift myself upwards, but I don't get very far. One second my stomach is pressed against the hard stone edge, the next, two warm hands are curled around my hips tugging me back gently.

"Don't leave," Sterling begs, his voice strained as I slide down his chest and he wraps his arm around my waist, pressing me against the tiled wall. His broad chest is firm against my back, and I can feel the beat of his heart echo inside my own chest.

"Sterling, this isn't a good idea," I warn, my whole body stiffening from his touch, not because I don't want him this close to me, but because I *do*. "Let me go."

"I don't fucking want to, Harlow," he replies, his breath sliding over my skin as he drops his forehead to my shoulder. "I've tried to give you space. I've fucking tried."

I'm not sure that makes me feel any better.

My pulse spikes at his close proximity, at the way he grips the side of the pool with one hand and presses me against the tiles, effectively trapping me. I should force him away. I should tell him to back off. But again, just like in Dalton's office, I do neither of those things.

"Someone will see," I say, more than a little breathlessly to be honest.

"I've given the staff a night off. We're the only ones here, Harlow," he counters, easing back just enough so that I can turn in his arms.

"Which is another reason why this is dangerous," I add, forcing myself to meet his gaze as the water laps gently around us both.

His eyes shine brightly, the silver striations within them sparkling under the pool light. Water droplets trickle from his hairline, snaking their way down the sharp cut of his cheekbones.

He's so beautiful.

"Look at you," he murmurs, reaching up to push a strand of wet hair off my face.

"Sterling..." My voice trails off as he presses his body against mine.

"When I told you this wasn't over, Harlow, I meant it."

"But I did," I lie, forcing strength into my voice.

"You don't mean that. I know you don't."

"Please don't do this. I can't–"

I don't get to finish my sentence because he slams his mouth against mine, kissing me roughly. And for just the briefest of moments I allow myself to receive his kiss, to absorb what it feels like to have his body pressed so tightly against mine, his cock hard against my stomach.

But despite how good it feels, common sense prevails and I find the strength to push him away.

"No," I say firmly.

"No?" he questions, looking at me with a mixture of shock, disappointment, and worse, *pain.*

"Harlow–" he adds, bridging the gap between us, crowding me once more.

"I said no, and I meant it, Sterling. I don't want this," I cut him off, forcing strength into my voice as I meet his gaze, hoping to God he doesn't see the truth in my eyes.

"I don't believe you," he persists, and I have to force myself to remain strong in my convictions, because if I let him get under my skin one more time, I'm lost.

"I love my mother. I like your father. I don't want to ruin their relationship or mine with them for that matter, by pursuing something with you. I won't be that person, Sterling."

"But you'll keep letting your mother ruin *your* happiness?" he counters, shaking his head in disbelief.

"She's my mom, Sterling," I protest, knowing full well that if the shoe were on the other foot my mother would have no issue being selfish and hurting me. But I'm not like her, I can't be responsible for her unhappiness. I'm still hopeful that one day we'll get back to the relationship we had when I was a kid, because I miss that version of her so, so much.

Sterling shakes his head, lifting his palm to cup my cheek. "Yes, she is, and if she gave a shit about you she'd *want* your happiness."

"How could she ever be comfortable with us being together? Regardless of her past behaviour towards me, this is still wrong."

"So you'll give up any chance of happiness to appease your mother? That's no way to live, Harlow," he persists, caressing my skin with the pad of his thumb.

"It's *my* choice. This can't happen," I reply, fighting the urge to lean my face in his palm, and accept his affection.

"Don't do this, Harlow. Don't walk back into my life, give me hope, and then shatter it all in one fucking week."

"Sterling, this is for the best," I say, placing my hand over his and pushing it away.

"Harlow, don't turn your back on me, on us."

I swallow hard, forcing myself to be strong because one of us has to have the strength to end this before we hurt anyone else. It's already too painful.

"We can be friends," I offer, hoping he'll forgive me one day for all of this.

He lets out a bitter laugh, his eyes glistening with determination as he rocks his hips against mine so that I can feel his arousal. "No, Harlow, we can't just be friends."

"Sterling, I'm so sorry for everything," I whisper, hating myself.

"I'm not sorry," he whispers roughly. "Not for meeting you, not for taking you back to my apartment that night, not for having sex with you, not for what happened in Dalton's office last week, and not for the way I feel about you. I'm. Not. Sorry."

"Stop it," I beg, feeling my resolve begin to crack.

"The only thing I'm sorry for is leaving it a week before I came to talk to you. You've spent the whole time convincing yourself we can't be together when I should've spent that time showing you that we can."

"I–"

"Mr Blade?"

"Fuck, it's Stephanie!"

Sterling exhales sharply, pushing away from me whilst I'm left reeling from his words. He gives me a look, one that says, *this conversation isn't over.*

But it is. There's nothing left to say.

Allowing my body to drop lower beneath the surface of the water, I tell myself that we were hidden by the wall of the pool, and the raised hot tub behind us. That doesn't stop me from panicking though. Stephanie knew I was taking a swim, and she no doubt would've noticed I hadn't eaten my sandwich she'd made. It doesn't take a genius to figure out we're in the pool together. The sheer fact we weren't swimming when she stepped out of the kitchen tells her that we were at the very least talking, I just hope we were obscured enough that she didn't notice how close we were whilst doing that.

"What is it, Stephanie?" Sterling asks, swimming towards the other end of the pool, drawing her attention away from me.

"I've left your supper in the den as you requested. I just wanted to let you know before I left."

Sterling hauls himself out of the pool and reaches for his towel, snatching it up, the residual tension from our conversation making his movements jerky, harsh.

"That wasn't necessary, but thank you," he bites out.

"I didn't mean to disturb you," she replies apologetically, flicking her gaze my way, sensing something amiss. "I apologise for interrupting."

"It's no big deal, we were just taking a swim and catching up," I reply, hoping she buys it as I plaster on a shaky smile.

Sterling nods his head in agreement, barely glancing my way as he wraps the towel around his waist, slides his feet into his shoes, and follows Stephanie inside. I hear her apologising softly again, and Sterling muttering something in response before the sound of the kitchen doors click shut, and a strangled sob releases from my lips.

"Oh God," I cry, slamming my palm over my mouth as I realise how close we were to getting caught, and how close I was to giving in once again.

FIFTEEN

"What you saw..." I begin, trying to find the right words to explain away my intense interaction with Harlow as I escort Stephanie to her car. At this point, I'm not even sure that I want to hide anything, especially not from someone I've known almost my whole life.

"Is none of my business," Stephanie replies, eyeing me as she reaches in her handbag for her key.

"It's complicated," I admit, swiping a hand through my hair.

Stephanie nods, her gaze soft, her smile gentle as she regards me. She's been a constant in my life, and whilst her official role has only ever been head housekeeper for my father, over the years she has unofficially been a friend to me, and my mother too. And right now I could really use a friend, because I honestly don't know how to handle this situation the right way.

I want Harlow, I know she wants me too, no matter how much she protests otherwise, but truthfully, how can we make this work? My father would never allow it, he would go out of his way to destroy me if he found out how I feel about Harlow, let alone if we attempted to have a relationship. Fuck knows what he'd do to her. Whatever relationship they have is one built on bullshit and lies. My father doesn't care about anyone but himself.

"Is this why you've locked yourself away in your studio this past week?" she asks me, sensing my need to talk.

"Partly, yes," I agree with a sigh, recalling how I spent the time painting images of Harlow, the urge to paint to try and rid myself of my need for her was intense. But like it was back in New York, painting her image has only made me crave her more. Fuck, I know it's a risky thing to do, but my father has never once stepped into my studio. Besides I keep it locked and I'm the only one with the key. "But–"

"But?" she questions.

"But also because I thought if I gave Harlow some space she'd be more open to..."

What, talk? Accept the attraction between us? Want to have a relationship with me? Feel as desperate for me as I am for her? "...Christ, I don't know. This whole situation is fucked-up."

"It's not my place to tell you what to do, Sterling, but I am assuming you met Harlow before the wedding."

"Yes."

"And that you already made a... *connection*?" she asks, lowering her voice even though the other staff have already left and there's no need for her to.

"Yes, we have."

"And your father and her mother...?"

"Have no idea. They think we met for the first time at the wedding," I explain, blowing out a breath, "When in actual fact we met months before, around the same time their relationship began. I didn't know she was Melody's daughter at the time, and she didn't know I was the son of the man her mum was dating."

"I see, that makes things very complicated."

"Yeah, it does."

"So how does Harlow feel?" she asks, cocking her head to the side as she glances up at me.

"For the most part, I think she's scared. Of her feelings towards me, of hurting her mother or my dad, though fuck knows why she gives a shit about what he thinks," I grumble, wishing she knew what he's really like. If she did, then perhaps she'd be less inclined to take his feelings into consideration. Feelings that he doesn't actually have given he's a cold-hearted bastard.

"I can't speak for her mother, but I do know that your father wouldn't appreciate a relationship between you and his wife's daughter."

"Tell me something I don't already know," I agree darkly.

"So what are you going to do?" she asks.

"Make her mine."

"But your father..."

She pauses, searching for the right words, her loyalty to my father as his employee, and probably a whole dose of fear, causing her to pause momentarily. He's fired plenty of staff over the years for doing much less than being honest, ruining their lives in the process too by ensuring no one else will hire them.

"You can be frank with me, Stephanie, we both know what my father's capable of. This conversation will go no further. Honestly, I could just really use some advice."

She nods. "I have witnessed many things working for your family over the years, and I'm fully aware of your father's disposition–"

"His *cruelty* you mean?"

"Yes, his cruelty," she soothes, reaching for me and squeezing my arm in acknowledgment. "I guess what I'm saying is that you know the risks if you pursue something with Harlow. He's a very powerful, influential man, and I know your relationship is already strained to say the least. I don't want you hurt anymore than you have been by his words and his actions over the years."

"So what are you saying, that I should just ignore how I feel? That I should let go of the only woman I've ever felt such a strong connection with? I don't know if I can do that."

"Does she know?" Stephanie asks, looking at me pointedly, and I know she's referring to my synesthesia. She's the only member of staff that's aware of my condition.

"No," I shake my head.

"Why? Don't you think it's important that she does?"

"It won't change how I feel about her," I protest.

She gives me a sympathetic look. "Sterling..." she warns, and I know where she's going with this.

"You think she'd reject me, is that what you're getting at?"

"No, that's not what I think at all, but your synesthesia is an integral part of who you are. If you're not willing to share that side of yourself with her, what makes you think that the risk of forming a real and lasting relationship with her is worth the cost of your father's wrath if you can't, at the very least, be completely honest with her?"

"I know you're right, but my synesthesia isn't my most pressing concern. My father and his reaction is. I don't know what he'd do if we were to pursue a relationship, but I do know it wouldn't be good."

"Herein lies the problem," she muses.

"So what do I do?"

"Sterling, you're a grown man, and you will come to the right decision in your own time. I think, perhaps, you need to really decide if the consequences of your actions are worth the risk. *Is Harlow worth it?*"

"Yes," I reply instantly, because despite everything, I know that she is. "This isn't just a sexual attraction, Stephanie."

"I wasn't suggesting that it is. I just think that you need to be certain of your feelings, your intentions, and the consequences of your actions."

"I am."

"Then I guess you have your answer..." Her voice trails off as she takes my hand in hers and squeezes it gently. "But you need to remember that this isn't just about you, you *have* to consider Harlow's feelings too. Not only that, you have to consider how your father, and her mother will treat her if you were to commit to a relationship. Do you really want her to experience his cruelty like you have on countless occasions over the years? You know how hateful and vindictive he can be."

"Of course I don't want–" I begin, but she cuts me off with a shake of her head.

"Not wanting her to experience your father's cruelty, and having the ability to prevent it are two very different things, Sterling. Just think about this some more, okay?"

"So what you're saying is we both have to forgo any kind of happiness just in case my father turns on us both?"

"I'm afraid, Sterling, that's exactly what I'm saying, because you know as well as I what he's capable of."

With that, Stephanie gives my hand one last squeeze before opening the door to her car and sliding into her seat, leaving me reeling.

After my conversation with Stephanie a few nights ago, my resolve to make Harlow mine has wavered. Not because I feel any differently about her, but because Stephanie's warning about my father hit home. This isn't just about me, and I've been going back and forth for days now trying to figure out what the fuck to do.

The truth is, whilst I've learned how to handle my father over the years, Harlow hasn't. She has no idea of the lengths he would go to to fuck us both over. Do I really want her to find out?

"Fuck," I mutter, pushing off my duvet cover as winter sunlight streams through a strip in my curtains, dust motes dancing in the air around me as I stand.

Reaching for my phone on my bedside cabinet, I notice that it's almost midday and I've missed several calls from Dalton, and a few from my father. Deciding that the last thing I want to do is speak with my father, I hit the dial on Dalton's number. He picks up within seconds.

"Sterling, I've been trying to reach you for fucking hours!" he shouts down the line.

"Good morning to you too, arsehole," I grumble, regretting my decision to call him back. Knowing him he's got himself into some kind of shit with a woman, and can't call Drix like he usually does to get himself out of it.

"Lia's in hospital. Daisy too," he bites out.

"What?" I exclaim, tensing.

"Lia's cunt of an ex turned up at their house this morning whilst Drix was out, he hurt Lia. Drix called me to let me know. I wanted to go to the hospital and check on her and Daisy but he fucking warned me away, Sterling."

"How badly is Lia hurt?"

"I don't know much other than she's going to be okay. Drix

got there in time, beat him to a pulp. Called the police on the bastard. He's been arrested."

"Good."

"You know that's not how we usually deal with shit like this, Sterling. We don't get the police involved, we handle this kind of thing ourselves."

"Drix made the right call. The last thing he needs right now is to go to prison for murder."

"I would've killed the cunt."

"Just calm down, okay. Take a breath."

"Don't tell me to fucking calm down. Daisy is in the hospital, Sterling!"

"Did he hurt her as well?"

"No, she was upstairs locked in a room with Toby, but he told me she's pretty shaken up. I should be there."

"Because Drix is your best friend..."

"No, arsehole, because Daisy is going to be *my wife!*"

"You sound like you care," I say, wincing at how that sounds. He might fuck around with women, but I know that he wouldn't want to see Daisy hurt.

"Of course I care. She's my best friend's sister. She's my... Fuck! *Fuck!*"

"I think, for now, you need to respect Drix's wishes. Just give him time."

"He'll *never* forgive me for this."

He doesn't need to tell me what Drix won't forgive him for. We're both well aware that Drix hates the fact that he's going to marry Daisy.

"Then maybe you should reconsider," I offer.

"No."

"No?"

"I'm marrying Daisy. It's happening whether he likes it or

not. Besides, we've already signed the contract. There's no backing out now."

"You want your inheritance that badly?"

The line goes quiet. "You don't understand," he eventually says.

"You're right, I don't. What gives?"

"Look, I gotta go. I've got things to do. Thanks for calling back."

"Is there anything I can do?"

"Call Drix, he'll talk to you. Make sure they're okay, will you?"

"I can do that."

"Good–"

"Dalton?" I interrupt, preventing him from hanging up.

"Yes?"

"Take care of Daisy. She's a good person."

I can hear Dalton mutter something under his breath, before his voice sounds down the line. "I will." With that he hangs up.

"Goddamn it," I exclaim, scrolling through my contacts until I find Drix's number, pressing the call button. It rings a few times before he eventually answers. "Drix, I just spoke with Dalton. How can I help?"

"You can keep Dalton away from the hospital. I don't want him here, Daisy doesn't either."

"He's concerned, Drix."

Drix heaves out a breath. "I can't have him here right now. I'm too fucking angry."

"I get it. How is Lia doing?"

"He hurt her, Sterling. If I'd taken any longer to get there he might've killed her," he replies, his voice cracking.

"But you *did* get there in time. She has you now, Drix.

You'll never let anyone hurt her again."

"I swear to fuck, Sterling, I wanted to end him. I've never felt more rage in my goddamn life. Who beats on a woman like that? FUCK, I should've killed him!"

"He'll go to prison for a long time, Drix," I soothe, trying my best to reassure him. "Lia and Toby need you to be present in their lives, not behind bars too. You did the *right* thing."

"He better hope he does," Drix grinds out.

"Do you need me to do anything?"

"I appreciate the offer, but I've got things covered."

"And Lia and Toby, are they–"

"Staying with me forever. I'm not letting them go, Sterling. I love them so fucking much."

"I know you do. Is Daisy okay?"

"She's shaken up, but she's stronger than people give her credit for. She'll be okay."

"And this marriage?"

"Is still going ahead. Daisy and Dalton signed the contract that Carl drew up a few days after your dad's wedding," he says, confirming what Dalton had told me. "He's released me from my obligations and I feel like a cunt for it. Daisy wouldn't back down, and Dalton is too much of a selfish prick to put a stop to this."

"He's your best friend, Drix," I remind him, though I *get* it. Drix is extremely protective of Daisy, and we all know what Dalton is like.

"He *was* my best friend," he cuts out. "Daisy is doing this out of her love for me, Lia and Toby, but Dalton? We all know money talks where he's concerned, and Carl won't let him see a penny of his inheritance unless he marries and gives him an heir to carry on the family name."

"I didn't think they'd actually go through with it. I'm sorry, Drix."

"Daisy's due to move in with Dalton this weekend. Their engagement party is the week after, and their wedding is going to be arranged for a few weeks after that."

"That soon?"

"Yeah, that soon."

"Fuck, man, that's tough."

"Daisy insists she has her own reasons for marrying Dalton..." Drix pauses, then sighs heavily.

"Want to talk about it?" I offer, sensing there's more to this that I don't fully understand.

"It wouldn't be right. I don't want to break Daisy's trust."

"I understand. Just know that I'm here for you if you need me."

"I appreciate that." Drix says. "How are things with you and Harlow?"

"Hey, you don't need to worry about me, you've got enough going on," I reply, palming the back of my neck in agitation.

"Listen, I could use the distraction right now. Lia is having an x-ray done on her ribs, and Daisy's sitting with Toby whilst I wait to speak with the doctor, so what gives?"

"Things are complicated."

"I bet. Have you talked anymore?"

"I want to, but every time we're alone together things get... *heated*," I explain.

"I see," he muses. "That intense, huh?"

"Yeah, it's been that intense. Truth is, I've spent most of the time avoiding her. I gave her space last week thinking that's what she needed, but then as soon as we were alone together the other night... Well, put it this way, I can't fucking control myself."

"I get it."

"You do?"

"Listen, I knew early on that Lia was the woman for me. I fell hard and fast. So, yeah, I get it. I'm assuming that you're struggling with the fact that she's now your step-sister?"

"Not so much that," I admit. "Because, frankly, I couldn't give a fuck that our parents are married. It doesn't alter what's happened between us or how I feel about her."

"But?"

"But Harlow's struggling with it all, and there's the added complication that my father is a bastard. We all know that he would go out of his way to ruin both our lives if we pursued anything."

"Yes, I imagine he would..." Drix pauses, then clears his throat. "Do you want my advice?"

"I'd appreciate it, yes," I reply hoping he can give me some clarity.

"Almost losing Lia has made me realise that fighting for someone you care about is the *only* thing that matters," he continues. "I thought that Lia and Toby would be better off without me, I was so fucking wrong, Sterling. I can't even begin to imagine my life without them in it."

"So, what are you saying?"

"If you think you can make this work with Harlow, and you're as serious about her as you seem to be, then *find* a way to be with her. After that, find a way to deal with your dad."

"I wish it were that simple."

"Mate, nothing worth having is ever easy."

"Did you just quote Theodore Roosevelt?" I ask, smiling a little when I recognise the familiar saying.

"Pretty sure I just quoted Hubert Hammer," Drix replies,

chuckling as he recalls his late father. "Then again, Dad did have an obsession with the American presidents."

"Yeah, he did, didn't he?" I reply, smiling at the memory of Hubert, and his many quirks. Like Ben's father Walter, Hubert was one of the good ones. He adopted Drix and Daisy when they were kids and showered them both with love and affection that neither of them received from their respective birth parents. It was a fucking tragedy when he died.

"Though I'm pretty sure that Dad would have a few choice words to say to Dalton about this sham of a wedding," Drix grumbles.

"Pretty sure he would've had a few choice words to say to Carl too," I add.

"Yeah, he would've," Drix agrees.

"Well, I'd better let you go. Thanks for the advice, Drix," I say.

"You're welcome. I guess I'll be seeing you at the engagement party then?"

"I didn't realise the invites had been sent out?"

"They haven't yet as far as I'm aware, but I don't need one. I'm there regardless. I might not agree with what's happening, but I'll be going to support Daisy."

"Then I'll be there too... Oh, and Drix?"

"Yes?"

"I know that Dalton has a reputation, but he might surprise all of us and do right by Daisy."

Drix releases a bitter laugh. "The *only* thing that will surprise me at this stage is if Dalton calls off the wedding, and we both know that's never going to happen."

SIXTEEN

The incessant trill of my phone alarm penetrates my sleep-addled brain and I jerk upright as though I've just had a twenty volt cattle prod stuck up my ass.

"What the hell?!" I mumble, blinking, as I try to find the source of my discomfort. It's pitch black and very clearly still the middle of the damn night, so either I've accidentally programmed in the wrong alarm time, or it's not actually my alarm but someone calling me.

Throwing myself towards the faint light peeking out from beneath my phone's wraparound cover, I grab my phone, flipping it open. It's my mother calling. I let out a groan. *Of course* it is.

"Mom, this better be an emergency," I say, switching on my bedside lamp.

"An emergency? What are you talking *scha-bout?*" she replies, slurring her words.

Great, she's drunk.

"It's the middle of the night!" I exclaim, unable to hide my annoyance as I flip back my duvet and stand. I've spent another day alone, which makes it four days since my conversation with Sterling in the swimming pool. Four lonely days of watching movies alone. Eating alone. Reading alone. And now is the time my mother chooses to grace me with her attention?

"Not where I am, it's not."

Give. Me. Strength.

"So what did you want?" I ask, pacing back and forth. Any patience I might've had if she'd called during the day like a reasonable human being has now been eaten up entirely by her selfishness.

I'm positive most people would hang up, and I'm considering doing just that when she says, "Robert tells me that there's going to be a wedding soon," she hiccups, and then giggles. If I could roll my eyes any harder they'd fall out of my head.

"Mom, couldn't this have waited until–"

"Apparently Carl's son, *Dalton*, is getting hitched and as Carl and Robert are best friends we've been invited to the wedding!" she interrupts.

"Dalton's getting married?" That comes as a surprise given everything Daisy said about him.

"Yes, and by *we*, I mean Robert and I have been invited to the wedding. It's going to be such a grand affair..."

My footsteps still as I let that tidbit of information sink in. I shouldn't be bothered given I barely know Dalton, but I am more than a little upset that my mother chose to call me in the middle of the night to essentially say I haven't been invited to his wedding. Feeling more than a little agitated, I stride over to the other side of the room, rip open the curtains before unlatching the lock and pushing open the window. A cold breeze flutters over my skin and I drag in a deep breath, trying in vain to calm myself down.

"This could've waited until the morning," I remind her, peering out of the window, but unable to see much other than my reflection in the glass.

"Oh stop being such a bore! Dalton is a very wealthy young man, and his family are extremely influential–"

"And I should care because?"

"Because these people are my friends, and this is going to be quite the event," she trills.

"*Robert's* friends, you mean?"

"My friends too now that we're married," she responds sharply, suddenly sobering up.

"Hmm," I murmur, perching the edge of my bottom on the windowsill and pressing my cheek against the cool glass.

"Carl is throwing Dalton an engagement party next weekend in fact," she rattles on. "Of course he invited us both, and whilst I do love a party as much as anyone, we're not cutting our wonderful honeymoon short just to attend. It really wouldn't be fair for either of us. Besides, we're having such a wonderful time together. Robert is so attentive, so loving, so generous, Harlow, and I am so *very* much in love."

"I'm sure they'll understand," I say. "So, is there anything else you wanted...?"

"Aren't you going to ask me who Dalton's marrying?"

"Who is he marrying?" I reply, humouring her as my breath fogs up the glass. I press my hand to the same spot, watching as my handprint lingers for a moment before fading away.

"Daisy Hammer. Drix's younger sister," my mother replies gleefully.

"*Daisy?* Are you sure?" I ask, pushing upright.

That can't be right. She hates him.

"You know her then?"

"I met her at the wedding. She was really nice."

"Nice isn't the word I'd use to describe her, when *calculated* seems to fit so much better."

"Mom, that's—" *Unkind,* but of course she cuts me off. Again.

"According to Robert her late father wasn't as wealthy as many people had thought and, well, *I* think that she's marrying into the Gunn family for *money.* Isn't that so distasteful?"

"That's a very unfair assumption to make given *your* history," I throw back, and even though Daisy had categorically said to me that she hates Dalton, she didn't seem like the type to marry someone for money. Then again, it's really none of my business. Perhaps they have history and she's secretly in love with him, denying it to everyone she meets. Perhaps he's secretly in love with her? Or perhaps it really is over money. Whatever the reason, I'm in no position to judge, and I won't get drawn into idle gossip just to entertain my mother.

"Are you insinuating that I've only ever married for money, because if you are–"

"Goodnight, mom. Enjoy the rest of your honeymoon," I say, cutting her off before promptly hanging up and putting my phone on silent so I don't get disturbed by her calling again.

"Why?" I mutter out loud.

Why does my mother love to make me feel bad? Why is she so intent on making me feel unworthy? I just don't understand.

I remain where I am for a few moments, my gaze fixed on my reflection in the window as I try to steady myself. My mother really can be such a bitch, and this brief conversation with her has made two things painfully clear. First, she can't see past her own needs and wants to even consider my feelings, let alone my sleep schedule. And second, she's deliberately tarnishing someone's reputation—someone she barely knows—

which only reinforces what I've feared all along. She will never approve of me and Sterling.

Never.

And whilst I've always known that to be true, I can admit that there was a small, naive part of me that had hoped she'd want to see me happy now that she's found her own happily ever after.

"So, *so* stupid," I mutter as I stride back to bed.

Reaching for my bedside cabinet, I open the drawer and pull out the bottle of sleeping pills I use when sleep evades me, which frankly has been a lot lately. Popping one into my mouth, I grab the glass of water I always have beside my bed and take a sip, swallowing the pill, then I climb under the covers, allowing myself a brief moment of self-pity before I close my eyes and wait for the oblivion of sleep.

Sterling

I can't fucking sleep. I've tossed and turned all damn night and nothing has helped. Not the four shots of whisky I chucked back a few hours ago, and definitely not the hand job I'd given myself in the hope that an orgasm would relax me enough to sleep. The truth is, all it had done was remind me of Harlow, and my complete and utter obsession with her. Which is great for my art, but fucking terrible for my sleep habits.

The truth is, I've no idea how she would react to seeing herself on canvas. Fuck, all it would take is a short walk to the edge of my father's property where she'd find my art studio filled to the brim with paintings of *her*. And if she were to take the time to inspect those paintings a little closer, she might just catch the faint scent of my cum too.

It may appear unconventional to some–using my cum in that way–perhaps even unsettling, but to me, each painting is a sacred depiction of my deepest affection for Harlow. They're an embodiment of my admiration, my reverence, and yes, my longing. These paintings aren't mere art; they are a testament to everything I feel for her, and I will not apologise for that.

Glancing at my watch, I notice that it's almost two am, and realising that sleep isn't going to come tonight, I pull on my trainers, step outside my studio and take a walk. Fifteen minutes in, I start to regret not grabbing a coat, and whilst my hoodie keeps me warm inside my heated studio, it's no match for the biting winter chill as I traverse the gravel pathway that circles Adaga Hall.

I could tell myself that I took a walk in this direction out of habit, and whilst that's partly the truth, it's not the complete truth. The real reason I'm here isn't just to check on Harlow; I'm here because I intend on entering her room whilst she's fast asleep so I can get my fill of her.

I *know* that it's wrong.

I *know* what that makes me.

But I can't seem to stop myself.

I'm not even sure that I want to.

And just as I'm about to head inside and do exactly that, her curtains are drawn apart, and light spills out onto the grass just a few feet before me.

"Fuck," I whisper, taking a few steps back, making sure I'm completely hidden within the darkness and nowhere near the rectangle of light spilling across the lawn.

I watch her with interest as she throws open a window, the cool breeze lifting her hair from around bare shoulders. "This could've waited until morning!" she says.

"Who are you talking to?" I mutter, feeling a pinch of jealousy, my cock stirring as I catch sight of her simple white nightie, her nipples peaked from the cold. Fuck.

"And I should care because?" she continues, completely oblivious to the fact I'm standing in the dark below her window and staring up at her with a semi. Whoever's on the other end of the line is doing a spectacular job at pissing her off, and going by the tone of her voice, and the completely unreasonable time to receive a phone call, I can only determine that it's her mother. My suspicion is confirmed when she goes on to say, "*Robert's friends, you mean?*"

"Of course," I say, fuming on Harlow's behalf, not to mention mine given my plans have been thwarted.

Rightly or wrongly, I need to see Harlow tonight, and whilst it's not in a way that's deemed socially acceptable in any fucking universe, it's the only way I can give her the space she appears to need without compromising my sanity. The logical, un-stalkery, level-headed part of me knows that what I'm doing is wrong, that I'm breaking every level of trust there is, but the obsessive, possessive, compulsive parts of me are far too loud to ignore.

I'm in deep. So fucking deep, it's scary.

So I don't leave like I should. Instead, I watch as Harlow sits on the window ledge and presses her cheek against the glass, and something about the way her shoulders curve inwards has my heart thundering in sympathy.

"I'm sure they'll understand. So, is there anything else you wanted...?" she asks after a moment, pressing her hand against the foggy glass. The fucked-up, stalkery part of me lifts my hand, fingers spread, as I imagine her palm pressed against mine.

"Who is he marrying?" I hear her say, and my hand drops as

it dawns on me that her mother must be telling her about Dalton and Daisy's upcoming wedding.

News sure does travel fast, though I shouldn't be all that surprised given Carl and Robert are close. Well, as close as any man can be without a beating fucking heart.

"*Daisy?* Are you sure?" Harlow asks as she stands, and right before she steps away from the window, I see the confusion on her face.

"Fuck," I grumble, agitated not only because Melody has interrupted Harlow's sleep, but because tonight she's interrupted my plans too. But that doesn't stop me from waiting for Harlow's light to go out, and it certainly doesn't stop me from creeping into her room an hour later either.

SEVENTEEN

As quietly as I can, I slip inside Harlow's bedroom, shutting the door behind me with a gentle click, my heartbeat pounding so loudly in my ears that I press a hand to the middle of my chest, willing it to calm down. For long, agonising moments, I stand with my back pressed against the door, allowing my eyes to adjust to the dim light. Fortunately for me, Harlow didn't close the curtains after her call, and the room is illuminated by moonlight that dusts her sleeping form in a silvery glow, only serving to make her even more beautiful.

"Christ," I murmur, watching her as she sleeps, completely unaware of my approach.

With each step I take toward the bed, a profound sense of relief washes over me, a calming kind of warmth that seeps into my body and quiets my restless mind. Her hair spills across the pillow, the silky strands shimmering like threads of spun gold.

Pausing at the edge of the bed, my gaze lingers on the gentle rise and fall of her chest, and the way her lashes rest delicately against her cheek. Her peacefulness shifts something inside of me, and all the stress of the past few days slowly lifts from my shoulders.

"I've missed you," I whisper.

Reaching out, my fingers graze the duvet that barely covers her hip, my artist's gaze absorbing every detail of her sleeping form. There's a softness to her features that makes her look innocent in a way I've never seen before.

Fuck, how I wish I could press my mouth against hers and awaken her with a kiss. Instead, I settle on tucking a loose strand of her hair behind her ear, the softness of it sending a rush of warmth through my fingertips and straight to my cock. She shifts onto her back, but doesn't wake up, and for a moment I stand there captivated by her. She's so damn beautiful. So fragile in this quiet moment. So completely unaware of my presence.

That fact shouldn't turn me on, but it does. *God help me*, it does.

I glance away from her sleeping form briefly, if only to calm the urge to touch her again, and notice a glass of water and what looks like a bottle of sleeping pills beside it. That might explain why she's so soundly asleep, and I can't help but feel a little envious that she can find such relief when I've found it almost impossible.

The drawer of her bedside cabinet is partially open too, and I notice a leather bound notebook tucked inside. Intrigued, I carefully slide open the drawer the rest of the way and pull it out, before closing it again. The leather is soft to the touch, and I open up the notebook to find pages and pages of what appears to be poems, or perhaps even lyrics. I walk towards the window so that I can use the moonlight to read.

Flicking it open to a random page, my eyes fall to her neat cursive.

> *One night of passion, a chance to be me,*
> *I stripped myself bare to reveal,*
> *The person others never see.*
> *He touched me like I was precious,*
> *Deep inside, he pulled me free,*
> *Free to be.*
> *To be me...*
> *But how can I hold on to someone,*
> *Who makes me feel so undone?*
> *How can I be his, when I've never been anyone's?*

My breath catches as I notice the date. She wrote this the day after we met for the first time.

"Fuck," I mutter, aching for her in that moment.

I flip the pages at random, reading line after line, absorbing a part of her that she's hidden from the world. Every word is like a heartbeat that echoes in my chest, each line pulling me deeper into her soul, revealing thoughts and feelings she's kept locked away. There's a rawness to her words, a vulnerability that makes my chest tighten.

> *Electricity races beneath my skin,*
> *A flash of blue, a spark within,*
> *That flares beneath the darkness of sin...*

She wrote this the day after the wedding, and I can't help but wonder if this is about us, about the undeniable magnetism we share. "Damn it, Harlow..." I murmur.

When I reach the last entry, my fingers tremble as I trace the lines with my fingertips. The words are simple, but no less powerful.

> Lost to the heat of his desire,
> I want his touch so much I'm on fire.
> Troubled by the intensity of his stare,
> Yet I want his attention, please strip me bare.
> Catch me alight, catch me alight,
> Oh stranger in the night…

I'd known it all along, of course. She feels it too, this pull between us, the way we're drawn to one another, not by choice, but by something deeper, something inevitable. I glance back at her, still sleeping peacefully, oblivious to the fact that I've expressed my feelings for her in much the same way. She uses words, and I use paint, both of us creating something that speaks without needing to be said aloud, something that exists between us in the lines of a notebook, and in brushstrokes of colour. Something secret, yet painfully exposing if anyone were to take a closer look.

Closing the notebook gently, I'm suddenly aware of how much of her I've just uncovered. It's almost too much, but I can't stop myself from wanting more as I pad across the room, my footsteps muffled by the thick carpet beneath my bare feet.

"You're a poet," I whisper, placing the notebook exactly where I found it. "You're *my* little poet."

Mine, she's mine, I think, that possessive, obsessive part of me wanting to claim her in sleep, just as I have claimed everything else about her. I know that *this* is the moment I should leave.

Yet I don't. *I can't.*

"Harlow?" I whisper, a small part of me, the part that is a decent human being with morals and boundaries wants her to wake up, to put a stop to this.

But then she moans, *"Please..."* and my heart stills, that one word igniting my desire into a blazing inferno, and turning every single piece of morality I thought I had into ash.

Seconds tick past, her legs shifting beneath the covers as the duvet slips between her parted thighs, exposing more skin, teasing me with more temptation.

"Can you sense my presence, my little poet?" I ask, reaching for her once more, the back of my knuckles grazing against the exposed skin of her thigh. Her cotton nightie has risen upwards revealing her hip and part of her stomach. It's only then I realise that she's not wearing any underwear.

"Fuck, what are you doing to me?"

In the confines of my jeans, my dick throbs. I'm so fucking turned on, so fucking desperate to take this further, to see what it would take to wake her up, but there's not even a flicker of awareness. And so, with a compulsion I cannot deny, I splay my fingers across her stomach relishing in the feel of her warm, soft skin against my palm.

Resting it there, I wait.

"What will it take to rouse you?" I mutter after a full minute.

I can feel her stomach move as she breathes, and every impulse inside of me wants to take this further to see how far I can push it. So, I slide my hand lower, cupping her bare pussy, the heat of her core sending my pulse skyrocketing. My balls tighten, my dick jerks as she moans again, her body seemingly aware of my presence.

"Look at you, my little poet, so fucking beautiful," I whisper, leaning over and brushing my lips gently against her cheek, and even though she's deeply asleep, her legs part, widening for me

as my middle finger slips between her pussy lips.

I hold my finger there, feeling her clit pulse as something primal unravels within my chest, a kind of ownership. This is where I belong, right here cupping Harlow's pussy whilst her body calls to mine.

Another soft moan releases from her mouth and I draw back, my gaze following the soft curve of her neck and lower to her breasts. Her nipples tighten beneath her nightdress, tempting me, and on instinct I take one into my mouth, tasting her through the cotton as I gently swipe my finger through her folds, gathering liquid before rolling the pad of my finger over her clit.

"Fuck, I want you so badly," I whisper against her chest, feeling her slicken even more beneath my fingers as I take her other nipple into my mouth, sucking hard.

Yet she remains asleep, so deeply under that even when I slide my finger into her soaked core she doesn't wake up. Despite that, her hips rock as I gently pump my finger inside of her, her body reacting unconsciously to my touch.

"Are you dreaming of me?" I ask, half-hoping she'll wake up and welcome me into her arms. "Do you dream of me like I dream of you?"

"Sterling," she mumbles, and my heart jackhammers inside my chest as I raise my gaze upwards, expecting her to be wide awake, staring at me in the dark. She isn't, and I drag in a shaky breath,

knowing that our connection is so powerful that despite being fast asleep she's still somehow aware of me.

"You're dripping for me, Harlow. Fuck, you make me so

hard," I groan, my cock aches, so hard it's verging on painful. But this isn't about me, not really. This is about Harlow.

Everything I do, all that I am, is for her.

Only her.

Determined to make her come, I press the heel of my hand against her clit, giving her the pressure her body needs to climax whilst I finger-fuck her gently. Her moans get louder, only adding to the sensuality of the moment, heightening everything. Heightening the way I feel about her, how turned on I am, how hungry I am to see her come apart, how desperate I am for her to wake up, take me in her arms and claim *me* as *hers*. Just like she has in her poems.

I've never wanted to belong to another person as much as I want to belong to Harlow. It's inconceivable to me that we might never get the chance to be each other's person, and I'm fully aware that I'm risking everything doing this, that I've crossed a line that I've no right to cross. But even if I wanted to stop now, I couldn't. I'm too far gone, too desperate for her to reach the pinnacle, *needing* to give her my undivided attention when it's so sorely lacking from the other people in her life. Because whilst this act is intensely sexual, it is also coming from a place of affection, of care, no matter how fucked-up it might seem. So I rub her clit with the heel of my palm. I finger-fuck her, revelling in the way she leaks for me, her pussy so wet, so warm, so fucking mine.

"I'm here, I see you. I want you to come for me, my little poet."

Yes I came into her bedroom for selfish reasons, but bringing her to orgasm is my gift to her. To the woman who has sunk so deep inside of my psyche that nothing and no one will unravel the binds that tie us together. If I had my way, I would show her every second of every day how much she means to me, how deeply affected I am by her presence.

I want her to feel seen.

I want her to feel desired.

I want to be her person.

I want to be *hers*.

It's with those thoughts that I work her body, sliding another finger inside of her, stroking that bundle of nerves deep inside her pussy. My gaze never leaves her face as her mouth parts and her muscles clench me tight. Her body is both liquid and coiled tight as she stiffens with pleasure, a rush of liquid covering my fingers. And with one last full body tremble, my little poet comes, back arched, head tipped back, a soft cry releasing from her lips.

EIGHTEEN

My eyes slowly drift open as winter sunlight pours through the window, warming my skin. For a moment I just lie in the pool of light, feeling a deep sense of relaxation. My body feels liquid, relaxed in a way I haven't felt in some time. Which surprises me given my mother's phone call in the middle of the night. I went to sleep feeling agitated, expecting to wake up in much the same way, or at the very least tired given my sleep was so rudely interrupted, yet I feel neither of those things.

"Must be the sleeping pill I took," I murmur, shifting slightly as I adjust my duvet cover which is draped across my stomach, the edge caught between my legs. The action causes the soft Egyptian cotton to drag over my bare pussy, and the friction makes me jolt, not because it's uncomfortable in any way, but because I feel so sensitive down there.

It's strangely... *arousing*.

I let out a soft breath, my clit pulsing as slide my leg back under the duvet and try to make sense of what I'm feeling. With tentative fingers, I feel between my slightly parted legs and gasp when wetness greets me.

"Oh," I whisper, as a zing of pleasure cascades down my spine from that gentle, yet explorative touch.

For a moment I keep my fingers pressed against my mound, trying to understand why I've woken up in such a state of arousal. Perhaps I had a dirty dream? That must be it.

Pressing my eyes shut, I try to recall if I have, and as I lie still waiting for the memory of that dream to appear in my consciousness, a strange feeling of something out of the ordinary flickers at the edge of my consciousness. Something that makes my nipples tighten and my clit flutter. Something that makes me feel *needy*, desperate somehow. And the *only* thought that enters my head at that moment is Sterling.

"Oh God," I mutter, my clit pulsing at the memory of the passionate kisses we've shared, making me wetter, making my hips rock against my hand.

I know that I should be shutting thoughts of Sterling down, that entertaining them, even if they are just private fantasies, won't do me any good in the long run. But, I can't seem to stop images of him from fluttering across my mind as I tentatively toy with my clit, gasping at how sensitive it is, how aroused I am, how much I wish it was him touching me right now.

Sterling and his startling blue eyes.

Sterling and his chiselled jaw, and perfect body.

Sterling and his thick fingers and beautiful cock.

Sterling and the way he looks at me like I'm the only woman who exists in the world.

"It's just a fantasy," I whisper, trying to rationalise my feelings. "Nothing can come of it. Nothing."

But that doesn't stop me from adding more pressure to my clit, rubbing against it in the way I like. I'm only human, I can't just switch off my attraction to him, and right now I don't even want to. Biting gently on my lip, I reach for my opening, gathering the wetness to lubricate my puffy clit, the slippery sounds only adding to my arousal.

Masturbation is something that I rarely allow myself the pleasure of. Not because I think it's dirty or wrong, but because I've never really had anyone that I've fantasised about enough to want to get off.

But this morning...

This morning I'm teetering on the edge of an orgasm just thinking about the man I cannot have, and even though there's a small voice in the back of my head warning me not to indulge, that it will only make things worse, my body isn't listening, it's reacting, and I don't have the strength to fight it.

Tentatively, I slip my finger inside my core, pumping it slowly in and out, and whilst it's pleasurable, it's not enough to make me come. I can't angle my hand the right way and keep pressure on my clit, so I roll onto my stomach. My tight nipples pressing into the cotton sheet, the slight friction only adding to the intensity of the moment.

"Oh fuck, yes," I hiss as I press my hips against the mattress trapping my hand between my pussy and the bed, allowing me to finger my hole and also stimulate my clit with the heel of my hand. I don't allow myself to think about what I must look like. I just give in to my desire and with my cheek pressed against the pillow, and my hair covering my heated cheeks, I allow my mind to wander. With every second that passes, sensation builds, merging with every memory I have of Sterling and us together.

His hand cupping my jaw, his nose brushing my cheek.

His mouth on mine, his tongue brazenly licking the seam of my lips.

His head between my legs, my core pulsing as he sucks my clit into his wicked mouth.

His hand squeezing my breast, his saliva coating my nipples.

His cock pushing inside of me, my muscles squeezing him tight.

I let my thoughts spiral, my memories tumbling into fantasy as I imagine his body laying over mine so heavy that I almost can't breathe. I imagine his chest pressed against my back, his arm hooked beneath my body, whilst his fingers wrap around my throat, squeezing. I imagine gasping for air as he positions himself between my parted thighs and enters me from behind with one hard thrust.

"Oh God," I moan, my fingers jabbing into my entrance, frantic for release as I press my hips harder into the mattress, my palm and fingers slippery with arousal.

"Please..."

Something flickers in my memory.

"Please..." I beg, the word slipping from my mouth once again as my body tightens and my fantasy twists into something else.

That word, it's triggering something I don't understand, but I'm too caught up in sensation to truly grasp what that is, too tightly coiled with pleasure, too overwhelmed with need.

It's as though I'm on the precipice of something. Something that sits between wakefulness and dreams. Something that my body reacts to and my mind has trouble understanding.

A dark room.

Hands on my body.

A voice... My voice?

"Please..."

My hips grind harder, my breath comes quicker, my clit throbs as my fingers thrust in and out, in and out.

"Sterling," I groan.

And there right at the edge of my consciousness I hear a voice reply as though he's right here in this room with me now, *"I'm here, I see you."*

"Sterling?" I question on a groan.

"I want you to come for me, my little poet."

My little poet?

Those three words send me over the edge, and I come.

I come so hard that I slam my eyes shut, my clit spasming, my body trembling, my voice calling out his name. Minutes later, when my breath has evened out, and my body has recovered from my orgasm, I sit up in bed wondering how my fantasy could feel so damn real.

After showering and getting dressed in a pair of worn denim jeans, warm socks and a soft, green sweater, I grab my phone and head downstairs to make breakfast. My mind is a jumble of thoughts as I try to unravel why Sterling's voice had seemed so real in that moment, and why his words had seemed so much more like a memory rather than a fantasy. He's never referred to me as his little poet, why would he? He doesn't know that I write lyrics, he only knows that I sing. And why *poet?* Maybe deep down that's how I see all songwriters, as poets, and it's my subconscious conjuring up his voice in a moment of heightened pleasure. Maybe I'm just overthinking this, maybe I'm just overtired.

Maybe...

Stepping into the kitchen, I head for the coffee machine that sits on the counter, and grab a mug from the cupboard, then pour myself a generous amount, adding some chilled creamer from the fridge. Taking a sip, I take a seat at the kitchen island where I can look out onto the view and try to make sense of everything, needing a moment to just think before I make myself some breakfast.

To be fair, it's been a few days since I last spoke with Sterling, so it's little wonder he's on my mind. That combined with the sleeping pills I took, the stressful call from my mother, it's no great surprise my imagination is making up things that aren't real. Still, it's thrown me. I'm supposed to be trying to put all thoughts of Sterling out of my head, and not indulging in fantasy that I shouldn't be entertaining.

Strumming my fingers against the counter, I heave out a sigh when my phone vibrates in my pocket. Reaching for it, I pull it out and raise the screen to my face so that it opens. A notification for Instagram immediately pops up and my heart sinks.

"Curiosity killed the cat," I mutter, my finger hovering over the notification as I debate whether to read it or not, because I know who this message is from. My stalker.

Curiosity wins, and I click on the notification.

You read these messages I send, yet you don't respond. Why is that? Don't you realise what you're doing to me? Fuck, I want you... I want you so bad that you're all I can think about.

Do you not believe me when I say how hard you make me? Do you need proof of how much I want to fuck you, is that it? Because, believe me when I say, I'm hard right now...

My hands shake as I read the message, dread making goose-bumps scatter across my skin. I can see that he's typing out another message, and I sit staring dumbly at my phone waiting to see what he sends next, but a movement beyond the window catches my eye and I look up.

It's Sterling, phone in hand as he walks around the swimming pool, oblivious to me watching his every move. My heart skips a beat as I watch him typing something into his phone, a frown creasing his forehead as he stops walking.

My first thought is how attractive he looks, how his tousled brown hair is whipped up by the breeze, how sharp the cut of his jaw is as he stares at his phone. Then, as though in slow motion, a smile draws his lips wide just as his thumb presses the screen right at the same time that my phone vibrates.

Flicking my eyes back down, I'm confronted with a close up photo of a man's erect dick. It's long, thick, and veiny, precum jewelling the crown.

"Oh my God!" I exclaim, both appalled and suddenly very, very afraid.

Told you...

My hands begin to shake as I lift my gaze back up to Sterling. The smile he was wearing fades to something that looks close to agony as he pockets his phone and strides towards the house.

I freeze.

No way.

It's just a coincidence.

He wouldn't.

It *can't* be...

But he's the only one who knows my pseudonym. He said

he searched for me, is it so inconceivable that he searched for me on social media sites, that he found my account?

I wait for long agonising seconds for another message. Another message that will prove it isn't Sterling who is sending me these messages. That whoever it is, is someone I don't even know. That it's just some stranger who has no idea who I am. And yet...

Another message doesn't come.

Nothing.

I watch Sterling get closer and closer, willing my stalker to send me a message so that I know it can't possibly be Sterling. It can't be the man who made me feel so wanted, so seen, so adored, so desired.

But there's nothing.

My finger hovers over the phone. If I message back now, and I see him answer that will tell me all I need to know, right?

I debate for all of two seconds, hoping to God I'm wrong. That the person who's sending me these messages, isn't the man walking towards me now.

I have to know.

I have to.

With shaking fingers, I type out a response.

Leave me alone.

Then I click send, holding my breath.

Sterling is almost at the kitchen door. My heart stops. My whole body stiffens as I wait for him to reach into his pocket to retrieve his phone. Seconds tick by as his hand rests on the handle to the door, his gaze meeting mine.

My heart is in my throat as I glance at my phone screen, a

sick feeling rising up my chest as I place my phone on the counter, then flick my gaze up to his once more.

He frowns, but he doesn't reach for his phone, instead he opens the kitchen door.

"Harlow?" he asks, concern flickering across his face.

I look back at my phone. My stalker doesn't answer, and Sterling steps inside the room.

"Are you okay?" he asks, pulling the door shut behind him. "You look..."

"I'm fine," I bite out, not knowing what to do, what to say, as I snatch up my phone and pocket it.

It can't be him. It isn't him. Please, don't be him.

"What's wrong, you're shaking," he points out, his gaze following my movements.

"Nothing. I'm fine."

"Harlow," he warns. "What is it? You look... *upset*," he whispers that word, and it only makes me feel even more wary of him, as though he knows something.

There's a weird kind of tension between us, and not the sexual kind of tension we've shared before. Is he afraid that he's been caught? Did he not respond to the message just because he saw me sitting in here holding my phone? Is everything I thought about him untrue? Is he hiding the real person he is from me, the person who would send gross messages about forcing himself upon a woman? Who would send dick pics?

It can't be him, can it?

I should confront him. I should confront him right now.

"I should go," I say instead, pushing back from the counter, the stool scraping across the tiled floor. I'm shaking so violently that my teeth start to chatter.

"Harlow, wait. Talk to me, *please*," he begs, rounding the counter, reaching for me. But there's something in his eyes, something that makes me shudder. It looks a hell of a lot like guilt. His touch sends me spiralling, the cool feel of his palm seeping through my jumper and into my skin as I flinch from his touch.

"Don't touch me!" I hiss, taking a step back. He takes another step towards me, the guilty look on his face turning to concern.

"Harlow, what is it?"

"I..." My voice gets caught in my throat as he takes another step closer, crowding me against the kitchen island. The bottom of my spine hits the marble countertop, and I let out a frightened yelp as his hands rest on either side of me.

"Is this about the other night in the pool?" he questions, but there's something careful about the way he asks me, as though he's trying to gauge my reaction.

I shake my head. "Who were you texting?" I blurt out.

"Texting?" he asks, cocking his head, something close to relief fluttering across his features.

It confuses me. If he was my stalker, if it is him sending me those messages just now, and I caught him in the act, why would he be reacting this way, as though relieved?

"Yes, who were you messaging a moment ago. Who, Sterling?" I bite out, my heart pounding so loudly that I can barely hear myself think.

"Dalton," he replies immediately.

"Dalton?" I parrot back.

"Yes, Dalton. He texted me about his engagement party coming up."

"To Daisy," I reply, frowning now. My head is all over the place. I know that isn't a lie given my conversation with my mother, but I was convinced it was him sending me the messages.

"That's right, to Daisy. You know then?" he asks, something flickering across his face as his eyes drop to my mouth, and my teeth buried into my bottom lip.

"My mother called me in the early hours of this morning and told me about the engagement party, and the wedding, and the fact I haven't been invited to either," I reply, and then before I can stop myself, because I need to know if he's telling the truth, I say, "Can I see?"

"See?" he replies, a sudden rash of anger written across his face.

"The messages. Can I see them?" I insist, forcing myself to ask once again. His anger is warranted because who demands to see someone's phone like this? But I have to know.

He hesitates briefly before nodding. "Sure. Here," he replies, pulling out his phone and holding it up to his face so it opens, before passing it to me.

I take it from him, his fingers brushing over mine briefly, my skin tingling from the contact. I'm still afraid, still having lingering doubts, but my body doesn't seem to react in the same way at all. Pressing on the messages icon, I scroll to the first message which is clearly from Dalton.

> The engagement party is this
> Saturday evening. 7pm. Black tie.
> You're welcome to bring a plus one.
> Harlow perhaps?

My cheeks heat as I read his response, aware that Sterling is studying me as I do. His head is tipped down, and his hand has crept closer to my side, his thumb brushing against my hip with the movement.

A whole dose of relief, a shedload of guilt, and a sharp pang of disappointment hit me all at once. He isn't my stalker. He doesn't want to take me as his guest to his friend's engagement party. And worse, he's been avoiding me. That hurts. It shouldn't, but it does.

"I'm sorry," I apologise, not knowing what else to say. Because I am sorry, for believing that he could be my stalker, that he's even capable of scaring me like that, for making him feel like he has to tiptoe around me. This is his home, not mine.

He takes his phone from my hand, slipping it back into his pocket. "Harlow, do you want to tell me what's going on?" The anger before has disappeared, replaced instead with concern.

"Nothing's going on. I just..." I begin, feeling so embarrassed that I can barely look him in the eye. "Like I said, my mom called to tell me last night, and I guess... I just thought that maybe... Sorry, I'm just feeling a little..." My voice trails off, I don't have a good excuse as to why I demanded to see his phone, other than the truth, and that's not something I wish to share right now, or ever.

"Hey, listen. I know how that text might sound, but I–"

I tip my head down, more heat creeping into my cheeks as I avoid his gaze. "You don't need to explain yourself to me, and you have every right to be angry. I haven't made things easy. This is your home and I've made you feel like you have to keep your distance. It was also incredibly rude of me to ask to see your phone. My mom just got into my head a bit..." I mumble, and whilst that's partly the truth, it's not the whole truth.

"I'm not angry at you, Harlow," he says roughly.

"You're not?"

"You've done nothing wrong. *Nothing.*"

"I totally understand why you wouldn't want to take me as your plus one. I haven't even been invited to the engagement party or the wedding. Which is fine, of course," I add quickly, trying to sidestep him.

Sterling's hand grasps my hip, holding me in place. "Look at me, Harlow," he commands gently.

"Sterling, let me go," I whisper.

"Not until you look at me."

I raise my head, slowly meeting his gaze. "I told you, you don't need to explain yourself to me. It's fine."

"No, it's not," he replies, shaking his head. "It's not fine that you've been made to feel unwanted. It's not fine that your mother called you to tell you about this engagement party and the wedding in the middle of the damn night, and it's definitely not okay that she made a point of telling you that you haven't been invited."

"It's okay–" I try to protest, but he shakes his head.

"But more than that it's not okay that you think I've been avoiding you, because I haven't."

"But you said–"

"I said that I've been keeping my distance, not that I've been avoiding you. Those are two very different statements, Harlow," he replies, his free hand grazing up my arm, before settling on my cheek. "And me telling Dalton that I don't think it's a good idea taking you as my plus one to his engagement party isn't because I don't want you there, it's because if you're by my side, I won't be able to keep my damn hands off you."

"Oh..." My voice trails off as he brushes his thumb against my bottom lip, and my heart hiccups inside my chest.

"You know how I feel about you, Harlow. I've kept my distance because I thought you needed space. But when I tell you that nothing's changed, that I want you, I need you to believe me. Do you believe me?"

"Yes," I reply, the word slipping out of my mouth before I can stop it.

"Good, because if I had my way we wouldn't have spent a second apart these past couple of weeks," he grinds out, his thumb pushing past the boundary of my lips as I gasp. "If I had my way I'd be spending every second of every damn day buried inside of you because that's the only place I've ever felt at home."

I groan then, my eyes fluttering shut as I suck his thumb deeper into my mouth and he presses his hips against mine, his cock hard against my stomach.

"And for the record, Harlow. If I had my way, you'd attend this engagement party, and the damn wedding, not just as my guest, but as *mine*."

With that, he pulls his thumb from between my lips and slams his mouth against mine, swallowing up any frail attempt I might have had to stop him.

NINETEEN

That kiss.

Fuck, that kiss was like a shot of heroin straight into my heart, and I've thought about nothing else since. Well, that's not entirely true. I've thought about what I would've done if we hadn't been so rudely interrupted by my arsehole friend, Dalton, and that is, strip Harlow bare, lift her onto the kitchen counter and bury my face in her delectable pussy.

Of course, Dalton's call had the same effect as chucking a bucket of cold water over us both. Harlow had insisted I answer, and with every second that Dalton complained about Daisy making his life difficult, Harlow had stepped further and further away from me until she'd slipped out of the kitchen and disappeared back to her room. Now, here I am sitting opposite Dalton and Ben in Bandits Bar whilst he asks our advice on how to handle his soon-to-be wife.

"Don't you think you should've thought about this before you signed the contract agreeing to marry Daisy?" Ben asks, straight to the point. "I mean, we all know she's a force of nature."

"Tell me something I don't know," Dalton snaps back, grabbing his glass of bourbon and chucking back a mouthful, before slamming it back onto the table. "I came here for some advice, not a lecture."

"So let me get this straight, she kneed you in the bollocks, and now you've got a bruised ego. Is that about the sum of it?" I ask, my lip twitching with a smile. I'd like to have seen that.

"The only part of my body that was bruised were my balls, which have thankfully recovered," he counters with a glare, but there's no denying the slight flush of pink to his cheeks from embarrassment.

I'm surprised he even told us to be honest, because I know for a fact that Ben won't let that juicy tidbit of information go. He'll take great pleasure in reminding Dalton for months about how Princetown's charming playboy finally got his comeuppance.

"Not sure how you're going to come back from that to be honest. She clearly hates you," Ben smirks.

"Again, not fucking helpful. I'm well aware of how Daisy feels about me, and Drix will chop my bollocks off if he finds out I upset her. I need to fix this as best I can, and it's not as if I can ask his advice right now given he hates me too. So here I am with you two arseholes," he says, glaring at us both, "I'm hoping that between the three of us we come up with a plan."

"You need a plan on how to take care of a woman?" Ben asks incredulously. "Here's me thinking that you were well versed in that area, but maybe you're not the Casanova you think you are, huh?"

"You know what? Fucking forget it," Dalton says, pressing his hands against the table and moving to stand.

"Sit down, Dalton," I say, throwing a look at Ben who just sniggers like a fucking school kid. To be fair it is pretty amusing, but I've got things to do, namely getting back to Harlow, and I really just want to get this conversation done, so the sooner he sits his arse back down in the chair, the better. "We came here to help. We'll help. So tell us exactly what's been going on because I'm getting the impression that bruised balls are the least of your concerns right now, am I right?"

Dalton grits his jaw, but he sits. "I bought Daisy an engagement ring, and last night I proposed at 'M'. We kissed to seal the deal."

"So let me get this straight, you took Daisy to a private members club, proposed to her in front of a room full of people, and then kissed her to *seal the deal?*" Ben asks, finger quoting the air as he flicks his gaze from me to Dalton and back again. "Even I know she'd fucking hate that, and I haven't been best friends with her older brother for over twenty fucking years. Daisy has *always* been incredibly private, not to mention the fact kissing her was taking a fucking liberty."

"We *have* to make this look real," Dalton argues, looking more than a little uncomfortable. "I couldn't exactly propose and then not kiss her, that would be fucking weird."

"Did you get down on one knee too?" Ben asks, flicking me a look.

Dalton clenches his jaw, heaving out a breath before answering. "Yes."

"And what did she say?"

Dalton looks at Ben like he's grown another head. "What the fuck else did you think she'd say? *Yes*, of course."

"To be fair, I still thought she might see sense," Ben replies with a shrug.

"So you took her to dinner, proposed, and then what?" I ask, because I can tell there's more. Dalton is looking far too shifty for there not to be.

"Some arsehole waiter spilled a drink on her shirt, and so I bought her a few replacements, gave them to her this morning…" he replies, dropping his gaze to his drink.

Ben's brows lift, as surprised as I am by the thoughtfulness. "And?"

"And then nothing," he mutters.

"And you can't kid a kidder. Fess up, Dalton," Ben insists.

"Then I said she should have a massage in the hotel spa because I thought she'd benefit from some relaxation," he replies, jaw clenching.

Ben and I exchange looks.

"What else?" I ask, because there's no way this is the end of the story. Dalton hasn't called us here to get a pat on his back for his efforts so far, he's fucked-up somehow, that much is clear.

"And I found out that she'd specifically asked for that beefy masseuse, Tomasz, to give her a massage," he retorts tightly, before gritting his teeth once again, that muscle in his jaw jumping with agitation.

"Uh oh," Ben says, taking a swig of coffee to hide his smirk. "Another man's hands on your woman, couldn't have made you all that happy."

"She's not my woman. She's my fake fiancé," he snaps.

"Tell that to someone who'll believe you," he retorts under his breath.

"So what did you do?" I ask, leaning back in my seat as I watch him swipe a hand over his face.

"I fired him," he cuts out.

"You fired a man for doing the job he was hired to do?" I ask, lifting my brows as Ben and I exchange another look. I'm pretty sure he's thinking exactly what I'm thinking, and that is Dalton is in fucking denial.

"He put his hands on Daisy, so yes, I fucking fired him."

"Because she's *not* your woman, but *is* your fake fiancé?" Ben insists, needling him.

"I'd just like to point out," I interject, "That this marriage is going to be very real, very soon. So unless you want that to change you have to accept that there's nothing fake about your engagement or your impending marriage."

"Semantics," Dalton mutters, scowling at us.

"Well, is there anything else you'd like to add before we give you our advice?" Ben asks.

"No."

I narrow my eyes at him. "Are you sure?"

"That's about it," Dalton replies, doing that same shifty eye movement he always does when he's hiding something. I momentarily think about pushing the subject, but I want to get back to Harlow, and I've already spent way too fucking long sitting here.

"Well then, mate, first I think you need to be honest," Ben offers.

"Honest? I *have* been honest," Dalton counters, looking about as uncomfortable as one person can get.

"That's debatable," I say, and Dalton glares at me.

"I mean be honest with Daisy about the whole Tomasz situation. I'm assuming she doesn't know that you fired him for *doing his actual job*," Ben says pointedly.

"I don't need to explain my reasonings, I'm the fucking manager, and he's a member of my staff so that means I can do what the fuck I want," he retorts, folding his arms across his chest defensively.

"That's true, but if you want to try fixing your relationship with Daisy, so that you can at the very least be in a position to become friends given you're about to spend a lot of time with her, then you need to start with being honest about what you've done," I say.

"Not sure that's a good fucking idea," he grumbles.

"She'll only find out for herself, and when she does, she'll be pissed. Better it comes from you, don't you think?" Ben points out reasonably.

Dalton nods. "Fine. I'll tell her, but if she thinks I'm going to rehire him, she can think again."

"That's your prerogative," I say with a shrug. "But can I make a suggestion?"

"Shoot," he retorts, emptying his glass.

"Take her out to dinner. Do it right this time. Be honest about what you did, and for fuck sake, try to consider her feelings in all of this."

"Not sure she considered my feelings when she kneed me in the bollocks the other day," he cuts out.

"You and I both know you probably deserved it," I counter, and Ben smothers another laugh.

"You're both loving this, aren't you?" Dalton fires back, glaring at us both.

"What's that saying? If you can't handle the heat, stay out of the fucking kitchen?" Ben suggests.

"Okay, so I take her out, be honest and try to smooth things over. Got it," Dalton says, ignoring Ben altogether.

"And I'd suggest not trying to kiss her again if you want to keep your bollocks," I add.

"Talking of kissing, how's that going for you?" Dalton retorts, arching a brow as he throws heat my way.

"Yeah, how is Harlow?" Ben asks, flicking his gaze to his phone that's resting on the table in front of him. "I've not heard a whisper from her since the wedding. Thought she might've texted me by now."

"Why the *fuck* would she text you? How does she even have your number any-fucking-way?" I retort, my hackles rising. He better not have made a pass at her. Best friend or not, I will deck him.

"I gave it to Harlow when we danced together the night of the wedding."

"You did fucking what?!" I grind out, about ready to launch myself across the table.

Ben raises his hands, palms facing me as he says, "It wasn't like that, dickhead, I'd never make a move on the woman you're interested in. Jesus, who the fuck do you take me for, I'm not Dalton?"

"I resent that remark, dickwad," Dalton grumbles.

"Look, I just figured she might need a friend, *that's all*," Ben adds, ignoring Dalton's complaint.

"*I'm* her fucking friend," I cut out, that possessive part of me needing to stake my claim. Wanting nothing more than to keep her all to myself. Which is fucking shitty after how her mother has treated her, but I'm not sure I can share.

"Pretty sure you're her fucking step-brother too," he retorts. "Not that *I* give a shit, but I think you need a little reminder about the predicament you're in right now, yeah?"

"I'm handling it," I retort.

"Like fuck you are. You're wound up tighter than a grandfather clock," Ben comments knowingly.

"And how, exactly, are you handling it?" Dalton asks, pitching a brow. "Because the last time I saw you together at your parent's wedding Sterling Junior was about to punch a hole in your trousers, and Harlow looked like she'd just had a very pleasurable org–"

"Shut the fuck up, Dalton!" I hiss.

"Fuck me, you really are in fucking trouble. Your dad will skin you alive, mate," Ben says, eyes widening. "You sure you know what you're doing?"

I pinch the bridge of my nose, and press my eyes shut in an attempt to calm myself down. I'm still riled up over the kiss Dalton interrupted earlier, not to mention the fact that I just found out that Ben gave Harlow his number. To top it all off, being reminded of my father or what he might do if he found out about me and Harlow isn't helping matters. I know for a fact that it won't take much more for me to lose my cool and take my frustrations out on either one of my friends. Probably both at this rate.

"I've no fucking clue what I'm doing," I admit.

"I thought you said you were handling it?" Ben asks.

"Yeah, his dick most likely," Dalton remarks with a smirk, and Ben barks out a laugh.

"You know what, fuck you both," I snap, standing.

And with that I stride from the bar, letting the door slam shut behind me. Half an hour later I'm pushing ninety miles an hour on the motorway heading towards fuck knows where.

TWENTY

For the first time in over two weeks I leave Adaga Hall and take a short taxi ride into the village which has pretty cobbled streets lined with a variety of independent stores and numerous cafés. It's just how I've always envisioned a pretty English village, and I regret not making the time to explore earlier.

I haven't seen Sterling since he left to meet Dalton a couple of days ago, and when I asked Stephanie this morning if she knew where he was, she explained that he'd left a message to say that he had business to attend to and would be back in time for the engagement party tomorrow night.

So here I am, strolling along the main thoroughfare, and getting some much needed fresh air, and more importantly, time to think. The village itself is relatively quiet, which is a relief because I can barely string together a series of coherent thoughts, let alone exchange small talk with someone I might've met at the wedding. But I figure just being out in a different environment and not hiding away back at Adaga Hall will help me to sort my thoughts and feelings out. Not to mention the fact

I've been avoiding my mother's calls. She has left me several messages this morning, but I haven't listened to any of them. I really can't face a conversation with her. Whatever gossip she wants to share with me will have to wait.

With my winter coat wrapped tightly around my waist, I head towards an interesting looking music store that has ivy wrapped around the entrance, beautiful hand-crafted instruments displayed in the window, and a faded sign that reads *The Cosy Chord*. I can't help but smile at the play on words, because the store does indeed look cosy and nothing like I'd expect a store selling musical instruments to look like. It has the ambience of an antique bookstore, but instead of leather bound books and first editions lining the old oak bookshelves, they're filled with rows of beautifully crafted instruments. There are violins with polished wood gleaming like amber, hand-carved mandolins, tambourines with shiny brass zils, and other hand-made instruments that seem to wait patiently for a hand to play them.

Curious, I push the door open, and a soft bell rings above me, its chime blending with the faint strum of a guitar that floats through the air, as if the store itself is humming a welcoming tune. My eyes are immediately drawn to an upright piano in the corner, its ivory keys gleaming like a set of perfectly polished teeth. It's been a while since I last played, and though there's a baby grand back at Adaga Hall, I haven't yet felt at ease enough to sit down and play.

"Hello?" I call out, noticing that there's no one standing behind the counter. "Is anyone there?"

After a moment, a man steps out from behind a door I assume leads to an office or storeroom. He's cradling a spruce and mahogany acoustic guitar, the leather strap keeping it snug against his body.

"Hey, sorry about that—I was out back tuning this beauty. How can I help you?" he asks, pushing a messy flop of jet-black hair off his forehead. It falls right back into his eyes, which is a shame, since they're a striking shade of grey-blue.

"I was just passing by and, well, your store looked really interesting and I thought I'd take a look."

"It's not my store. Belongs to my uncle, a moody arsehole who barely comes here anymore and hides away in his estate tucked away on the outskirts of the village, " he explains.

"Ah, I see. Well, your uncle has incredible taste. The instruments are really stunning," I reply, my gaze coasting around the store, only to fall on a beautiful tawny owl with piercing gold eyes perched on a shelf next to a fiddle. I gasp. "Is that a real owl?"

He follows my gaze and chuckles. "That is, in fact, a very *dead* owl."

"Why do you have a dead owl in a music store?"

"My uncle is a taxidermist," he replies, pulling a face. "Fucking creepy, huh?"

"Does he k—?"

"Kill the animals? Fuck, no. He's actually a conservationist and takes in injured wildlife. Sometimes they don't survive and, well, I don't think he can't bear to part with them. I'm pretty sure he prefers animals over humans any day of the week..." He replies, his voice trailing off as we both study the owl.

"Wow, okay. Kind of creepy, but also somehow not..."

"My uncle *is* creepy as fuck, so that's fair. Anyway, he refuses to come into town anymore, so I run the store for him. The pay is shit, though I do get a small commission for every instrument I sell. Not that I'm bothered, really, because I get to spend my nights performing at Bandits with my band. Makes up for the shit wage," he shrugs.

"Wait, are you a member of *Princetown Bandits*?" I ask, remembering Ben telling me about the band he manages when we were dancing together at the wedding.

"You've heard of us? Don't tell me you're a fan who's travelled all the way from the US just to see us play? Nice accent by the way," he replies with a cocky kind of swagger that makes my cheeks heat. He's most definitely got that cool, rock vibe going on with his faded tee, tattoos trailing down his arms, torn denim jeans and scuffed up leather boots.

"Erm, well..." I pull a face, not wanting to offend him, but equally not wanting him to think that I'm some groupie, one that's a good few years older than him at that.

He tips his head back and laughs. "I was just joking. Sorry, I couldn't help myself."

"Oh, right. Sure," I laugh, my shoulders untensing.

"So how did you hear about us?"

"I met your manager, Ben, at my mother's wedding a few weeks back. He told me all about your band."

"Ah, that'd explain it," he replies, then he cocks his head to the side and studies me. "Wait a minute, are you the woman Ben wouldn't shut up about? He said your voice was shit-hot."

"He did?" I let out an embarrassed laugh, waving away the compliment.

"Yep," he says, popping the p.

"That was nice of him."

"Believe me, he was *very* impressed. Anyway, ummm...." His voice trails off as he holds his hand out to me to shake. "Sorry, he did tell me your name but I'm a forgetful bastard, and I'm blanking on it."

I take his hand, shaking it. "Harlow Richards, and you?"

"Blake Black," he replies, giving my hand a squeeze before releasing it.

"Very Rock 'n' Roll," I say with a soft smile.

He shrugs. "Fits the vibe of a bass player, I guess."

"You play the bass?"

The grin that seems to be permanently painted on his face widens as he pulls a pick from out of his pocket and strums a few chords on the guitar, his deft fingers moving up and down the frets with accomplished ease. "The guitar, violin and cello too, but in the band I'm the bassist. Sexiest instrument by far in my opinion. Though my bandmates would probably disagree. How about you, do you play an instrument as well as sing?"

"The piano. Though it's been a while to be honest," I explain, eyeing the piano in the corner of the store.

"Want to give it a play?" he asks, following my gaze.

"I don't know. I'm probably a little rusty."

"How long has it been since you last played?"

"About a year, give or take."

"Well, that beauty over there hasn't been played in forever, and whilst I'm a talented bastard and can play most instruments, I've never quite got the handle of percussion, string is more my area of expertise. These fingers prefer to strum and pluck, if you know what I mean?" he says with a flirtatious wink. "Give it go."

I can't help it, I laugh. "Sure, I guess it wouldn't hurt to try."

Blake gives an exaggerated nod, his grin widening. "Exactly. Plus, if it sounds terrible, I'll just blame it on the piano."

"Yes, let's do that," I agree, still feeling a little hesitant as I take a seat on the bench and rest my fingers gently over the keys.

I don't immediately begin to play, I just allow my mind to clear and take a few deep breaths before I arrange my fingers into a familiar chord pattern. Once my nerves have settled a little, I begin to play, tentatively at first, but as I continue a deep sense of comfort settles around me and I let the notes roll through my fingers, playing the chords without thinking too much about it. The rhythm flows with surprising ease, and soon enough, my hands find the familiar pattern of a song I used to love to play: *Your Song* by Elton John.

I glance over my shoulder at Blake, whose gaze is locked on the movement of my fingers.

"Not bad for rusty," he smiles, his voice low, almost in awe.

I smile, though it's more to myself than for him as I continue to play the familiar tune. "I guess it's like riding a bike. Once your muscle memory is triggered it all just comes back to you."

"Yeah, I guess you're right," he murmurs, dropping his gaze to his own hands as he begins to play the guitar alongside me. His talent is raw and honest in a way that makes my pulse quicken in admiration.

For the next few minutes we continue to play together, and with every moment that passes I feel this rush of joy unfurling inside of me. A joy I haven't felt in a long time. It feels so good that I start humming to the melody, and when I look up at Blake he mouths *sing*, so I begin to sing, the

words slipping from my lips in a husky whisper. My voice is soft at first, then when I begin to feel more comfortable, I let myself go and really sing.

And God, it's freeing.

It feels so good.

Every now and then, I glance up at Blake who could rival the Cheshire Cat from Alice in Wonderland with his perfectly wide, white-toothed grin. His enthusiasm gives me confidence, and I return his smile with one of my own, loving the warmth blooming inside my chest from happiness. Singing and playing the piano is a joyous experience for me.

It's an expression of who I truly am.

And I miss it.

Eventually, the song comes to an end, and I'm left with the soft echo of the last chord lingering in the air. "That was nice," I say softly, resting my hands in my lap.

"Nice?" His eyes widen as he leans a shoulder against the piano. "I was thinking more along the lines of *incredible.*"

I laugh, shaking my head. "It wasn't *that* great. But I appreciate your kindness."

"You're selling yourself short, Harlow. You play like a professional, and you sure as fuck sing like you were born to do it. Damn, girl!" he exclaims, blowing out a breath. "No wonder Ben got a hard-on for you. You're the shit!"

"A hard-on? Now don't start spreading rumours, jackass, this one's taken," a familiar voice says as Blake's head snaps up towards the door, and I look over my shoulder to see Ben stepping inside the shop.

Taken? My cheeks heat.

"Of course she is," Blake mutters.

"How are you doing, Harlow? I see you've found the bassist of Princetown Bandits."

"I'm good, thanks, and yes, Blake and I were just..." My voice trails off as I stand, suddenly feeling more than a little awkward as he glances between us both. Not that there's anything going on whatsoever given we've only just met, and he's too young, and I'm more than a little attracted to someone else entirely.

"Jamming together," Blake interjects. "You were right, Harlow sure is talented."

"Told you," Ben agrees with a grin, before focusing his attention on me. "You know the offer still stands. I'd love for you to play at the bar. In fact the Princetown Bandits are gonna be playing some gigs in London soon, and I don't have anyone to replace them, so you'll be doing me a favour if you'd consider stepping in at least for one night."

"Fuck, yes!" Blake agrees.

"Oh no, I couldn't," I reply, shaking my head.

"Why?" Blake asks, removing his guitar and placing it on a stand. "You'll blow everyone's minds with that voice of yours."

"I don't know. It's... I just... You really think I should?" I find myself asking.

"Abso-fucking-lutely," Blake says, shoving his hair off his face and grinning.

"The punters would love you," Ben adds in encouragement.

"Come on, say you will. What have you got to lose?" Blake asks as Ben looks at me expectedly.

"When were you thinking?"

"Next weekend?" Ben beams at me, his green eyes twinkling.

I chew on my lip as both men wait for my reply. What harm could it do? I've already sung at my mother's wedding, and it's only one night. I'm just doing Ben a favour. That's all.

"Sure, why not," I find myself agreeing.

TWENTY-ONE

Glancing at my reflection in the mirror, I straighten my tie and do up the buttons on my suit jacket, smoothing down the lapel. The last thing I want to do right now is go to Dalton and Daisy's engagement party. But I promised I'd be there, so that's where I'm headed as I stride across my studio and grab the keys to my car from the coffee table.

Having arrived back at Adaga Hall an hour ago, I decided not to seek out Harlow knowing that there wouldn't be a chance in hell I'd end up at the engagement party if I did. It's felt like forever since we shared a kiss in the kitchen, and whilst the time apart has been fucking torturous for me, I just need to make it through the next couple of hours before I can finally have a conversation with her. That doesn't stop me from feeling guilty about the fact I'm not taking her as my plus one. I feel like a fucking arsehole for not insisting she come, but I'm also acutely aware that if she did, there's no way I'd be able to hide my attraction for her, or keep my hands off her for that matter.

Especially not when I'm so fucking wound up I can barely breathe.

"One step at a time," I tell myself as I climb into my car and start the engine.

Twenty minutes later I pull up outside the entrance to Highwood Manor Estate, and hand my keys to the valet. After taking a glass of champagne from one of the staff members, I head into the ballroom in search of Ben, finding him talking with Lia and her kid, Toby, a couple of minutes later.

"Sterling, didn't think you'd show. Where the hell have you been?" Ben asks, as Lia greets me with a kiss to the cheek, and I ruffle Toby's hair.

"Just a work thing," I reply vaguely, not sure how much, if at all, Lia knows about my situation with Harlow. Though, if I know Drix like I think I do, he would've kept our conversations private.

Ben nods, understanding that I'm not in a position right now to tell him the truth. "Well, I'm glad you're here," he replies, squeezing my shoulder good-naturedly.

"I can see Carl's invited most of the private members club," I remark, glancing around the ballroom.

"Everyone looks really lovely," Lia says, her eyes lighting up in awe at the men and women sweeping past in ballgowns and tuxedos.

"Not lovelier than you, Lia. You look beautiful," I say, admiring her long sleeved, black ballgown that hugs her figure. She's a beautiful woman, both in looks and personality, and I can totally see why Drix is so enamoured with her. It makes me think of Harlow back at home alone, and guilt climbs up my throat once again.

Her cheeks blush pink. "Thank you."

"They might *look* lovely, but I can promise you most of the people here are far from it. Present company excluded, of course," Ben adds, adjusting his cufflinks as he scans the crowd. "Trust me, they're all about status and how many zeros are in their bank accounts."

Lia raises an eyebrow, her lips quirking into a playful grin. "Well, I'm glad I'm here with you both then."

"And Drix," Toby points out, hopping from one foot to the other.

"*Especially* Drix," she agrees, her smile softening.

"Speaking of which, where is the handsome bastard–?"

Toby gasps, pointing at Ben with his chubby little finger. "You swore. Mama, he swore!"

Ben pulls a face. "Apologies."

Lia waves his apology away with a laugh. "Don't worry, I'll add a pound coin to the swear jar on your behalf. Toby already has quite a tidy sum from all the swearing Drix does."

"Is that so? Pretty good way to clear out Drix's bank account," Ben muses, winking at Toby who grins. "So where is he? I'm surprised he's not glued to your side like he usually is."

"He went in search of Daisy. She hasn't arrived yet," Lia explains.

"And Dalton?" I ask.

"Mingling with the crowd, piling on the charm, you know the drill," Ben explains.

"Oh wait, I think I see them. Dalton's with Daisy and Drix now, " Lia says, her gaze darting over my shoulder. "Should we go and join them?"

"Absolutely," I say, stepping to the side so that she and Toby can guide the way.

"Lia, Toby!" Daisy exclaims as we approach. She steps out

of Dalton's hold and throws her arms around Lia in a hug before crouching down and wrapping her arms around Toby.

"Your dress is so pretty!" Toby exclaims as she draws upright, his small hands touching the delicate fabric of her dress.

I can't help but notice that she's not adhered to the black and white colour theme, and I smile at that. Her dress is a stunning royal blue with a stone encrusted bodice that catches the light and sends colour sprawling over everyone around her. This dress is most definitely a fuck-you to stuck-up arseholes who're staring at her with varying levels of disdain, and I admire her for it.

"Thank you, Toby. You look very handsome too," Daisy replies, beaming.

I can't help but notice how Dalton flicks a look her way, a muscle in his jaw feathering. Fuck, he's tense.

"We've missed you," Lia says.

Daisy's smile softens. "I've missed you too."

"How about we get together soon?" Lia asks as Toby glances between the pair, grinning widely.

"Can I come? I promise I'll be good," he says, hopping on his feet. He's such a cute fucking kid, and so happy. I can't ever remember smiling as much as he does. He's a credit to Lia.

"Of course! Maybe a play date at the park, followed by some food at Daphne's cafe in town?" Daisy suggests, ruffling Toby's hair.

"Yes, please," he agrees, as Lia takes his hand in hers and glances at Drix. They exchange a loving look, and it only serves to remind me of what I'm missing in my own life.

"We'll organise it soon. I imagine we have lots to catch up on."

"We do," Daisy agrees, and I can't help but notice the pointed look she gives Lia. I sure as fuck hope Dalton has been treating her well. Though knowing my friend he's probably already fucked up again.

"Daisy, you look good enough to eat," Ben says, interrupting my thoughts as he steps forward.

Daisy's cheeks heat as he leans in and kisses her in greeting. "Thanks, Ben."

"Careful, Ben," I interject with a smirk as Dalton mutters something under his breath. "You know how Dalton gets."

"Not with my sister, he won't," Drix grumbles.

I smother a smile, then drop a kiss against Daisy's cheek. "You scrub up well."

"Thanks, Sterling. How are things with your family? Your stepmother and stepsister seem lovely," she says.

"They're settling in," I reply, not elaborating.

"Are you sticking around for a while?" she asks softly.

I've always liked Daisy, she's sweet and kind, and I know the hopefulness in her gaze is genuine. She needs as many friends at her upcoming wedding as she can get and even if I wasn't staying for Harlow, I would've made sure to attend their wedding regardless.

"Of course, I wouldn't dream of missing your wedding," I reply, cutting a look at Dalton, who clears his throat.

"I hate to steal Daisy away, but there are other guests we need to greet. We'll catch up soon, yes?" he says to Drix, before looking between me and Ben.

Drix doesn't reply, but Ben nods. "Actually, Harlow has agreed to sing at Bandits Bar, you should all come, might make her feel more at ease if there are some familiar faces in the crowd."

I stiffen, my head snapping around to glare at Ben. *What the fuck? Since fucking when?*

"She has? When was this arranged?" I ask, trying and failing to hide my surprise given the shit-eating grin Ben throws my way.

"Few days ago. She's performing next weekend, in fact," he replies. "I asked her to fill in whilst the guys are doing some gigs in London."

I clench my teeth so fucking hard I almost break a tooth.

"Princetown Bandits are gigging in London?" Drix asks, surprise in his voice.

"Yeah, a record label is very interested in them. I'm going to meet with the label and the guys when they return," Ben explains. "It's been a long time coming."

"That's amazing, they're really good," Lia adds.

"If you don't mind me coming too, I'd love to hear Harlow sing again. Her voice is stunning," Daisy says.

Lia's smile broadens "Oh me too. She gave me chills when she sang at the wedding."

"Pretty sure she gave a few of us more than chills," Ben comments with a smirk, and I almost reach out and punch him in the face. "Anyway, of course you all should come. It'll be a great night."

"Well, I guess we better head off. I'll hopefully see you all soon then?" Daisy asks.

"You bet, Daise," Drix replies as Dalton leads Daisy into the crowd. We all watch them walk away as Drix says, "Drink, anyone? Because I could sure fucking use one."

"Drix!" Toby exclaims before throwing his hand over his mouth and giggling.

"Sorry, bud," he replies, wincing, before casting us both a look. "You coming?"

I shake my head. "We'll catch up with you in a moment, okay?"

"Sure thing." Drix nods then guides Lia and Toby to the corner of the room.

"I'd like a word, Ben. In *private*," I snap before he can even open his mouth and put his foot in it one more time.

"Oh fucking hell, Sterling. Don't lose your shit. It's just a gig," Ben retorts, but he follows me anyway.

As soon as we step outside, I round on him. "What the actual fuck, Ben?!"

"It's no big deal–" he begins, but I cut him off with a shake of my head.

"No big deal? You know what it does to me when she sings."

"Then don't come to the gig," he offers with a shrug.

"There's no fucking way I'm letting her go to Bandits Bar alone," I counter darkly.

He rolls his eyes and I almost reach out and throttle him. "She *won't* be alone."

Exactly! She's far too beautiful, and way too talented not to get any unwanted attention.

"Regardless, I'm coming!"

"Okay, great. Now are you going to chill out?"

"No. I'm pissed off that you're having conversations with Harlow behind my fucking back!"

"Lower your damn voice," Ben warns, nodding to a couple of guests who've just arrived. He waits for them to enter before he continues. "It's innocent okay. I bumped into her a couple of days ago in *The Cosy Chord*, we got talking and I explained the band are gigging in London, and that I needed a stand-in. She agreed. That's all there is to it."

"She was at The Cosy Chord? Was Blake there?" I ask, knowing what a flirtatious bastard he can be. The kid has got a reputation, and I don't like the fact she was alone with the little shit.

"She is allowed to leave the fucking mansion, Sterling," he points out. "And, yes, of course Blake was there."

"Fuck sake," I mutter, feeling more than a little agitated.

"Actually, they were playing together when I walked in. Harlow was singing, and she was fucking incredible, Sterling. Did you know she could play the piano?"

No, I fucking didn't.

"They were *playing* together? She was *singing*?" I ask instead, my voice rising in agitation as jealousy thunders through my veins. I'm both jealous of the fact that Harlow felt relaxed enough to sing and play the piano with Blake-fucking-Black, but also so damn proud that she could. I know how hard it is for her to reveal that side of her. The two warring emotions make my stomach churn.

"Listen. I get it, okay," Ben sighs, giving me a sympathetic look. "I know how you feel about her–"

"No, you don't get it, Ben," I say, pinching the bridge of my nose momentarily. "I can't fucking breathe when I'm around her. I've spent the last four days trying to sort my head out, and the only reason I didn't bring her tonight was because I knew what would happen if I did. That doesn't stop me from feeling like a complete fucking shit for leaving her behind though."

Ben rests his hands on my shoulders, squeezing gently. "You need to think about what would happen if you pursued this and your dad found out."

"Of course, I have," I hiss.

"And have you figured out what you're going to do yet?"

We lock gazes and my nostrils flare.

"I'm going to stay away," I eventually say, blowing out a shuddering breath.

"That's tough," he replies, but despite his sympathy, I see how his shoulders relax and I know he thinks it's the right thing to do. Which is bullshit given his recent actions offering to pay for time with another man's wife.

"Yeah," I agree, knowing that it's a lie. Knowing that as soon as I can slip away I'm going to go back home and finally claim Harlow as mine.

TWENTY-TWO

Stepping into the parlour, I flip the light switch on, illuminating the room. In the corner, the grand piano commands attention—a beautiful instrument I've longed to play since my arrival. Its sleek black surface gleams under the soft overhead light, and I've often wondered if anyone in the family can actually play it. I suspect it's more for decoration, as neither Sterling nor Robert has ever mentioned any musical talent. To be honest, my brief conversations with Sterling have rarely strayed into personal interests. It feels like whenever we're in the same space, the air crackles with tension and an intense attraction. Small talk is the last thing on our minds.

Maybe stepping in here wasn't the best idea I've ever had, but I've spent the last four days alone, driving myself crazy thinking about Sterling, and I need a way to channel my frustrations. Playing the piano seems like a better way to do that than going for a swim. I'd rather avoid the temptation of being practically naked in the pool with Sterling again. That's if he ever decides to show his face.

Besides, writing lyrics and crafting melodies is cathartic for me, and after playing the piano at *The Cosy Chord* the other day, I've decided I'm not going to repress that part of me anymore.

As I settle onto the piano stool, my fingers hovering over the keys for a moment, the familiar feeling of anticipation bubbles up within me, providing me with a much needed distraction.

Pressing my fingers lightly against the keys, I start with a gentle melody, something soft and introspective. The sound fills the room, and for a brief moment, I forget my worries, lost so completely to the music.

Then I feel it—someone watching me intensely, and I know without looking up that it's Sterling.

The same familiar thrill rushes over my skin and my fingers stumble over keys, caught off guard by the way his presence shifts the atmosphere, the connection we share snapping to life as I glance over at him leaning against the doorframe. His arms are crossed as he watches me with a brooding kind of intensity that has my pulse quickening. Dressed in tailored black trousers, a white shirt rolled up to his elbows, with his tie loosened around his neck, he's the perfect combination of masculinity and effortless beauty that draws me in like gravity, making it impossible to look away. Knowing that the engagement party is tonight, I briefly wonder why he left so early given it's only just past ten o'clock.

"Don't stop," he murmurs.

"But shouldn't you be–"

"Please, Harlow. *Play*," he demands softly, his gaze piercing yet contemplative as he pushes off the doorframe and approaches on bare feet.

The slight creak of the floorboards beneath his weight echoes in the sudden stillness of the room as he settles beside me on the piano stool, our knees nearly touching. I can feel the heat radiating from him as I press my fingers against the keys, forcing myself not to glance at him. I can sense his curiosity in the way he studies me, and it makes my heart race as I play once more.

"What are you playing?" he asks after a while, his voice low and smooth like the melody that lingers in the air between us. I'm acutely aware of how close he is, the scent of his cologne mingling with the fragrance of polished wood and ivory keys. "I don't know this melody, is this something you wrote?" he asks.

I hesitate, my instinct to retreat kicking in. I'm so used to being belittled by my mother that my immediate reaction is to leave, to protect myself from the pain of being ridiculed for my art. With Blake, whilst still nervous, I'd felt a surprising sense of calm, and that's probably because he's a musician too, but also because I'd played a tune that wasn't mine. This is way more personal since the melody is something I've written.

"Harlow?" he insists, reaching for me, his fingers barely grazing against my wrist, before dropping away.

"Yes," I finally admit, biting my lip. "I wrote this."

"It's beautiful," he replies, his tone gentle as I risk another glance at him, his gaze shifting from an almost pained kind of longing to a curious interest.

"Thank you," I whisper.

"Will you play some more?" he asks.

"I think maybe I should–"

"Because I just need a moment to figure something out," he interjects.

"Figure out what?" I ask as a strange, unreadable expression passes over his features.

He lifts his hand, rubbing the back of his neck, the muscles in his forearm flexing and relaxing beneath his skin as he does so. I've always found a man's forearms and hands attractive, especially when they're as strong and as veiny as Sterling's are. *Arm porn*, I muse, then internally berate myself for even going there.

"If I can do *this*..." he says pointedly.

"Do what?"

"Be in the same room as you and not want to pull you into my arms and kiss you until both of our knees are weak," he blurts out, his arm falling back to his side.

"You want to kiss me?"

"I want to do much more than that, Harlow, but I'm trying very hard to respect your wishes," he admits, and I don't know what's more devastatingly attractive, the fact that he's holding himself back and respecting my wishes–which are shaky at best–or the smile he gives me that reveals those two beautiful dimples in his cheeks.

"Then I guess I should distract you, huh?" I reply as I begin to play once more.

"Hmm," he hums, both of us aware that we're stepping into flirtatious territory, and neither of us doing a damn thing to stop it.

After a minute or so, I can feel Sterling leaning closer, each note seeming to draw him in like a thread weaving us closer together. He begins to tremble, his fingers curling into fists as I let the music swell.

"Sterling?" I question, confused by his physical reaction, by the way he seems to study me.

"Keep playing," he replies, his voice rough as his fingers grip his thigh.

"Okay," I reply softly, pouring my emotions into the melody.

I'm fully aware that this is dangerous, that I should get up and leave, but yet again I can't seem to bring myself to do that.

"Did you play this for Blake?" he asks after a while, and there's a note of jealousy in his voice that should be a huge red flag, but only makes me feel more desired.

"You know about that?"

"Ben told me. So did you?"

"I played an Elton John song, so no I didn't play this for Blake," I reply softly.

"Do you ever share the music you've written with others?" he asks, his voice barely above a whisper.

I shake my head, a faint laugh escaping my lips as my fingers move over the keys. "Honestly, no. I usually keep it to myself. My music is..."

"Personal to you?" he offers.

"Yes, very much so."

He shifts slightly, turning to face me as his knee brushes against my thigh. "Then why are you sharing it with me?"

"Because you were the first person to truly *see* me and not make me feel like my dreams are pointless, or worse, that I'm just not good enough."

He takes a breath, and I can feel the tension between us charging the air with something electric. "You have this light, Harlow, a vibrancy. It's hard not to notice. Fuck, you've no idea how you affect me."

Not entirely sure how to respond to that without giving in and throwing myself into his arms, I continue to play, letting the music flow around us both as the room fills with a rich, resonant sound. I don't sing, mainly because I'm not sure I'll ever be ready to share the lyrics given how personal they are. For now, I just allow myself to be swept away by the melody, soaking up

Sterling's attention as he listens intently. Then, as the final notes drift into silence, I rest my hands in my lap, and wait.

"That was... Wow, Harlow!" Sterling breathes, his expression a mix of admiration and something deeper, something that sends my pulse racing as our gazes clash. For one long, heart-pounding moment we stare at each other, but when he leans closer, I shift away from him, putting space between us.

"Do you play?" I blurt out.

"I'm guessing chopsticks don't count?" he replies with a rueful grin.

"Not really, no," I agree with a light laugh. "What about Robert?"

He shakes his head, his smile dropping "Definitely not. To be able to play a musical instrument you need to be able to feel a variety of emotions, and my father is only capable of hate, loathing and disgust."

"That sounds ominous."

Sterling scrapes a hand through his hair and lets out an even breath. "I could lie to you and say that the issues I have with my father are mine alone, but I'm not going to do that, Harlow. He hurts people, and he gets a kick out of doing it."

"Are you talking about your mom?"

He nods, and without thinking about it, I reach for his hand and place mine over the top. It's meant to be an affectionate gesture, one to show solidarity and support, but the second our hands meet that spark that always lingers between us burns brighter.

"Not just her," Sterling replies, turning his hand beneath mine so that we're palm to palm.

"Has he hurt you very badly?" I ask, my breath catching as he weaves his fingers with mine, and brushes his thumb over my knuckles.

"Put it this way, Ben's dad has been more of a father to me than my own over the years," he replies. "I've always been a disappointment, and I've certainly never lived up to my father's expectations. He has gone out of his way to make sure that I know exactly how he feels about me, and none of it is good."

"I'm sorry, Sterling. I didn't think he was that kind of man."

"Believe me when I say, my father is adept at manipulation, at making himself look the pillar of the community when deep down he's a master of deceit. He uses charm to mask his cruelty, playing the role of the perfect father and husband in public, whilst behind closed doors he's cruel and unyielding. It's exhausting to navigate the facade he maintains, and even more exhausting to constantly question my own worth in the process."

"I had no idea. I'm so sorry," I repeat.

"You've nothing to apologise for. Just, *please*, be cautious when it comes to trusting my father."

"Should I be worrying about my mom?"

"I wish I could tell you that he'll make her happy, but truthfully there will come a time when he'll break her just like he broke my mother. Just like he breaks everything he touches."

"That doesn't feel good to hear," I admit, because whilst my relationship with my mother is far from perfect, I don't want her to get hurt.

"From what you've told me, she hasn't been the best mother to you either. Perhaps they deserve each other."

I know he's right, and I hate the fact that despite everything she's done and said to me over the years, I still miss the mom I used to have. I wish I didn't care about her the way I do, but I can't help it. Instead I ask, "So why are you still here? Why haven't you returned to your life in New York?"

"I thought by now I've made that pretty obvious, Harlow.

There's only one reason that I'm staying, and that reason is you."

"Sterling, no," I reply as firmly as I can muster whilst withdrawing my hand from beneath his. "You need to go back to your life in New York, to your job..." I pause, realising that I don't even know what he does for a living. There are a lot of things I don't know about Sterling.

"Don't tell me no," he counters roughly, catching my wrist as I stand, deciding that it's probably time I left before things get too heated between us.

"We've been through this already," I reply, looking down at him, and resisting the urge to run my fingers through his hair. "Besides, even if our parents weren't married and we could be together, I still don't really know anything about you. So what does that tell you about us?"

"It tells me that we've been wasting time avoiding each other when we should've used this time to get to know each other better."

"I don't even know what you do for a living!" I blurt out, my voice rising in pitch as I struggle with my conflicting emotions. One minute I want to throw myself into his arms, and the next I want to put a stop to this once and for all.

"I work in the arts," he replies. "Next question."

"I'm not playing this game," I reply, trying to tug my wrist free from his grasp.

"Next question, Harlow," he demands, reaching up for me with his free hand, and grasping my hip as he tugs me closer until I somehow end up trapped between his legs and pressed up against the piano, his muscular thighs preventing me from leaving as he looks up at me.

"I told you I'm not playing this game," I repeat, folding my arms across my chest and turning my face away from him.

"Would you rather we don't talk at all?" he asks, his hand squeezing my hip before coasting downwards and sliding around the back of my leg, cupping the point where my arse and thigh meet. His fingers wrap around the fleshiest part of my leg, centimetres away from my core. The only material between us is the thin cotton of my joggers, and panties.

Fuck.

"Fine. How was the engagement party?" I ask, treacherous heat building in my core.

"It would've been a hell of a lot better if I had you by my side. But we both know that would've been a mistake because, apparently, I *can't* keep my hands off you," he says, his fingers flexing against my thigh. "Next question."

"What's your favourite colour?" I blurt out, hoping to move on to safer topics.

"I told you before, berry red."

Fuck. Fuck. Fuck.

Right now I'm pretty sure my cheeks are *berry red* as I recall the intimate part of my anatomy he likened to the same colour that night we slept together. A smile pulls up his lip as he notices the stain of colour creeping across my skin.

"Anything else you'd like to know?"

"How long have you been best friends with Ben?" I ask, clearing my throat and rapidly changing the subject as I look down at him.

"Since we were toddlers."

"And what about Drix and Dalton?"

"They're older than us both by about five years so we didn't really start getting close until Ben and I were in our late teens. We bonded over whisky and fast cars, whilst our dad's bonded over business and the billions they had in their bank accounts."

"And how long have you lived in New York?"

"I don't live there anymore, Harlow. I live here, *with you.*"

"You can't just drop everything for me, Sterling. You've built a life there–" I begin, but he cuts me off with a shake of his head.

"I've been *living* in New York, that's not the same thing as having a *life* there."

"What do you mean by that? You have friends, right? What about your work colleagues? Your apartment? You can't just not go back."

"I told you I was a loner, and I meant it. I can count on one hand the friends I have, and all of them are here in Princetown. Besides, my apartment is on a year's lease. It has three months left. I have no desire to return there."

I huff out a breath, hating that he's been so isolated, so alone. "And your work?"

"I can do that wherever I live."

"What is it that you do exactly?"

"I told you, I'm in the arts."

"That's very non-specific."

He shrugs. "I deal with paintings."

"So you're an art dealer."

"Pretty much," he agrees.

"So why choose New York?"

"It was as good a place as any."

"Sterling," I warn, sensing that he's keeping things from me. "Why do I feel like you're hiding something?"

"Would you prefer it if I said what's really on my mind?" he counters, his gaze heating dangerously.

"Perhaps not," I mutter, trying to ease myself out of his hold, but he just stands, the stool toppling over behind him from the force as he braces his hands either side of my body on the lid of the piano.

"Because the truth is, no matter what excuses you come up with about why we shouldn't be together, I'm not letting you go. I refuse," he says, inching closer.

"Sterling..."

"You can try to tell me that we don't know each other well enough, and to that I would say that we have years to get to know each other because, again, I'm not letting you go."

"This is–"

"You can tell me that this connection between us is wrong, and I will answer it the same way each time: you're mine, and nothing and no one is going to change that."

"Yours?"

"Yes."

"I'm not–"

He growls, actually fucking growls as he reaches up and cups my throat, his long, thick fingers holding me with a possession that should scare me, but doesn't. *Why doesn't it?* I honestly don't have an answer to that, all I know is that I feel his dominance in this hold, his absolute determination to make me understand that he's not backing down, that he wants me, and there is something incredibly attractive about that. I'm the object of his attention, his desire, and for most of my adult life that hasn't been the case.

"Once again, let me make something perfectly clear. I don't care that our parents are married. You are *not* my sister, Harlow. You are the woman I want, irrespective of how that may or may not affect others."

"Stop this. Stop it right now," I say, trying to push him away but he leans over me, the action making me sit on the keys, the random, disjointed notes only adding to the intensity of the moment.

"No, I won't. You wanted honesty, you're going to get it," he replies, sliding his hand from around my neck to the back of my head as grabs a fistful of hair, tugging on it so that I'm forced to look up at him. "I want you. There is nothing that you can say or do that will change that fact. I want there to be an us."

"And what about what *I* want?" I ask, my breath hitching not from fear, but from excitement.

"You want me, at least be honest about that," he states.

I do. I really, really do.

"No," I say instead, and maybe my defiance isn't just a knee-jerk reaction to his chest-beating possessiveness, maybe it's because a part of me wants to see what will happen if I push his buttons. Maybe I want his hand back around my throat and that gleam of possession in his eyes.

"Liar," he bites out before slamming his lips against mine and claiming my mouth in a searing kiss.

God this kiss.

It makes me weak.

Every protest I had, every argument against why we shouldn't be doing this, why we can't be together evaporates. This kiss is passionate, yes, but it's also filled with so much more than lust for one another, there's a sweet kind of forgiveness, a heart-thumping kind of honesty, and a deep kind of understanding.

"You are becoming everything to me, Harlow," he admits against my lips.

For a fraction of a second, my heart stops beating. "What did you just say?"

"You heard me," he replies, pressing another soft kiss against my lips.

"Sterling..."

"I mean it, Harlow."

"But you don't know me, not really," I protest softly.

"I know you," he replies, shifting back slightly. "I know that I can't look at you without wanting to bury myself deep inside of you because that's the only time I've ever felt at home. I know that you're an incredibly talented artist. I know that your voice bewitches me every time I hear you sing. I know that you're a gifted pianist who hides her talent from everyone because your mother has only ever made you feel like you're not good enough. I recognise the pain you carry from a parent who hasn't loved you the right way, because I feel that too."

"Sterling, don't," I whisper.

"I know that you hide your light because if you didn't you'd outshine everyone around you. I know that you're so selfless that you will forgo your own dreams and desires to protect your mother's ego. I know that you have tried so hard to fight this connection between us because you're afraid of hurting people who don't deserve it. But I also know that the way we feel about each other is stronger than fear, that I have faith we can make this work somehow. I know that you've never felt seen, not truly, not for everything and all that you are." Palming my cheeks gently, he adds, "And I know that I *see* you, that I *want* you."

"But–" My chest heaves as heat rises up my chest and neck.

"So, while I may not know your favourite colour or the names of the friends you grew up with," he says, cutting me off. "I do know you. I know the parts that matter the most, and please believe me when I say that you are worthy of affection, of support, of encouragement and kindness. You don't have to settle for anything less than real connection, and you no longer have to feel the rejection of selfish men who don't truly see you. You deserve to be desired, to feel cherished in every way, and I want to be the man to give that to you. *I* want to be the one to show you that. *Me.*"

"I don't know what to say," I reply softly, feeling overwhelmed, still not entirely believing his words despite every-thing he's said.

"You don't have to say anything, you just have to believe me," he replies before pressing his hips against mine, palming my cheeks and kissing me breathless.

TWENTY-THREE

Harlow can protest all she likes, she can throw excuses my way, she can try to avoid me, but we both know that we're inevitable, and I'm done giving her space.

Our parents return home from their honeymoon in a couple of days, and we're going to have to figure out how to handle them, but that's a future us problem. Right now I'm getting lost in Harlow, and I'm not coming up for air until she's more than satisfied. I promised her multiple orgasms the night of our parents' wedding, and that's exactly what she's going to get.

Right the fuck now.

"Sterling, the staff..." Harlow gasps, pushing against my chest.

"I sent them home," I reply, guiding her to her feet, and closing the fallboard on the piano so Harlow doesn't continue to play the keys with her beautiful, peachy arse.

"So you planned on seducing me tonight?" she asks a little breathlessly.

"I guess that all depends on whether you let me?" I counter, dropping my mouth to her neck and pressing an open mouth kiss to her pulse that races beneath my tongue. I expect her to say no, to come up with another excuse, but she surprises me.

"I want you to," she whispers, her fingers curling into my hair as she lets out a soft moan.

"You have to be certain, Harlow. Because there's no turning back after this. Do you understand me? I need to know you're in this with me. No matter what."

"I am. I want to be. *Please*," she whispers.

Fuck, the way that sounds has my cock jerking in my trousers, and I'm reminded of the night I crept into her room and made her come when she'd unknowingly whispered that exact same word.

I lift my head, leaning back slightly so that I can look at her and the subtle colours that thread and weave around her body. They're less vibrant than the times before, yet they're no less beautiful. This time it's like looking at a Monet painting, the muted soft blues, dusky pinks, pale yellows and pinks are a masterpiece all of their own.

"I expected you to argue some more," I reply, cupping her face with my hands, smiling a little.

"Me too... But then you said all those beautiful things, then kissed me and every single argument I had ready just floated away, " she murmurs back. "Does that make me weak?"

"No, Harlow, that makes you mine."

She nods, then slides her hands up my forearms until her fingers wrap around my wrist and she gently lowers my hand to her throat. "Then I guess I'm yours," she says, her mouth parting as I squeeze her throat just a little.

Fuck. Me.

"You like that?" I ask, feeling her thready pulse pounding

beneath my thumb as my cock punches against the zipper of my trousers.

"I like it," she admits, as she guides my other hand to her breast. "I like *you* way more than I should."

"Not nearly enough," I argue. "But after I strip you naked, lay you on the top of this piano and eat you out until you scream my name, you're gonna like me a whole lot more."

She gasps, and I drop my hands to her jogging bottoms, curl my fingers around the waistband, removing both them and her knickers in one quick sweep of material. She steps out of them, her eyes heady with lust as I reach for the hem of her t-shirt and pull it up over her head, her hair swishing with the movement. She isn't wearing a bra, and my cock leaks at the sight.

"I've been dreaming about your beautiful tits for days now. It's been torturous," I say, whilst tracing the mound of her breast.

"Just my tits?" she asks, a teasing glint in her eyes.

"No, not just your tits," I admit, loving this flirty, playful version of her.

"What else?" she asks as I palm her breasts, my thumbs circling her hardened nipples.

Bending over, I drag her nipple into my mouth, sucking on it until her whimpers beg me for more. "I've dreamt about sucking on your nipples and making you so wet that when I finally get my mouth on your pussy it's dripping for me," I reply before coasting my mouth to her other breast.

"Is that so?" she questions, her chest heaving as I drag her other nipple into my mouth, causing her to moan once more.

"Are you wet for me, Harlow?" I ask, every word teased with a lick of my tongue.

"Why don't you find out?" she throws back, placing her

hands on my shoulders as though urging me to crouch before her, but I have other plans.

Reaching between us, I cup her mound. Her gaze flashes with heat, and she adjusts her stance a little so that her legs part. "Fuck, Harlow. You're dripping," I exclaim, my middle finger slipping between her folds. I gather up the slick heat and smother it over her clit.

"Sterling..."

Her mouth parts and I claim it, licking my tongue into her mouth, swallowing her moans as I gently stroke her clit. She throws her arms around my neck hauling me closer, so that my arm is trapped between our bodies.

"You want more?" I tease, smiling wickedly against her mouth.

"God, yes," she pants. "I want it all."

With my gaze locked onto hers, and our lips millimetres apart, I slide two fingers deep inside of her with one swift motion, pressing the heel of my palm against her clit as I do. She cries out, her hands dropping to my shoulders as she rises on her tiptoes, the wet, slippery sounds of her arousal making my cock thicken painfully. The intrusion is verging on rough, yet she doesn't tell me to stop, in fact she just drops to her feet, forcing my fingers deeper inside of her dripping cunt.

"You like that?"

"Yes," she hisses, spreading her legs wider as I pull my fingers almost all of the way out, and then spear them back inside of her in one steady thrust. Her tits bounce from the force as she throws her head back.

"You want me to finger-fuck you like this?" I repeat, lifting up my free hand and cupping her throat as I pull my fingers out of her, then shove them deep inside her pussy once again.

"Yes, I want to feel..." she moans, her voice trailing off as her eyes flicker shut, giving me a moment to study her beautiful face that is currently doused in soft sunset colours.

"You want to feel what, Harlow?" I demand, my hand between her legs stilling, whilst the one around her throat tightens a little.

Her eyes snap open, her mouth parting as she looks at me. The way her pupils enlarge and she presses her thighs back together around my hand tells me all I need to know. She's as turned on by this as I am. So she likes it a little rough? My *dirty* little poet.

"Tell me," I insist, releasing her throat a little, my own desire making my head swim with lust and my body fucking tremble with the need to be inside of her.

"I want you to overwhelm me, Sterling," she whispers back, licking her lips as her gaze darts from my eyes to my lips and back again.

"Overwhelm you?" I ask, my voice rough as I start to pump my fingers inside of her once again.

"Yes," she moans. "I want to feel so desired that you can't stop, that you can't control yourself."

"Like this?" I ask, shunting my fingers inside of her, my gaze fixed on her face as her fingers curl into my shoulders and she groans. "You want it hard, Harlow? You want me to prove to you how much I fucking want you. Is that it, huh?"

"Yes. I want that. I want that so much. I want you to ravish me, Sterling."

Ravish? That word conjures up visions of a long haired villain stepping into a virgin's room, tying her to the bed under a pale moonlight and having his wicked way with her. It reminds me of the night I crossed a line and coerced an orgasm from Harlow's sleeping form.

Fuck, that memory just makes me harder.

"Then that's what you're going to get. Now sit your arse on the lid of the piano, and spread your fucking legs," I command, pumping my fingers into her pussy three more times before dropping my hands and stepping back.

"You want me to sit on the piano?" she asks, stumbling a little.

"You heard me. Up!" I demand, grasping her hips to steady her briefly, before picking up the stool that I'd knocked over earlier and setting it back on its feet.

"But–"

"I won't ask you again," I growl, then grasp her elbow in my slick hand. "On. The. Piano."

She nods, her throat bobbing up and down as she steps onto the stool, her hands pressing against the shiny lid of the piano. I adjust my hands, taking the opportunity to coast them over her arse as she kneels onto the fallboard. She leans forward and briefly gives me a stunning view of her slit from behind, before she twists around and turns to face me.

And fuck, she's a vision.

She's desire and sex.

She's swathes of colour and subtle beauty.

She's the darkness of sin and licking flames of lust.

She's *mine*.

Stepping towards her I grip her knees that are pressed together, hiding her pussy from view.

"I thought I told you to spread your legs, Harlow," I say, and her mouth pops open as I shove her legs apart, my gaze falling to her ripe slit, to the glistening berry red of her pussy, and the bead of wetness that gently slips from her hole and slides over her perineum towards her puckered arse.

"Look at you, dripping for me. Did my fingers fuck you good, Harlow?"

"Yes," she whimpers as I slide my palms up her inner thighs towards her sex, pressing them against the tendons pulled taut beneath her skin.

"But you still haven't come," I mutter, using my thumbs to gently pull apart her outer lips so that I can memorise the form of her pussy, and the slippery wetness that greets me.

"No," she agrees, her chest heaving.

"What will it take to make you come for me?" I ask, dropping my head closer to her slit, and blowing warm air over her clit.

"Your mouth on me," she pants, her chin dropping to her chest as she looks down at me.

I look up at her. "And what will I get in return?"

"Anything, *anything* you want."

"Anything?" I question, my thoughts tumbling back to the night when I slipped into her room and stole an orgasm.

"Anything," she breathes.

Licking my lips, I drop my gaze back to her pussy as another bead of liquid gathers at her hole, then slowly slips downwards, a glistening trail that I desperately want to chase with my tongue. A zing of pleasure rushes down my spine and gathers in my balls at the thought.

"Then one night when you've fallen deep asleep I'm going to creep into your room, and fuck you until you wake up screaming my name," I promise, and before she can even begin to respond, I bend forward, press the tip of my tongue against her puckered arsehole, collecting the bead of wetness, before sliding my tongue up her slippery slit and sucking her clit into my mouth.

She drags in a startled breath, her hands flying backwards to keep her upright. "Sterling, fuck, that's... Oh, fuck... that feels so good," she cries.

"You like that, huh?" I muse, grinning like the fucking cat that got the cream as I return to her arse, rimming her hole.

"No one has ever..." her voice trails off as I slide a finger through her pussy lips, gathering the wetness before using it to lubricate her virgin arse.

She jerks from the slight penetration as I ease the very tip of my finger inside of her. "This tight hole will be mine one day soon. Not tonight, but soon," I promise before removing my finger, my heart pounding in my chest like a fucking jack-hammer as I inhale her scent and try to calm the carnal need to rip my trousers from my legs, pull her off the piano and impale her on my cock.

"Not yet. Not fucking yet," I mutter against her skin.

Harlow's hips jerk, and she whimpers, "Sterling."

"What Harlow? What do you want?" I ask her.

She moans, mumbling something incoherent.

"Use your words. What do you want?" I growl against her quivering pussy.

"You, Sterling. I want you!"

I lose it.

My ears fill with the frantic throb of my pulse as I slide my palms underneath her arse perched on the edge of the lid, then throw her legs over my shoulders. The action makes Harlow fall backwards onto the piano lid, her arms no longer able to hold her upright as I bury my face into her delectable cunt and feast on her pussy like a man *obsessed*.

Her taste explodes on my tongue, musky, feminine, fucking delicious, and it drives me wild. Every bottled up, hidden away, disguised and suppressed part of me breaks free from the constraints I've locked myself up in, and colour explodes behind my eyelids, like a New Year's Eve night sky lit up with fireworks.

I feel free. Unchained.

Free to claim Harlow.

Free to give in to my base desires.

I'm wild. I feel raw. *Untethered.*

I'm fucking crazy in my lust.

So fucking crazy that I frantically lick her pussy, alternating between plunging my tongue into her hole, and sucking on her puffy, swollen clit as I fuck her with my fingers.

She thrashes beneath me, her fingers curling into my hair as she bucks her hips and cries out with pleasure. I can feel her internal walls tightening around my fingers, her heels digging into my back, and her thighs tightening around my head until I almost can't breathe.

But I give her what she wants.

I don't let up.

My fingers pump inside of her in a steady, firm rhythm as I flick her clit with my tongue so fast that her whole body begins to tremble. Fuck, she's going to come soon and when she does I'm going to take my fill of her. But not yet. Not yet.

"Still my favourite colour," I murmur as my fingers still inside of her, and I press a kiss against her clit, savouring the moment, enjoying how she quakes beneath me.

"Sterling," she begs. "Don't stop."

"Look at you," I groan, my cock begging for relief as I remove my fingers and place the flat of my tongue against her hole. I hold it there, nudging the tip of my nose against her clit as she rocks her hips for some relief.

"Sterling, please!" she cries, her fingers yanking at my hair as she makes her needs known.

And I give her everything she desires, knowing that I will do anything to make her happy, to make her mine.

With colours tumbling behind my closed eyelids, I lick up

her slit over and over again, lapping at her like a starved animal. I don't care how feral this makes me look, how base, how fucking unhinged. I just give in to this animalistic desire and lap at her, slaking my thirst on her wetness, slipping my tongue into her core whilst my hands curl over her upper thighs.

"Like that... Oh God, Sterling, just like that!" she moans, her hips undulating against my face, seeking more stimulation.

My thumb finds her clit, my fingers spread out across her lower belly as I circle the tight bundle of nerves and fuck her hole with my tongue. I don't recognise the sounds emanating from my chest, all I know is that I won't stop until she comes apart screaming my name.

I won't stop until her body is lax from an orgasm, until her muscles are nothing but water, and even then I won't give her any respite, because I intend on pulling my cock free from the confines of these fucking trousers and impaling her on my dick.

"Sterling, Sterling, Sterling," she pants, and with every flick of my tongue, she climbs higher and higher until I suck her swollen clit into my mouth, forcing her over the edge.

With her hips jerking and her fingers gripping my hair tight, Harlow comes loudly, screaming my name and that makes me want to roar with pride, with *ownership*.

Every scream. Every cry of pleasure. Every moan, groan and whimper. They're all mine. I'm claiming them right here and now.

"Mine," I mutter against her pussy, pressing a gentle kiss against her clit as she releases my hair.

Her body goes lax, her muscles turning liquid as her legs slide from my shoulders and she lets out a soft breath. Gently, I place her feet on the fallboard, pressing a kiss against each knee. She needs a moment, and I'll give her one. But that's all she's getting. Just a moment, because we're not done. Hell, we're only just beginning.

Stepping back slightly, I reach for the button of my trousers, unhooking the clasp and unzipping them, before shoving both my trousers and boxers past my hips and down my legs, Harlow's cum seeping into the material, and scenting the air.

"Fuck," I groan, my cock springing free as I grip the base, giving it a squeeze as my gaze travels over the dips and curves of Harlow's body. She's draped across the lid of the piano like a decadent renaissance painting, her beautiful features painted with orgasmic bliss.

I can't wait to paint her like this.

"You're so damn beautiful," I say, bridging the gap between us, not willing to allow another moment to pass. I release my cock, kicking off my trousers and boxers.

Harlow stirs, pushing up onto her elbows, her hair mussed up and her cheeks flush as she gives me a heavy lidded smile. "That was—" she begins, but I cut her off as I grasp her hips in my palms and tug her towards me, lifting her off the piano and into my arms.

"Just the beginning," I finish for her, as she instinctively wraps her legs around my waist and I take one step back, dropping my arse to the stool. Her slick pussy slips down my chest, warmth seeping through my shirt from her wet heat.

"Sterling," she gasps, still sensitive, the friction making her judder.

"We're not done," I say, cupping her arse cheeks, keeping her core just above my bobbing cock as she looks down at me with a heady lust that has my balls tingling. "I'm going to fuck you now—"

Somewhere in the house a door slams.

Harlow stiffens, her head snapping towards the door. "Oh my God, Sterling. Who's that?" she gasps.

"Hello, Harlow are you here?"

"Is that...?" Harlow's face pales, her eyes widening. "It's my *mother*. Why is she here?"

The sound of heels clicking against the marble floor has Harlow scrambling off my lap. "No, no, no, no!" she hisses, frantically reaching for her clothes.

"Stay here. Get dressed, I'll head her off," I bite out, gathering my trousers and pulling them on. I quickly zip myself up, then snatch up my boxer shorts, shoving them into my pocket as I stride towards the door. Flicking my gaze over my shoulder I briefly watch as Harlow pulls on her clothes with shaky hands. Our gazes meet briefly, and hers are wide with terror.

"Fuck," I mutter, knowing that whatever plans I had have well and truly been thwarted.

For tonight at least.

TWENTY-FOUR

"Mom, Robert, why are you back so early? We weren't expecting you home until next week," I say, stepping into the living room, avoiding Sterling's gaze altogether as I greet my mother with a kiss to her cheek before stepping back. I reach for my hair, tucking the wayward strands behind my ear, praying that I don't look like I've just had the best orgasm of my life.

"If you'd bothered to listen to the messages I left you, you'd know that a storm was about to hit our resort so we decided to come home a little earlier," she snaps back as I flick my gaze to Robert who gives me a tight smile. Fuck, he looks pissed-off.

"Oh... I'm sorry. I was meaning to call you back but I've been a little busy."

"Too busy to take your mother's calls?" she retorts, folding her arms across her chest and scowling at me. "It could've been an emergency, Harlow! If we'd stayed it most certainly would've been!"

"It's my fault. I've been showing Harlow around Princetown," Sterling interjects, unruffled by the lie that slips off his tongue with ease.

How can he be so calm? It was only moments ago that he had his head between my legs. If we hadn't heard them... God, I can't even think about what could've happened.

"Is that so?" Robert asks, looking between us, an unreadable expression on his face before he turns his attention back to Sterling. "Did you take Harlow to the engagement party too?"

"No. I didn't go," I say, shaking my head.

"I see," Robert replies, and I can't tell whether he's happy about that or not.

"I didn't feel up for it, headache," I mumble.

"You could've made an effort and shown your face," my mother says with a huff. "What will people think? That's terribly rude, Harlow."

"How can it be rude not attending an engagement party that I wasn't even invited to?" I retort, anger unfurling in my chest.

"Of course you were invited," Robert says, glaring at Sterling as though it's his fault.

"No," I shake my head, hating that he assumes Sterling is at fault. "Mom called me a few nights ago to tell me all about Daisy and Dalton's engagement party and wedding, and the fact that I hadn't been invited."

Robert scowls. "Melody, is this true?"

My mother visibly blanches. "Harlow must have misunderstood. That isn't what I said at all."

No, of course it wasn't.

I bite back my retort and push down my disappointment, not wanting to start an argument. All I want to do is have a shower and go to bed. I can't deal with my mother right now, and I certainly don't think that I can stay in this room a moment longer trying to pretend that Sterling didn't just eat me out on top of the baby grand piano whilst I screamed out his name.

"Harlow?" Robert insists.

"Mom called in the middle of the night. I must have misheard because I was so tired," I lie.

"Exactly," my mother says, her shoulders dropping with relief.

"Besides, I'm sure I wouldn't have been missed."

Sterling opens his mouth as though to say something, but then changes his mind. Instead his mouth snaps shut and he throws me a heated look. My cheeks warm from the tension between us, at the way Sterling then glares at my mother. I told him what she'd said, and he believed me. Right now he looks like he's about to call her out on *her* lie.

"It's getting late, and I still have a headache. Would you mind if we catch up in the morning?" I quickly ask, hoping that everyone will decide to go to bed too.

My mother waves her hand in the air. "Yes, that's fine. I'm rather tired from all the travelling anyway." She turns her attention to Robert. "Darling, are you coming?"

"In a moment, there's something I need to discuss with Sterling," he says, leaning over and pressing a kiss against her cheek. "I'll follow shortly."

"Very well," she replies, striding past me without so much as a look, let alone wishing me a goodnight.

I watch her leave, suddenly feeling like I should stay. I don't like the way Robert is glaring at Sterling. Is he always this frosty towards him? Sterling had told me as much, but this is the first time I've truly experienced it, and it's horrible.

"Did you enjoy your honeymoon?" I ask Robert, trying to temper the growing tension and draw his attention towards me and away from Sterling.

"It was lovely, thank you for asking, Harlow," he replies, his gaze softening as he looks at me.

"I'm glad."

"However, I do really need to speak with Sterling..."

His voice trails off as he gives me a pointed look, and I know when I'm being dismissed. Even so, I cast a look at Sterling for any kind of sign that he wants me to stay, because despite feeling out of sorts, I will pull myself together so that he doesn't have to face his father alone. Besides, unless Robert is able to read our minds, there's no way he's aware of what's transpired between us. At least I hope not.

"Sterling?" I question, noticing a muscle feathering in his jaw.

"Goodnight, Harlow," he retorts, turning away from me and striding over to the bar in the corner of the room, dismissing me as well.

Sterling

Knocking back the generous glass of bourbon, I wait for my father to tell me what's on his mind, because I sure as fuck am not about to open the conversation and give him any ammunition to use against me. I know him too well—he's the type of person who waits for someone to hand him the rope, then stands back and lets them hang themselves with it.

"You've gotten over yourself then, I take it?" he asks, picking up the bottle of bourbon and pouring himself a glass as he eyes me with a neutral expression. I don't trust his intentions, not one fucking bit.

"If by gotten over myself you mean accepting Harlow into

this family, then yes, I guess I have," I reply evenly, refusing to rise to the bait.

He nods, swilling his bourbon before taking a sip. His expression relaxes, and to the untrained eye you'd be fooled into thinking he was content with my answer under the guise of wanting a *happy* family. But I know better. The subtle tightening around his eyes, the way his jaw ticks just slightly—it's all there, a carefully masked tension that warns me to tread carefully.

"I didn't expect you to still be here. Why haven't you returned to New York?" he asks, changing tactics.

"One of my closest friends is getting married in a few weeks. What would be the point?" I throw back. It's the best excuse I have, and it's the one I'm sticking with because I'm not about to tell him the real reason I'm staying. Not yet, anyway. He's not the only one who can play this game.

"Are you going back?"

"I haven't decided."

"I see."

The sheer fact that he doesn't push the subject has me on high alert. This conversation isn't about me returning to New York, this is about something else entirely. I wait, refusing to give him any rope to hang me with.

"So, Harlow..."

And there it is.

"What about her?" I ask, forcing myself not to react in any way.

"You didn't take her to the engagement party, why?" It's a loaded question, and we both know it. My father isn't a fool, he could tell something is up between us, but right now he isn't entirely sure what.

"She had a headache," I shrug, backing up her lie. "I wasn't going to force her when she was feeling unwell."

"Hmm," he mutters, taking a sip of his bourbon as he eyes me over the rim. "No hidden agenda?"

I didn't think he'd be so bold, but here we are. So, how do I play this? I could keep pretending that I'm okay with her being *family* or I could turn this discussion to my advantage, and throw him off track, which happens to play nicely into my plan because what Harlow needs most is *time*. Time to get to know me better, time to strengthen our bond, to become a united front, and if my dad thinks for one second that we like each other more than step-siblings should, he'll do everything in his power to end it, and destroy us both in the process.

I grit my jaw, allowing anger to seep into my features, pretending to snap. "I spent the whole fucking day with her yesterday, playing happy-fucking-families. Do you honestly think I'd *want* to take her to an engagement party too?" He lifts a brow, and I can tell he's not quite convinced so I add a nail to the coffin, hoping to fuck he buys it. "Mum called, *she* asked me to play nice. Though God knows why given you've treated her like shit and none of this bullshit has been easy on her. So, I played nice for *Mum*. But if you think I'm going to accept Harlow as my fucking step-sister, let alone Melody as a stand in for mum, you can think again. That's the first and last time I'm making an effort."

"I should've known your mother was involved. You've always been a *mama's boy*."

"It's a damn sight better than following in your footsteps," I throw back, allowing the familiar feelings of hate and disgust to seep into my voice. "Besides, I'm *not* the one with a hidden agenda."

"And what's that supposed to mean?" he bites, his mask slipping as he takes the bait.

"Why did you marry Melody?"

"Because I'm in love with her. That's what two people tend to do when they're in love."

I can't help it, I scoff. "Oh come on, we both know you're incapable."

He slams his glass onto the bar. "You'll do well not to antagonise me, son."

"What's your angle?" I push, cocking my head to the side. "It can't be Melody's money, given you have plenty of your own. Is it the status you'd gain from marrying a Hollywood starlet?" He opens his mouth to respond, but I hold my hand up, silencing him. "No, wait, it can't be that given *nothing* is comparable to what you've achieved in life. I mean, I could be invited to paint the Cistine-fucking-Chapel and that still wouldn't be good enough in your eyes, so I can't imagine starring in some two-bit nineties TV series would warrant your approval."

"Firstly, Melody's talent can hardly be compared to your..." He waves his hand in the air dismissively, "...*Sickness*."

I grit my teeth, feeling the sharp slice of pain I always do when he belittles me. I hate that he's still so easily able to hurt me, but I allow it because it only feeds into the lie I'm creating to protect me and Harlow.

He smirks. "And secondly, she's *Hollywood royalty, not* some wannabe artist who doesn't have the balls to showcase his work because he knows that the only person who'd buy it is his *mother*."

Fuck. Him.

"Are we done?" I snap.

"For now," he replies, smirking.

I stride towards the door but as I reach it, he calls out to me.

"One last thing, son," he says.

"What?" I reply, throwing him a glare over my shoulder.

"Whilst you're living under my roof, you will give Melody and Harlow the respect they deserve, you will treat them both with kindness, you will fucking act with grace and charm whenever you're around them, and you *will* spend time with Harlow playing happy-fucking-families whenever the fuck *I* tell you to."

"And if I don't?"

"Then your precious mother will find out what it's like to live as a fucking pauper when I stop paying her the rather generous monthly allowance she's become accustomed to."

My shoulders stiffen, and whilst his demands have given me the ability to spend time with Harlow without it throwing up any red flags, I don't like the fact that he's threatening my mother's happiness by taking away the money she's owed from marrying such a cold-hearted bastard. A knot tightens in my stomach, and I feel the weight of his words settling like lead in my chest. I've been walking this tightrope for years, always caught between loyalty to my mother and the disdain I have for him.

"You wouldn't dare."

His eyes narrow, studying me. "Just remember I will hit you where it hurts the most if you don't do as I fucking say. By refusing me, your mother suffers. All I want is peace in my house, and if this is the only way I'm going to get it, then so be it."

I nod, trying to ignore the simmering fury inside. *Peace?* This is nothing more than control, and he's not going to stop until he has it all. What he fails to realise is that neither will I, and more importantly, he has played right into my hands.

TWENTY-FIVE

"So, what exactly have you been doing whilst we've been away?" I hear Melody ask Harlow as I step into the kitchen a couple of days later. Harlow is making herself a coffee and her mother is leaning against the counter eyeing her with a mixture of frustration and disdain. "You know we have staff who can do that. Why do you insist on doing it yourself? I suppose you've been cleaning your own room too?"

"Because I want to," Harlow replies tightly, her back to me. "It's just a cup of coffee, and yes, as a matter of fact I have. I don't need anyone to wait on me hand and foot."

"You always did love Cinderella. I never could quite understand why the prince would marry a pauper when he could've had his pick," Melody scoffs, and her meaning is clear. God, what a bitch.

"Pretty sure the prince married Cinderella because she was the only woman who *didn't* want to marry him for his money or for notoriety," I remark darkly as I scowl at Melody, before resting my gaze on Harlow. "Plus she was fucking beautiful inside and out."

Harlow gasps and Melody visibly pales before she waves her hand in the air with a fake smile.

"You know what I meant."

"Oh I know *exactly* what you meant."

Melody clears her throat as she slowly drifts her gaze from my face to my bare chest, then to my workout shorts, before trailing her eyes back up again. "Did you sleep well?" Her voice lowers a few octaves, as she blatantly checks me out. Does this woman not have any shame?

"I've been up a few hours already, working out," I say, reaching for the towel chucked over my shoulder and swiping at the beads of sweat gathering on my forehead.

"Yes, you have been, haven't you?" Melody replies, her brow arching as her gaze flickers with appreciation. I try not to throw up on my feet.

"I was about to take a swim, then head into the sauna, but I think I might grab a coffee first," I say, heading towards the counter. There's no fucking way I'm leaving Harlow alone with this bitch.

Harlow peers at me over the rim of her cup as she watches me approach, and I can't help but notice the flicker of both desire *and* fear in her gaze. Thank fuck her mother is looking the other way.

"Well, there's plenty here," Melody says, waving her hand in the direction of the coffee machine. "Perhaps Harlow can pour you a cup seeing as she's so insistent on playing housemaid."

"Like Harlow, I prefer to get my own coffee," I bite back, wanting to prove to Melody that, unlike her, I also don't need to be waited on, but the insinuation is lost on her as she continues to ramble on.

"... Your darling father has arranged for a spa day for me at the hotel whilst he catches up on some business. I'm rather looking forward to relaxing. Harlow, you couldn't be a darling could you, and take a look at the emails my agent sent? I think she wants Robert and I to do an interview with one of the national newspapers next week. Oh, and I really think that you should be getting back to work too. Just because I've been away on honeymoon doesn't mean you should be slacking."

"*Slacking?*" Harlow tenses, her mouth opening as though she wants to say something to the bitch. *Please, Harlow, just tell her to fuck off.* Instead, she just sighs. "Sure, I'll take a look."

"It'll do you good to get back to work instead of moping around the place, and doing jobs that other people have been paid to do," Melody says, only adding insult to injury.

Fuck me, if this woman says one more nasty comment I'm going to lose my shit. Instead, I grit my teeth, and grab a cup from the cupboard, reminding myself that I have to curb my thoughts right now despite how much it pains me to do so.

"Excuse me," I murmur, stepping in between Harlow and Melody as I help myself to some coffee. Harlow edges out of the way, making a point of not looking at me, and it's taking a great deal of effort not to reach out and pull her in for a hug. She sure looks like she could use one, and I know I certainly do.

Fuck, it's hard not to act on my desires, and whilst I've purposefully stayed out of her way these past couple of days after my conversation with my father, this morning, admittedly, I had hoped to get a few moments alone with her. There are things we need to discuss.

"Perfect, well, I'll leave you to it," Melody replies, pressing her fingertips against my arm. It's all I can do not to jerk away from her touch, which lingers a lot longer than necessary. "Actually, Robert was looking for you. He's in his study. I was heading there myself."

"I'll drink this first," I say, giving her room to pass.

"I think it was rather urgent," she insists when I make no move to go with her, and instead lean against the kitchen island.

"I'm sure it can wait a few more minutes," I cut out, my patience slipping.

She looks at me, her eyes narrowing a little before she nods her head. I get the distinct impression that she's not used to being defied. "Well, I'll tell him you'll be along shortly. Have a nice day, won't you?" she says directly to me, ignoring Harlow entirely.

With one last smile, which I don't bother to return, she leaves.

"Harlow," I begin, my voice rough as I reach for her arm.

Her gaze drops to my hand, heat spreading across her cheeks. "I don't think this is a good idea," she whispers, tensing beneath my touch.

"We need to talk," I snap, my lingering anger at her mother making my request sound harsher than I'd intended. "Why the fuck do you let her speak to you like that?"

She jerks her head up, eyes widening at the anger in my tone, and try as I might I can't seem to dampen it enough to make her relax in my presence. I'm not angry at her, not at all. I'm angry at her mother for being such a bitch. I'm just about to tell her as much when I hear said bitch's voice echoing along the hallway.

"Darling, I was just telling Sterling that you were looking for him."

Harlow tenses, and I withdraw my hand.

"Fuck sake," I mutter.

She looks at me, fear dancing across her flushed face as our parent's exchange small talk, but I don't have any time to put her at ease before my father strides into the room a few moments later.

"There you are," he says, eyeing me, his brow lifting as he notices my state of relative undress.

"Here I am," I reply, taking a sip of my coffee as Harlow shifts on her feet beside me.

I'm not sure if she's uncomfortable because of the tension between us, if it's because her mother just talked to her like she's a piece of shit, or that my father isn't bothering to hide his annoyance as he glares at me.

"I've been meaning to have a conversation with you, but it seems you've been avoiding all of *us*," he remarks, the warning to his tone not going unnoticed.

If he knew the real reason I've been keeping myself out of the way, I'm sure this would be a very different conversation right now. Instead, I shrug. "I've been busy. What do you want?"

"Too busy to spend time with your *family*?" he asks, giving me a pointed look. "I'm sure Harlow would've appreciated you making an effort. Wouldn't you, Harlow?"

"And I'm sure Harlow has better things to do with her time than hanging around with me. Right, Harlow?" I retort, throwing her a look that can only be interpreted one way.

She flinches at the carefully constructed hostility, and I feel like a fucking prick. But I'm doing this to protect her. If I'm too eager to spend time with her then his suspicions will be aroused, but if I don't show at least some annoyance or resentment at being forced to play happy families then that'll only add to his suspicions. Either way, it's a fine line I have to walk, and believe me I'm teetering on the edge. I'm not sure how long I can do this before I make my true feelings known.

"It's fine," she mumbles. "I've been busy catching up on some emails. Mom mentioned that her agent wants you to attend an interview together..." Her voice trails off as he scowls.

"Absolutely not. Any interviews that we do together I will decide upon."

"Of course," Harlow whispers, wincing at the tone of his voice.

"Please forward me the details as soon as you have a moment," he adds with a patient smile, that mask he loves to wear slotting into place. Harlow's shoulders relax a little, and I hate that she doesn't see through his pretence.

"Sure. Um, okay," Harlow replies.

"Perfect. Now, back to the point at hand," he says, focussing his attention on me. "Sterling a word."

"In a minute. I'm just having this coffee, spending time with Harlow. That's what *you* want isn't it?" I reply, making no move to leave. Out of the corner of my eye I notice Harlow curl in on herself, her shoulders rounding, and not for the first time I feel like an absolute cunt.

"It's fine. I'll go," she says.

My father's nostrils flare sensing her unease as he fires me another filthy look. "Finish your coffee, then come see me in my office," he commands, before striding out of the kitchen.

I wait a few moments before turning to Harlow who looks about ready to bolt. "Harlow," I begin.

"You probably shouldn't antagonise him," she replies, placing her coffee on the counter as she takes a step away from me.

"He'll survive, but I'm not sure I will if you don't give me a moment of your time," I say softly, placing my own cup of coffee on the counter and stepping towards her.

"You don't have to feel like you should be spending time with me," she replies, and there's no hiding the hurt in her voice.

"Harlow, that isn't–"

She holds her hand up, shaking her head. "I know what I heard."

"That isn't what I meant," I reply, my fingers curling into fists in frustration. Fuck, I don't want to make her feel unwanted. That's the last thing I want.

"But it *is* what you said," she counters, clearly hurt.

"Harlow, listen," I say, taking another step towards her, but she steps away from me again, and just when I'm about to haul her into my arms, something beeps loudly.

Harlow's hand flies to her back pocket, and she pulls out her phone as though grateful for the interruption. Her gaze drops to the screen and I'm tempted to snatch the phone out of her hands and throw it across the room for interrupting us, but when her thumb slides over the screen and her eyes widen, I hesitate.

"What is it?" I ask, noticing how her face pales. She jerks her head up, her gaze meeting mine. "Harlow, what is it?" I press, hating the panicked look in her eyes. God, I've royally fucked-up here.

"Nothing..." she replies quickly, pocketing her phone.

"Harlow," I warn, but she takes two strides away from me, rounding the kitchen island, preventing me from grabbing her arm and forcing her to answer me.

"It's just a work thing. I should go," she says before she practically runs from the room, almost knocking into Stephanie as she leaves.

"Sorry," Harlow mutters, then disappears.

"What on earth?" Stephanie exclaims, startled. She gives me a round-eyed stare, and I swipe a hand over my face.

"*Fuck!*"

<hr>

Harlow

In the privacy of my room I stare at the message on my phone, my stomach churning. After I responded the last time telling whoever this arsehole is to leave me alone, I hadn't heard anything back. I'd thought that he'd given up, or at the very least hoped he'd gotten bored, a part of me had selfishly hoped that he'd found someone else to bother.

But I was wrong.

> I can't leave you alone. I've tried. But how can I do that when we belong together, you and I? I'm already so close to making you mine, and when we're finally together, you'll sing for me every day my sweet songbird. Perhaps I'll even build you a cage?

As I stare at the message, my eyes blurring with tears, another message pops up. This one is worse than the last.

> Do you like my nickname for you? I thought it was apt. Then again, you go by Friday, don't you? Or perhaps I should call you by your real name, Harlow...

I let out a cry of fear, dropping the phone to the floor.
He knows who I am.

TWENTY-SIX

"You're doing what?" my mother asks, her voice shrill as she narrows her eyes at me.

I drag in a steady breath, trying my best not to lose it in front of Robert and Sterling who are finishing off their meal as we sit in the dining room together. I'm feeling extra out of sorts today after receiving that latest message from my stalker, and the last thing I need is a confrontation with my mother.

"Ben asked me to cover for Princetown Bandits who are in London right now. It's no big deal," I explain, refusing to feel intimidated by her obvious disapproval of me singing tonight.

"You're singing at Benedict Pike's *bar?*" she repeats incredulously.

"Yes, Mom."

This is the third time I've reminded her this week, but it's as if she has a switch that turns off her attention whenever the conversation isn't about her. God knows I've spent the entire week listening to her talk about her honeymoon, her plans to renovate the mansion's south wing, how she's going to buy a horse with Robert tomorrow, and how far behind I've got with my work.

The truth is, even if I wasn't performing tonight, I would probably be out somewhere drinking to settle my nerves and numb my frustration. My patience has been pushed to its limits, not just by my mother, but also from trying to hide my feelings for Sterling. Since our parents returned home from their honeymoon, he has been pretending like we haven't been intimate on numerous occasions, and worse, acting like a jerk. I understand the need for secrecy, of course I do, but his coldness towards me is unexpected, and has been like a knife to my heart, especially after everything he'd said.

"I wish you'd told us earlier," Robert interjects. "We would have both loved to hear you sing again, wouldn't we Melody?"

I don't bother to tell him that I had told my mom on several occasions.

My mother's scowl drops as she evens her features and gives him a smile that most definitely doesn't reach her eyes. "We've already confirmed to the Olderburys that we're dining with them this evening. We can't cancel now."

Robert nods. "Indeed. Perhaps another time?"

I mumble something in response before pushing back from my seat as I stand. "I should probably get going. Ben wanted me to arrive a little earlier to set up..." My voice trails off as I look at Sterling. He runs a hand through his hair, avoiding looking at me.

"Sterling, you will accompany Harlow," Robert demands.

"I have plans," he cuts back, and I can't help but flinch at his response.

He's been like this all week whenever we've been around each other. Apart from that brief moment in the kitchen the other day when he'd stuck up for after my mom was being her usual bitchy self, he has acted with the same kind of disinterest. It's like he's a different person, and I'm reeling from it.

"It's fine," I mumble.

"Your plans have changed, Sterling," Robert cuts back, a note of warning in his voice. "Take Harlow to Bandits Bar. Stay for the performance. Then bring her home safely."

Sterling huffs out a breath, then stands. "It would be my pleasure," he replies sarcastically, plastering on a smile that would ordinarily make me melt, but instead makes me feel cold inside.

Was everything he said to me a lie? God, I feel so foolish.

I cringe. "It's fine," I repeat. "I can take a cab there and back."

"Absolutely not," Robert snaps. "I shan't have my step-daughter entering Bandits Bar unaccompanied–"

"Harlow is a grown woman, she doesn't need a chaperone," my mother interjects, but I get the distinct impression it isn't to support my right to travel without someone babysitting me, and more about Robert showing concern for my well-being. Which he has been doing a lot of lately. It's confusing given everything Sterling has told me about his father, but right now he's the only one who seems to give a damn about my happiness.

"Sterling will take Harlow, and that's the end of it," Robert replies, brooking no arguments.

"Then let's go," Sterling adds, striding around the dining table and heading towards the door.

When I don't immediately follow, he turns around and says, "Are you coming?"

"See you both later?" I ask, flicking my gaze between Robert and my mother, feeling more than a little awkward as Sterling glares at me impatiently.

"Actually, we'll be staying at the Olderbury's tonight. Stuart is accompanying us both to the breeders tomorrow, he is quite the equine expert according to Robert," my mother trills, her voice pitching with excitement.

"I'll see you tomorrow some time then," I reply before following Sterling out.

A couple of minutes later we're climbing into Sterling's silver Tesla, the air thick with tension as he drives us down the private road that runs through the grounds of Adaga Hall and onto the main thoroughfare.

"Harlow," he begins, the tone of his voice apologetic.

"It's fine. I get it," I reply, waving my hand in the air between us. "Next time I'll just get a cab."

"That's not what I was about to say," he says, reaching over and palming my knee, squeezing gently. My body instantly reacts, and I hate that my cheeks flush from his touch.

"Then what is it?" I ask, willing my pulse to calm down.

"It has to be this way right now," he continues, his thumb gently rubbing circles over my jean clad thighs.

"Treating me as though you hate me?" I ask, feeling the pinch of my unhappiness sharpening my response.

"You know I don't hate you, Harlow."

"Do I? You've barely said a word to me since our parents came home, and any time we've been in the same room it's as though it's torturous for you."

"It *is* torturous!" he shouts, causing anger to bubble inside my own chest.

"I'm so sorry to be such a fucking burden!" I yell.

"A burden? You're not a burden. Damn it, Harlow. I'm trying to protect you!"

"Protect me?" My pulse quickens as he flashes me an agonised look. "I thought you didn't want me anymore."

"No! Fuck, no! Of *course,* I want you."

Sterling releases my thigh and presses his foot on the gas, only to turn the wheel sharply to the left at a small road a minute later, leading to what looks like a secluded picnic area. Parking the car, he pulls up the handbrake, switches off the lights, but keeps the engine running. The outside world is pitched into darkness, the only light coming from the full moon that's shining brightly in the night sky.

"Sterling what are you doing?"

"I *want* you Harlow," he says, unhooking his seat belt and turning to face me.

"But–"

"I want you," he repeats, reaching over the centre console and cupping my cheek, the heat from his palm instantly soothing. "If our parents hadn't walked in on us, I would've continued to show you how fucking much. I've been acting the way I have to throw my father off. He suspected something."

"He knows about us?" I ask, eyes widening.

"If he knew the truth, there's no fucking way he'd insist on me spending time with you. My father hates to see me happy."

"I don't understand."

"That night when they returned home from their honeymoon, and my father wanted to speak with me, I pretended that I disliked you so he wouldn't know the truth. I told him that I didn't want to play happy families and in return he threatened to cut my mother off, saying he would stop paying her monthly allowance following their divorce if I refused."

"He did what?" My mouth drops open as Sterling's gaze fills with a mixture of anger and pain.

"This is what he does, Harlow. He uses what you love most against you. I've had to act this way so he doesn't suspect the depths of my feelings for you. If I were too eager to spend time with you, he'd know. This way he thinks he's forcing me to spend time with you, when in actual fact it's *all* I want."

"God, I'm sorry," I say, my anger retreating as quickly as it came.

"Don't be. None of this is your doing. Do you hear me? None. This is the first opportunity I've had to speak to you about this without either your mother or my father interrupting us. But that isn't an excuse. I should've found a way to get you alone to explain."

"I shouldn't have jumped to conclusions. It's just hard for me to believe that..." *You actually care*, but I don't say that out loud. Instead I sigh.

"You think after everything that I said to you, that I would willingly hurt you? Do you really think that I don't want to tell your mother where to stick her nasty comments, or wrap you in my arms and protect you from them? Harlow, I meant everything that I said. Just bare with me, okay?"

"So what are we then?" I ask after a beat, needing to know what this is exactly. I feel so out of my depth, and I've no idea how we move forward. There's so much stacked against us.

"What do you want us to be?" he replies, leaning closer as he brushes his lips against mine.

"Each other's?" I offer. It's the best I can do. We can't be official in any capacity, so it's not as if I can call him my boyfriend, but we're more than lovers, that much is becoming abundantly clear.

"Yes, we are. But for now, in secret, okay?" he says, brushing his lips against mine.

"Okay," I agree, sighing against his lips, wishing we didn't have to hide. "What about your friends? What are you going to tell them?"

"They already know how I feel about you," Sterling

answers. "But at this stage it's too risky to let them know any more than that. As far as they're concerned I want you, but that's it. I'm not going to tell them that we're together. Not yet, anyway."

I frown. "You don't trust them?"

"It's not about me not trusting them. I don't trust my father, and if he suspects anything, they'll be the first people he'll put pressure on. They've got enough going on in their own lives right now. The last thing they need is my father's attention."

"What if I were to talk to Robert?"

He shakes his head, his fingers digging into my scalp, as his eyes flash with concern. "Absolutely not. No, Harlow."

"But maybe I could—"

"I know you think you have a good relationship with him," he says, cutting me off, "But, Harlow, please believe me when I say that he has no redeeming qualities. None. You have to trust me on this."

"Okay," I reply, understanding his reasoning but feeling more than a little uncertain, not about how I feel for Sterling– I'm past the point of fighting this–but because his father seemingly holds so much power.

"I'm sorry," he says softly, sensing my discomfort. "It won't always be like this. Once I've figured out how to deal with my father, we can be open about our relationship."

I nod, trying to brush off the uneasy feeling in my chest as he presses a tender kiss against my lips, a kiss that soon turns heated.

"Harlow," he groans against my mouth, his hand dropping to cup my throat in the way I like. "Fuck, Harlow. All I want to do right now is strip you naked and bury myself inside of you."

"I want that too. But we really should go," I reply, every single part of me wanting to give myself over to him, to find comfort in his arms but I reluctantly place my hand against his chest and gently ease him back. "Ben is expecting me."

"What time is he expecting you?"

"In about twenty minutes," I reply.

"Then we have at least ten minutes to spare," he says, his voice husky as he grips my throat a little tighter.

"Sterling, we're in the middle of nowhere," I protest weakly, my pulse spiking even more.

"Exactly. There's no one here but us, Harlow."

"Sterling–"

He slams his mouth against mine, cutting off my protest.

I don't fight it.

Kissing Sterling is like drowning and floating all at once. I can't breathe, and that isn't because he's giving me a hand necklace, it's because he makes me feel lightheaded with his lust-filled groans and talented tongue. When we kiss I forget about our parents, about my arsehole stalker. I'm lost to his heat, his desire and my own spiralling need. Groaning, he pulls back slightly, then reaches around my side, pressing a button that has my seat slowly edging backwards.

"What are you doing?" I whisper, my clit throbbing just from the way he's looking at me.

"I'm making the most of the next ten minutes," he replies, releasing my throat, and reaching for the zipper of my jeans, undoing them. "Did I tell you how fucking incredible you look in these jeans?"

"You just did," I reply softly, gasping as he slides his fingers beneath the waistband of my panties, knowing that he'll find me soaking for him.

"Fuck, Harlow. Are you always this ready to be fucked?" he groans, his finger slipping between my folds and swiping against my sensitive clit.

"Not usually, not for anyone but you," I admit. Around Sterling I'm in a perpetual state of arousal. I'm so attracted to him, it's ridiculous. I've spent most nights bringing myself to orgasm just thinking about him touching me, tasting me, *fucking* me.

"Damn straight," he replies, focusing his gaze on me as he gently strokes my clit. "This pussy is mine. You're mine, Harlow."

I gasp at his possessive words, at how he so easily makes me melt beneath his touch. God knows I've tried to fight this. I've tried to be a good daughter. I've tried to do the right thing. He's my step-brother, he's off-limits, and yet knowing that turns me on even more. It shouldn't. I know it shouldn't, and logically my head tells me that we met before we became family, but I have to admit to myself, to the deepest, darkest parts of me, that it only makes me want him more.

"Tell me you're mine. Tell me that you'll never let another man touch you like this. Tell me that there is no one else for you, that from this point onwards we are each other's, no matter what."

But his fingers are so talented, his gaze so intense, that I can't seem to bring myself to answer as he teases my clit. I'm too lost in the overwhelming need to give myself over to him, to receive the pleasure that he's so determined to give me, and that I'm more than willing to accept.

"Harlow, tell me!" he demands, his whole hand cupping my pussy possessively.

There isn't much give beneath the confines of my jeans, and the heel of his hand is firm against my clit, making me moan loader.

"Harlow," he insists.

"Yes, Sterling," I groan, rocking my hips as I search for

relief. My eyelids flutter shut as I whimper, "I'm yours. We're each other's, no matter what."

"You've left out an important part," he adds with a growl, my eyes snapping open as he leans over me, his face inches from mine. It's so dark, and he's so close that I can barely make out his features as the moon slips behind a swathe of cloud. "If you want to come you need to promise me that there will *never* be anyone else."

"There won't!" I cry, so close to coming that I'm panting.

"Promise me!"

"I promise. There will never be anyone else. Only you. Just you!"

He nods sharply then his mouth crashes against mine as he shoves two fingers inside of me with one firm thrust.

I come apart, an orgasm rushing outwards from my core in a shockwave of intense pleasure that makes me shudder and shake. He swallows my cry, kissing me roughly, his fingers still pumping inside of me, coated in my cum. Sterling drags out every last drop of my orgasm until I have to twist my head to the side and suck in much needed oxygen.

"And I promise that I will never look at another woman as long as I live," he states, nipping my earlobe as he withdraws his hand and captures my jaw with his sticky fingers.

Slowly, he turns my head to face him, and through the fog of lust, and lingering pleasure, I'm rewarded with a smile so pure, so brilliantly beautiful that my heart swells with something more than lust, something more than like, something that feels close to love.

"Good," I reply softly, accepting the gentle brush of his lips against my own before he leans over me, and presses the button that makes my seat shift upright once again.

"We should probably get going," he says with a rueful grin, as he settles back into his seat and clips in his seatbelt.

"What about you?" I ask, my gaze dropping to his crotch and his erection.

"Our parents aren't home tonight, so I was planning on accompanying you to your room and having my wicked way with you," he retorts, flipping the headlights back on as he puts the car into gear.

I bite on my lip, my cheeks flushing a deeper pink at the thought. "Then I hope you'll let me return the favour," I say, thoughts of his thick dick shoved so far down my throat that I'm choking on it.

"The favour?" he cocks his head, grinning.

My eyes flick to his erection once again, and I lick my lips. "I haven't tasted you yet," I reply.

His eyes widen. "Fuck, Harlow, are you trying to make me come in my pants?"

"I'd rather you come inside of me," I deadpan.

"Jesus-fucking-Christ," he grumbles, gripping the steering wheel tightly. "Do we *have* to go to Bandits Bar?"

I can't help it, I laugh. "I'm afraid I promised, and I happen to keep my promises."

"Fine, fuck. Let's do this."

I settle into my seat, smiling to myself as Sterling manoeuvres the car so that we're heading back out onto the main road, the headlamps momentarily lighting up a dirt track that cuts through a bank of tall pinewood trees. I notice that it's wide enough for a vehicle to pass through.

"Where does that lead?" I ask, pointing in the direction of the partially hidden road.

"That leads to Craven Mount-Black's estate," Sterling replies.

"That's a name straight out of a historical romance novel if ever there was one," I reply, eyebrows hitching.

"I don't think Craven has left his estate in years, let alone in a relationship as far as I'm aware. That man is not 'social'. Rumour has it he prefers animals to humans."

"Colour me intrigued," I reply. Sterling flicks me a look, his brow hitching as I grin at him. "What?

"Actually you met his nephew, Blake."

"Wait, Craven Mount-Black is Blake's uncle, the *taxidermist*,?" I ask, eyes wide.

"Yes, and extremely wealthy. Years ago my father once tried to do business with him, but Craven refused, and he's been an outcast ever since. Not that I imagine he cares. Like I said, he barely leaves his estate, preferring his own company for the most part. Frankly, I don't blame him. The whole billionaire circuit is fucking draining to be a part of."

"So Blake is his only family or does Craven have any other relatives?" I ask as we head out onto the main road, towards town.

"As far as I'm aware, yes. Blake's dad passed away a few years ago which actually makes Blake heir to the Craven-Black fortune. Ben told me that when Blake arrived in town a couple years ago Craven set him up with a job at *The Cosy Chord*, and bought him a house in Princetown. Blake's mother was so heartbroken from his father's death that she took her own life. Craven is all the family he has left. Though I don't think they have a particularly good relationship from what I've heard."

"That's terrible," I reply. "Poor Blake."

"Don't feel too sorry for him, that flirtatious bastard uses the orphan angle to get women into bed," Sterling replies, pressing his foot on the gas as we speed towards the centre of town.

"Sterling, I'm sure that isn't true! He seemed lovely when I met him."

"Just ask Ben, he'll tell you the same. Anyway, let's get off the subject," he says, shooting me a look that tells me he's still a little put out that I spent time with Blake a few days ago. "What songs are you planning on singing tonight?"

For the rest of the short drive I reel off my playlist. All of them covers, and every single one having some kind of meaning for me.

"You're singing True Colours by Cindy Lauper?" he repeats, side-eyeing me briefly.

"Yes, why? You don't like that song?"

"On the contrary," he replies softly. "I happen to love that song."

TWENTY-SEVEN

It's the early hours of the morning by the time I reach Harlow's bedroom. Her lights are off, and I can hear her soft breathing as I slip inside her bedroom. I had every intention of going to bed with her the moment we got back from the bar, but my synesthesia had other ideas. Instead, I made up an excuse that I wasn't feeling well, and that I'd see her in the morning. Which was partly the truth, at least.

She hadn't been able to hide her disappointment, and yet again I'd felt like a prick for lying to her. I know that I should just tell her about my condition once and for all but right now, despite everything I know to be true about Harlow, I'm still uncertain as to whether she'd accept my synesthesia and how it affects me when so many other people haven't. It's unfair of me to make that assumption, but I'm just not ready to reveal that side of me, especially since my studio is filled to the brim with paintings of her in varying degrees of undress.

My obsession aside, I wasn't in a fit state to have any kind of conversation with Harlow, let alone confessing my sins about painting my cum onto her image. Frankly, I was so consumed by the colours her voice had conjured, that I'd barely managed to get us home safely. Now that I've purged myself of them, by spending the last few hours painting another image of Harlow, I'm more able to think straight. And, selfishly, the only thought I had was finding comfort in her arms. Her presence brings me peace, and I know I have no right to search for that when I'm keeping such a huge part of me hidden, but here I am.

Crossing the room as quietly as possible, I strip naked, placing my clothes on the armchair in the corner of her room before sliding into bed behind her. She's so deep asleep that even when I curl my body around hers, she doesn't stir.

"Harlow?" I whisper, wanting to apologise, wanting to tell her everything.

Her body is warm and relaxed as she shifts in her sleep, and I press my lips against the curve of her neck, dragging in her scent through my nose. Despite feeling the exhaustion I usually do after an episode, my cock hardens against her arse.

"You sang so beautifully tonight," I mutter, my palm settling against her stomach, feeling the soft rise and fall as she breathes. "I'm so sorry I didn't tell you that."

More guilt climbs up my spine. I'd been concentrating so hard on not crashing the car on the way back from the bar that I hadn't even told her how fucking incredible she was. After everything we'd discussed earlier in the evening, I can't imagine how hurtful that must've been.

"When you sang True Colours, it felt like every word was meant for me, Harlow," I confess, my fingers tracing patterns over her stomach. It's too dark to see what she's wearing, but her legs and arms are bare, and her top has risen enough for me to know that it's a shorts sleep set rather than a nightie.

My balls tighten, and I can't help but gently grind my cock

against her arse. She shifts again, her breath releasing in a soft sigh, and I press my lips against her ear. "Wake up, my little poet."

For a beat I keep still, waiting for the moment when she realises that I'm in bed with her, but just like before she remains deeply asleep.

"I don't know if I can stop," I say, my palms sliding up the centre of her chest until my fingers cup her throat. The soft beat of her pulse, and the gentle rise and fall of her chest only adding to the indescribable need to bury myself inside of her. "You consume me, Harlow."

Releasing her throat, I slide my hand back downwards, my fingers dust over her stomach just above the waistband of her sleep shorts. I should stop. I should wake her instead. I should confess my secrets, but my body has other ideas.

Right at the moment I'm about to slip my hand beneath her sleep shorts, she shifts beside me, rolling onto her stomach, the side of her face pressed into the pillow beneath her head.

"Harlow, are you awake?" I question, pushing off the duvet as I rise up onto my knees beside her. A shard of moonlight penetrates the gap in her curtains, and I notice that her hair has fallen over her face.

Straddling her, I hover above her arse, my knees pressed into the mattress either side of her hips as I lean forward and gently push her hair off her face. She lets out another soft sigh, her lips slightly parted, her eyelashes feathering against her cheeks. Unable to stop myself, I lean over and kiss her temple, willing her to wake up.

"Harlow, I need you," I say, my voice hoarse, thick with desire.

But when I pull back she merely mutters something indistinguishable and I'm left with a decision. I could settle back beside her, go to sleep, and wait until morning to sink inside of her, or I could give in to my darkest desires and take her now.

The darkness wins out.

I carefully move down the bed, pushing off the duvet covering and making room to remove her sleep shorts without disturbing her. My heart pounds in my chest as I gingerly wrap my fingers around the waistband and slowly slide the fabric off her hips and thighs. As the material reaches her knees, I shift my position to kneel beside her, easing the shorts off her legs and feet. She stirs slightly in her sleep, and I wait until her breathing becomes steady again. My entire body trembles with nerves as I finish the task, but when she shows no signs of waking, I know she is still sound asleep

"Are you wet for me, my little poet?" I ask, slowly trailing my fingers up her inner thighs. Her legs are parted slightly, allowing me to slip my fingers between her thighs to find out.

"Fuck, you are," I breathe, my cock swelling with more blood as I finger her gently from behind.

When her hips start to rock, and a sweet moan releases from her lips, I can't stop myself from easing her legs apart until the gap is wide enough for me to kneel between them.

A small voice in the back of my head is telling me to stop, to at the very least wake her up, but that night when I'd eaten her out on the piano, she'd told me she wanted me to ravish her, and in response I'd warned her that I was going to creep into her room, slide inside of her and fuck her awake, and that's exactly what I'm going to do.

As gently as possible I lower my hips, holding the top half of my body up on outstretched arms as the underside of my cock rests against her crack. I leave it there momentarily as I drag in a breath, my arms shaking from the effort of not giving in and slamming my dick inside of her.

"Harlow, I'm going to fuck you now," I warn, and this time my voice isn't quiet.

Something shifts in the air, and I hear Harlow's breath catch just as I adjust my hips, the crown of my cock slipping through her folds and grazing her entrance.

"Sterling?" she questions, her voice breathy, needy, *alert*.

I tense, breathing hard. Fucking trembling. "I'm here, Harlow," I manage to utter.

"You came."

"I'm about too," I blurt out, my fucking mouth running away from me. Then I realise exactly what that means. "Fuck. I'm not wearing a condom!"

What the fuck was I thinking? Jesus Christ, I'm an arsehole. I move to pull away, guilt, shame, lust, desire, agony and desperation all swirling inside my chest.

"Don't stop," she begs, reaching back, her fingers grazing my hip as she tugs me towards her.

"What?" I gasp, the tip of my cock penetrating her hole just a little. It's all I can do not to come there and then.

"I'm on the pill. I'm clean. Don't stop," she begs, her nails digging into my skin slightly before her hands fall away.

"I am too," I reply.

"Good, now fuck me, Sterling. I *need* you."

I don't need to be told twice. With one powerful thrust, I slam into her, sheathing myself right up to the hilt. "Harlow!" I cry, her thready gasp and tight, slick pussy making my eyes roll back into my head.

"Oh my God, Sterling!" she groans into the pillow, her legs parting further as she gives me better access.

"I'm sorry," I say, not for fucking her awake, but for not complimenting her on her singing, for not telling her about my synesthesia, for being so obsessed about her that I've painted my cum into her image on canvas, for keeping the darkest parts of me secret from her.

"I'm not," she replies, misunderstanding me. "I've been waiting for you."

"I meant–"

"Please, Sterling. Just squeeze my throat with your beautiful hand, and fuck me."

"Jesus, Harlow," I exclaim, my voice strained as I lay my body over hers, slip my arm beneath her chest, wrap my fingers around her throat, and fuck her.

With every shunt of my hips, Harlow's internal walls clench tightly as though trying to pull me deeper inside her body. Even though I'm the one with almost my entire weight on her back, I feel as though I'm being completely engulfed by her.

She might feel ravished by the carnality of this act, from the frantic fucking as our skin meets and I pound into her with uncontrolled movements. She might be gasping for air and simultaneously moaning as I gently squeeze and release her throat. Her body might feel slick as my cock slams inside of her tight, wet heat, and our skin glistens with sweat.

But I'm just as consumed by her.

I'm so fucking gone for this woman.

I'm as sure of that as I am of my affection for her.

Fuck that, this isn't just affection or attraction. This is more. This is obsession. This is adoration. This is possession, veneration.

This is love.

I love Harlow Richards.

I may have only known her for a short period of time, but that means nothing to me. I don't live by the same rules as everyone else. I've spent my whole damn life suppressing my feelings, trying to hide who I am, and being forced to conform to society's norms. But I refuse to suppress this feeling a second fucking longer.

That realisation has me rearing upwards and taking her with me, our bodies still joined as she follows the movement until I'm sitting on my haunches and she's spread over my thighs, her knees pressed into the mattress, her back to my chest and her slit stretched open wide, my cock buried deep. Fuck, I wish we were positioned in front of a mirror so that I could see how that looks. For now my imagination will have to do.

"Sterling, please," she cries, the sound of my name on her lips is a fucking beautiful melody all of its own.

"You want it like this?" I grind out, my arms wrapped around her chest to keep her steady as I thrust up into her over and over, and she meets every thrust by slamming her hips against me.

"Yes," she hisses, her hands flying upwards as she tangles her fingers into my hair and tugs.

"Deeper, harder, Sterling. Don't hold back," she whimpers, and my balls draw up so tight against my body that for a moment black spots dance in front of my eyes.

"Then get on your hands and knees, Harlow," I demand, unwrapping my arms from around her chest, and pushing forward. She braces her hands on the mattress, my dick still inside of her as I raise one leg, my foot pressed into the mattress by her knee. Then, I reach forward and gather her hair in my grasp, thrusting into her, my fingers bruising her hip as I lose control.

I rut into her with deep, powerful strokes, and she takes every single one of them, pushing back against my hips just as roughly.

"I'm going to come!" she screams.

"Then come for me, Harlow," I plead, my movements more

and more uncontrolled as my eyes start to roll back in my head. "Let me feel you shatter around me. I want you to break apart. Fuck, I need you to come for me. I can't take any more, please just come!"

"Oh, oh, oh, ohhhhhh," she cries, her body tensing, her breath hitching, her walls spasming violently around my cock as a wave of pure ecstasy seems to engulf her body causing a jolt of intense pleasure to shoot through me.

I can't hold back any longer; the sensation is too much.

"I'm going to come too," I gasp out before pressing my cock one last time inside of her, and coming with a body-shuddering roar that mingles with her own cry of release.

Minutes later Harlow's body is draped across mine, her leg thrown across my thighs, her fingers tracing patterns across my chest. We're both covered in a sheen of sweat, satiated, relaxed, content.

"Can I ask you something, Sterling?" she asks after a while.

"Of course," I reply as she eases the top half of her body upright and looks down at me.

"Have you ever come into my room at night before?"

For a beat I don't answer. I consider lying to her, but in the end I just nod my head. "I have, yes."

She bites on her lip, an unreadable expression crossing her features.

"I shouldn't have... I... Fuck, Harlow, I'm sorry."

Reaching up I cup her face, as she lets out a slow, laboured breath. "Did you touch me, Sterling? Did you touch me in my sleep?"

"Fuck," I murmur.

"Did you?" she insists.

"Yes, Harlow. I did. I couldn't stop myself. It was wrong. I know it was wrong. Fuck, *I'm sorry*."

She shakes her head, but she doesn't pull away like I expect her to do. Instead, she licks her lips and lowers her mouth to mine, kissing me gently.

"It was the night when I was on the call to my mother, wasn't it?" she asks, pulling back.

"Yes," I admit.

"I woke up the next morning feeling aroused. I was so wet, Sterling. I thought I'd dreamt it, dreamt you. But I didn't, did I?"

"No, you didn't..." My voice trails off as she stares at me. There's no anger in her gaze, just a kind of knowing. It settles the guilt inside of me. "Do you hate me for it?"

"I don't hate you for it, no. In fact, I want you to do it again, Sterling."

"You do?"

"Tonight was the best sex of my life. Waking up to you in my room, with your body pressed against mine. I knew at that moment you'd been in here before, that you'd touched me in my sleep. That you made me come."

"There's something else," I say, needing to confess.

"What?" she asks, as I push her hair behind her ear.

"I found your notebook. I read some of what you wrote. You have a gift, my little–"

"Poet?" she finishes for me.

"Yes, my little poet."

"I thought I'd dreamed that too..." she replies, dropping another kiss to my lips. "Sterling, no one has ever made me feel the way you do. No one. I don't want this to end."

"It won't," I reply fiercely. "You're mine."

"I'm afraid..." she whispers out, her expression changing as she lowers her body against my chest once more, and I fold my arms tighter around her.

"I won't let our parents come between us. I swear to you, Harlow. I promise I'll protect what we have, no matter what."

"Promise?"

"I promise," I say vehemently, meaning every word.

Except that night I didn't realise that she was talking about something else entirely, and that Harlow was hiding a secret that could destroy us both.

TWENTY-EIGHT

"You look beautiful, Harlow," Sterling murmurs, his fingertips grazing over mine as we stroll towards the entrance of the church.

It's Dalton and Daisy's wedding day and according to my mother the whole town has been gossiping about their relationship, and the real reason they're getting married. I choose to believe it's for love, and even if it isn't, it's none of my business anyway, but all the gossip has only served to remind me what Sterling and I would have to face if our secret got out.

"Thank you," I reply, my pulse spiking from his brief touch as I steal a glance at him. He's wearing a navy blue suit that brings out the blue of his eyes, making them even more striking than usual.

I wish I could twine my fingers with his, instead I reach up and tighten the deep burgundy shawl that matches the colour of my dress around my shoulders to fend off the cold.

"I've missed you," he adds, and even though we only saw each other yesterday, I know what he means.

Since that night Sterling crept into my bedroom a couple of weeks ago, we've only managed to steal brief moments of time with each other. But it's never enough, and I know that we're both feeling the loss of each other's company. In front of our parents, he keeps up the charade of resenting spending time with me, and in turn I hide my true feelings for him. It hasn't been easy, and I can't help but feel a sense of impending doom looming over us that seems to increase with every passing day. I still haven't told him about the messages I've been receiving, afraid that if I do, he'll want to confront the issue directly, and I'm scared that in doing so it will destroy the fragile balance we have created. I'm not ready just yet to face the consequences of our relationship being exposed.

On top of that my mother has been demanding as usual, and I've been busy fielding emails, scheduling upcoming events in her diary and managing her busy schedule. So much for her becoming a lady of leisure, though Robert doesn't seem to mind. He's too busy with his own business dealings, and is often in his office for hours a day working. It's apparent that their honeymoon period is well and truly over.

Meanwhile, Sterling and his father have reached a tense truce, but the animosity between them still simmers beneath the surface. They barely speak to each other, but when they do their conversations are filled with sly digs, and barbed comments, making our occasional dinners together more than a little awkward.

"I've missed you too," I reply, keeping my voice quiet as wedding guests gather on the steps of the church to greet Carl, Dalton's father, before stepping inside.

"Ah, Sterling, Harlow, so nice to see you both," Carl says, as we reach him.

"Carl," Sterling says tightly, his jaw clenching as Carl leans in to kiss my cheek in greeting.

"You look rather fetching, Harlow."

"Thank you," I murmur, feeling wholly uncomfortable at the way he's looking at me.

Sterling steps closer, resting his palm on the base of my spine. It's a possessive move, one that doesn't go unnoticed by Carl. He hitches a brow, and I don't like the assessing look in his gaze.

"Dalton informed me that you sang at Benedict's bar not too long ago. Quite the entertainer are we?"

"I was just standing in for the band that usually plays. It's not something I intend on doing again."

"Why, you were incredible!" Sterling interrupts, slamming his mouth shut when he realises his mistake.

Carl cocks a brow. "I'm surprised you even enjoyed it given your—"

Given his what?

"Carl, thank you so much for the invitation," a familiar voice says, cutting Carl off as he turns to greet Councillor John Hoxton and his wife Elodie, who looks as uneasy as I feel.

I frown, partly from wondering what Carl was about to say, but mostly from how Councillor Hoxton's gaze hones in on me, his eyes flickering with recognition. I force a smile in return but am more than a little grateful when we use the distraction to escape.

"I can't believe Carl invited that prick," Sterling mutters under his breath as we step through the heavy wooden doors of the church, the scent of fresh flowers mingling with the soft strains of music filling the air.

"You don't like him, I take it?"

"No," Sterling retorts, his hand falling away as we follow the other guests inside the church.

"Me neither," I admit

Sterling's feet still as he snaps his head to the side to look at me. "Why?"

"He just made me feel a little uncomfortable when I was introduced to him at mom's wedding."

"Uncomfortable how?" Sterling asks, as we head towards a pew at the back of the church, neither one of us wants to sit anywhere near our parents who are already seated towards the front.

"Nothing he said in particular. There was just something about him I didn't like."

Sterling scowls as we take a seat. "That man has a reputation."

"Reputation?"

"For stealing things that don't belong to him," he replies rather cryptically, eyeing the subject of our conversation as John passes us by with his wife, Elodie. I can't help but notice how tightly his fingers are wrapped around her elbow, or the wince of pain on her face that she tries to hide with a smile when she notices me staring.

"Are you talking about Elodie? Has this got something to do with Ben?"

"In part, yes," Sterling explains, his voice lowering as more guests fill up the rows in front of us. "Ben was dating Elodie for years. We were all convinced they were going to marry, and then all of a sudden she left him for that prick."

"Why on earth would she do that?"

"I don't know. Ben has never gotten over it. He's planning on making a move though," Sterling reveals, wincing a little when he realises he may have said too much.

"A move how?"

"Now's probably not the time to talk about that," Sterling replies, flicking his gaze to a couple who've settled at the other end of the pew that we're sitting on. "I'll tell you later, okay?"

"Sure," I agree. "So, what was Carl about to say before he was interrupted earlier?" I ask instead.

"Remind me what he said," Sterling murmurs, side-eyeing me.

"He seemed surprised that you enjoy listening to me sing. I don't know, it was as though he was going to say more..." My voice trails off as Sterling shifts in his seat.

"Carl is my dad's best friend. They talk. I made a mistake in complimenting you, so he was probably referring to that. I'll be more careful next time."

"Yes, of course. That makes sense, I suppose," I reply evenly, and if it wasn't for the tense way Sterling is holding himself, I might've believed him.

As it is, I feel like I'm missing something, or that he's hiding something from me, and I'm not sure what makes me feel worse, the fact that he's keeping something from me, or the fact that I'm doing the same in return.

For the next few minutes as we listen to the string quartet hidden away in the balcony above us, waiting for Daisy to arrive, I can't help but steal glances at Sterling whose gaze is fixed on Dalton standing at the altar. A muscle feathers in his jaw, tension oozing from him. I know that being around a lot of people is difficult for him, and I long to place my hand on his thigh to comfort him, but of course I don't.

"Are you okay?" I ask instead, resting my hand on the pew between us, my pinky grazing against his thigh. He looks over at me, some of the strain around his eyes softening as I caress his leg with the gentlest of touches.

"I'm good," he whispers out, something flickering in his eyes, something that looks an awful like longing.

After a beat he places his hand over mine, and I can't help but wonder if his heart is pounding as much as mine is, because the slightest touch from Sterling has my body reacting.

Dropping my gaze to the Bible tucked into the back of the pew in front of me, I blow out a shaky breath, trying to calm my racing pulse. I long to lean into Sterling's side, but for now, the warmth of his palm against mine will have to do. Moments later the processional music begins to play, and every guest turns to watch Daisy enter the church with her brother Drix, offering us both a welcome distraction.

"Wow!" I gasp, studying Daisy's breathtaking wedding gown.

It's unlike anything I've ever seen before, and is simply exquisite. The bodice hugs her figure perfectly, leading into a long chiffon skirt that seems to gracefully dance around her legs with every step she takes. But it's not just the style of the dress that makes it so stunning; it's the gorgeous pastel shades of pink, blue, yellow, green, and lilac that blend together seamlessly to create a gorgeous ombré effect.

"Stunning," Sterling murmurs, a smile spreading across his face as we watch her approach Dalton, who is staring at her so intently that I wonder if he's even aware of anyone else in the church.

The way they look at each other throughout the ceremony and during their wedding vows reveals a connection stronger than what I imagine many of the gossiping attendees had anticipated. Dalton's gaze never falters from Daisy's face, and she in turn looks up at him with flushed cheeks and shining eyes just like any other bride would look at their husband on their wedding day.

"You may now kiss the bride," the vicar eventually says with a smile.

Dalton steps forward, reaching up to cup Daisy's cheeks. There's a moment of stillness when she tips her head back to look up at him, and he leans forward and whispers something against her mouth that makes her gasp, before kissing her.

And boy does he kiss her.

It's heated, undeniably passionate, and I shift in my seat feeling a sudden sense of *loss*. Here are two people sharing an intimate moment in front of a church full of people, and here I am terrified that someone will see us holding hands.

"Harlow..." Sterling murmurs, drawing my attention to him. I'm met with agony in his gaze and I know he's thinking the same thing too.

"It's okay," I whisper back, but my response is drowned out beneath the sounds of everyone clapping, which slowly peters out when Dalton raises his hand.

"Can I have your attention, please?" he says, his voice rising above the noise. The guests fall silent, waiting as Dalton lifts his chin in what appears to be a defiant gesture. Beside him Daisy frowns, an uneasy expression on her face.

"What's going on?" I whisper.

"I've no idea," Sterling replies.

"My wife and I will be heading directly to our honeymoon," Dalton continues, his voice cutting through the whispered conversations. "The reception party will still go ahead, and of course you must all attend to celebrate our marriage, but we won't be in attendance."

"Excuse me?" Carl rises from his seat in the front row, his voice clipped, angry. "We have the press waiting, Dalton!"

Dalton glares at his father as Daisy's face pales, and the rest of us just watch on with varying degrees of surprise. I can see my mother look up at Robert, her eyes widening with shock and dare I say it, glee. She'll be living off this moment for weeks.

"This isn't up for discussion. We're leaving now," Dalton snaps, and I can't help but notice how he tightens his grip on Daisy's hand, pulling her closer. She steps into his side, her body leaning into his and I have the urge to do the same with Sterling. The way Dalton's father is reacting, and the way the whole congregation is muttering their disapproval has me on edge.

"The hell you are!" Carl seethes.

"Daisy's happiness is my priority, and staying here for a second longer so the vast majority of you can all pretend to be happy for us both whilst gossiping behind our backs is something that I will not tolerate. I will also not allow the press to invade our privacy. I don't give a fuck about the deals you've made without our permission, *father*," Dalton retorts with a snarl.

"Oh my God," I whisper, equally horrified by the fact that Dalton is even having to address the gossiping at his own wedding, and impressed by his boldness in standing up to his father. I don't know Dalton all that well, or Daisy for that matter, but I do know a man in love when I see one.

The tension in the church is palpable, with murmurs and gasps rippling through the guests.

"Why you ungrateful–" Carl begins, but Dalton holds his hand up, cutting him off.

"Enjoy your evening everybody," he says, before striding up the aisle, Daisy's hand firmly grasped in his.

"Well isn't this quite the embarrassment," my mother says under her breath as we sit at one of the circular tables in the beautifully decorated ballroom of Carl's palatial mansion.

Next to her, Robert is currently talking with Councillor John Hoxton, whilst his wife Elodie is chatting with a woman I've never met before. Sterling is sitting stiffly beside me, giving monosyllabic responses to a business acquaintance of Carl's.

Neither of us want to be here.

Even Drix, Lia and Ben made their excuses, leaving shortly after Dalton and Daisy. I wish Sterling and I had the chance to do the same, but as usual my mother and his father made that impossible, and so here we are.

"What on earth was Dalton thinking? His father has paid an awful lot of money for this reception," she babbles on. "And did you see her dress? What a monstrosity–"

"Mom, stop it," I warn, the last thing I want right now is to get drawn into a conversation about Daisy and Dalton's absence, especially not when Carl is approaching the table, and neither do I want to listen to her making fun of Daisy's beautiful wedding dress.

"Are you enjoying yourselves?" Carl asks, his words a little slurred as he grips the back of Robert's chair and glances around the table. I notice that his tie is undone, and the top bottom of his shirt loosened.

"The meal was delicious, and the company even better. We're having a wonderful time," my mother replies with practised ease, her smile drifting into place as Carl glances at her, his eyes more than a little glassy.

"Well, I'm glad someone is," he retorts with a scoff.

"Carl, let's go for a walk," Robert says, easing back his chair as he moves to stand. It's obvious he's attempting to get Carl out of the room before he says or does something to embarrass himself. I consider asking Robert to take my mother with them.

"Actually, I was coming over here to ask if Harlow would sing," Carl replies, looking over at me.

"Oh no, I couldn't," I say, shaking my head. It was one thing to sing at Bandits Bar for a small crowd of people as a favour to Ben, quite another in front of a group of people who prefer to gossip about things that don't concern them.

"Well, I'm not sure that's a good idea. Harlow isn't used to singing for such a large audience. Besides it's just a hobby," my mother states, her mouth pressing into a hard line.

"She sang at your wedding, and there were over a hundred more people there," Carl points out, his gaze coasting over me in a way that makes me feel more than a little uncomfortable.

"Yes, I for one would *love* to hear you sing again," Councillor Hoxton adds, giving me a smile that is more snakelike than friendly. I suppress a shudder. "I'm sure Robert would too, he's always boasting about your singing ability, Harlow. Dare I say he's quite the proud step-father."

"He does?" my mother asks, barely able to disguise her surprise, or the way she snaps her head around to stare at Robert.

His gaze moves between us, a flicker of annoyance crossing his expression at my mother's reaction. "Of course I'm proud. We *both* are," Robert adds, pointedly looking at my mother.

Sterling stiffens beside me, and I can't bring myself to look at his expression. It must feel awful for him to hear that Robert has been complimenting my singing to his business partners, when all he can do is throw snide remarks his way every day.

"Thank you, but even so. I'd rather not," I insist, shaking my head.

Beneath the table, I feel Sterling's hand press against my

thigh, which up until this moment I hadn't realised was jiggling up and down with anxiety. I don't know why I feel so anxious, it's not like any of them can force me to sing.

"Oh, but you must, we'd all love to hear you sing once more. Wouldn't we, Elodie?" Councillor Hoxton continues, his gaze flicking to his wife.

Beside him Elodie nods. "Yes, of course." Yet, when her husband's attention is back on me, she shakes her head. It's minute, the movement, but I catch it nevertheless. So did Sterling too, given the way he squeezes my thigh.

"Do you take requests? I'd love to hear *Songbird*. Elodie and I walked down the aisle to that song, didn't we, my love," Councillor Hoxton says, his eyebrows lifting as he stares at me.

I feel all the colour drain from my face.

Songbird?

Oh my God, is he...?

My anxiety turns to outright panic as I push back from the table, standing abruptly. "I'm actually not feeling all that well. I'm sorry. I can't sing for you," I say directly to Carl who's knocking back another mouthful of whatever alcohol he has in glass.

Sterling's hand remains under the table, and I feel his knuckles gently brush against the side of my thigh before he stands too. "Would you like me to take you home?"

"That's not necessary," Robert interjects, looking between us both. "I'm happy to do so."

"Robert!" my mother exclaims, clearly put out. "She's quite capable of calling a cab. Why ruin our evening too?"

"I'm sorry I thought you made *me* her designated chauffeur?" Sterling retorts, making sure to add that little tidbit for everyone to digest. "Stay with your wife, I'll make sure Harlow gets home safe."

"Yes, exactly. Sterling should take Harlow home," my mother adds, waving her hand in the air as though she's trying her best to waft us both out of the ballroom like annoying specs of dust.

Robert clears his throat. "Fine, of course."

"Harlow," Sterling says, his fingers briefly cupping my elbow. I flinch from his touch, feeling more than a little jumpy as Councillor Hoxton continues to stare at me. Sweat beads on my forehead and trickles down my spine, and with every passing second I'm beginning to feel more and more nauseous.

It's him. *He's* my stalker. I know it.

Sterling's hand falls away, and Robert smiles. "You know it's terribly heartwarming to see you looking after your sister so well."

"She's not my–"

"Nice to meet you all again," I cut in, before striding off and ending the conversation altogether.

"Harlow, talk to me, what's going on? You were quiet the whole way home," Sterling says as he follows me into my bedroom half an hour later.

"I just don't feel well. I have a headache and I'm a little nauseous," I whisper, turning my back to him as I head into my ensuite.

My hands are trembling and I do feel like throwing up, but not because I have some sudden stomach bug. All I keep thinking about are the messages I've received, how I've been suppressing how frightened they've made me feel, and that Councillor Hoxton said that his wedding song was *Songbird*. I knew the moment I met him that something was off about him, and his behaviour tonight has only cemented my fears.

He's my stalker.

God, what am I going to do? He's a business acquaintance

of Robert's, and someone I'll likely see again. There's clearly something going on with him and his wife, she is always so jumpy around him. Does he hurt her? Does he want to hurt me too? Then my mind decides at that point to remind me of every message he's sent.

Will you scream when I force my dick inside of you? Will you enjoy it?

Do you need proof of how much I want to fuck you, is that it? Because, believe me when I say, I'm hard right now...

Bile rises up my throat, and I throw a hand over my mouth but it's no use, I can't stop it. Dropping to my knees, I lift the toilet seat and throw up.

"Jesus, Harlow," Sterling exclaims, dropping to his knees beside me, his hand resting on my back as I empty my stomach.

When we're finally together, you'll sing for me every day my sweet songbird. Perhaps I'll even build you a cage?

I retch again, tears spilling from my eyes as Sterling keeps rubbing my back. What the hell am I going to do? This is so fucked up.

"Oh God," I murmur, dragging in deep lungfuls of air.

"Easy," Sterlings says, his voice soothing as I push back upright onto my haunches.

I wipe the back of my hand across my mouth, noticing that there's some puke in my hair. "I'm sorry."

"What for? You're not feeling well, Harlow. You don't need to apologise to me," he replies, his gaze coasting over my features.

"What must you think of me?"

"I think that you're sick, and that you need me to take care of you," he replies, helping me to my feet. "Let's get you undressed and into bed, okay? Then I'll go and make you some toast, see if that helps to settle your stomach."

"I'm not sure I can stomach any food. I think I should take a shower, I have puke in my hair," I point out, acutely aware of how disgusting I must look.

Sterling frowns as I sway on my feet, another bout of nausea washing over me. "Then I'll get in with you. I don't want you passing out."

"Sterling, our parents will be home soon. You can't."

He frowns, then gently urges me back onto the lip of the bath. "Stay there, I'm going to lock your bedroom door. If they come home early and try to check on you, we'll at least have some warning."

"Sterling..."

"It'll be okay. Just give me a moment," he replies. A moment later he returns, having already removed his suit jacket and shoes. "Let's get you undressed."

I don't have the energy to argue, so I sit quietly as he drops to his knees and gently slips off my heels, placing them to the side of the bath. Pushing upright, he takes my hands in his warm palms and helps me to stand.

"Turn around, Harlow, I need to unzip your dress."

I nod, following his instructions. Ever so gently Sterling removes my dress, cupping my elbow as I step out of the material. Then his fingers trace over my skin as he unclasps my bra and removes my panties. Completely naked before him, he brushes past me and turns on the shower.

"You okay?" he murmurs, pulling off his tie then unbuttoning his shirt.

"I've been better," I reply, giving him a shaky smile.

I watch him as he removes his clothes, and places them on the vanity. My gaze traces over his bare chest and his growing erection. Heat climbs up my cheeks.

"Apologies, I can't help how my body reacts to you. Please

ignore it, Harlow," he says, giving me a rueful grin as he takes my hand and leads me into the shower.

Warm water cascades over us both, and I heave out a tremulous breath. "Thank you for looking after me," I whisper. "It's not something I'm used to."

Sterling frowns before gently tugging me against his chest, his arms wrapping around me as he presses a tender kiss against my forehead. "I'm here for you, Harlow."

"I'm going to miss this," I mumble against his neck.

"Miss this?" he questions, drawing back slightly.

"On Monday I'm travelling to London with Robert and mom for that interview they're going to do for a magazine article. Robert gave it the go ahead, and I finalised the details just yesterday. We're going to be away for a few days, maybe even a week as we've tacked on a meeting with her agent and another newspaper."

"A few days? Can't you get out of it?"

I shake my head, feeling my heart sink at his disappointment. "I'd love nothing more than to spend that time with you, but this is my job. I have to go."

"Fuck, Harlow. I'm going to go crazy without you," he replies, pulling me back into his arms.

"Believe me, there's nowhere I'd rather be than with you. You make me feel wanted, cared for. You make me feel *safe*, Sterling. Thank you for looking after me tonight."

Neither of us say another word, and as we stand beneath the shower, wrapped in each other's arms, I push away the thought of my stalker, allowing the rhythmic sound of the water to drown out the unease creeping in. In Sterling's arms I do feel safe, but deep down, a small, unsettling voice whispers that I'm anything but.

TWENTY-NINE

Placing my paintbrush on the table, I take a step back and look at the canvas before me. It's another rendition of Harlow, the one I started the night we returned from Bandits Bar a few weeks ago. Ordinarily I don't stop painting once I start, my synesthesia usually forcing me to work on the painting until it's complete, but this piece has taken me weeks to get to this point, and that in itself is an anomaly.

When Harlow left for London with our parents a week ago, I returned to the studio, needing to lose myself in my art to escape the emptiness I felt in her absence. I haven't left since. The only breaks I've taken were to eat the meals Stephanie insisted I have, to relieve myself, and to grab a few hours of sleep when exhaustion finally caught up with me. The blisters on my hands, the paint on my skin and in my hair—it's all proof of how much I've missed her. In a couple of hours, she'll be home, and I'm nearly frantic with the need to see her again, to hold her, to kiss her, to lose myself in her.

Tilting my head to the side, I study the vibrant colours in

the soft morning light. The brush strokes are still fresh in some places, if a little haphazard, as though I can't quite decide how to capture the lightness that has slowly crept into my life since Harlow's been in it.

"Beautiful," I mutter, letting my fingers trace the contours of Harlow's face. The same face I've memorised in the quiet moments when we're together, when the world outside falls away. I think about the way she laughs, the way her eyes soften when she looks at me, how completely free she is when she sings. I think about the way her body reacts to my touch as though every brush of my fingers against her skin ignites a fire within her, something I feel only too keenly myself.

Her absence these past few days has made everything feel off-kilter. The silence in the studio, the emptiness I feel—hell, even the light feels different without her.

I pull my hand away, taking in a deep breath. The air smells of paint and sweat, a scent I've always associated with creation. But today, it's tainted with the gnawing ache of impatience. I need her back. I need her in my arms where she belongs.

Behind me, the door creaks open, and I turn, half-expecting to see her standing there, as if my thoughts alone could summon her here. But it's just a draft, and I let out a short laugh at myself, shaking my head. I'm losing it.

My amusement is interrupted as my phone buzzes on the table, and I glance at the screen, seeing Ben's name. It's been a while since we last talked. He's been busy with the bar, and trying to get a record deal for Princetown Bandits, and I've been busy painting in my studio distracting myself until Harlow's return.

Snatching it up I answer. "Ben, what's up?"

"I've got some bad news," he instantly replies.

My spine stiffens. "What kind of bad news?"

"It's Daisy, she's in hospital. Fuck man, it's not good."

"What are you talking about? I thought Dalton and Daisy were still on their honeymoon."

"They came home yesterday. Daisy collapsed at home. She's had a..."

"What?" I exclaim, running a hand through my hair.

"She's had a miscarriage, Sterling. Drix tells me it was early, but there were complications."

"Jesus, I didn't even realise they were..." I let my voice trail off. It's none of my business whether or not they've been intimate. "How are they holding up?"

Ben heaves out a heavy sigh. "Not well. I don't know all the details, but Drix tells me that they found out Daisy has an underlying medical condition which was picked up following the miscarriage and subsequent operation. She may never be able to conceive again."

"Fuck, Ben. That's awful. Is there anything I can do?" I offer, feeling fucking helpless.

"There is actually. Drix asked if one of us could check in on Lia and Toby. Despite her ex being in custody, he's still worried about them. I can't do it because I'm stuck at the bar. Can you head over there, make sure they're okay?"

"I'd be happy too," I reply.

"Thanks, I'll let him know. There is one other thing," he adds.

"What is it?"

"Dalton wanted to let you know that they're not telling Carl the real reason she's in hospital, and has asked you to keep this between us. Right now he's trying to figure out how to handle the fact that Daisy might not be able to conceive an heir. We both know his cunt of a father won't take the news well given an heir is all he wanted out of this marriage."

"Of course, I won't say anything."

"I suspect this whole situation is going to get worse before it gets better, and they're going to need us when it does."

"I'll be there. Maybe once Daisy's had time to recover physically and they've both had time to process everything we could get together for dinner, just our group, figure out the next steps?"

"Yeah, that sounds good. Just give them some time before you suggest it. I don't think either of them will be up for socialising for a while yet."

"That's understandable," I agree, and we both fall silent as we digest the news.

"Sterling?" Ben questions after a while.

"Yeah?"

"When things like this happen it makes you re-evaluate your life choices, doesn't it?"

"It certainly puts things into perspective, yes," I agree.

"And on that note, I've decided to stop fucking around and call Hoxton, get things in motion."

"When?"

"As soon as possible. I have the funds, I have a plan, and this time *I'm* going to be the thief. He stole her from me, and I'm going to steal her right back."

"You've got this all figured out," I observe, thinking about my own relationship with Harlow. Truth be known, I've been biding my time in dealing with my father under the guise of giving Harlow space to get used to *us,* when in reality I've been too shit scared to tell her the truth about *me.*

"When you want something enough, you find a way, right?" Ben replies.

"Even when it's messy?" I counter.

"Elodie's worth it. I guess you've just got to figure out if Harlow is worth it too," he replies.

"But I thought you agreed that I shouldn't–" I begin, but he interrupts.

"I know what I said at the engagement party, but today we've both had a reality check. I'm done fucking about. Are you?" he asks, before clicking off the call.

Swiping a hand through my hair, my thoughts wander back to Harlow. It's about time I tell her the truth about who I am, and I need to trust that she'll still want me when I do.

"Oh, so you think Daisy's pregnant too?" I hear Melody say as I step into the lounge in search of Harlow a few hours later. "Because I was thinking exactly the same thing. How else would she manage to pin down such a man?"

"Watch what you say about my friends," I snap, not bothering to hide my anger as Melody turns to face me, her phone pressed to her ear. Her eyes widen for a fraction of a second before she mutters something to whoever is on the other end of the line then hangs up.

"Sterling, I didn't realise you were there," she says, forcing a smile as if that alone could erase the harsh words she just spoke. I honestly don't know what my father sees in her. She might be beautiful, but her personality makes her ugly.

"What exactly do you think you've heard?" I retort, my hackles rising. If she has any idea how close to the truth she is, then things are going to blow up for Dalton and Daisy sooner rather than later.

"It's just silly gossip," she replies, waving her hand in the air. "I'm sure they're very much in love."

My shoulders relax a fraction. The gossip mill clearly hasn't found out about Daisy's hospitalisation just yet, and I'm hopeful Dalton is able to come up with something convincing to cover the fact she's just miscarried their baby. The last thing either of them need is the elite of Princetown finding out and making things a hundred times worse for them.

"Where are the others?" I ask, noticing that neither Harlow nor my dad are in the room.

"Robert is just parking the car in the garage, and Harlow is still in London."

My head snaps back around as I look at Melody. "Why is she still in London?"

"Robert seemed to think that she was still a little out of sorts, and he thought taking in the sights of London, and doing some shopping might help her to deal with whatever's on her mind. She's been distracted all week," Melody replies, rolling her eyes. "So he's paid for her to stay another night at the Godolphin on Marleybone."

"When will she be back?" I ask, trying to keep my cool.

"Tomorrow evening. Which is rather inconvenient given there's still a long list of things I need her to do for me. Honestly, Sterling, Harlow really needs to get her priorities straight, she's becoming entirely too selfish in my opinion. I'm going to have a word with Robert to stop coddling her. I think he's overcompensating because she's grown up without a father figure," she continues on.

I turn on my heel not bothering to listen to a second more of her vitriol as I rush out of the door. Pulling out my car keys from my back pocket. I reach the garage just as my father is stepping out.

"Where are you going?" he asks.

"I'm heading over to Drix's place, he wants me to check in

on Lia and Toby whilst he's at the hospital with Daisy. I'll be gone for the night."

"Why is Daisy at the hospital?" my father asks, surprise lifting his brows.

"Call Carl, I'm sure he'll fill you in," I retort, before brushing past him and climbing into my car, not bothering to tell him that once I've made sure Lia and Toby are okay, I'm driving to London to see the woman I love.

THIRTY

Gazing at my phone, I chew on the inside of my cheek, my nerves frayed from the bombardment of messages I've received from my stalker over the last few days. There are so many that my eyes fill with tears, and my body trembles with anxiety.

> Why do you insist on ignoring me, my sweet songbird? I'm contemplating clipping your wings so that you don't have a chance to fly away.

> Though, I rather think you enjoy the chase. Are you behaving this way because you only wish to sing for me? I think perhaps it must be that.

I think about all the ways I'd take you when you're finally mine. I really hope you fight me. The thought of you pinned beneath me, my cock in your tight cunt whilst you scream for help turns me on.

Does that turn you on?

Soon, my sweet songbird. Soon…

Bile rises up my throat as I throw my phone across the room. It lands on the chaise positioned beneath the window, before dropping to the floor with a thud.

"Sick bastard," I exclaim, swiping at my cheeks as I try and fail to steady my nerves.

I haven't left the hotel since Robert and my mother returned to Princetown this morning, and in all honesty I wished I'd gone with them. My insistence on accompanying them both home was met with Robert's abject refusal, and in the end I'd agreed if only to stop him and my mother from arguing over whether I should take some time off or not.

Despite everything that's going on with me, I don't want to be the cause of any upset between them. So here I am, utterly terrified, staring at the messages and wishing I'd just told them both what's been going on. But I'm a grown woman, and I should be able to handle this myself. I realise now that I should've reported this to the police a long time ago. Today I'm going to do exactly that.

With that decision made, I push up from the bed and head into the bathroom with the intention of splashing my face with cold water, but a knock at the door has my steps faltering.

"Shit," I mutter, forgetting that I'd ordered room service.

Tucking my hair behind my ears, I let out a steadying breath, hoping the member of hotel staff won't question why I look so disheveled.

"One moment, please," I call out, unlocking the door and pulling it open, only to find Sterling standing there.

"Harlow..."

"What are you doing here?" I ask, a mix of shock and relief flooding through me. I hadn't realised how much I needed him until now.

He takes one glance at my face, and without hesitation, reaches for me, his hands gently cupping my cheeks. "You've been crying," he murmurs, his voice laced with concern.

"Sterling..." My voice cracks as I waiver on my feet.

"Fuck, Harlow, what's wrong?"

"I–" I begin, but he steps into my space, walking me backwards until my back hits the wall and the door slams behind him.

"Tell me why you've been crying," he insists, concern scattering across his handsome face as I try to fight back a sob. "Is it your mother? Has she said something to upset you? Was it my dad, did that fucker do something to upset you?"

I shake my head, my hands flying up to press against his chest as I try to form words, but it's no use, his concern has a damn opening up inside of me and I just throw myself at him, seeking comfort from the only person who has ever made me feel wanted.

Sterling doesn't question me further, he simply pulls me into his arms and holds me whilst I break. All the fear I've been holding onto leaks from my eyes in scalding tears, and I sob into his chest. I'm trembling so hard that my knees buckle.

"Hold onto me," Sterling says, as he swoops down and lifts me off my feet, my body held horizontally across his chest. In a few strides he has me settled on the bed, my back pressed against the headboard. "Stay there, I'm going to get you a drink of water."

I simply nod, watching him as he strides across the room to the bar where miniature bottles of alcohol and soft drinks are kept chilled in a fridge. Pulling out a bottle of water, he twists off the cap, then returns, offering it to me.

"Thank you," I whisper, reaching for it with trembling fingers. I take a sip as he sits down on the edge of the bed, watching me carefully. When I've had enough, he takes the bottle from me and rests it on the floating shelf next to the bed.

"Harlow, can you tell me what's going on?" he asks, his grip on my hands gentle but firm as his thumbs trace soothing circles across my skin.

I take a shaky breath, trying to steady myself. "It's... I..." My voice cracks, but he doesn't rush me—he just waits, his concern palpable. "I have a stalker..."

"What?" His voice is a low, dangerous growl now, and I feel his fingers tighten around mine. Whatever he expected to hear, this clearly wasn't it.

"Someone's been sending me messages. They're... Oh God, Sterling, I'm scared," I manage to choke out, tears streaming down my face.

"Messages? What kind of messages?"

"Disturbing ones," I rasp out.

"For how long?" His question is short, sharp, his voice laced with a barely contained fury. I force myself to meet his gaze, knowing his anger isn't directed at me, but at the person terrorising me.

"Months."

"*Months*?! Harlow..." His voice trembles with a mix of anger and concern, his jaw clenched, as if the idea of someone hurting me is more than he can bear.

"At first I just thought it was some random person on the internet, and I ignored them, hoping they'd grow bored. But the messages have become more frequent, more sexual, more *threatening* and I didn't know what to do. "

"Sexual? Threatening? I'm going to fucking kill them," he seethes. "Who is it?"

"I don't know for certain," I explain, forcing myself to speak through my tears, a sudden well of shame gathering inside my chest. "They're coming through on an old Instagram account I used to post to."

Sterling cups my cheek, ducking his head so that our eyes meet, a fierce expression in his eyes. "Tell me everything, from the beginning Harlow. Help me to understand so that I can deal with this bastard."

And so I tell him.

I tell him about my Instagram account. I tell him about the fact I haven't used it in years, and then how I received the first message months ago. I explain that in the beginning they seemed harmless, but over time that the messages have gotten steadily more intrusive.

"There was a point that I thought maybe you were the one sending me the messages," I admit in a whisper, guilt climbing up my throat.

"Never. I'd *never* do anything to hurt you, Harlow," he exclaims, rearing back as though I've slapped him.

"I know that. I know. I'm sorry for even thinking it," I quickly say, more tears pooling in my eyes.

"Why did you think it was me?" he asks.

"Initially, I thought you'd come across my account somehow, and after I left the way I did that night we first met, I thought perhaps you were trying to hurt me..."

"Harlow, shit. No..." His voice trails off, but I catch something in his eyes that gives me pause.

"What?"

"I did find your account," he admits carefully, as though he's afraid that I might react badly. "And I did send you a message, but nothing like this. I swear to you."

"You messaged me?" I whisper.

"Yes. Once. You never responded. Then you were singing at our parents' wedding and, well, there was no need for me to message you there anymore."

"Why didn't you say something?"

"I guess it didn't matter at that point."

"I wish you'd told me, it might've saved me from still thinking you were my stalker even after I'd moved in."

He frowns. "Do you really think so little of me?"

"Please let me explain," I say, feeling awful.

He nods. "Okay."

"Do you remember that time in the kitchen when I asked to see your phone?" I ask.

"I remember."

"I'd received some messages that morning, and you happened to be approaching the kitchen. You were on your phone at exactly the same moment..."

"*That's* why you asked to see my phone?"

"Yes," I nod.

"But you don't think it's me now?"

"No, no I don't," I confirm, reaching for him. My palm slides across his cheek as I lift up onto my knees and shift closer to him on the bed. "I trust you. I wouldn't be telling you this if I didn't."

"Fuck, Harlow. Why didn't you tell me this earlier?"

"I thought I was handling it. But the messages have gotten worse, and I think…"

"What? What is it?"

"I think I might know who it is, but I can't be certain," I add, as his eyes flare dangerously.

"Who?" he demands.

"At Dalton and Daisy's wedding reception Councillor Hoxton said something that made me think it could be him."

"Councillor Hoxton?" Sterling questions, his expression hardening. "What exactly did he say?"

"He mentioned that the song he walked down the aisle to was Songbird," I explain.

"Yes, I remember, why would that make you think it's him who's been sending you these messages?"

I chew on my lip, knowing that it's dangerous to accuse someone with no actual proof. "It could've been a coincidence, and if he didn't make me feel so uncomfortable I wouldn't even have considered it a possibility."

"Why did him mentioning that song trigger you, Harlow?" he presses.

"Let me show you," I say, climbing off the bed so I can grab my phone. Picking it up, I return to Sterling, clicking open the app and going to the messages. I scroll through them, finding the one where he calls me his sweet songbird.

"That motherfucker!" Sterling exclaims, taking the phone from me as he reads that particular message, before scrolling back to the beginning. I wait quietly, watching his expression change as he reads. By the time he's finished, his gaze is simmering with rage.

"Sterling, what should I do?"

"You're not going to do a damn thing. I'm, however, going to confront the bastard," he growls.

"I have no proof, Sterling. I don't want you accusing someone when it might not be them."

"I will not sit back and let him send you these twisted messages. I will not let him threaten you—"

"I'll go to the police," I interject.

"No."

"What?"

"I said, no, Harlow. All they'll do is give you a crime number, then file this away. At best they'll get his account shut down. That won't resolve the fact that he's out there just waiting to hurt you. Not to mention that even if you were lucky enough to get a restraining order on him, which is highly unlikely given we don't have any proof that it's him, he'd still be able to hurt you. That bastard has friends in high places."

"Including your father," I whisper.

"Yes, including him," Sterling retorts, scowling. "Does my father know about this? Does your mother?"

"No," I shake my head. "I haven't told anyone but you."

"Good, because telling either of them isn't an option. I don't trust my father not to use this against us both somehow, and I sure as fuck don't think your mother would help. I will sort this out. *Me.*"

"I don't want you to put yourself in a difficult position, Sterling. If you accuse Councillor Hoxton and he's not the one sending these messages, he'll just tell Robert. Not only will that create more problems with your father, but it will also raise questions about us."

"I can't sit back and do nothing, Harlow. I won't," he replies, dropping the phone to the bed and tugging me onto his lap. I go to him willingly, needing him more than I've ever needed anyone in my life. "It's already too fucking hard not to be able to call you mine officially, and now I have to contend with someone threatening the woman I love. No, I won't do it."

"*Love?*" I whisper.

"Yes. I love you, Harlow," he says emphatically, as my heart trips up inside my chest. "Even if I still have to hide how I feel from everyone else–*for now,*" he adds vehemently, "I refuse to hide that from you. I love you. I need you to know that. I'm not expecting you to say it back—"

"Sterling," I cut him off but he continues to speak.

"I just want you to know that I'm in love with you. I'm so fucking in love with you that I'm ready to shout it to the world and fuck the consequences. Not only that, I'm ready to batter down that prick's door, reach my fist down is throat and rip his dick out of his body from the inside out for even daring to scare you—"

"Sterling, listen to me," I demand, adjusting myself on his lap so that I'm straddling his thighs with my own. "Firstly, you're not going to do anything rash. We'll figure out how to handle this together. Secondly, and most importantly, I'm in love with you too."

"What?" Sterling asks, his eyes widening a fraction at my confession.

"I love you."

He grins, his anger momentarily forgotten. "Say it again."

"I love you."

He presses his kiss against my lips briefly, before pulling back. "Again, louder this time."

"I love you!" I laugh, all my fears slipping away as he gently lays me back on the bed, his body poised over mine, the silver streaks in his blue eyes sparkling.

"Stay right there, Harlow," he says, before pushing upright

and pulling out his phone from his pocket. "I just need to make a quick call."

"A call?"

"Room service," he says by way of explanation as he heads towards the bathroom.

"I've already called for food," I say.

"It's not that kind of room service," he replies rather cryptically, and when I frown he just grins. "Trust me okay?"

"I do trust you."

"Good. I'll just be a moment."

"What on earth?" I whisper, and despite feeling a little shaky still, I can't help but smile to myself. Things don't seem as scary now that Sterling knows the truth, and somehow, the weight that had been pressing on my chest is a hell of a lot lighter knowing that Sterling is in love with me, and that I'm hopelessly in love with him too.

THIRTY-ONE

By the time room service has been delivered and we've shared the burger and truffle chips that Harlow had ordered, it's nearing dusk. Outside, the street lamps flicker to life, illuminating the bustling streets below, whilst the distant hum of traffic fades into background noise.

"That's just awful," Harlow murmurs after I tell her about Dalton and Daisy's miscarriage. "They must be devastated."

"They are. On the drive over, I spoke with Drix who's keeping them both company at the hospital. He said they've decided to tell Carl that Daisy had an appendectomy."

"Why?" she asks, taking a sip of her wine, a frown knitting her brows together.

"Because if Carl found out the truth—that Daisy miscarried and may never be able to have children again—he'd force them to divorce so Dalton could remarry and give him the heir he's so desperate for."

"Wait, what?!" Harlow asks, her face draining of colour as

she shifts in her seat. "He would actually do that? What kind of person does that?"

"The kind of person who only cares about himself. The same kind of person as my father. They're friends for a reason, Harlow. Both of them have been corrupted by wealth, but it's the power they wield that makes them so cruel. I know that might be hard for you to understand given that so far my father has been good to you."

"I believe everything you've told me about your father," Harlow says, "And I would never devalue your experiences with him just because I've only ever experienced kindness."

"But?" I question, feeling anxiety unfurling in my chest as I wonder where this is going.

"There are no buts. Believe me," she continues, giving me a sympathetic smile. "I'm fully aware of what it's like to have a parent who's seen one way by the rest of the world but who you experience completely differently. My mother is a perfect example of that, and I'm sorry your father is as harsh and cold toward you as she can be with me."

"She's a bitch to you, Harlow. She treats you like an employee, not a daughter. She puts you down, she outright ignores you, and God forbid if anyone compliments you. Fuck, I've never met someone who is so jealous that she'll twist any compliments you might receive into an opportunity to belittle you, I fucking hate it."

"I know," she agrees, setting her wine glass down with a soft sigh. "And I'm partly responsible for the way she treats me."

"Her behaviour is not your fault," I respond, my voice sharp.

"But—"

"No, Harlow. You are not to blame. Could you be more assertive with your mother? Sure. But should you have to be? Hell no. A parent's job is to love their child, not to seize every chance to make them feel worthless, and it sure as fuck isn't your job to make excuses for her behaviour, especially not when you lay the blame at your own feet."

Harlow lets out a shuddering breath. "I know you're right. I guess I've spent so much time letting the mother I have now treat me terribly, all while wishing the mom I used to know would return. She hasn't always been this way and it feels as though I've been mourning that person, all while still holding onto the hope that she hasn't completely disappeared."

"I understand, Harlow. I really do. Hell, I've longed for a different father myself. But while you may have once had a loving mother, I've never known what it's like to have a loving father."

"I'm so sorry, Sterling," she replies, and for a brief moment Harlow turns her attention towards the window, the fading evening light casting a soft, golden glow on her skin.

"If I ask you something, will you be honest with me, Sterling?" she eventually asks.

"Yes," I reply.

"I know Robert hurt your mother, and I'm not downplaying how much that's impacted your relationship," she says, her eyes studying me closely. "But there's something more, isn't there? Something you're holding back. Will you tell me what it is?"

Even though I've mentally braced myself for this moment, my stomach tightens with anxiety. She's told me she loves me, and I want to believe that means she'll love and accept all of me —even the parts I've had a hard time accepting myself, but like Harlow I've suffered years of emotional and mental abuse at the hands of a parent, and it's hard to let go of the fear that if I tell her about my synesthesia she'll reject me just like my father has.

"There is something that I've kept from you," I admit, dragging in a shaky breath. "Something about me that makes me different from everyone else. It's hard for me to open up because in the past when I have, all I've been met with is ridicule, cruelty and disgust."

"Your father?" she asks.

"Not just him. I had a rough time growing up. Part of the reason I choose to keep to myself and have few friends is because I've been treated cruelly by a lot of people. Let's just say that my time at school was something I'd rather forget."

"What is it that makes you different, Sterling?"

Just at that moment, there's a knock on the door. "Let me answer that, and I'll tell you everything, okay?"

"Sure," she replies, and I feel the heat of her stare as I stride towards the door.

"I have your delivery, Sir. Where would you like them?" a member of the hotel staff asks me.

"I've got this, thanks," I reply, taking the 3ft canvas and easel from him, resting them against the wall before grabbing the bag of oil paint and brushes that I paid over the odds for from a local art shop to get them delivered here on such short notice. He waits for me to tip him, so I pull out a couple of fifty pound notes from my wallet and hand them to him.

"Thank you, sir," he says, taking them from me with an appreciative smile before I gently close the door.

"What's this?" Harlow asks, as I tuck the canvas under my arm and grab the other items.

"This is who I am. This is the real me, Harlow," I say, setting up the easel and placing the canvas on the shelf, securing it in place.

"You're an artist?" she questions, her eyes widening as she looks from me to the oil paints and brushes that I set up on the table between us.

"I am..." My voice trails off as she frowns.

"I don't understand why anyone, least of all your father, would treat you so badly for being an artist? It doesn't make any sense."

"I have a condition called synesthesia," I explain, my fingers coasting over the oil paints before I pick up a medium-sized paintbrush, the wood smooth in my grasp.

"Synesthesia? What is that?"

I pause for a moment, trying to find the right words. "It's when the senses are...mixed up, I guess. For me, it means I can see colours when I hear music, or someone singing."

Harlow looks at me, processing. "So, you see colours... from sound?"

"Not everyday sounds, specifically music and when I hear someone singing," I explain, taking a seat opposite her. "When music plays, I can see this whole spectrum of colours. It's not just random, though. Each note has its own colour, its own texture even. And it's always there, constantly, whether I want it or not. Painting what I see helps me to deal with it."

She shifts forward in her seat, her curiosity growing. "But that's incredible... Why would your dad treat you so poorly because of it? Isn't it a gift to be able to experience music that way?"

"Not to my dad it isn't. When I was a kid, hearing music would send me into a tailspin of overstimulation." I pause, setting the paintbrush back on the table as I recall those early years when everything seemed so frightening, and my dad had been especially cruel. "I'd be bombarded with this over-whelming flood of colours. It was like a sensory explosion, and it was too much to handle. There was no way for me to cope with it back then, no way to explain it because I didn't understand what was happening to me..." My voice trails off as I look down at my hands for a moment, fidgeting nervously.

"Sterling, I'm so sorry. That must've been terrifying," Harlow says, her brows pinching together with empathy.

"More times than I can count, I'd do things that made my dad embarrassed or ashamed of me. I'd flap my hands around, trying to disperse the colours, but when that didn't work, I'd just collapse, curling up into a ball on the floor, covering my ears and hoping the world would stop spinning long enough for the sensation to pass." My hands tighten into fists as I remember the helplessness of those moments, and I drag in a steadying breath, forcing myself to continue. "Most of the time, I'd end up fainting from the overload, the colours just becoming too much for my body to process."

Harlow gasps, her eyes flashing with recognition. "You fainted that night we met, was it because I was singing..." Her voice trails off when I nod.

"Yes."

"I had no idea about any of this. Your father never mentioned anything."

"He's still ashamed of me, of my condition, so of course he wouldn't. As you can imagine, my father... Well, let's just say he wasn't exactly equipped to deal with a child who didn't act 'normal.' Looking back now, I know it's because he just didn't want to."

"God, Sterling. I'm so sorry," Harlow exclaims. "Did he never even *try* to understand you?"

I bite my lip, swallowing the pain of his abject refusal to see me as anything other than a problem he needed to fix. "He sent me to countless therapists, made me undergo a barrage of tests with various specialists, all in hopes of fixing me. But none of it helped because I didn't need fixing, Harlow. I needed understanding, patience, *love*, and he couldn't bring himself to give me any of that."

"What a cruel bastard, Sterling. I'm so angry for you," Harlow gets to her feet, traversing the table as she ducks down before me and cradles my hands in hers.

"Eventually, when I was old enough to articulate what was happening to me, my mother..." I pause, my voice softening as I think of her. "She figured out that I needed an outlet—something to release everything I was feeling and experiencing. She brought me some art supplies, and together we found a way to manage my condition. When I paint, I can purge myself of the colour, easing that part of me."

"She sounds like a wonderful woman," she says, her thumbs gently stroking the backs of my hands.

"It was the first time I felt like someone truly understood me, and yes, my mother is wonderful. Without her love and support I don't think I'd be here today."

"Oh, Sterling..." Harlow murmurs, her eyes filling with tears at my confession.

"You can understand why school was tough for me. Kids can be particularly cruel when they know someone is different," I explain, gritting my jaw at the memory of that period of my life. "Over the years, I've found ways to manage my condition. If I'm out where I know I might hear music, I normally wear noise cancelling headphones. In New York, the night we met, someone bumped into me on the street, knocking off my headphones. That's when I heard you singing, and the colour your voice conjured was so fucking beautiful, Harlow, that I was helpless against it."

"But I've sung so many times in front of you without realising the effect it has on you. That night when I played the piano..." Her voice trails off and she winces. "Have I caused you pain, Sterling?"

"Please don't misunderstand me, when I was younger it was

difficult to manage, yes. But ever since my mother figured out how to help me, I've been able to use art to express this side of me. It's lessened the negative impact of my condition, and enabled me to earn a living as well. I can't lie and tell you that your singing doesn't have a profound effect on me, both emotionally and physically, or that I'm not drained after an episode, but I want you to know that I'm grateful for the beauty your voice evokes, and I'm so fucking glad I heard you singing that night."

There's a pause as she takes in what I've said. Then she reaches up, her voice soft as she cups my cheeks in her palms. "I think this is incredibly special, Sterling. You see the world in a way no one else can."

I smile, a small, bittersweet smile. "I try to tell myself that. It's just hard when one of the people who should love you, no matter what, would change you into someone you're not rather than accept you for who you are."

Harlow gives me a small nod, her gaze drifting to the canvas. "Well, I think you're brave for sharing this part of yourself with me, and I'm so grateful that you have. I would never want to change you, Sterling. *Never*. Do you hear me?"

"I do. Fuck, Harlow..." I release a shaky breath, the fear and anxiety I've been carrying around with me melting away as she rises up on her knees and kisses me gently, her lips soft against mine.

She pulls back, her eyes searching mine. "No more secrets, okay?"

I nod, my hand trembling slightly as I brush a strand of hair behind her ear. "There's one more thing I need to tell you."

Her expression softens, and she waits, patient and calm. "Okay."

I take a deep breath before continuing. "Back home, on the

grounds of Adaga Hall, I have an art studio. And right now... it's filled with paintings of you."

She blinks, her voice barely a whisper. "Of me?"

I nod, my heart pounding. "Yes, you. Ever since we first met, you've been my muse, Harlow. Every colour, every painstaking brushstroke—it's all been about you. Fuck, I've even..."

"What, Sterling?"

A flood of colour heats my cheeks, but I refuse to feel shame. Instead I meet her gaze and say, "I've been so consumed by you, so obsessed with everything about you that it wasn't enough to just paint your image on canvas. I needed to leave my mark, a piece of me if you will." Dropping my gaze to my hardening cock, I fist my dick over my trousers. "So I'd fuck my hand until I came, and painted my cum into your lips knowing that a piece of me will forever be a part of you."

Harlow gasps.

"Does that disgust you?" I ask, bracing myself for rejection.

She shakes her head, her breath hitching. "No, Sterling, that doesn't disgust me. It turns me on."

"Thank fuck," I mutter, swiping a hand through my hair, the relief I feel is palpable. Reaching in my pocket, I pull out my bunch of keys, and reach for the spare to my art studio. Releasing it from the clasp, I hand it to her. "This is the key to my art studio back home."

She takes it from me. "You want me to have this?"

"Yes. My studio is my sanctuary, Harlow, my safe place, and I want it to be that for you too..."

"Thank you, this means so much," she replies, grasping the key in her palm and pressing it against her chest.

"When we get back, I'll show you where it is, okay?"

"I'd like that," she replies, her gaze flitting to the easel and the canvas resting on it. "So, what happens now?"

"I ordered these art supplies because I want to share who I truly am with you in the only way I know how. I've never allowed anyone to witness me create, Harlow. It's an incredibly personal experience, and I am often so overcome with colour that I can paint for hours straight, days even, until I'm satisfied. I want to share that part of me with you, but in order to do that, I need your help." I pause, meeting her eyes once more, and then she smiles and it's as if the entire room is bathed in sunlight. "Will you sing for me, Harlow?"

"At this point, I'll do anything you ask," she says, repeating the exact same words to me as she did the night we met.

THIRTY-TWO

"What song would you like me to sing?" she asks, climbing to her feet.

My answer is immediate and certain. "True Colours."

She gives my hand a gentle squeeze, her eyes lighting with affection. "It makes sense now why you love this song so much."

"When you've spent your entire life suppressing who you truly are, hearing the words of this song feels like an acknowledgment, you know?" I explain, adjusting the height of the easel in front of me, so that I can remain seated whilst I paint.

"I understand exactly what you mean," she replies, her gaze soft with understanding as she studies me for a moment. Then, without another word, she takes a few steps back and begins to hum the intro. The gentle sound fills the space between us as we lock gazes, and I realise that she's giving me a moment to acclimate to the sound, to settle into the rhythm before the song fully envelops me, and I'm grateful for her thoughtfulness. As the hummed notes continue to float in the air, a tingling sensation spreads over my skin, the first glimmers of colour beginning to awaken within me.

They're tentative at first, nothing more than a faint shimmer, barely discernible, but as she begins to sing the lyrics, they become richer in hue. Soft gold and pale ochre float outwards from her body in a haze of warmth that has me gasping. She's singing with such tenderness, it's as though she's offering me a piece of herself–a part that's meant to heal, to comfort, and in turn my synesthesia is conjuring colours to reflect that.

I swallow back the emotion rising up in my chest, instead reaching for my paintbrush, my fingers curling around the smooth wood. A sense of peace settles inside of me as I pick up a tube of paint, its colour the closest to what I see wrapping around Harlow now.

When the first dash of colour spreads across the canvas, I feel another emotion stirring deep within me, *pain*. The lyrics are a reminder of all the years I spent hiding, pretending to be someone I'm not, just to keep others from seeing the truth of who I really am. The vulnerability of it is overwhelming, but here with Harlow, it feels safe. She makes me feel safe, and as her voice envelops me, I allow myself to feel everything I've kept buried for so long.

There's anger, fear, rage, pain, disappointment, exhaustion, betrayal, and finally *hope*.

I'm hopeful because of her, because of Harlow.

Tears pour unbidden down my face, and Harlow pauses, her voice cracking.

"Sterling, should I stop?"

"No, please, keep going," I rasp, needing to see this through, craving her voice and the comfort she brings me despite the tears. "Don't hold back, Harlow."

Harlow nods, the beauty of her voice washing over me as I

swipe at my tears and continue to paint. My hand moves almost automatically, and I barely register the motion. For once, there's no frantic energy in my strokes. This time, painting isn't a purge of emotion or colour, it's something else entirely, it's a profound sense of peace.

I'm so engrossed in what I'm doing that I don't immediately register Harlow undoing her shirt whilst still continuing to sing. It's only when her hands fall away, and the material parts showing her smooth skin and simple cotton bra, that I realise what she's doing.

Something flickers in her gaze as though she's seeking permission. I nod, and with slow deliberate movements, Harlow strips, adding a sensual dynamic to the moment that has my heart pounding, and my cock stirring with need. Now every note is bathed in carnal promises, the colours changing to deep plums, rosy pinks and velvety reds as her voice drops an octave, adding a potency to the lyrics that I've never heard before.

"Fuck, Harlow," I murmur, my heart hammering in my chest as I watch her strip until she's naked before me, the last note of the song lingering in the air between us.

"You are baring the deepest parts of yourself with me," she replies, her chest rising and falling as I study her. "I want to honour you in the same way."

"God, I'm so in love with you," I murmur, every inch of me aching to pull her close and lose myself in her. But then, with her lips forming a perfect circle, Harlow begins to sing *The Night We Met* by Lord Huron, and I'm swept away once more, caught in a whirlwind of colour, with Harlow at its heart.

For the next couple of hours I continue to paint, and during all that time Harlow sings for me. Song after song, her haunting voice fills the room, only pausing occasionally so she can take sips of water to keep her throat from drying out.

By the time my brain registers the pain in my arm muscles from keeping them aloft for so long, Harlow is laying down on the bed, her arms stretched above her, her chin tipped up as she sings *Wicked Game* by Chris Isaak.

The sultry cadence reminds me that I'm still hard, painfully so, and I rest my paintbrush on the table then shift the canvas to one side. Dragging in a deep breath, my gaze coasts over Harlow's pebbled nipples, the rivets of her ribcage, and the soft curve of her belly that rises and falls with every melodic breath.

Reaching for the zipper of my jeans, I slowly undo them, my hand sliding beneath the waistband of my boxers as I pull my cock free. Groaning, I give my dick a squeeze, before pumping the shaft, my gaze never leaving Harlow's perfect form. Her expression is one of pure joy that slowly softens into a heady kind of desire as she tilts her head to face me.

We lock gazes as the last line of the song settles around us, and then with feline grace, she rises to her hands and knees, and crawls to the end of the bed.

"Stay where you are," she commands softly as she climbs off the bed, her hips swaying seductively as she walks towards me.

"Harlow, it's not finished," I say, flicking my gaze to the painting.

"I won't look until it's done," she promises, her hair framing her face as she looks down at me.

"Then what are you doing?" I ask, my brain short-circuiting as she drops to her knees before me and presses her palms against my thighs. "Make room for me."

"Fuck, Harlow," I murmur, finally catching up as I widen my legs, and she smooths her hands over my jean-clad thighs.

"I want to taste you," she whispers, reaching for my cock, her fingers grazing briefly over my hand before I let her take me in her hold.

Gently gripping the base of my cock, she leans forward, licking the crown, and I swear to fuck I'm so sensitive, so turned on, that I almost come there and then. My hips jolt, my cock slipping into her mouth as she hums around me.

"It won't take much for me to come," I admit, my cock leaking pre-cum, my heart pounding at the sight of her naked and kneeling before me.

"Hmm," she hums, her lips sliding down my cock as she takes me deeper into her mouth.

My hands fly to her hair, a low moan ripping from my lips as my stomach muscles clench and release. She doesn't ease me in, licking and sucking slowly. No, Harlow deepthroats my cock until I hit the back of her throat.

"Fuck, Fuck, Fuck!" I exclaim, my eyes rolling into the back of my head from the sensation of her throat and tongue wrapped so tightly around my engorged length.

She pulls back slightly, the ridges of my cock slip over her tongue. The heat of her mouth, the slippery warmth and the cascade of sensation making dark spots dance in front of my eyes. I'm fucking wrecked, in all of the best possible ways, and I don't try to control her movements. Instead, I simply cup the back of her head, watching with wide eyes as she slips up and down my cock, coaxing out an orgasm.

With every dip and rise of her head, my breaths become more laboured, my stomach muscles tensing as my balls lift high and tight against my body. "Harlow, I'm going to come," I warn her, and she simply lifts her gaze, her eyes meeting mine as her tongue lashes around the sensitive crown of my cock.

"Fuuuuuccckkkkk!" I roar, my hips jerking as my orgasm rips out of me and I come in Harlow's mouth, the colours that lingers still shimmering and sparkling behind my closed eyelids.

I drag in a few tremulous breaths as Harlow pulls back, looking up at me with watery eyes.

"That was incredible..." I say, my voice trailing off as Harlow opens her mouth and slides out her tongue, offering me my release.

Fuck. Me.

"You want me to paint my cum into your image?" I ask.

She nods once, and I slip two of my fingers inside her mouth, scooping up some of my cum, then lean over her and swipe it across her breasts and stomach that I've painstakingly painted onto canvas. "There."

"Good," she murmurs, before pushing up onto her feet, making sure to avert her gaze as she steps towards the bed. With heavy-lidded eyes I watch her climb onto the bed, her slit glistening before she turns back around and settles onto the bed.

"Make love to me," she whispers.

"Every fucking day, forevermore," I reply hoarsely, as I climb to my feet and strip for Harlow. Taking my time, I revel in the way she watches me, her hand slipping towards her pussy as her legs spread.

"You're so beautiful," she murmurs, her fingers slipping between her folds as she touches herself. "Everything about you is so beautiful to me."

"Ditto, my little poet," I reply, my gaze drifting from her sweet pussy to the unused paintbrushes still lined up on the table. I reach for the one with the rounded beavertail handle, it's bristles soft to touch. Grasping it in my fist, I climb onto the bed, kneeling between her spread thighs.

"Did you know that paintbrushes were used by man as early as the stone age?" I ask, lightly trailing the bristles up the inside of her leg.

She shakes her head, her eyelids drooping in pleasure as she swirls her finger around her clit. "No, I didn't," she breathes.

"Imagine that, the earliest forms of humankind used pigment to paint scenes on the walls of caves as a way to record their experiences. It's incredible, no?"

"It is," she agrees, her breath hitching as I continue to gently trail the soft bristles upwards, drawing circles against her thighs, and over her stomach until finally reaching her peaked nipple.

Leaning forward on my knees I press my hand into the mattress beside her head, coasting the bristles over her nipple as I gaze down at her. She shudders, her back arching as I tenderly paint the colours that I still see into her skin.

"Golden yellow," I murmur, staring into her hazel eyes.

"What?" she replies, her cheeks flushing a pretty blush pink.

"That's the colour I see swirling around your nipples right now, Harlow," I explain.

"You still see the colours even though I've stopped singing?" she questions softly, her mouth parting on a whimper as I move the paintbrush across her chest, swirling it around her other nipple.

"They linger for a while afterwards, yes, and right now you're doused in colour. It's intoxicating. You're intoxicating," I rasp out, so fucking overcome with love for this beautiful woman.

"Describe them to me," she breathes, her fingers moving between her legs, the sound of her arousal making my cock thicken once again.

I gaze down at her, my heart swelling with love and gratitude, my gaze filled with a plethora of colours that douse her skin in a breathtaking display of light and shade. "The yellow is like warm rays of sunlight on an early summer's day," I say, using the paintbrush to swirl the colour across her breasts. "And here," I say, stroking the paintbrush across her clavicle and throat, "It merges with sunset pink."

"Sunset pink?" she muses, her voice soft as I lower my mouth to her lips, kissing her reverently.

"Yes, just like the kind of pink you might see as the sun slips past the horizon," I explain. "And your lips, they're a deep rose red," I add, pulling back as I drag the paintbrush down the long column of her neck and between her breasts, tracing the curve of her ribcage.

"What do you see now?" she asks, her chest heaving.

Swirling the soft bristles over her skin, I paint ever decreasing circles over her stomach, stirring up more colour. "And here, it's a warm ochre."

"My God, Sterling, what you see, it's incredible," she whispers, as I trail the paintbrush lower.

Nudging her hand out of the way, I stroke the soft bristles over her clit. "Still berry red," I say, my cock twitching at the glistening wetness.

She shudders beneath me, her hips rocking as I swipe the brush through her folds over and over again, making the bristles sticky with her arousal. Her breath comes in short soft pants, her back arching in pleasure.

"Please, Sterling," she begs.

Twisting the paintbrush in my hand, I place the thick handle against her entrance, tentatively rimming her hole with the rounded tip, wanting to make sure she's okay with this.

Her eyes snap open as she lifts up onto her elbows.

"Is this okay?" I ask.

"Don't stop," she whispers, watching as I slide the smooth wooden handle of the paintbrush into her slick heat, gently fucking her with it.

Her gaze is transfixed on the handle disappearing and reappearing from her tight cunt. Her body shudders with every thrust, her breathing ragged as she cries out in both pleasure and surprise.

"Faster, Sterling," she begs, her fingers digging into the sheets beneath her.

I comply instantly, increasing my pace, the handle slipping in and out of her in a steady rhythm. It's so fucking erotic that my jaw slackens with need, and when I press my thumb against her clit, adding just the right amount of pressure, she drops back to the bed, a groan releasing from her plump lips.

"Sterling, I'm going to..." she gasps, her face flushed and eyes glassy.

"Then come for me, Harlow," I urge, watching as she reaches the peak of pleasure, her back arching and her stomach muscles clenching.

"Sterling," she cries, her eyes rolling back as an orgasm washes over her, her pussy pulsing around the handle. Her hands grab my wrists, her fingernails digging into my skin as I hold the paintbrush there, and she rides out the final waves of her orgasm.

Slowly her body relaxes as her breathing begins to regulate, and I gently remove the paintbrush, placing it on the bed beside her hip. Adjusting my body over hers, I brace my forearms by the side of her head and kiss her tenderly, my aching cock slipping between her parted folds.

"I'm not done," I say, nipping on her lower lip before sliding my tongue inside her mouth.

As we kiss, tongues languid and searching, the crown of my dick presses against her entrance. Slowly I slide inside of her inch by inch until I'm fully sheathed. Her legs wrap around my arse, and she tangles her fingers in my hair, her whimpers against my lips fucking music to my ears.

"Harlow," I groan, so turned on that I'm already close to coming again.

She moans, her eyes locked on mine as I move within her, her walls tightening, our bodies moving in perfect synchronicity, each thrust bringing us both closer to the edge.

"This is where I belong, Harlow, buried deep inside of you," I mutter against her lips, revelling in the feeling of her internal walls tightening around my cock.

"I love you," she whispers back.

"Say it again," I demand roughly, pleasure racing down my spine with every rock of my hips.

"I love you," she exclaims, smiling up at me.

"And I love you," I reply, then with one final thrust I come, Harlow following shortly after.

THIRTY-THREE

Isn't it funny how time seems to both move in slow motion, yet passes through your fingers like sand? One minute, you're holding on to every second, trying to make them last, and the next thing you know, they've slipped away. Hours can feel like an eternity, but days pass by in the blink of an eye. Maybe it's this fleeting quality of time that makes each moment between Sterling and I all the more precious. But I crave more than fleeting moments. I want every minute, every hour, every day with him, forever more.

Yet still we hide our love.

"What are you thinking about?" Sterling asks me as we steal another precious few hours with each other, just like we have every single day this past month. Sometimes we take a walk together in the woods surrounding Adaga Hall, the huge pinewood trees hiding us from sight. Other times we meet at his studio, situated a mile from the main building. The first time I entered I was overcome by his talent, the paintings of me utterly stunning, and somehow capturing the parts of me I thought I'd kept hidden.

Tonight, our parents are out of town, and we're using the opportunity to invite his friends over for dinner. It's the first time we've all got together since Daisy's and Dalton's wedding day. According to Sterling, the tragedy of Daisy's miscarriage has put a strain on their relationship, and Dalton is desperate to fix things. He's hoping that being around people who care about her will help.

"Us," I reply, a note of sadness in my voice as I set the final dinner plate onto the table. "I want to be free to love you, Sterling. I don't want to hide anymore."

He rounds the table, pulling me into his arms, and I sink into them, my cheek pressed against his shoulder as he holds me. "We are so close to having that, Harlow. Please, bear with me."

"It's so hard though..." My voice trails off as I heave out a sigh.

"I know, but we are one step closer to finding out who your stalker is, and once I know that you're safe, and that bastard is dealt with once and for all, we'll tell our parents together. One thing at a time, okay?"

"Have there been any more messages?" I ask, drawing back slightly to look up at him.

Ever since I revealed what's been happening, Sterling has taken over my account. We both agreed that the only way to draw this man out of hiding was to pretend I welcomed his attention. I couldn't bear to respond to my stalker, so Sterling has been acting as if he's me. For weeks he's been pretending that I'm slowly 'coming around,' and though it makes me sick to my stomach, it's the only way we can lure him out.

"Yes, several," he replies, pulling out his phone and clicking on the app, showing the messages to me.

I read over the last few, wincing at the one where I claim to have missed him messaging me after a week of silence. Bile rises up in my throat, hating that Sterling is having to do this on my behalf.

"You think he's buying it?" I ask, chewing on my lip as I lift my gaze from the screen.

"I believe so," he murmurs, pointing to the latest message. I read it.

> My sweet songbird, there are a few things I need to finalise before we can finally be together. Once I have, I will claim you as mine. Be patient, my love.

A shiver tracks down my spine. "What do you think he's talking about exactly?" I ask.

"I have my suspicions," Sterling replies, cryptically.

"Do you want to share those with me?"

Chewing on his lip, Sterling regards me for a moment before nodding. "Do you remember at the wedding when I told you about how Benedict is going to make his move on Elodie?"

"Yes," I reply, my brows pinching together as I wonder where this is going.

"Ben has in fact offered two million pounds to Hoxton to spend a month alone with Elodie. He plans on using the time to steal her back from him."

"What on earth, Sterling? You can't just buy people!" I exclaim, shocked that Ben would even consider doing something so outrageous. It's one thing to try and win her back, quite another to *buy* her back.

"I know that, and believe me when I tell you that Ben is doing this with good intentions. He loves Elodie, he always has."

"But what about *her* feelings in all of this? I can't believe that Ben has even considered this, let alone going through with it. I don't know how I feel about that."

"Ben is a good man. He wouldn't be doing this if he didn't think that there was any other way."

"And what kind of man would accept money in exchange for time with his wife?" I ask, pissed.

"The kind of man who sends sexually explicit and threatening messages to the woman *I* love," Sterling retorts, his jaw gritting with anger.

"We still don't know it's him," I whisper, feeling my stomach churn. I don't like Councillor Hoxton, but if we're wrong the consequences could be catastrophic.

"We don't, you're right, but everything you've said points to him, and pretty soon we'll know for sure if this plan I have works out. Please trust me. If our suspicions are right, then it would seem that Hoxton has agreed to this exchange with Ben so that he can make his move on you. It makes sense, discard Elodie so that he can replace her with..." His voice trails off as he looks at me.

"...Me?"

"Yes, I believe so."

"Sterling, that's so messed up."

"I know, but you're safe. I'm not letting you out of my sight. That man won't get anywhere near you, I promise."

"Have you told Ben what you suspect, or any of the others?"

Sterling shakes his head. "Right now, the less people who know, the better."

"And have you told them about us?"

"No, and I won't until we've dealt with Hoxton. We can't

tell Ben in case it impacts his plans, and we need that to go ahead if we're going to draw Hoxton out."

"I don't have a very good feeling about this. It's as though we're complicit in what Ben's doing, and while I appreciate that he's doing it with good intentions, buying someone still makes me feel uncomfortable. She's a human being, not a possession."

"I get that," he replies, soothing his hands up and down my arms. "But whichever way you look at it, Elodie is better off without Hoxton. Ben just wants the opportunity to get her out of his grasp, even if it's just to set her free from that man."

"So you're saying that if this all backfires on Ben, he'll just let Elodie go?"

Sterling heaves out a breath. "No, he *will* fight for her."

"What about Drix and Dalton, could we not tell them what's happening? It might help ease the burden somewhat."

Sterling shakes his head. "Telling them isn't an option either. Drix has just gotten out from beneath Carl's hold, and the last thing he needs is more shit blowing up in his face if he were to get involved in our problems. Which leaves Dalton, and he's got way too much going on right now."

"You're right," I agree, my shoulders slumping in defeat. "I just hate the thought that you don't have anyone to talk to about all of this."

"I have you, and that's more than enough, Harlow," he replies, dropping a kiss to my forehead.

"So, tonight we're just two people who happen to be connected by our parents, and are putting on a united front for your friends."

Sterling cocks his head to the side. "Tonight I'm a man who's hopelessly in love with his step-sister and can't do a damn thing about it since she's playing hard to get," he says, a smile pulling up his lips as he swats my arse playfully.

"Great, blame it all on me," I reply, shaking my head with a laugh.

"Never. Now, let me finish up here, and you go and get ready."

"That was delicious," Drix says, leaning back in his seat, his plate completely empty. I watch as he throws an arm over the back of Lia's chair, their ease with each other the complete opposite to how me and Sterling are behaving right now. We're both tense, guarded with each other, and I hate it.

"Yes, thank you for having us," Lia adds, leaning into his side, her kind eyes drifting between me and Sterling who's sitting beside me. "This was all so delicious. Please pass on our thanks to your chef."

"Of course," Sterling replies, grabbing his glass and knocking back the last dregs of wine. He's been distracted ever since he went to the billiards room to talk with the guys earlier, and I'm sensing that there's more to how he's behaving than keeping up the charade between us. Once they've left, I intend on finding out what's bothering him.

"So are you settling in okay?" Lia asks me.

"Everyone has been very welcoming," I reply, almost jumping out of my skin when Sterling reaches beneath the table and gently brushes his knuckles against my thigh, my cheeks heating at the brief contact.

"Well, we're all happy to have you here, aren't we, Sterling?" Ben says, his eyes twinkling with mischief as he tips his head with a wink. My cheeks flame even more. "So what now? A game of billiards?" he adds.

"I'd really love to hear Harlow sing. You have a beautiful

voice." Daisy murmurs softly, and my gaze flicks to her. She looks so incredibly sad, and my heart squeezes in sympathy. All night she's been quiet, distracted. I can only imagine the pain she must feel.

"I don't think that's a good idea," Sterling cuts in as he moves to stand. "I'll go and set up a game."

Despite knowing his abruptness is all part of the act, I can't help but frown.

"Personally, I would love to hear you sing again," Lia interjects, giving me a warm smile, clearly confused by Sterling's urgent need to leave the room. "Daisy's right, you have an incredible voice."

"I don't know..." I begin, glancing at Sterling who smiles tensely.

"Yeah, maybe not tonight, eh?" Drix says, seemingly picking up on Sterling's discomfort.

"*Please*, I'd really like it if you could sing for us," Daisy comments. She's so forlorn, and if my singing could make her feel a fraction better, then how can I possibly refuse her?

"Okay, sure. The parlour has a piano..." I reply, pushing back my chair as I stand.

"You play the piano too?" Lia asks, eyes widening. "Wow, I've always wanted to learn how to play a musical instrument."

"You still can," Drix says, giving her shoulder a squeeze.

"I could teach you," I offer. Both Lia and Daisy seem like really nice people, and it's about time I made some friends of my own. What would be the harm?

"Really? That would be wonderful!" she exclaims, grinning.

"I guess we're listening to you sing then," Sterling mumbles, and we all head into the parlour.

Pulling out the stool beneath the baby grand piano, I settle onto the seat, a hushed silence descending as my fingers hover

over the keys. Everyone else is seated on the huge sectional waiting patiently, and I take a moment to briefly glance at Sterling. His expression is fixed in place, but there's no hiding the look in his eyes. It's as though he's bracing himself, and I'm acutely aware of the effect my singing will have on him. This time there's no easing him in like I did at the hotel.

Resting my fingers gently on the keys, I begin to play the opening verse of *Someone You Loved* by Lewis Capaldi. As the music swells, I pour every raw emotion I've been holding inside into my voice. The ache of loving Sterling but having to hide that love echoes within every note I sing. Each press of the keys, each breath I take, becomes a silent confession of a love I can't speak out loud, but can only show through this song.

I wish everyone could understand. I wish they could see the depth of our love. How the moments we've stolen away from the world have slipped through our fingers too quickly, days blending into nights, and weeks fading into months, all while our love remains hidden. With each passing line, I let go, surrendering to the music, allowing it to speak for me until eventually the song comes to an end, and I rest my trembling hands in my lap, waiting for someone to break the silence that quivers with suppressed emotion.

"Damn," Ben mutters whilst tension crackles in the air.

I feel the heat of Sterling's stare, and can't help but look at him. His mouth is slightly parted, his fingers curling into the arm rest, knuckles white. I want to ask him if he's okay, but Lia starts applauding, preventing me from doing so.

"You're amazing!" she exclaims, jumping up from the couch and rushing towards me. I stand, and she pulls me into a hug as the others rise to their feet, murmuring their agreement. I'm still not used to receiving compliments, but Lia's kind words are a welcome relief.

"Thank you," I say softly, my gaze gravitating back to Sterling who remains frozen in his seat. My throat constricts at the agony in his gaze. I sway on my feet, wanting nothing more than to go to him.

"I... I need some air," he manages to rasp out, before striding from the room.

Ten minutes later, everyone has left, the evening cut short by Sterling's abrupt departure. After spending the next half an hour helping Stephanie clear the dishes despite her assurances that she's happy to do it alone, I slip on my coat and head towards Sterling's studio, knowing he'll be there purging all the colours my singing has stirred within him tonight.

THIRTY-FOUR

My chest heaves as I stare at the canvas before me. My naked torso and arms are covered in bright crimson paint, the colour blending with the sweat that slides over my skin. Harlow's performance tonight has unleashed a rage within me.

Not at her, *never* her, but at everything else.

At my father for being the coldhearted bastard he is.

At Melody for treating Harlow with such contempt.

At Councillor Hoxton who wants to hurt the woman I love.

At Dalton's father for thinking only of himself and forcing Dalton and Daisy to make a decision that could break the both of them.

And most of all, at myself for not acting sooner.

I should've claimed Harlow the second I saw her at our parents' wedding. I should've made it clear that we belonged together and maybe Councillor Hoxton would've backed the fuck off.

I'm angry, so fucking angry.

After hearing Harlow sing, I came straight here to unleash

the turmoil I felt from every beautiful, poignant note that she sang. Daisy might have asked her to sing, but that performance was for me. I felt every drop of longing, I heard every uttered cadence telling me how trapped she feels by our secret, by the man who's been terrorising her. Fuck, I'd wanted to go to her. I'd wanted to pull her into my arms and kiss her pain and fear away. I wanted to soothe her. But I fucking couldn't. I could only watch as she poured her heart and soul into her performance, my own desperation making me stiff with tension, with rage. I still feel it now, despite trying to purge myself of it. Every stroke before me is a violent declaration of how much she means to me, how far I'm willing to go to keep her safe.

Dropping the paintbrush that's dripping with crimson and black paint, I snatch up my phone and open the app, clicking through to the messages. I'm done with this shit. It's time I draw the bastard out once and for all. Moving towards the far wall where more paintings of Harlow are situated, I take a photo of the very first painting I did of Harlow, and press send. Then I wait. Within minutes I see that he's typing a response. My anger blazes as I read.

What is this?!

I can feel his shock and confusion through the message. Good. I hope the motherfucker feels a fraction of how I'm feeling now. If he's as consumed by Harlow as he appears to be, seeing her image that I captured in a state of arousal will incense him. It will force his hand. Blowing out a steadying breath through my lips, I wait a moment before responding, but in the meantime he sends another message.

Who the fuck painted you like this?
Have you been disloyal to me,
Harlow? Are you trying to make
me mad?

"Yes, motherfucker, that's exactly what I'm doing," I grind out, my thumb flying over the screen as I type out a message in response.

No. I'm afraid. That's why I sent you these photos. He's been acting strange around me, making lewd comments under his breath, pretending to our parents that he hates me when all the while he's been painting images just like this. There are so many of them. I didn't know.

He responds instantly.

Who? Tell me who!

Rolling my head on my shoulders to ease the tension, I reply.

My step-brother, Sterling. Tonight I overheard him speaking with his friends. He's going to sell these paintings at a private viewing. People will assume we're together. How could he do this to me? It's sick.

For long moments, I wait. I can see him typing out a response, but nothing comes back straight away. He seems to be typing a message, then thinking better of it. I wonder what thoughts are rolling through his head right now. I hope he's fucking raging, but more than that, I hope he takes the bait.

When?

His short response has a wicked smile curving up my lip. "Got you," I mutter.

When? I reply.

When is he having this private viewing?!

Next Saturday in an art gallery in London. What should I do?

He replies within seconds.

I will sort this out. Leave it with me my sweet songbird. I'll protect you from that deviant bastard and from anyone else who thinks they can own a piece of you. I'll buy every damn painting if that's what it takes.

"The fuck you will," I grind out, slamming my phone onto the table, and cracking the screen in the process.

"Sterling, is everything okay?"

My head snaps up as I watch Harlow step into the studio, gently closing the door behind her. Her eyes are wide and her cheeks tinged pink from the cold as she takes me in. I know what I must look like, standing here covered in paint, trembling still from the aftermath of hearing her sing, from being so fucking angry at everyone and everything, of both wanting to protect her and struggling with my feelings that I've had to keep hidden. Hell, from needing to claim her as mine in front of our friends.

"No, Harlow. I'm not," I admit, resting my arse against the table as I drop my head.

"I shouldn't have sung. It's my fault," she says, her voice laced with concern as she comes to me.

Within moments her arms are wrapped around my back, her hands running up and down my spine. I melt into her embrace, hauling her close.

"It's not that. It's not you."

"Then what is it? Talk to me, Sterling," she begs, pulling back slightly so she can read my expression.

"I'm so fucking angry," I admit, my body trembling with suppressed rage.

"Was it something to do with the conversation you had with the guys earlier? You seemed so tense after you spoke with them, what happened?"

I nod. "Partly."

Cupping my cheek she strokes the pad of her thumb against my skin. "Tell me," she urges.

"Do you remember when I told you that Dalton is afraid that if his father finds out about Daisy's miscarriage that he'll force him to divorce her and find another wife?"

"Yes," she nods, her brows pinching together with concern.

"Well, part of the reason they got married in the first place was so that a debt Drix owed Carl would be paid in full, so long as Daisy agreed to marry Dalton and provide Carl with an heir to carry on the family name."

"They married to clear a debt that Drix owes?" she repeats, shock widening her eyes.

"Yes. It would also mean that Dalton would receive his inheritance."

"I thought he was in love with her."

"He is, very much so."

"But you said–"

"Daisy agreed to marry Dalton because she loves her brother and wanted to free him of the debt so he could be with Lia, and Dalton initially agreed to the marriage for selfish reasons," I explain.

"And now?"

"And now he's so in love with her that he's willing to do *anything* to keep her, including walking away from his riches. The problem is, if he does, then the debt Drix owes still stands. Carl holds all the fucking cards."

"What are they going to do?" she asks.

"*I'm* going to help them."

"How?"

"I can cover most of the debt with my own savings from paintings I've already sold, but I'll also have to sell these," I explain, watching her carefully for a reaction.

"By these, you mean the paintings of *me*?"

"Yes..." My voice trails off as I let that news sink in.

Harlow thinks for a moment, her eyes drifting around the studio. She has every right to refuse, to insist that I don't sell them, but instead she reaches up with her other hand and palms both my cheeks.

"If it will help them, then do it. Sell the paintings, Sterling."

I should feel relief at her agreement, but all I feel is guilt because I hadn't sought her permission before promising I'd help Dalton, least of all using the sale of these paintings as an opportunity to draw out that cunt Hoxton.

"What?" she questions, sensing there's more.

"I should've consulted you first..." My voice trails off as I grit my jaw.

"Sterling, just tell me."

"I can't wait any longer, Harlow," I blurt out, cupping her wrists and feeling my stomach churn with desperation. "This is the only way I could think of to force Hoxton's hand, so that he makes a move and we can deal with the bastard once and for all. Fuck, I don't know if I've done the right thing."

"How are you forcing his hand?" she asks, her gaze flickering with a sudden unease that makes my throat constrict with panic.

"Fuck," I exclaim.

"Sterling, how?" she insists.

"I sent him a photo of that painting," I say in a rush of breath, pointing to the painting that has captured Harlow in pure ecstasy. The one where her head is thrown back in surrender, her mouth parted on a moan, her beautiful face surrounded by an array of colours that represent the intensity of our first time together. It's an incredibly personal piece that I never intended for anyone else to see, least of all that cunt, but I also knew that it was the only one that would ignite a reaction from him, and finally draw him out of hiding.

Harlow gasps, her hands dropping from my cheeks as she takes a step back, processing my words. For a moment I think she's going to walk away, and I wouldn't blame her, but instead she lifts her eyes to meet mine, pulls back her shoulders and nods.

"I trust you, Sterling. I trust that you're doing what you think is best to protect us," she says firmly, determination and gritty resolve shining in her eyes.

I feel a surge of gratitude and love for Harlow at that moment. Despite my reckless actions and questionable decision, she trusts me with this and that means so fucking much to me. Without hesitation, I bridge the gap between us, pull her into my arms and slam my lips against hers.

The second our lips meet, a current of electricity shoots through me, igniting a crazed kind of passion that has Harlow responding with equal fervour. Her hands grip my shoulders as our bodies press together with a powerful connection that cannot be contained. Everything that has happened tonight is eclipsed by our feelings for each other, and in its place is a raw, wild kind of need that drives us closer together. Harlow's hands slide into my hair as I lift her effortlessly, her legs wrapping around my waist as we continue to kiss. Carrying her to the table, our kisses become frantic as I lean over and swipe my arm across the surface, knocking paintbrushes and tubes of oil paint to the floor. Our fingers race over one another, fumbling with buttons and zippers as we strip off our clothes until there's nothing left but skin on skin. I devour her with hungry kisses, nipping and licking her skin as I trace the curve of her neck and the swell of her breast before clamping my mouth around her nipple and sucking hard.

"Sterling!" she hisses, arching into me, her voice begging for more. I oblige without hesitation, drawing her nipple deeper into my mouth.

Our moans fill the room, mingling together in a frantic cacophony of sound whilst the air around us thickens with palpable heat. The faint scent of her arousal mixes with spilled paint creating an erotic cocktail that only serves to turn me on more. My hands roam over her body, tracing the curve of her hips and the softness of her thighs as I push them apart, my fingers finding her wet and wanting.

Smashing my lips back against hers, I slide two fingers inside of her slick pussy whilst she clings to me, her nails digging into my skin. Her moans intensify and my cock drips with pre-cum, begging me to drive the thick shaft inside of her.

"I need you, Harlow. I need you so fucking much," I rasp out as I remove my fingers and grip my dick, her slickness coating my shaft as I fist myself.

Her eyes seek mine, heady with lust and love. "Fuck me, Sterling. Please, just fuck me!" she cries.

Reaching up, I press my palm against the middle of her chest, urging her back against the table, then I line my cock up with her entrance, wrap my fingers around her throat, and slam into her with one firm thirst. My cock drives home, slipping effortlessly into her wet heat.

She gasps, the force of my entrance shoving her across the table, causing my fingers to slip from her throat. So I reach for her hips, holding her in place with a bruising grasp as I rut into her. There's a desperate edge to our fucking, a culmination of so many pent-up emotions, and I feel them all. There's frustration and fear, need and longing, desire and love. It churns within my chest, around us both, thickening the air and stealing the oxygen from my lungs. This isn't just two people fucking, this is a claiming, an intense declaration of our undeniable connection.

"Goddamn it," I roar as her legs tighten around my arse and I thrust deeper, slamming into her at a frenzied pace.

"Harder," she hisses, as her hands grasp my back, holding on tight. She needs this as much as I do.

I oblige, each stroke eliciting a high-pitched moan from Harlow that only fuels my need to chase the intense orgasm that's coiling around the base of my spine. The pleasure builds with every thrust, my moans turning to grunts as every last thread of my control snaps.

"Sterling!" Her voice is a breathy plea and I respond by folding myself over her, each slide of my cock an aggressive claim on her body and soul. Harlow claims me right back, her internal muscles squeezing me tight from her oncoming orgasm.

"Mine!" I grunt, slamming into her. "Mine. Mine. Mine! You're mine!"

With one last final thrust, I empty inside of her with a roar, my cum coating her internal walls. "Yours!" she screams in response, her body tensing and shuddering with her own powerful orgasm.

Pure pleasure washes over me as I shudder inside of her, riding out the last waves of my orgasm until I can't hold myself up any longer, and collapse against her chest, spent and utterly satisfied.

It takes a while for us both to find the strength to get dressed, but we do so quietly. I help her to pull on her jeans, my touch gentle as I graze the bruises blooming on her hips from my grip.

"I'm sorry," I apologise.

"I'm not," she replies, pressing a chaste kiss against my lips.

"Are you certain that you're okay with all of this?" I ask, as she pulls on her t-shirt and jumper.

"I am. I want this to be over so that we can finally be together."

"Me too, but if I'm going to keep you safe, I don't want you anywhere near the viewing. I want to deal with that bastard alone."

"Do you honestly think this plan will work?" she asks softly. "Do you think he'll actually attend the viewing?"

"I'm certain of it," I reply, hoping to fuck I'm right.

THIRTY-FIVE

"What on earth is wrong with you, Harlow? You've been jumpy all week!" my mother exclaims, throwing her hands up in the air in frustration.

"Nothing is wrong, I'm just tired, that's all," I reply, closing the lid to my laptop and reaching for my phone resting on the table between us. After packing up and shipping the paintings earlier this week, Sterling left for London this morning, and I'm a nervous wreck. The private viewing of Sterling's art has already commenced, and I'm terrified of what's going to happen.

My mother continues to speak, but I barely register her words as I glance at the last message Sterling sent me just over an hour ago.

> Everything is going to be okay. I'll call you as soon as it's over.

"Harlow, are you listening to me?! We have company arriving very soon!"

"Company? What do you mean we have company?" I ask, my head snapping up.

"Robert has invited Councillor Hoxton and his wife Elodie to dinner—"

"No!" I exclaim, pushing up from my chair as fear cascades down my spine.

"What do you mean, *no*?" My mother looks at me aghast. I've been so distracted that I hadn't even noticed that she's dressed up to receive guests.

"I... I'm..." I stammer, struggling to come up with a reasonable explanation for my reaction.

I know I need to calm down, but how can I when Councillor Hoxton is on his way here, even though he's supposed to be in London for the viewing? Panic floods my mind as anxiety tightens in my stomach. Even if I manage to reach Sterling, he's over two hours away. What am I supposed to do?

"Harlow!" My mother yells, grabbing my shoulders and shaking me. I blink rapidly, trying to regain control and think clearly.

"Hello? Where are you both?" I hear Robert call from down the hall.

"I'm not feeling well," I snap, breaking free from my mother's grip. "I'm going to my room to lie down. Have a nice evening."

"Absolutely not. You will attend this dinner. It's incredibly rude not to," my mother insists, but I ignore her and rush toward the hallway, colliding straight into Robert's chest.

"Harlow, are you okay?" he asks me, his hands flying out to grasp my shoulders as he steadies me. "You look as though you've seen a ghost."

"Stop coddling her, Robert. She's not feeling well, *appar-*

ently, and is refusing to have dinner with us and our guests," my mother says, joining us both.

My gaze lifts to Roberts, his eyes searching mine. A frown creases his forehead. "You're unwell?"

"Yes, I'm suddenly feeling a little lightheaded," I whisper, taking a step back as his hands fall from my shoulders. It's not a complete lie, I do feel lightheaded just not for the reason he might think.

"Robert, is everything okay?" a familiar voice asks.

Behind Robert, Councillor Hoxton appears, his snakelike gaze assessing me. My skin crawls with unease and I feel all the colour draining from my face. Frozen in place, it's all I can do not to throw up.

"Oh, everything's fine, John. Just a bout of dizziness, Harlow was just heading to her room to lie down for a bit," Robert explains smoothly, stepping to one side as he gives me room to pass.

"There must be something in the water. Elodie has been feeling under the weather too. She wasn't able to make it this evening after all."

"Oh no, that's terrible, poor Elodie," my mother states, though there's a distinct undertone of annoyance that is hard to miss.

"Indeed, it is a shame," Robert adds, throwing a look at my mother. Seems like I'm not the only one who can sense her insincerity.

"I think I should go for a walk outside, get some fresh air," I interject quickly.

Robert studies me for a moment, a flicker of suspicion crossing his features. He's not stupid, he knows something is going on, but I'm not about to stick around long enough for him to press the matter. I need to get hold of Sterling.

"Alright, take a walk. Perhaps when you return you can pop into the dining hall and let us know that you're okay?" Robert asks, giving me a gentle smile.

"Sure," I murmur before striding down the hallway in the opposite direction. With every step I can feel Councillor Hoxton's gaze boring into my skin, and it's all I can do not to break into a run.

Once outside, I make my way toward Sterling's studio. It isn't until I step inside and lock the door behind me that I finally allow myself to take a shaky breath. With trembling hands, I pull out my phone and dial Sterling's number, but after a few rings, it goes to voicemail.

"Sterling, it's me. Councillor Hoxton is *here*. I don't know what to do. I'm scared. Please call back," I say, before hanging up and clutching the phone to my chest.

I leave it a few more minutes before trying again, but once again it goes to voicemail after a few rings. Frustrated and anxious, I send Sterling a text as well.

For the next half an hour I pace back and forth in Sterling's studio, my mind racing with all the possible scenarios that could unfold with Councillor Hoxton's unexpected appearance. Is this just more mind games? Has he figured out that we're on to him? What if he's here tonight to finally follow through on his threats?

"This can't be happening," I cry, trembling so violently that I have to take a seat on Sterling's threadbare couch.

Surely Councillor Hoxton wouldn't act on his threats with my mother and Robert both here? It's not as if he can really hurt me while they're around, can he?

Wait..!

What if we *were* wrong and he isn't my stalker? What then?

Try as I might, I can't dampen the sense of dread gnawing at me, and just when I'm about to give in to a full-blown panic attack, my phone rings. It's Sterling.

"Oh, thank God," I say, snatching it up and pressing it to my ear.

"I got your message. I'm on my way, Harlow. Where are you now?" he asks me, his voice tight with worry.

"I'm at your studio," I reply, relief flooding through me at the sound of his voice.

"Good. Have you locked the door?" he asks.

"Yes."

"Okay, stay where you are. Do not leave the studio. You'll be safe there. I'm coming as quickly as I can."

"I won't. Sterling what does this mean? If he hasn't bought the paintings then could we have the wrong person?"

"All the paintings have been bought," he replies tensely.

"By who?"

"A few from some of the guests tonight, but most from an undisclosed buyer. It has to be Hoxton. It was stupid of me to think he'd actually attend the viewing. This is my fault, Harlow. I've forced his hand and put you in danger. Fuck!" he shouts, his fear amplifying my own.

Forcing myself to calm down, I say, "Just get here safely. I'll wait until you arrive."

"I love you," he replies.

"I love you too."

Dropping the phone onto the couch, I grab a thick blanket that's draped over the arm of the sofa and wrap it around my shoulders, trying to ward off the chill that has settled deep into my bones. Minutes tick by agonisingly slowly as I stare blankly at the wall, waiting for Sterling to arrive. After an hour and a half has passed, my eyelids begin to droop, weighed down by my sheer exhaustion, but just as I feel myself slipping into an uneasy slumber, the sound of a key twisting in the lock jolts me awake.

"Sterling?!" I say, sitting bolt upright.

The door creaks open, an icy blast of air cutting through the studio as a figure stands in the doorway. But it's not Sterling.

It's Robert.

"Robert? What are you doing here?" I ask, as he steps into the studio, a look of relief on his face.

"You didn't return, and when your mother said you weren't in your room she insisted I go and find you. I must admit I had a moment's regret buying such a huge mansion, so many rooms to get lost in. I might've known you'd be here," he replies, stepping into the studio and shutting the door behind him.

I watch him as he turns his back to me, and locks the door. It takes me a moment to register what he's doing, but when I do, all the blood drains from my body.

"Robert, unlock the door," I say, trying to hide the sudden tremor in my voice as Robert turns to face me, a sinister grin spreading across his face.

Seconds slip past slowly as realisation dawns.

No. Please, no.

"Oh, Harlow, you really didn't think you could escape me, did you? It was very remiss of Sterling to think that I didn't have a key to his studio," he sneers, the concern in his eyes evaporating as he advances towards me with slow, deliberate steps.

"W-what are you talking about?" I ask, panic surging through me as I stand, the tremble in my voice giving away my fear.

Robert's eyes gleam with malice as he reaches into his pocket and pulls out his phone, his finger swiping over the screen before he flips it around to face me. "Does this seem familiar?" he asks.

My gaze drops to the photograph that Sterling sent of the painting he did of me. The one we thought we'd sent to Councillor Hoxton. Bile burns that back of my throat as I realise the true extent of the danger I'm in.

"You're my—"

"You've been playing a dangerous game, Harlow," Robert interjects, circling around me like a predator closing in on its prey. "Do you think I'm not aware of how you've been carrying on with my son right under my nose? Do you think that I can allow that to continue?"

"*You've* been sending me the messages?" I manage to choke out.

"Yes, though the shock on your face tells me that you didn't figure that out until just now. It's clear to me now that you thought it was John going by how you reacted to his presence this evening." His smile widens, revealing a malevolent side that Sterling had warned me about on so many occasions. "Whilst Hoxton is a deviant bastard, it wasn't him."

"You're sick!" I exclaim, unable to help myself.

"I must admit it's been the most fun I've had in years. Though I had hoped you'd think it was Sterling sending the messages, and that you'd sever your relationship with him once and for all. That was a fatal error in judgement on my part," he retorts.

"I don't understand. You sent me that first message way before you married Mom, before Sterling and I were officially introduced at your wedding. You're not making any sense. None of this is making sense."

"You really were so enamoured with him that you didn't even notice me sitting at the bar that night, huh?" he asks, cocking his head to the side as he regards me.

I blink at him, my thoughts whirling, and then I remember the lone man at the bar.

No! No way.

"That was *you*?"

"Indeed."

"How did you even know I'd be there that night?"

"When I decided to commit to a relationship with your mother, I made it my business to know everything about her, *and* by extension you. I had some checks done, and it's amazing what you can find out if you know the right people. I was made aware of your account on Instagram, so I asked my employee to do a little more digging. That led me to find out about your secret identity, and it wasn't all that hard to find out where you were singing next given my extensive contacts and access to some rather talented hackers. Intrigued, I wanted to hear you sing in person, so I made a quick diversion to the bar before heading over to see your mother at the hotel. You can imagine my surprise when I saw Sterling stumble into the club and leave with you a few minutes later," he adds, narrowing his eyes at me. "It doesn't take a genius to figure out where you were going off together, and so I had to act."

"How could you?" I hiss, utterly sick to my stomach.

"Very easily, Harlow. I am a man used to getting what he wants, and I do not want you having a relationship with my son!"

"Please, Robert, I never meant to come between you and Sterling. We love each other," I plead, desperation seeping into my voice.

Robert's expression darkens, his eyes narrowing as he looms closer. "Love each other? You think what you have is love? It's nothing but a pathetic infatuation, and it ends now."

"We didn't mean for this to happen. We met before you

made anything official with my mom. I didn't even know Sterling was your son until the night before your wedding. I know that this is unusual," I say, trying to appeal to his better nature, hoping that there's a part of him that is decent.

"Yet you've been sneaking around with each other ever since!" he shouts.

"If you didn't want us to be together then why force Sterling to spend time with me under the guise of wanting a happy family? Why not just confront us both?"

"Because I believed once you'd found out about his illness, you'd see how fucked-up he is and end the relationship yourself just like everyone else in his life has. That boy is incapable of having any real relationships. He's an embarrassment."

"He has friends!" I argue, anger mixing with fear. "He's a good man. He's loyal, brave, and talented. How dare you say such things. How dare you treat him the way you have!"

He waves his hand in the air dismissively. "They're acquaintances at best, and only tolerate him because of my relationship with their fathers."

"You're wrong. They care about him. *I* care about him."

"I really don't understand what you see in him. He's pathetic, nothing but a stain on this family name."

"And you're a coldhearted bastard!" I retort, my fist curling at my sides.

"I am who I am. Your mother doesn't seem to mind," he adds with a shrug.

"She doesn't know the real you, clearly. She'll be horrified when she finds out about what you've done, and has seen all the messages you've sent to me. She'll divorce you."

"You and I both know that's not true. Your mother doesn't care about you, all she cares about is herself. But *I* care about you, Harlow. I've done this all for you. Why can't you see that?"

"Sending me threatening messages is caring about me? Telling me that you want to force yourself on me, that you wonder if I'd scream if you did? How does that show you care about me?!"

"Like I said, I wanted you to believe it was Sterling, he does have a rather obsessive nature."

"You're lying. There's something you're not saying. None of this is making any sense. Maybe at first that was your intention. But if you've known about us all along, have suspected that we'd grown close, why keep sending them?"

He chuckles then, and the sound is manic. I take another step back praying that Sterling arrives soon. I just need to keep him talking long enough until he arrives.

"Well, admittedly that's because I'm a sick fuck, Harlow," he replies, laughing at himself as though what he's just said should be amusing and not down right scary. "Besides you were mine first, until he stole you from me."

"What do you mean, I was yours first?" I ask, utterly thrown now by where this conversation is heading. My head is spinning from everything he's said as I try to grasp the implication of his words. Robert's eyes gleam with a twisted kind of satisfaction as I take another step away from him.

"Don't you recall the night we met in Hollywood?"

"The night you met my mother, you mean?" I reply.

"Yes, her too, but it wasn't just Melody that I wanted. It was you."

"Me?" I whisper.

"You are a remarkable young lady, Harlow, or should I say my *sweet songbird*, and I'm a hot-blooded male. When I heard you sing that night at *Smokey Joe's*, I can admit that I was enthralled, turned on even. So I wrote those messages in part to make you think it was Sterling, but once I realised it wasn't working, I decided that I rather enjoyed the whole thing."

"No," I reply, shaking my head. "You're sick!"

"So you've said," he replies, taking another step towards me. "But now I'd like to experience what my son apparently has. I'm a jealous man, Harlow. I don't like what belongs to me being used by someone else."

"Oh my God. You're here to *rape* me? Do you think I won't fight you?"

"I truly hope you do. It's getting rather boring rutting into your mother. For all her flirtation she's a sack of potatoes in bed."

"And then what? You expect me to keep quiet, to not call the police and get your sorry ass thrown in jail? You're insane!"

"That would be incredibly difficult for you to do when you're dead."

"Dead?" I whisper out, my thundering heart stilling with abject terror.

"You've forced my hand. This could've gone so differently. I could've made you happy. You give me no choice."

"You won't get away with this!"

Robert throws his head back and laughs maniacally, and I frantically look around the room for anything I can use to protect myself with. My gaze lands on a metal palette knife that Sterling sometimes uses to press the oil paint onto canvas. It's small but sharp, and it's about the only thing I could use to try and protect myself with. I edge closer to it.

"What do you intend to do with my body?" I ask, trying to distract Robert enough so that I can grab the palette knife. "Do you honestly think you can get away with this?"

Robert sighs. "I'm a billionaire, Harlow. Money can buy an awful lot of things, including men who will cover up this little...

indiscretion," he says, his creepy smiles so unhinged that my teeth begin to chatter.

Despite my fear, I clench my hands into fists, rage filling me now. "You truly think you can just buy your way out of this? That you won't get caught? That someone won't suspect." My voice trembles, but I fight against the fear gripping my heart.

Robert's smirk falters for a moment, as if he's genuinely considering my words. "You truly have no idea how dark the world is. It's rather sweet, your innocence. Shame I'm going to have to snuff it out." He takes another step towards me, and I know I have to act quickly.

With a burst of adrenaline, I launch myself at the table, my fingers wrapping around the palette knife as I snatch it up. Twisting on my feet I lunge at Robert, slicing his cheek with the sharpened edge. He reaches for his face, shock reflected in his eyes before they turn steely.

"You surprise me, Harlow. I'm going to enjoy this," he says, his eyes flashing with a predatory gleam as he lunges at me, but I dodge his grasp and swing the palette knife at his head.

He catches it with his hand, leaving a shallow wound on his palm. I seize the opportunity to kick him in the stomach, sending him stumbling backwards, coughing and spluttering. Then I run, focussing only on my escape as I drop the palette knife and reach inside my pocket for the key.

Throwing one last look over my shoulder to make sure Robert is still on the floor, I lift the key to the lock, my hand shaking so much that it takes me three attempts to get it inside. Finally the lock gives way, and right at the same moment, as my hand wraps around the handle, Robert's arm wraps around my throat.

A blood curdling scream parts my lips as his other arm wraps around my waist and he lifts me off my feet.

"Got you," he snarls into my ear as he drags me kicking and screaming across the room. With one rough shove, he chucks me to the floor, then clambers over me, straddling my thighs. I buck my hips and claw at his face, fighting with every last ounce of energy I have.

"Keep fighting, sweet songbird," he goads before lifting his hand and slapping me so hard that my head snaps to the side, black spots blurring my vision.

"This is going to be so much fun–"

"MOTHERFUCKER!!!!!"

One moment I'm struggling to stay awake, and the next Sterling has his arm wrapped around Robert's neck, lifting him off of me and pulling him away.

"I'll kill you!" Sterling yells, squeezing tighter as Robert desperately tries to break free, his face turning a deep shade of purple.

"Sterling!" I whisper, watching in horror as Sterling's eyes fill with unbridled fury and he tightens his grip around Robert's neck.

Then, as though in slow motion, I see Robert let go of Sterling's arm and elbow him forcefully in the stomach, causing Sterling to momentarily loosen his hold. Seizing this opportunity, Robert quickly headbutts Sterling, the back of his head meeting Sterling's nose with a sickening crunch. The sound echoes through the room, and Sterling stumbles back, blood pouring from his broken nose. Robert turns towards him.

"You little piece of shit," he rasps out between gasps for air. "I should've had you locked up in an institute when you were a kid."

"Fuck you," Sterling snarls, swiping at the blood that's trickling over his lips and chin. "This ends right now."

"I was saving this for Harlow, but I guess I'll use it on you first," Robert sneers, and from my position on the floor I can see him reaching into his back pocket, pulling out a flip knife that he snaps open with a flick of his wrist.

"Sterling, look out!" I scream, scrambling to my feet as Robert lunges towards Sterling.

I don't think. I act.

With adrenaline surging through my veins, I rush towards Robert, shoving him as hard as I can, my palms slamming into him with enough force that it sends him sprawling towards the table. I'd only meant to buy Sterling some time, but when I hear the sound of his skull meeting the sharp corner of the table, I know that I've done far more than that.

Robert's body slumps to the floor, his sightless eyes staring up at the ceiling as blood pools around his head, crimson spreading across the floor.

He's dead.

I'm not even aware of my own screaming until Sterling pulls me into his warm embrace, muffling the sound against his chest.

THIRTY-SIX

One month later

"And you're positive that this is over?" Harlow asks Walter, who's sitting opposite us both in the office of the law firm he owns. Beside him Ben watches us closely, his jaw gripped tight as his father nods. He has been a good friend this past month, and I'm so fucking grateful to him, to Drix, Lia, Dalton and Daisy too. They've rallied around us both, offering their love and support. Pity that the rest of Princetown have only seen fit to twist this horrible experience into a gossip that has had the paparazzi hounding us, so much so we've had to seek shelter at Walter's home until the storm passes.

"It was self-defence, Harlow. What happened was *not* your fault," Walter replies firmly, his gaze flicking to our lawyer, Charles, who nods in agreement.

"Absolutely. Robert's stream of messages, the fact that he attacked you and Harlow so viciously combined with the amount of money he paid to obtain every single one of your paintings have all led to the same conclusion," Charles explains. "The judge has ruled his death as a result of self-defence after months of harassment. This is over."

I nod, my hand squeezing Harlow's as she sits quietly by my side. "Thank you for managing this all so quickly," I say, looking from Walter to Charles.

"You're welcome. Now I have some final paperwork to finish. If you'll excuse me?" Charles asks, gathering up the file in front of him before standing.

"Of course," Walter agrees, waiting for him to leave the office before breaking the silence. "I know that this past month has been really difficult for you both, especially you, Harlow. But I want you to know that the people who care about you the most, do not blame you for any of this."

"He was your friend," Harlow whispers, and even though we've talked about this over and over, she still feels immense guilt despite knowing that if she hadn't acted then my father would have tried to kill us both. If I could change what happened, I'd do so in a heartbeat. I've struggled with the fact that Harlow is carrying the burden of killing my father, albeit by accident. All I ever wanted was to keep her safe, and I failed.

"Regrettably, yes," Walter replies with a sigh. "But that man doesn't deserve your guilt, and no matter our past relationship, I do not condone his actions in any way. Harlow, you did what you had to do, and for what it's worth I'm *proud* of you."

Harlow lets out a small sob, and I wrap my arm around her, hauling her into my side. "My mother isn't," she whispers. "She still blames me."

"Your mother will get over it," Walter snaps, his feelings for Melody about the same as my own, that is, we both despise her.

The way she treated Harlow in the aftermath of that night

was disgusting. The police were called, statements were taken, and rather than Melody comforting Harlow after everything was explained, she'd attacked her in a fit of rage. If we never see that woman again it will be too soon.

Harlow lets out a shuddering breath. "She'll never forgive me."

"It isn't you that should be seeking her forgiveness, not after how she's treated you, Harlow," Ben says firmly, fully aware of what has happened, and how her mother has behaved since.

Despite my father's prenup, she has become a very wealthy woman, a fifth of my father's money now lining her bank balance. Thankfully Walter's lawyers were quickly able to put a gag order in place, preventing Melody from profiting off of the events of that night after we found out she was courting one of the gossip magazines. She's since left for Los Angeles, taking her riches with her. Good fucking riddance.

Unsurprisingly, my father left me very little in his will, most of my inheritance was wrapped up in clauses that I never fulfilled. Mainly taking over his businesses, of which I never wanted anything to do with. The deeds to Adaga Hall will be passed onto me as the surviving heir as was written in a water-tight contract penned over a hundred years ago by my great, great grandfather who had the foresight to ensure that the property would only ever be owned by a Blade, despite my father's apparent attempts over the years to try and get around that particular stipulation.

And despite knowing that my father bought all the paintings of Harlow, they are now back in our possession, the millions of pounds he paid to secure them used to assist Daisy and Dalton, freeing both them, and Drix, from Carl's hold. At the very least something good came out of this whole mess.

"Are you planning on moving back into Adaga Hall?"

Walter asks me, quickly adding, "You are of course welcome to stay with us for as long as you need. There is absolutely no rush."

"Actually, we've decided to do some travelling for a few months before returning to Adaga Hall," I explain. "We need to get away for a while. We're meeting my mother in Sydney, Australia towards the end of our trip. She's always wanted to visit the country, and Harlow and I are keen to spend some time with her."

Walter grins. "That sounds like a great plan. Let us know when you're returning, and I'll host a dinner party to welcome you home."

"I will. Thank you, Walter, for everything," I reply, climbing to my feet.

Harlow rises too and after a quick exchange of goodbyes, Ben follows us out of the building and onto the quiet backstreets of Princetown, where our cars are parked.

"Fancy a drink at Bandits?" he asks, eyeing us both.

"Harlow?" I question, acutely aware that today has been taxing on her mental wellbeing.

"Actually, I think that would be really nice," she replies, giving us both a wavering smile.

"Mind if the rest of the gang join us?" Ben asks, giving me a look that tells me he's already invited them.

"Of course not," Harlow says. "We wanted to say goodbye before we left anyway."

"Excellent."

Ten minutes later we're locked in at Bandits Bar. It's closed for the evening, and we're surrounded by our close friends. Behind the bar Ben is gathering drinks for everyone, whilst I chat with Dalton and Drix, and Harlow is talking with Lia and Daisy.

"How's Harlow doing?" Drix asks me, casting his gaze her way before giving my shoulder a squeeze.

"She could be better," I admit. "It's been rough, you know?"

"I bet, mate."

"She's strong, and she has you," Dalton chimes in, his voice filled with reassurance.

I offer them both a small smile of gratitude as Ben approaches with the drinks. Setting the tray on the table, he hands them out.

"How about some music?" he suggests, eyeing the jukebox in the corner of the bar before pulling a face. "Sorry, Sterling, probably not the best idea I've ever had."

"Actually, I thought maybe I could sing?" Harlow says, rising to her feet. She gives me a questioning look, always aware of my condition, and checking in on my wellbeing. "It's been a while, and I guess I just wanted to..." Her voice trails off as she chews on her lip.

"We'd love that," I tell her, offering my reassurance. I'm aware that singing for her is not just a way to express her feelings, but is also a source of comfort. I haven't heard her sing since that night at the hotel. I've missed her voice—and, if I'm being honest, the colours it brings to life. I haven't been able to paint in weeks, despite my attempts. Even though music still triggers my synesthesia, nothing captures the vividness of colour quite like Harlow's voice. Nothing.

Ben grins, ducking back behind the bar to fetch a microphone, before handing it to her. Then he takes a seat next to me, whilst Lia drops onto Drix's lap and Dalton pulls Daisy into his side.

"I'm going to sing acapella, if that's okay," she asks, looking between us.

Everyone mutters their approval. "Of course," I say.

Harlow looks into my eyes, her gaze filled with a tenderness that takes my breath away. "If it weren't for your synesthesia, you might never have walked into *Smokey Joe's* the night we first met, and I may have never known this love, this feeling I have for you now," she says, dragging in a steadying breath. "I need you to understand that I love you for everything you are. There's nothing about you that doesn't have my heart. This song... it's everything I want to say to you. You may create masterpieces, Sterling... But you, you are *my* work of art," she continues.

A beat later she raises the microphone to her lips and begins to sing, and by God, the colour that appears before my eyes pales in comparison to the beauty of her voice as she sings *Work of Art* by Benson Boone.

Her beautiful voice is like a conductor of my synesthesia and I absorb every breathtaking colour, every enchanting note that dances in the air around us. The room seems to fade away, leaving only me and Harlow. I can feel her love pouring out of her. Every word, and every note, painting a vibrant masterpiece in my mind that no brush could ever replicate.

As the last note fades into the air, a hush falls over the bar. Harlow's voice lingers like a whisper, carrying with it a depth of emotion that leaves us all spellbound. I catch Daisy swiping a tear from her eye and Lia clutching Drix's hand tightly.

My chest heaves as I stare at the woman I love. A golden glow, sparkling with silver, flows around her, beckoning me to my feet. Only a few weeks ago, I'd have to suppress my emotions around her, I'd have to hide my love, but I don't have to do that any longer.

Harlow sets the microphone down gently, and without a word, I cross the distance between us, palming her cheeks, as I say, "My love for you is more vibrant than any colour on the spectrum. You are my muse, Harlow, the beating heart that fuels my very existence, and I love you with everything and all that I am."

Then I press my lips against hers in a heart-stopping kiss, claiming her as mine.

EPILOGUE

There months later

"You have made Sterling so happy, Harlow," Sterling's mother says, grasping my hands tightly in hers as we sit on the steps of Sydney Opera House. "Thank you for seeing him the way I do."

"He's everything to me," I reassure her, the late evening sun warming our skin as we wait for Sterling to join us. He's taking a photograph of the sun setting across the harbour, and I can't help but notice how handsome he looks in his loose slacks and t-shirt, his hair tousled by the warm evening breeze. Today is the final day we get to spend together before Sterling and I head home to Adaga Hall, and his mother travels on to New Zealand for the next part of her trip. There's a bittersweet tinge to the air that settles around us both. Sterling and I will miss spending time with Clara, and I know she feels the same way too.

"I always knew he'd find his way, that he'd find someone who will love him as much as I do. I'm just terribly sorry for how things worked out with his father..." Her voice trails off as her eyes mist with tears.

"I'm so sorry, Clara. For everything," I whisper.

"Don't be. What Robert did was unforgivable. I'm not sad about his death, despite once upon a time loving him. The world is a better place without Robert in it. More importantly, my son is the best version of himself now, and that has so much to do with you, Harlow," she reassures me. "I have waited a long time to see the light in his eyes shine as brightly as it does now. Before you, I saw so much sadness still harboured in his heart, a sadness his father put there, but you filled them with light and I will be forever grateful to you for that."

"Oh, Clara," I cry, pulling her in for a hug.

"Should I be concerned?" Sterling asks aswe pull apart, swiping at our eyes.

Clara gives him a wavering smile. "Not at all, we were just righting the wrongs of the world, as women tend to do."

He nods, laughing. "Okay."

"Shall we head to the restaurant then? I think our table is booked for seven, is it not?" Clara asks, moving to stand.

Sterling takes her hand in his, helping Clara up. "There's something I wanted to do first. Mum, would you mind taking a photo of me and Harlow," he asks, handing her the camera. "I'd think it'd make a great picture with the sun setting behind the opera house."

"Of course, darling," she replies as he drops to his knees a couple of steps below me.

"Don't you think you should be facing that way?" I ask, motioning towards his mother who's currently pointing the camera at his back.

"Actually, I think this is the perfect position," he replies, grinning at me as he reaches for something tucked into his back pocket.

"What are you…?" But my voice trails off as my eyes widen at the small velvet box cupped in his hand. "No way," I gasp.

"I haven't even asked the question yet and you're already telling me no?" he laughs, not at all put off by comment. "I guess proposing to you on the steps of the Sydney Opera House with that beautiful sunset as a backdrop, was a bust then."

He moves to stand, but I grab his arm. "Don't you dare!" I warn playfully.

"Ask you to marry me, or leave?" he retorts with a chuckle.

"Oh my God, Sterling, stop teasing me," I reply, my eyes filling with tears as Clara snaps photo after photo, capturing the joyous moment.

"Yes, stop teasing her, Sterling," Clara says, her own voice light with happiness.

"Okay fine," he retorts, throwing a smile over his shoulder before turning back to face me. "Harlow," he begins, snapping open the lid of the box to reveal a stunning berry red ruby nestled between two sparkling diamonds set on a platinum ring.

"Yes?" I squeak, barely able to suppress my joy as I lift my gaze to meet his.

He blows out a short breath, nerves briefly flickering across his features before he reaches for the ring and pulls it out of the box. "Harlow, from the moment I laid eyes on you I knew you were mine. The colours your voice conjured may have drawn me to you, but it's *you* I love. I see you, every beautiful part. Will you do me the honour of becoming my wife?"

A few people milling around stop to stare, and I feel my cheeks heat from their attention. It takes me a moment to answer and Sterling pulls a face.

"I didn't think it would be this hard for you to make a decision," he says, holding back a laugh. "What do you say, Harlow? Will you spend the rest of your life making me the happiest man alive?"

"Yes!" I finally reply, throwing my arms around him and almost sending us both flying down the steps. "Yes, of course I'll marry you!"

The people around us cheer and clap, and when we finally break apart, Clara is quietly swiping more tears from her cheeks.

"Oh thank fuck," Sterling grins. "Would've been bloody embarrassing if you'd said no. Not that I would've taken no for an answer, that is."

"Oh yeah? What would you have done if I had said no?" I ask, as Sterling slips the beautiful ring on my finger, and presses his lips against my ear.

"I would've taken you back to the hotel and fucked you until you said, yes, yes, yes!"

I can't help it, I laugh.

"Then it's just as well I did say yes, because we have dinner reservations and I'm starving," I reply, and as we walk towards the restaurant, hand in hand, I feel this overwhelming sense of happiness and peace settling into my heart knowing that I will forever be his *little poet*, and he in turn will always be my very own *work of art*.

THE END

ABOUT THE AUTHOR

Bea Paige lives a very secretive life in London... She likes red wine and Hairdo sweets and loves to write about love and all the different facets of such a powerful emotion. When she's not writing about love and passion, you'll find her reading about it and ugly crying.

Bea is always writing, and new ideas seem to appear at the most unlikely time, like in the shower or when driving her car.

She has lots more books planned so be sure to follow her on social media to keep up to date.

Books set in the brand new world of Princetown

#1 The Thug And His Doll

#2 The Rogue And His Flower

#3 The Painter And His Poet

#4 The Thief And His Jewel

Books set in the same universe as the Academy of Stardom series - by chronological reading order:

The Brothers Freed Series

#1 Avalanche of Desire

#2 Storm of Seduction

#3 Dawn of Love

#4 Brothers Freed Boxset

Academy of Misfits

#1 Delinquent

#2 Reject

#3 Family

Contemporary Standalone

Beyond the Horizon

Finding Their Muse

#1 Steps

#2 Strokes

#3 Strings

#4 Symphony

#5 Finding Their Muse boxset

Academy of Stardom

#1 Freestyle

#2 Lyrical

#3 Breakers

#4 Finale

#5 Encore

Their Obsession Duet

#1 The Dancer and The Masks

#2 The Masks and The Dancer

Grim & Beast's Duet

#1 Tales You Win

#2 Heads You Lose

The Deana-Dhe Duet

#1 Debts and Diamonds

#2 Curses and Cures

Short Story

Force of Gravity

(available FREE via my website if you signed up to my newsletter)

For all up to date book releases please visit

www.beapaige.co.uk